All My Secrets

All of These Secrets

by Elaine H MacDonald

ISBN-13: 978-1533153234 and
-10: 153315323X

Contents

1. Shifting into Reverse 1
2. Morning at NorthWind 12
3. Blackberries & Other Sweet Things 25
4. Fleur's Investment 41
5. Prodigal Daughter 51
6. Running Shoes 70
7. Father and Daughter 88
8. Sister Love 106
9. Cinderella 121
10. Woman Talk 142
11. Distrustfulness 153
12. Sympathy for the Devil 170
13. Civic Duties 189
14. A Real-Life Whodunit 208
15. Opportunity Knocking 221
16. Concentric Circles 236
17. The Man About the Money 249
18. The Icing on the Cake 272
19. Engaged in the Process 291
20. What Fleur Knew 313
21. Battle in the Barnyard 325
22. When the Dust Settled 334
23. Evidence versus Truth 352

Family of SABRA 1917-1973 & MAURICE 1914-1973 DELGANEE

MATHIEU 1949 -1967		
ROSE 1953 m. 1977 Dan Palmer	MARIK 1980	
	ELIZABETH 1985 M 2005 Zach de Jagger	Lincoln 2006 Darrin 2008
	ROBERT 1987 m. 2011 Serena 1982	Owen 2013 Paisley Gwendolyn & Felicity Rose 2015
JOAN 1955 & 1981Rick Brothers	Daughter 1973, given to adoption	
JANICE 1955 & 1980 Andy Brothers		
MELINDA Karlsson 1957 m. 1978 Jack Karlsson div 1988	EDWARD 1978 m. 1998 Tiffany div. 2002	Connor 1998
	HELENE 1980 m. 2002 Alex	Daughter 2004 Son 2006

Family of GWENDOLYN 'Nonny' 1926 & LINCOLN PALMER 1920-2005

GERARD 1943 m. 1969 Sally Henderson	GERARD 1971 ELIZABETH 1973 BRENT 1976 SARAH 1979	9 Grandchildren
DAHLIA (Blabon) 1947 m. 1975 Bill Blabon 1950	197979	
FLEUR (Bell) 1950 m. 1978 Frank Bell 1943-2013	Brad Bell 1972	
	CAROL Bell 1979 m. 2004 James Bullard div 2012	Daughter 2004 Daughter 2007
DANIEL 1952 M. 1977 Rose Delganee	MARIK 1980	
	ELIZABETH 1985 m. 2005 Zach deJagger	Lincoln 2006 Darrin 2008
	ROBERT 1987 m. 2011 Serena	Owen 2013 Paisley Gwendolyn & Felicity Rose 2015
DAISY (Chalhey) 1954 m. 1975 Will Chalhey	EDWARD 1976 m. 1998 Wendy	Wallace 1999 Zoe 2003
	CODY 1982 m. 2007 Holly	Imogene 2005
	ERIC 1984 m. 2010 Veronica	
	CHAD 1987	

I years have been from home,
and now, before the door
I dare not open, lest a face
I never saw before

Stare vacant into mine
and ask my business there.
My business – just the life I left,
was such still dwelling there?
...Emily Dickenson

CHAPTER ONE

Shifting into Reverse

"Marik," Terri said, "Are you sure of this?" She leaned on the truck's open window, examining her friend's face with concern. "You know what they say – you can't go home again. I'm surprised that you want to, from what you've told me of your home and family! There's still time to change your mind."

Marik clicked the seat belt into place. Sure? Not a hundred percent, but sure enough. She was too self-disciplined to give voice to the doubts that she'd already stared down.

"I need to do this, Terri. Lately I've started to think I may have wronged them. Besides, in my heart of hearts, I've always been a small-town girl, not a city girl." She gestured at the street, lined with apartment buildings. "I've started noticing it more and more lately, the constant noise, the pollution and dirt, the stink of hot machines at work – this isn't what I want for the rest of my life. I've lived here for twenty years – more than half my lifetime! It's too long."

She turned the ignition key, and the engine coughed and caught. "I want to live in the country again." She looked apologetically at Terri, not wanting to leave without making one last attempt to have her understand. They had discussed it to death, and still her friend fretted, not wanting her to leave.

She drummed her fingers on the worn steering wheel. "I want to belong there, in Chesney Creek, in my family, again."

"Do you really think you can back up your life, and start over? That seems pretty naive to me!"

"Maybe." Marik conceded. "I'll find out. If there is one thing we've won, it's Choice. We've won the opportunity to choose how we want to live I choose this! It's an opportunity to start over, to live the life I was born to live. I believe I'm still young enough to make a different life for myself. I want to find out if I can fit myself back into the pattern where I began, where I was born to belong. "

"And if you can't?"

"It's not irrevocable. If I can't stomach Chesney Creek, it, I can always leave again. I can come back here if it doesn't work out. I can come and sleep on your couch, can't I?" She smiled, trying to lighten the mood. She didn't want to leave on the sour note of argument with this dear person who had been such a faithful friend for so long.

"We both know that's not going to happen," Terri said with sad resignation. She took her hands off the rusty red door of the truck, and stuck them into the pockets of her shorts. "You ought to have someone with you for the drive, at the very least."

"I have to do this on my own, Terri. I've explained that."

"You've explained that you're too pig-headed to ask for help!" Terri snapped. Her eyes misted. "I'm just worried about you, sweetie, that's all. You won't have anyone to talk to. You just bought this old truck, who knows if it is up to such a long drive? You'll be all by yourself out there. You ought to have someone with you, a friend or even someone like Ted since he knows the truck. Besides, where will you stay when you get there? You said you hadn't told them exactly when you were coming. They won't be expecting you tonight."

"Ter, we've talked about that," Marik replied gently but forcibly. She had made her plans. She wouldn't go to her parents' house, nor even to the farm, although that was the one place where she dared to expect an open-armed welcome, from Gran and Aunt Dahlia. No. She would find a hotel, a not-too-expensive one; surely there would be hotels now, in her small home town. Chesney Creek had grown, she knew, in the past 20 years. "I'll be fine. This is something I have to do on my own. It's my chance to put my ghosts to rest once and forever and start over where I left off. Maybe you can come for a visit when I'm settled." She eased the truck into first gear. "Thank you for helping me pack. Thank you for everything."

Terri stepped back, and Marik let out the clutch and pulled away from the curb. She wouldn't allow herself to cry, but Terri was blurry in the rear view mirror, waving goodbye. They had worked together for years, and shared the apartment for the past two years, after the breakup of Terri's marriage with Ted. They had been good years. Marik was proud of what she'd done to turn her life around, and Terri was no small part of that. Their friendship had been a source of strength for both of them. This parting was harder for Terri, Marik thought as she negotiated city's busy streets, harder than it was for her. She had the mad adventure of going back to the life she'd run away from, all those years ago, while Terri was still unsure of what direction she wanted to take. There would be no 'going back' for her. As she said, "Ted? Not a chance, that is so finished!"

She wrapped an elastic around her heavy mane of dark hair while she waited for the light to change so she could merge onto the highway, and wondered idly what Terri would finally decide to do. Life had changed so dramatically for all of them, with the huge, with the humongous, lottery win. Each of them, all six of them, were now multi-millionaires. It was fortunate, Marik supposed, that they had planned what to do if they won. They thought it was just day-dreaming, something to talk about between customers, or when they slid into the booth back by the servery for a quick coffee-break after the lunch-rush in the restaurant. Bob's Old Beanery was an upscale restaurant, despite its tongue-in-cheek name. They fed the downtown business community during the day, and at night, the restaurant was a destination eatery for people coming in from the suburbs. Their lottery-pool had been kept going for years, amongst the waitresses and kitchen staff. Sometimes they won a bit — anything over twenty dollars was shared out, anything less was kept to fund even more tickets for the next draw, with the same names on the back of the ticket. Someone had to check tickets twice a week, and collect their winnings. Most often that was Marik, by popular default or perhaps because she'd been there the longest. She could hardly believe it when she saw that they had all seven numbers; she'd checked and rechecked, unable to believe the evidence of her eyes. Thirty million plus. They'd actually won it!

The agreement was long-standing: If they won a BIG one, they always said, they wouldn't tell anyone for a month. Not anyone! Not spouses, not friends, and certainly not grouchy Scott, the restaurant manager, their boss. Instead, they made their long-promised appointment with Ken Rheddenk, the accountant who came in for lunch every Wednesday regular as clockwork. I'm proud of us, Marik thought. It wasn't often that six people could all agree to do something, and then all honour their agreement! Maybe that's why they'd won, because they were all honourable in that way. They continued showing up for their shifts and collecting their tips, exactly as they had agreed to do in all their daydreaming about "What We'll Do If We Win". Even Kelly, who wanted to go on a massive spending spree, agreed to hold off until Ken Rheddenk could set up their separate accounts. They all recognized the down-side of too much publicity, and wanted to hold on to their precious anonymity. They needed time to adjust mentally and emotionally to their new status as multi-millionaires. Ken, bless his heart, had handled everything for them, even keeping the press more or less at bay. Luckily, a series of weather-related tragedies on the east coast bumped their Big Lottery Win out of headline news.

With the miles flowing out behind her, first on the freeway and now on the quieter highway through the mountains, Marik still felt like she had to pinch herself to be sure she wasn't dreaming. Kenneth had advised them to invest their winnings, and live on the income. Even Kelly had agreed to that – as long as she could take a few thousands off the top for a convertible and the clothes to wear while driving it! They'd each taken an advance: Sid the dishwasher was going to attend an international Star Wars Convention in Belgium; Pat and Nancy, both with children, were buying homes in good neighborhoods, while Terri was eyeing a luxurious albeit small condo overlooking Stanley Park; and Marik was going home to Chesney Creek.

She'd gone back for Uncle Frank's funeral two years ago, and a few times before that, but only for the briefest of visits. The visits had been uncomfortable at best. She told herself she didn't fit in, that she was the black sheep, the unloved and unvalued member of the family. In recent months she'd begun to question that assessment. Something she'd learned in one of her many Community College classes had brought her up short. The pre-frontal cortex of the brain, the professor said, that part of the brain which is capable of rational, reasoned decisions, is not fully developed until a person is in their early 20s. Indeed, he said, it actually shrinks during the puberty years. Is it any wonder, he asked, that teenagers are notorious for making bad decisions? Marik had been only 15 when she ran away from home; is it possible that her judgement had been impaired? It was not only possible, she concluded. It was highly probable that her perceptions were flawed and her stories about how it had been, pure fiction.

Sadly, she didn't question her version of "the truth" about her parents and family even when, as her professor said, her pre-frontal cortex began to expand. In plain words, even when she was old enough to know better she continued to insist to herself, and to anyone else who asked, that running away from home had been an excellent decision. The utter horribleness of her home life was the absolute truth! Now she had to question that. It seemed quite possible that the 'truth' might be something quite different from what she'd believed for all these years. Going back to Chesney Creek now, in her mid-thirties, was an opportunity to re-examine her past with a mature brain. It was an opportunity too good to be missed, especially now that she could so easily afford to do it.

The advance that Kenneth Rheddenk arranged filled up her bank accounts with more than enough to cover the purchase of her pickup truck. She deliberately bought a used one. Ted came with her to check it out.

"The price is high for the year, but it's a good one, not a thing wrong with it that I can see other than that bit of rust around the rear wheel-wells." He emerged from under the raised hood. "You might be able to find a newer one for the money." He wiped his hands on the knees of his jeans. Terri had complained more than once about his habit of using his jeans as a grease-rag. "Then again, maybe not. If you are happy with a 12-year-old vehicle and you can afford it, I'd say Yes, go for it. Let me talk to him, I might be able to get the price down a bit for you." Ted was another one who was still in the dark about the big lottery win.

"No need for him to know," Terri declared. "He might think it's a good reason to charm me back into his arms, and let me tell you – it's not! We've agreed to keep this quiet, and that's what I'm doing. I haven't told a soul. And that's how it's going to be. Let them figure it out later, if they ever do. Especially Ted."

The old truck was part of Marik's disguise. She didn't intend to flaunt her new-found wealth in her old home town. Instead, like Terri, she intended that no one should know about it. She was going back as if she were still the Marik they knew, or thought they knew: runaway, recovered druggie, waitress. She gave the truck a pat on the dashboard. Good truck! It was eating up the miles, climbing the long hills and swooping back down into the valleys between. She loved this part where the highway followed the river, with the pasture-lands stretching away on the either side towards the hills, and the fast running water sparkling in the afternoon sunshine. The late summer grass was dry where it wasn't irrigated, short and wispy. Another few hours would find her back home in the valley, in Chesney Creek. She slipped one of her new CDs, into the player, and cranked the volume. Terri had given it to her, a Haydn symphony full of brass and horns, not the sort of music she usually listened to, but it was tonic for her flagging afternoon energy. Lunch was too long behind her. She smiled, thinking of how surprised the woman who'd served her must have been when she discovered the ridiculously generous tip. She would stop for coffee in the next small town. She needed to refill the gas-tank as well.

The sun was low in the sky behind her by the time she topped the last mountain pass before home. She pulled into the rest-area viewpoint, angling the truck in against the stone parapet. This had been one of her Dad's favourite places to stop, coming home from summer holidays by the ocean when she was a child. She unbuckled and got out to stretch and twist and bend her back. She had certainly gotten to know her new truck well during the long, long drive. She leaned against the rough stone, and wished for a moment that she still smoked. It felt like the moment for a contemplative cigarette, before she tackled the last hour, the descent down the winding highway into Chesney Creek, into the heart of her family, into her childhood. Not that she could be a child again, but she knew that for a little while she would be awash in memories of childhood, whether she liked it or not, whether they were pleasant or not. Some of them were pleasant, even more than pleasant. It would be wonderful to see Gran again. If it went as she hoped, she would soon find herself absorbed back into the family as an adult, and she would move easily into whatever future was waiting for her, back here in her hometown. She couldn't help but wonder what that a future might be.

The wide, familiar panorama of the valley spread out peacefully below, warmed by the slanting rays of the setting sun. The two mountain ranges, curving arms on either side of the valley, converge here where the long highway from the coast climbs up and over the high pass. The southern range is higher and steeper than its northern counterpart. Usually snow-capped, even at this time of year, it is heavily treed except for the patches where active logging has harvested the timber. The northern range of mountains flows down to the valley in soft round foothills, home to farms and ranches. The highway into the valley slopes down into the foothills in long curves, crossing and re-crossing Chesney creek, which grows larger and more tumultuous as it makes its way downhill before feeding into the lake.

There are other small towns further down the valley, and miles away, the city of Quinton sprawls where Chesney Creek converges into the river. Despite the fact that her hometown has come to serve as a bedroom community for the more intrepid of city commuters, Chesney Creek still retains its own identity, with small local businesses serving the people on the farms and ranches surrounding the town.

Marik climbed stiffly back into the truck and pulled out onto the highway. The sun was sinking beyond the western mountains, spreading the mountain shadows down the eastern slopes, down across the foothills and out across the valley. The lights of her home town were coming on, like a sparkling collar around the darkness of Chesney Lake Park. Somewhere in that collar were the lights of her parents' home, and the homes of the rest of her family, sister and brother, aunts and uncles and cousins, and all the people she had once known and would soon, God willing, come to know again.

It was fully dark when she turned into the hotel parking lot at the intersection of the Chesney Bypass and the old highway that ran through town. She hauled her two suitcases into the modest lobby, leaving the cardboard boxes full of books on the truck's narrow backseat. Funny to think that these were all her worldly possessions. So much of what she had owned, furniture, even her closet full of clothes, had not been worth keeping. It had all gone back to the charity shops from which it had come. Eventually, she would go shopping for replacements, find a new home, furnish it, and buy a new wardrobe, too. For now, all she wanted was a quick meal, a shower, and a long sleep. Tomorrow would be time enough to begin her new life.

CHAPTER TWO

Morning at NorthWind

Dahlia hoisted the ranch truck's reluctant tailgate and slammed it shut. The horses, busily pulling hay from the rack, paid no attention to the racket. She climbed into the cab, and headed back uphill to the barn. The sun was well above the horizon now. Morning chores were so much easier in the summer, with all the animals out on the grass. There were no stalls to clean, no icy water buckets to fill. A couple bales of hay delivered to the hay rack in the front field that stretched down along the drive to Mountain Retreat Road, then a couple of flakes for her good old Skudder to mess about with in the home paddock, and she was done. She parked behind the barn by the riding ring and put the pitchfork away in the feed & tack room, and headed across to the big old stone-and-brick farmhouse.

Coming through the mudroom, she shrugged off the old flannel shirt she wore outdoors and slipped into a cardigan. She pulled her long greying blond braid out from under the collar. Summer it may be, but by now, in mid-August, the mornings were starting to get chilly. She switched the kettle on.

Before going out to feed the horses, she always made a thermos of tea and tiptoed upstairs to leave the tray beside her mother's bed. At nearly ninety, Nonny no longer got up to make Dahlia's morning tea, as she had in previous years. Their roles were reversed now. Dahlia chuckled to herself, remembering the old lady's birthday party a year ago, when she had declared herself retired.

"It's your turn," she told the gathered clan, "to wait on me."

"For 'you'," Dahlia thought ruefully, "read Dahl, the Grown-Up Daughter at Home." Widowed before her time, she returned home to the farm 15 years ago to help nurse her father through his final illness. When he finally passed away, two long years later, she stayed on with Nonny. She knew from harsh experience how hard it could be to make the adjustment from wife to widow. By that time, Dahlia knew she wanted to stay on the farm just as much as the widowed Nonny did. The scale of farming that her parents had done was no longer economically feasible, especially not for two women, neither one of them young. Her oldest brother, Gerard, helped her to sell the cattle and equipment. The Kings, their next-door neighbours a mile up Mountain Retreat road, were happy to lease the grazing and hay fields. All that Dahlia and Nonny had left to look after were the chickens, the garden and orchard, and Dahlia's old horse, Skudder.

Dahlia had acquired Skudder when she first came home to help look after the old man. It was part of their agreement: if she came home, she must have a horse to ride. She'd ridden as a child, as most of the Palmer clan had, but Dahlia had been the one who had been most devoted to everything horsey. As a high school student, she had bought and trained two young horses, selling each of them for a good profit. The money she had earned had been her seed-fund for university. She had been able to work her way through to a degree in social work, but when her father's degenerating health became critical, she had been more than willing to give up her inner-city career and to come home to the farm. The only condition was that she had to have a horse to ride.

Skudder fit the bill: he was a rescue horse, in the care of the SPCA until Dahlia paid up his vet bills and brought him home. Good care had quite quickly turned the starving bone rack into a healthy creature with a fine gloss to his dark chestnut coat. When her father's querulous invalid demands and the heartache of his dying stretched Dahlia's temper to the limit, Skudder was there to save her from herself. A good fast gallop up into the pines, the fresh air and smell of warm horseflesh, had returned her to patience and sanity. Poor Father! He'd taken far too long to die. He'd been ready to go weeks, even months, before his merciful release from the pain of his dying. Meanwhile, her success with Skudder had inspired Dahlia to rescue other abused or neglected horses. That mission led to the establishment of Northwind Stables, and her own evolution as a riding and horsemanship teacher.

The kettle boiled. Dahlia sloshed a little hot water into the big brown teapot, swirled it around to heat the pot, then poured it out before throwing two teabags in, filling the pot, and topping it with the quilted cozy that would keep it hot for an hour or more. She could hear Nonny moving about overhead. She cocked her head, listening: was she ready to come down yet? Yes, there she was, the footsteps clearly heading for the bedroom door. Dahlia dashed up the stairs, just in time to see the bedroom door open.

"Good morning! Perfect timing, I've just come up to get the tray." She slipped past the older woman and grabbed the tray with its cup, milk pitcher and empty tea thermos off the foot of the bed. It was a blessing that her mother moved more slowly these days. Dahlia got ahead of her again before she reached the top of the stairs, and led the way downstairs slowly and carefully with the old woman behind her. The fear of Nonny falling on the steep stairs was always with her. Her friend's mother had died that way, taking a tumble downstairs, breaking bones and ending up in a hospital from which she never returned. Even a short flight of stairs could be dangerous. The vision of her mother losing her footing, being pitched headlong down the long steep wooden flight, haunted her like a nightmare. If only the old darling would agree to move her bedroom downstairs!

"I love the view of the mountains from up here," Nonny always said when Dahlia or one of the others expressed their concern with her negotiating the stairs twice or more each day. "I don't want to give that up. Besides, that back bedroom is too small for all my things." That was the worst, Dahlia thought, of a domestic-minded woman: she became too attached to the physical objects of her home, and forgot just how much they inconvenienced her. On the other hand, she thought ruefully, that seemed also to be the worst of horsey women like herself, who chose to ignore the amount of time, trouble, work, inconvenience, and yes, money, her beloved creatures cost her.

Happily, the horses were paying their own way these days, between the lessons, trail rides, leases, and the Ability Riders Program that was so dear to Dahlia's own heart. She had built Northwind Stables from the ground up, and she was proud of the accomplishment. The horsey experiences she offered were a much-loved benefit to the whole extended community, there was no doubt about that. But she didn't know how she was going to manage it this winter. Nonny had stubbornly stuck to her guns about decreasing her role and responsibilities for running the household, which meant Dahlia must do more indoor work.

Running the house in addition to her outdoors work was already stretching her energies to the limit. Even with the help of Alika and Bonnie, the two girls from the neighbouring ranches who had swapped barn-chores and housework for their riding lessons, Dahlia felt exhausted most of the time. In a few short weeks, the two girls were leaving home on their way to college and university and then what would she do?

Stable chores multiplied in the winter when the horses had to be kept inside. This year there would be no helpful neighborhood teenagers conveniently at hand to help in the barn and the house. A few years ago, her budget had stretched to hiring a helper. Serena had been wonderful, happy to work for a pittance as long as she could continue learning the ropes of stable management, and deeply attached to the old woman as well. Her presence on the farm had allowed Dahlia a freedom that she desperately missed now. The fear that her mother would take a fall on the stairs haunted her from the moment she headed out for morning chores until she got back in and could fly upstairs, hopefully in time to subtly escort her mother down for breakfast. If only she could talk her mother into moving downstairs! It wasn't worth arguing about anymore, however. That was a battle which, apparently, she could never win. Something drastic would have to happen to make the stubborn old woman change her mind.

"Daze and Fleur and Rose are coming out tomorrow to do the green beans again," she reminded her mother as she loaded their plates and cups into the dishwasher. Her sisters and sisters-in-law used the farm's extensive vegetable garden as a family allotment, sharing the growing season tasks, and then the harvest chores. The arrangement relieved Dahlia of the garden responsibility, and filled the pantries and freezers of the extended family with home-grown goodness.

"Marik too," Nonny corrected her. "I'm so glad she finally came back. Like you did."

"Dad was my reason to come back," Dahlia reminded her. "No one seems to know why Marik decided to change course."

"Doesn't matter," Nonny said shortly. "She's back, and that's that. I'm looking forward to seeing her tomorrow. We need to have a talk."

"Uh-oh," Dahlia laughed. "Should I warn her?" Her mother might take her role as family matriarch too seriously sometimes, but that role was surely her right. "What about lunch?" Dahlia's own role was that of homemaker. It was not a role she relished, but on the other hand, when her sisters were at the farm, Dahlia could temporarily let go of her concern and worry about her mother. Even if Nonny didn't actually help with the labour of picking and processing the beans, her home would be filled with happy activity, and she would be contentedly occupied with visiting and supervising their work, while they could keep an eye on her. It meant Dahlia could do some of the back-pile of barn chores, perhaps even get the hen-house cleaned out again.

Unfortunately, the sisters' work-party also meant that tomorrow she would probably not fit in her usual precious daily hour of meditation. All the more reason to make sure she made time for it today! After lunch, when Nonny was settled in the front room with her crochet, and Dahlia's daily dash of housework was done, she went gratefully upstairs to her bedroom. She loved the view from her window, overlooking the barn and the horse pastures below and behind it. The horses were grazing quietly, enjoying their period of rest before the after-school riders arrived. Dahl slipped off her house-shoes, and settled herself on the bed with one of Nonny's pretty crocheted throws over her legs, her heavy old laptop on the bed beside her. She breathed deeply to centre herself, and began her cleansing ritual, bringing energy up from the earth, the woman's way, up through her feet, and into each chakra in turn, imagining the colours becoming brighter, clearer, as she focused on each one.

Red: the Base - revitalizing energy flowing throughout her body, cleansing, strengthening

Orange: Creativity - clear, radiant, expansive

Yellow: Receptivity & Acceptance – openness, willingness to experience what life offered

Green: Connection - the energy of the heart-centre. Loving kindness flowing outward

Turquoise: Expression – speech & action as light shines through moving water

Indigo: Faith, Trust, Vision – choosing wisdom

Amethyst: the fountain of purity, Peace - surrender into all-goodness

She sat for a few moments, letting her breath flow softly as she attuned herself to stay within the vitality of peace and trust. She imagined a star-dappled veil of spangled light settling over her being as she relaxed even more deeply, face, neck, shoulders, arms, body, legs, feet, settling into a state of restful tranquillity. She pulled her laptop onto her knees, opened it and clicked on the icon marked "Guided", the Word file she used nowadays for her guided writing. She keyed in the date, and waited for the inspiration to guide her fingers. She had been guided this way, through the writing, most of her adult life. When she had first learned to open herself to the guidance, back in her early twenties in university, she had written on oversized pulp-paper scribblers, the sort used by preschooler, writing in big loopy sentences, half-a-dozen to the page. As she became more skilled, she had graduated to journals, using the same spiral bound notebooks that she used for classroom note-taking. In recent years, the laptop keyboard had become her preferred way to channel her guidance.

"Blessed, thank you for this time together. We would like to talk today about your concerns for your mother, which are truly unnecessary. We would like you to trust in that, to know that she is herself going through the very necessary processes which will resolve whatever concerns you have for her health and well-being."

Enigmatic as always, Dahlia thought ruefully. They didn't say specifically what would happen. "They" was the term she used for the source of her guidance. At one time, back in those early days, she had received the messages from a single Guide, as she called herself.

"I am one of a group of beings," she explained to Dahlia via the writing, *"whose role or assignment is to assist you in living your life, happily and peacefully and productively. We live, you might say, in an alternate universe which touches upon yours. We aren't dead people – deceased human beings – we are, rather, beings of*

a different order, whose assignment is to help and assist human beings."

For all Dahlia knew, her guides might be nothing more than figments of her active and creative imagination; nonetheless, she trusted them absolutely. They spoke, or rather wrote, with assurance, and their advice and assistance had always, always, served her higher good. It was her guide who suggested that she begin offering riding experience (you really couldn't call it 'riding lessons') to physically or mentally challenged people, and look what that had done for NorthWind Stables! That had been real, practical advice, something she would never have thought of, on her own. It brought in money via grants, and raised her public profile, so that more people knew about NorthWind. That helped feed the horses! More than that, however, her guides had taught her to understand her life in ways which certainly seemed to come from outside of any personal wisdom or intelligence she could lay claim to; whatever else 'they' were, they were kind, loving, wise, peaceful, and most of all, helpful.

"Let go of your worry for her, let go of your worry for yourself. We've said it before: the human habit of worrying serves no good purpose, and much bad purpose. It drains your energy. Please become more aware of your tendency to go down the neural pathways of dismay; put up roadblocks! Imagine that there are big yellow barriers with flashing lights at the start of any worry-road, and don't go there. You can just as easily imagine what

you'd prefer to have happen – just as you did last fall when Alika was competing, and doing so well. Please do that now, in regards to your life with your mother. All is well."

Over the years, she had read the work of many others who worked with writing guides, everyone from Edgar Cayce to Jane Roberts to Esther Hicks, and others as well who were not so popular, but who were well within the same tradition. Her guides told her years ago that there were many, many humans who accepted the guidance of beings like themselves. "However," they told her, "publishing is not necessary! Indeed, it would be counter-productive for you." She had a different path, a different way to live, they told her. Their writing was for her eyes only, not for general consumption. "Not at this time, maybe later." So far, 'later' had not come.

"Dear One, that is all from us for now. Only remember that we love you and that we are with you even when you are not on the computer! And that we have your best, your very best, interests at heart."

I know that, Dahlia thought, so why can't I trust it? Wouldn't it be wonderful if she could just float through her days, in a state of blissful trust? Not necessarily trust that life would be good – because stuff happened, no doubt about it, events occurred that she didn't like and wouldn't like – but how blissful it would be to simply trust that out of the times of chaos would come the new and better order of things.

Just like her unhappiness long ago, when she was widowed so young, and then lost her heart for her work, her career. The life she had lived out east had collapsed into the chaos of nursing Father in his illness, and then the further chaos of his death, and wondering what to do with the farm. Her guides had told her to trust, back then, and she'd done her best.

"*Do the next right thing,*" they told her. That had prompted her decision to help her mother to stay on the farm, and to work with horses as she'd dreamt of doing as a child. That had worked out very well, thank Goodness! The times of chaos were no fun. For now, she'd prefer life to go on as it was, more or less. More money would be nice. Nonny moving downstairs would be nice. She hadn't closed the Word file yet, and her fingers seemed to move back to the keyboard with a volition of their own.

"*Now before we go, we want to put your mind at rest. Did you notice that you were thinking that maybe the resolution of your mother's issues might be her death? We did! Rest assured, her time is not yet, she is not done yet with what she has to be and do and enjoy (yes, enjoy! That's in large part the point of human existence, but don't tell the serious folk, lol!) Please note, there is a big yellow barrier across the neural pathway of "when Nonny passes on." No need to go down that pathway, not now, not yet. All things, dear one, in their own time. Be in the present, and limit yourself to enjoyment of the not-present, past or future. If you ain't enjoyin' thinkin' about it, DON'T. Thank you. We love you, we cherish you, we are always on call for you.*"

It amused Dahlia that her guides used slang expressions and modern abbreviations. They picked up the thought and responded.

"All we have to use is the language that is in your mind. It is often inadequate, and sometimes it is fun. That is all from us for now."

She saved the file, and closed the laptop, then her eyes. She brought her attention back to her breathing, slow and even, as she repeated her breathing mantra:

Inhale, I love, exhale, myself.

Inhale, I love, exhale, my life.

Inhale, I love...my body.

I love....my mind.

I love....my personality.

I love...myself. I love my body, even as it is growing older. I love my afternoon rest. I wonder if Mom remembered to put something out to defrost for dinner. What if we were to make over the dining room as a bedroom? We could close off the archway from the front room, wall it in with a doorway. Would she be willing to move downstairs if we could make that big room into a bedroom? No, probably not. The dining room was the dining room, always had been and must continue to be. Poor dear stubborn old woman! Dahl's mind wandered as she slid from dozing into deeper sleep.

CHAPTER THREE

Blackberries & Other Sweet Things

Marik sat in her Aunt Daisy's breakfast nook, a cookie-sheet spread with wild blackberries on the table in front of her. The sweet, sticky steam of cooking berries filled the big old kitchen. It was her turn to pick out the bits of stem and leaf that had ended up in their pails despite their best efforts. Four dozen gleaming pints of jam already filled the counter, and her Aunt Joan was ladling hot jam into another dozen.

"How many more batches do you want to do?" Rose asked, coming into the kitchen from the back porch with another bin of hot jars. "We'll be running out of jars unless you have more hidden, Daze."

Marik had been home now for a week, the first awkward days behind her. She had phoned her parents' house from the hotel, that first day, to let them know she'd arrived and to ask if she could come and have lunch with them. Luckily, they were both at home, and had welcomed her visit. Both Dan and Rose came out to greet her when her truck rattled to a halt in their driveway.

Over sandwiches and tea, Marik gathered up her courage, took a deep breath and told them that this was more than a visit. "I've decided to move back here," she told them, "back to Chesney Creek."

Rose's reaction was a look of utter disbelief, followed by a rush of tears. Marik glanced at her father, but Dan was looking down at his plate. His wife was not a woman who wept easily.

"Call them tears of joy, or relief maybe. I can't tell you how I've longed for this day!" She wiped her eyes and gave her daughter and husband a tremulous smile. Marik was deeply touched. She couldn't remember ever seeing her mother so overcome by emotion. Tears warmed her own eyes as she stood, came around the table and leaned down to give Rose an awkward hug.

Her father was not a demonstrative man, but he stood up and gave her a quick, affectionate hug. "Glad you've finally come to your senses," he said, and they all chuckled a bit. She checked out of the hotel the following day, and moved her suitcases and book-boxes into their guest room. It wasn't the house they'd lived in when she was a child. They'd bought a new home in Sanson Vale a year or two after Marik left home, keeping the house on Fifth as a rental. Rose apologized for the fabric stash that filled half of the guest room's closet.

"You'll have your sewing room back before long. I'm going to look for an apartment or cottage. Know of anything?"

"Can you afford to do that?" Rose asked. "We're happy to have you here, you're more than welcome to stay with us until get on your feet, find a job. I'm sure we can find something for you, if I put it out to the family grapevine." Marik wasn't surprised that Rose expected her to be job-hunting. She would have to find a way to calm her practical mother's financial concerns about her, without giving away the fact that she wouldn't ever have to work another day in her life.

"I'm alright for now," she said. "I have plenty of savings."

"Don't be using it all up! You never know when you might need it." Rose had been anxious about money for as long as Marik could remember. Her financial anxiety had haunted their family like a malevolent ghost. "I'm in no rush about the sewing room. Stay with us just as long as you want. I haven't got a quilt on the go at the moment, too many other things to do in the summertime. "

One of the many things Rose liked to do in the summer was this annual blackberry-fest with her sisters and in-laws. Marik wiped her sweaty forehead with the back on one sticky, purple-stained hand. As Rose had said, there was always plenty to do in the summer time, especially if you were part of the Palmer clan! Too bad that the annual jam-making always took place on the most blazing hot days of August. Today was no exception.

They'd started early. The sun had risen on another hot late summer morning when Rose, Marik and several of her aunts from both sides of her family gathered at Aunt Daisy's big old house on the north side of Chesney Lake. Daisy had an omelet frittata, full of sausage and vegetables, waiting in the oven for them. The fragrance of fresh-brewed coffee blended seductively with the scent of toasted home-baked yeast buns. Marik's belly growled in anticipation. She was the only one of her generation taking part in the berry-picking this year. The cousins were scattered, and the ones who were still in the area were busy with their young families and their jobs. After their meal, she trailed behind the older women, enjoying the familiarity of the walk as they ambled down Daisy's back yard with their pails and onto the lakeside trail. From there, it was a short walk around to the old orchard where the berries grew ripe and sweet in the summer sun. High, tangled thickets of prickly blackberry vine mounded the fields here at the west end of the lake. Marik hadn't realized how much she missed all of this, the Park and Lake as well as the way the family worked together, making their common tasks more like play than labour.

They spread out among the thickets, within chatting distance, but not always within sight of one another. Armed with her plastic ice-cream bucket and a pair of secateurs, Marik followed the bark-mulched jogging trail to where, if she remembered correctly and if it was still there, the remains of an old log-built snake fence would give her access to the higher branches. The largest, sweetest berries were, of course, the ones that grew tantalizingly just out of reach.

She found the fence, only a little more decayed than it had been when she was a child. She was clipping back a tough, aggressive vine that blocked her access to a pendulous bunch of berries when she noticed the runner coming towards her, in shorts and sweat-dampened t-shirt, his big dog trotting easily at heel. Surely it wasn't a park ranger, coming to tell her off for daring to prune the overgrowth? He raised a hand in greeting without slowing his rapid, even stride. Marik returned the greeting and watched appreciatively as he moved away from her, his arms swinging easily in harmony with the thrust of the long muscular legs. Man and dog made an attractive picture. She was still watching when he slowed, paused, and then jogged backwards towards her. She tucked the secateurs into the pouch hung on the belt of her cut-off jeans and stepped down off the fence.

"Marik? Marik Palmer, am I right? It is you, isn't it?" His face was one she vaguely remembered. The grey eyes under the straight brows, thick dark hair, curling with damp sweat now, the prominent nose and strong chin, were the features of someone she hadn't seen for years. What was his name? She searched her memory. He hadn't left a strong impression, whom ever he was.

"Stan Albescu. We went to school together. I was a year ahead of you." He bent, hands on knees, catching his breath. He was obviously happy to renew the acquaintance, even at the expense of his exercise. By the look of his legs in the abbreviated nylon shorts, he was a dedicated runner. "And Trigger," he added. The dog grinned up at her, tongue lolling from the broad grey muzzle. Not a park ranger come to scold her, then. That was good.

Marik wiped her hands on the sleeves of the wind-breaker she'd borrowed from Aunt Daisy's house. It was too big and too hot, but it protected her arms from the thorny attacks of the vines. She returned his handshake.

"I saw you a couple years ago, in Vancouver, do you remember? I stopped you because you had a burned out turn-signal."

"You didn't give me a ticket." It was coming back to her now. She had borrowed Terri's little Vespa scooter for a quick run to the grocery store. The flashing cop-car lights behind her had spooked her badly, flashing her back to her earlier days, when she had been a runaway living on the street. In those days, the police were the enemy, to be avoided at all costs. He had walked up beside the scooter, asked for her licence, and then recognized the name and then her face. He reminded her that they were from the same small town. She had been surprised that he would remember her. He must have been fifteen or sixteen when she left, that spring when she should have been finishing her second year in high school. He didn't give her a ticket for the malfunctioning signal, although he probably should have. He let her off, on the strength of their shared schooldays, with only a warning to get the light repaired. The incident left her shaken. She'd gone home and phoned her sponsor, Sue-Ellen, to talk down the remains of her anxiety about being stopped by the police. She hadn't remembered his name.

"So – you're back in Chesney Creek now?" He pulled a water bottle out of his waist-pack, took a long swallow. "I moved back here a couple years ago, got on with the department here. It's a good place to live and a far easier place to work."

He leaned against a fencepost, his breath slowing. Apparently he had all the time in the world to renew an old acquaintance. "What brings you back?"

She gestured at the thicket of vines. "Blackberries. My aunts are having their annual jam-session, I got roped into helping." It still made her feel a bit nervous, talking to law-enforcement. Maybe this conversation was something to do with violating park rules. Once a cop, always a cop?

"I always regretted not giving you that ticket." His sun-darkened skin crinkled with smile lines around the dark eyes. "Yup, if I'd given you a ticket, I would have had your info, could have called you. Could have asked you out on a date." He slipped the water bottle back into its carrier, like a handgun into a holster. "So how about it, shall we meet up sometime, make up for lost time? We could go for coffee, get reacquainted, catch up on old news." He had his cell phone out, ready to enter her number in his data-base.

For one paranoid minute, Marik wondered if it was a set-up, if the local police somehow knew her history, and wanted to keep tabs on her. But that was ridiculous, it had been years since she'd been 'known to the police'. It was a date he was asking for. A date with a cop. Now that would be a turnaround, something she'd never imagined. It might have happened, though, to the woman she might have become if she'd finished her growing up right here in Chesney Creek. If she didn't have all that history of girl-gone-wrong behind her.

"Sure. I'd like that." In for a dime, she thought, in for a dollar, in her new old life. He keyed in the phone number for her parents' house, as she explained that she was new back in town, and not settled yet. She had cancelled her cell phone contract before leaving the city. That had felt good, a symbolic way of cutting off from her old life. She hadn't gotten around to getting a new one. She didn't need one, there was no one she needed to be connected with that way.

"I'm on afternoons for the next few days, but I'll call, we'll make a plan. It's great to see you again Marik. See you soon."

He jogged a few steps down the bark mulched path, and then picked up the pace, running easily with the dog at his heel. He gave her a wave before the trail turned and he disappeared among the trees, heading on around the lake. She climbed back up on the fence rail, and pulled a heavily-laden vine down to pluck the sweet berries. She could hear the aunts' voices in the distance. How many years had it been since she last picked berries for the aunts' annual blackberry jam sessions? Back then, picking had been the job of the cousins, she and her little sister Liz, Carol, Aunt Daisy's middle boys Cody and Eric, Helene and her beastly brother Ed. After a morning of berry-picking, the cousins had been sent to spend the afternoon on the beach at the lower end of the lake, the younger ones under the responsibility of their elders, while the Aunts brewed their jam and gossiped.

Marik and Helene and Carol were all of an age. She remembered lying on worn beach towels in the sunshine with them, browning their skinny 10- and 11-year-old bodies, giggling over nonsense. They'd made up names and phrases to describe their relatives: "Daisy's in a daze!" "The twins are in a spin, but Rick & Andy, they're just dandy." "Darling Aunt Flo, she's just a little slow."

They'd felt so brave and naughty, making up their daring ditties about their aunts, their uncles, even their very own parents. "Rose gots thorns!" "Grandma Nonny, she's a honey." "Jack the Jerk." None of them liked Uncle Jack, Ed and Helene's father. Even Helene recognized that there was something wrong about him, something not right about how he treated her mother. Marik remembered walking into the kitchen after school one day, in search of an after-school snack, and seeing her slim, elegant Auntie Lindy sitting at her mother's kitchen table with tear-reddened eyes, the inevitable cup of tea surrounded by sodden, used tissues.

"What's going on?" she mouthed to her mother, opening the refrigerator behind Aunt Lindy's back. What age had she been? Eight or ten, Marik guessed. An age when, for her at any rate, parents were simply fixtures. Subconsciously she'd been absorbing their attitudes, but consciously they were simply there – loved, not judged, accepted as they were. That was before she became a teenager.

When that happened, they were no longer simple fixtures in her life. Suddenly, their every flaw and fault loomed immense, magnified by her self-generated teenage drama into monstrous threats as every adult in her life was transformed into a member of the enemy army.

"That damned Jack's being a jerk again," Rose hissed, "Now get your snack and go upstairs. Men!" Lindy and Jack divorced a few years later. He had one affair too many, and patient, bullied Lindy finally gathered up sufficient courage to take a stand. Either the affairs stopped, or she and the children were gone. When the divorce was finally done, however, only Helene stayed with Lindy. Edward chose to live with his father.

It was the only divorce in the older generation, but apparently Jack wasn't the only spouse who could try a partner's patience. It wouldn't be until years later that Marik's hindsight became clear enough that she recognized the marital challenges her own parents faced. Not affairs – neither of them were that way inclined, thank God! It was finances that were the rub in their marriage, a constant and ongoing source of anxiety and stress that had forced her father, a heavy machinery operator, to take a camp job. He lived away three weeks out of four, leaving Rose at home to pay the bills and to carry the full responsibility for home and children. She too was working, in a part-time position at the library. Marik, the oldest, was expected to help with the housework every single Saturday morning. How she had resented that!

Looking back, she knew that her attitudes had added more weight to Rose's burden. It was past time, she knew, to make amends for the grief and sorrow she'd caused. As much as Ed had been a son of Jack the Jerk, like father like son, she was Rose's daughter, far too prickly, far too easily offended. Like the blackberries, she thought ruefully, with all these thorns. She picked up another berry from the almost-empty cookie-sheet. Someone had picked one that wasn't ripe enough for picking. She yanked off the stem and dropped it back on the tray.

"Shall I take these?" Aunt Joan, asked, reaching for the bowl of cleaned fruit. "Toss that one in too. A few red ones add zip to the flavour."

Marik dumped the accumulated dross from the cookie sheet into the compost bucket, and spread out another bucketful of berries. The ones she cleaned before lunch were simmering on the stove, her Aunt Lindy stirring them gently with a long wooden spoon. "Do you think this is ready?"

She watched with affectionate amusement as the three greying heads converged over the simmering jam-pot. Like the opening scene of Macbeth, Marik thought. "Bubble, bubble toil and trouble". She chuckled to herself. Toil and trouble pretty well described the harvest season. How she hated all the work of it, when she was a kid!

Pudgy Aunt Daisy brought the tea-saucer, frosty from the freezer, across the kitchen to the stove. Aunt Joan dipped up a hot sweet spoonful and poured it carefully onto the cold plate.

"Put it back in the freezer," Joan cried urgently, "quick-quick!" They were making old-fashioned boiled jam this time, with green apple pulp instead of commercial pectin to set it. It was an experiment, instigated by one of the twin aunts. "This had better work!"

"We've never done it this way before," Aunt Daisy told Marik, resting her hand on the younger woman's shoulder as she reached over to set the timer on the microwave. "Five minutes, right? Then it should be jelled, if we've done it right. Whose idea was this, anyway?"

Aunt Jan pointed an accusatory finger, "My twin!"

Aunt Joan laughed, pushing the damp curling grey tendrils off her brow with her forearm.

"My twin has always been the one to push the envelope, right Joansie?"

"That's because I got all the creativity!"

"And I got all the common sense, groupie-girl." A burst of laughter greeted this sally, and Joan lowered an eyelid in a conspiratorial wink at Marik. Rose, coming in with the big roasting-pan full of hot jars from the summer kitchen, gave the others a repressive older-sister look. Their generation had secrets that Marik's generation wasn't privy to, and as far as Rose was concerned, that's the way it should remain.

"Where do you want these hot jars?" Rose asked impatiently. She still carried a lingering sense of resentment brought forward from childhood. Even after all these years, she still envied the twins' closeness. She had been just three when they came along to usurp her place as the baby of the family, and they'd done it with a double whammy. Who could resist twin babies? Rose remembered the voices of the grownups, exclaiming over them. Weren't they just the most darling things ever? Adorable! Who could ignore twin toddlers, dressed in matching ruffles?

Yet as adults, raising their young families, the four Delganee sisters had grown close. Despite her thorniness, Rose's underlying generosity brought her sisters with her into the close network of Palmer clan unity. Her sisters and her sisters-in-law came together frequently to do their women's work, especially in harvest time. Marik's early memories were filled with family gatherings, cousins both maternal and paternal romping while their mothers cooked and visited and drank endless cups of tea together. Sometimes the fathers were there, but more often it was the women and children, while "the menfolk" as Gran called them were busy with their own concerns. These were the happy memories that she had pushed aside for too many years, the memories of the good times.

Aunt Daisy's big old house had been a favourite. In the summer time, there had been the lake, right down at the bottom of the garden. Even in the winter, the house was large enough so that the cousins, led by Daisy and Will's four lively boys, could be kept busy without being underfoot in the big kitchen. Now Aunt Daisy and Uncle Willard lived here alone. "The house is really too big for just the two of us," Daisy said, "but where else could we live? Will can't give up his workshops!"

"And we don't want to give up your kitchen," Jan added. "It's been five minutes, is it set yet?"

Daisy reached into the top of the refrigerator for the saucer. The glistening deep red blob oozed slightly as she tipped the frosty saucer.

"Good enough!" Joan declared. She popped the old silvery jam funnel into the top of a hot jar, and began ladling the hot jam from the kettle.

"Phew!" Daisy sank into the seat opposite Marik, and fanned herself with the place-mat. "Is it just me, or is it way too hot in here?"

"Middle age, Sweetie!" Jan declared.

"Old age, I'm beginning to think," Daisy responded. The years had changed all of the Aunts, but none more than Daisy. Marik had been shocked when she first saw her, despite her mother's fore-warning. In Marik's memories, Daisy was a slender, pretty young mother, silvery blond, blue-eyed and vivacious, aptly named. Now, the blond hair was cut short, permed and tinted an ashy blond to cover the grey, and Daisy weighed half-again as much, if not more. The full flesh of her upper arm wobbled as she fanned herself.

"We're afraid she's developing diabetes," Rose told Marik, "but she refuses to see a new doctor. That old Dr. Garmann of hers is just about useless. They say diabetes used to be one of the most under-diagnosed of all degenerative diseases, but there's no excuse for that now! Every doctor on the planet should know enough to test for it, it's virtually an epidemic! But you know Daisy, she's stubborn as a mule under that fey exterior. Used-to-be fey exterior," she amended.

So many changes, Marik thought. All of the aunts had grey hair, even if Jan and Joan were the only ones who flaunted it, long and loose on their shoulders. The older generation had grown older, and there was another generation coming up. It was hard to think of her parents as grandparents, but so they were, several times over. Her sister Lizzie and her husband were parents of two schoolboys, her brother Robbie and his Serena had a toddler and twin baby girls. She hadn't yet met this crop of second cousins, her own cousins' children. When the lottery win set her free to come back to Chesney Creek, she had presumed that the pattern of 'home' would be the same as when she left. How wrong she had been!

Daisy ran her plump fingers lightly over the second batch of berries that Marik was cleaning. "Good job tidying these up," she said. "I vote we freeze these, girls. We've done enough, they don't all have to be jam." The others agreed.

"We've got the darned beans to do again tomorrow, too, out at the farm. This is enough work for today." Rose set a low cardboard box on the counter, and began packing the warm jars.

"We've made more jam today than we did all of last season," Jan remarked, filling another box. "One extra set of hands makes all the difference, picking and processing. Good thing you've come home young Marik. We couldn't have done it without you."

Far from having to make a place for herself in the family pattern, Marik found herself being slotted into place as an adult woman as neatly as the jam jars were being fitted into their boxes. It was as if she had never been lost. Despite the changes the years had wrought, the heart of the family was as warm as it had ever been. Tucking the box of jam into the trunk of Rose's car, she wondered how she could have been so unaware of that warmth when she was fifteen. Why hadn't she turned to her aunts, or even her grandmother? But that was ancient history now. Regrets were useless. It was the future that concerned her. The big question now was how her family would take to the news that she was absurdly wealthy? Money had the power to change relationships, not always for the better. She would tell them, when the time was right. Meanwhile, she was accustomed to keeping her own council. It shouldn't be difficult to act her part. Wealth was the last thing they'd suspect. She stretched her arm out the window to wave to Daisy standing on the front porch. "See you tomorrow!"

CHAPTER FOUR

Fleur's Investment

Fleur tied the bow of her gardening apron, kicked off her pretty house-sandals, and pushed her feet into the soft rubber shoes that she used in the garden. She'd bought a new reflecting ball, a small one this time, to go amongst the asters, to reflect their glowing purple. The asters were the glory of her autumn garden. There was another gleaming ball poised to reflect purple, the big one on the tall pediment tucked in among the lilacs. The gardening season was bracketed in royal purple, lilacs at one end, the bushy asters at the other, but Fleur paid no attention to such limiting brackets. As soon as the snow-drifts began to melt and recede, Fleur came out to look for the green spears of early snowdrops and spring crocus. They sprang up from the brown earth, up from under the mulches of dead leaves she'd spread over the beds in the fall, even up out of the patchy, wet lawn.

How that invasion had annoyed Frank! Darling Frank. His one and only garden pride was his long smooth stretches of well-mown lawn. When he first bought the house for her, so many years ago, there had been a great deal more lawn. The sandbox, swing-set and playhouse had reduced his mowing chores, and then the vegetable garden had taken another piece. Her passion for flowers had grown over the years, each flower bed or border eating up more of the lawn area. Even the vegetable garden had given way, becoming smaller when Brad, with his teenage appetite, grew up and moved away, and smaller still when Carol grew up and got married. She and Frank had no real need for a vegetable garden. The garden up at the farm, tended with loving care by so many hands, gave everyone in the family more than enough, so now dahlias thrived where corn and spaghetti squash used to hold sway.

Fleur brought the two boxes out into the front yard, first the one containing the new reflecting ball, then the bigger one that held the pieces for the tripod pedestal. The boy at the garden shop said that assembling the tripod was a simple task. She doubted that. She ought to have talked to Rob or Sue, the owners. She'd been dealing with them for years. They understood her challenges. Maybe she could figure it out, by studying the pictures. She used the point of her secateurs to pull away the tape that sealed the top of the box. Inside, there were several plastic bags full of the pieces which, when correctly assembled, would cradle the gleaming silver ball amongst the bud-covered plants, just high enough to catch the sunshine and reflect the blossoms that would be bursting into bloom in the next week or so.

Fleur sat back on her heels. If only Frank were still here! It was over two years since he'd passed, and still at moments like these the grief of his loss threatened to overwhelm her. Frank had done so much for her, he had loved her, and oh, how she had adored him! There was no one now to stand between her and the confusing, impatient world. Fleur pulled off her soft leather glove, and reached into her gardening apron pocket for a cotton-flannel hankie. She'd hemmed it herself, one of dozens that she made over the years. Paper tissues, made of wood pulp, were too rough for her skin. They made her delicate tip-tilted nosed look all red and raw. Frank had admired her first because she was pretty. There were many things that Flo did not understand very well, but she did know how to be pretty. Frank had always come home to a well-dressed, well-groomed wife. He had been proud of her blonde beauty, and she had been pleased, and determined, to keep herself beautiful for him. Her nails were always well-manicured, and she never gardened without gloves. She always used a cotton hankie, even now when he, her love, was gone, and the hankie was wiping away tears. She couldn't stop them, especially at times like this when she needed him so much, with this pedestal to be assembled. She couldn't do it.

A newer-model car, deep turquoise, drove up the street, and parked in front of the house. Fleur rose to her feet. She wasn't very good at cars, didn't recognize this one, but she recognized the burly brown-haired man in the light summer suit who emerged from it. "James! How lovely to see you!"

"Mama Fleur!" He swung the gate open, and in two strides was with her, pulling her into a warm embrace. Oh how lovely to have a man's arms around her, to feel his vigorous strong life upholding her. He held her away from him then, and looked at her. "You've been crying again! What is it this time?"

She pointed at the boxes lying on the ground. "I can't figure out how to put it together."

James picked up the larger box, glancing at the instructions. All it needed was an ordinary Phillips-head screwdriver.

"But darling James, you can't do garden-work in your suit!" Fleur protested. He pulled off his jacket, handed it to her, rolled up the sleeves of his pale checked shirt, and a few moments later, planted the assembled tripod amongst the bushy plants. Fleur placed the gleaming ball on the mounts, and stepped back beside him to admire it.

"This is my seventh one!" she gloated, her glance caressing the abundant beds of flowers and shrubbery that surrounded them. As well as the reflecting balls – just one other here in the front garden – there were a few concrete creatures peeking out from under the hedge, a gilded plaster fairy perched on a fence post, and a pair of Dutch gnomes, male & female, leaning one towards the other as if for a kiss. Each one of the ornaments were dear to Fleur's heart, her own purchases no less than the ones that had come to her as gifts.

"How much do one of these things cost?" James asked, gesturing at the ball and tripod he'd just set up. Fleur told him, explaining that Frank had arranged her garden budget for her. He told her to take $150 out of the bank at the start of each month and put it in an envelope marked

"GARDEN." That was the amount of money she could spend each month on outdoor plants and decorations.

"In the winter, I sometimes have some left over," she confided. "Then I have more to buy bedding plants in the spring! But you didn't come here to hear about my garden. Would you like a cup of tea? Or, no, it is coffee you young people drink, isn't it?"

"That would be great!" His ex-mother-in-law made excellent coffee. She did all domestic things well. Pity that Carol hadn't followed her mother's example, they might still be together. "I do have something I want to talk to you about." He followed her into the sunny kitchen, slid into the breakfast nook, and glanced out into the big backyard while she busied herself with the coffee-grinder. The girls used to love coming here. Fleur was a perfect Grammy with a garden that was enchanting for youngsters. They loved the narrow pathways, the hidden nooks and crannies, the multitude of statues, ornaments, gnomes, and yes, more of those damned balls. What a waste! His ex-mother-in-law was chattering on about the girls – had he seen them recently, were they coming home to spend some time in Chesney Creek before school started? He fielded her questions, and when at last the coffee was brewed, and she had poured a cup for each of them, he began to explain why he had come to visit today.

"Mama Fleur, you mentioned that you get only $150 to spend on your garden each month. Would you like to have more?"

"Oh yes," she said enthusiastically. "I'd love a fountain to put it in the backyard. Back by the buddleia bush. The butterflies would love it!" She showed him a picture in one of her gardening magazines. The fountain she wanted featured a pair of gigantic butterflies, spouting twin antennae of water into a shallow bird-bath basin. Of course, she admitted, it was just a dream. It would cost far more than she could afford.

Frank had warned her to stay within her budget. If she had any questions, he told her, she was to talk with their lawyer. Edward Karlsson had his head on right about money. Like most of the town's old families, Frank had always done business with Bolster & Nod. The firm was an institution in the town. If a Chesney Creek citizen wanted legal advice, they went downtown, to the office in the solid old brick building that had been the firm's home for generations. When Ed Karlsson joined the firm, Frank transferred his company and personal business to the younger man. "He may only be an associate attorney now, but old Mr. Bolster is going to have to make him a partner before long," Frank predicted. It made sense to leave Fleur's affairs in the hands of a younger man.

"If you are worried about money," he told Fleur repeatedly during his last months, "you go talk to Ed Karlsson. He'll keep you straight." Karlsson was a family connection, through her sister-in-law

Rose. His dear simple Fleur would be safe with the young lawyer to handle her financial affairs. She had visited their offices, in the old red brick building downtown, often enough to be comfortable with Ed Karlsson and the other members of the firm. She knew them, and more importantly, they knew her.

"I can't spend more than darling Frank said," Fleur explained now. "I have to do just what he told me, then I'll be alright. I'll be safe."

James sipped his coffee. Oh yes, ma-in-law made a good cup of coffee. "It's good to be safe, Mama Fleur, but sometimes we need to look outside the box when it comes to money. I am sure Frank knew that! In fact, I remember him saying something to me about that very thing." James had been one of Frank's insurance salesman. That's how he met their daughter, his wife Carol. His ex-wife. He had expected to take over the company when Frank retired, but it hadn't worked out that way.

Fleur looked puzzled. "Outside the box?" she asked. It was a phrase that meant nothing to her.

"Like your Frank always told me: If you want to make money, you have to be brave. He said exactly that! You know I had a lot of respect for Frank. That's why I want to tell you about this. I have a proposition for you – a way that we can make a lot of money, you and I together. All we have to do is be brave about it, like Frank always said. And we'll be helping lots of other people as well. May I tell you about it?"

Fleur nodded agreeably. Men liked to talk about money. Frank had, and look at how well he had provided for them, always. It was good for men to think about money. She didn't really understand what James was saying. It had to do with a new computer system or "game" that a friend of his had invented, a way that would make it easy for people to design things, "even gardens" he said, to play their games. It was an investment. She understood about investments. You put money in, and then it made money. Frank had always had investments.

"This would be a loan, see? Don and I have been working on this system for a long time, and it is ready to go into production, but we haven't got the money to launch it. That's where you, and our other investors of course, come in. My sister's already in on this, I offered it to her first because she's family. I know it is going to really help them! And after all, you are part of my family. Could I have a little more of your excellent coffee?"

Fleur refilled the cookie plate as well. James complimented her on the chocolate ones. "A new recipe? I don't think I've had these before." It too was from one of the gardening magazines, she told him. She loved her gardening magazines!

"But to get back to what I was saying. This is strictly a loan. We'll pay you back once we go public, but in the meantime, you'll get the interest on it. We'll pay you good interest – 12%! So if you loan us, say, $200,000, then every month your investment – you! - will be earning..." He reached into the inside pocket of his suit jacket, and pulled out an instrument that Fleur didn't recognize. Not a pocket calculator, like Frank always used. This one was all screen, and no keys. The numbers that James quoted didn't mean very much to her. The fountain was so cute! It would be lovely at the back of the lawn, and the butterflies would love the trickling water. So would the birds! It might even attract more of them. She liked to watch them at the bird feeders during the winter. It would be wintertime before long. Maybe next month she would get a new feeder for them. She'd seen a picture in one of these magazines...

"So what do you think? I want you to get in on this! You can have your fountain by next spring! I'll even come and help you install it, how's that? It'll look great out there." He had Fleur's attention now. How exciting, she would actually get the fountain! James was wonderful to her, she hadn't thought the fountain was really possible!

"Yes it is," James said. "More than possible, it's going to happen! Because you are going to be earning really good money, just like Frank always did. I promise."

He explained that the first interest payments would start the following month. She should put the money in her garden envelope, he said. Then she could have more plants, more bird feeders, more ornaments of any kind she wanted.

"I'll be back this afternoon," he said, "with the paperwork." He finished the last of his coffee, and put the cup and saucer on the counter. "Now, you mustn't tell anyone about this, of course! We have to keep it secret until we are ready to launch it. Otherwise someone might scoop us."

"What does that mean? Scoop us? Like with a shovel?"

James laughed. He explained that it meant someone might steal their idea, might scoop it up and run away with it. Then those thieves would be the ones who made big money, instead of his Mama Fleur, and his sister, and the other investors.

"That would be terrible! Why would anyone do that?"

"Don't worry," James reassured her. "Just remember, mum's the word, mum-in-law! We mustn't let anyone else know about this!" He gave her a long warm hug before getting in his car. "I'll be back with the papers you need to sign, for the bank, in about an hour."

Fleur sang quietly to herself as she washed up their dishes. Darling James was such a dear man, even if he and Carol were divorced. She didn't get to see Carol and the girls very often. If only she hadn't moved away to Quinton! Brad didn't come to see her, either. But James did! He looked after her. Wouldn't Frank be happy, if he looked down from Heaven and saw her now. He'd be proud of her. She put the dried cups and saucers back in the cupboard, and wiped away her tears. She still missed Frank dreadfully at times.

CHAPTER FIVE

Prodigal Daughter

Marik picked up the coffee tray and followed her grandmother out onto the wide veranda that stretched across the front of the farm house. Nonny sank carefully onto the wicker loveseat, with its commanding view down the rolling foothills to the wide valley below. Marik placed the tray on the low wicker table, tucked the faded outdoor afghan over the elderly woman's legs, and handed her the delicate cup and saucer before settling herself in the matching rocker.

In the distance, beyond the lower folds of the hills, the lake gleamed in the sunshine, reflecting the dark evergreens that surrounded the still water. Along the water's edge, deciduous maple and poplar were already tipped with autumn gold. The park was laced with walking and riding trails, but at this distance, and from this elevation, it appeared to be virgin forest, peacefully embracing the quiet water. The town of Chesney Creek, on the far side of the lake from them, was partially visible, one- and two-story homes and shops, with a few taller buildings where the new highway curved away to the south. Luckily, the encircling hills rose up between the farm and the eastern end of town, where the new big box stores with their surrounding asphalt replace the orchards and farms of an earlier era. Nonny's kitten, a lithe black and white spotted creature, sauntered up the stairs onto the veranda and leaped lightly up to settle herself, purring, on the faded afghan beside her mistress.

"Happy to be back home?" Nonny asked. "Truthfully now." Marik chuckled at the old familiar phrase. Her father used it to, when he'd wanted her, or little Liz, or even Robbie, the baby of the family, to tell him the whole truth, and nothing but the truth. She hadn't thought of that phrase in years. It meant, 'this is important. Not just to you and me, but on a larger scale.' For Gran, a life-time church-goer, it meant the Truth as God-the-Omniscient knew it.

"All life includes suffering. Ask your Aunt Dahlia about that."

"That sounds like something more I don't know about, Aunt Dahlia's 'suffering.' What do you mean?" Once again, a family member was mentioning something casually, in passing, some reference to a common knowledge that she simply didn't share. These reminders of just how much of an outsider she was made her heart ache with loss. There was 20 years of family history, full of small incidents and large, that she'd missed by running away. She doubted that she would ever recover all of it.

"I'm sure your Aunt Dahl has experienced plenty of pain in her life," Nonny said wryly, "everyone has. But no, what I was talking about is a quotation Dahl has, a Buddhist thing, 'All life is suffering' or 'includes suffering', something like that. You know that even the good Lord suffered, because He chose to be human. Suffering is part of being human. There's no need for you to feel bad about causing pain. We all suffer at one time or another, and it's not always a bad thing. Suffering can be good for us. It improves us. At least," she added, struggling to be honest, "it can. It doesn't always work."

She sipped her coffee. The cup trembled the tiniest bit in her hand. Counselling the young was not her favourite task, although it seemed to be about the only one she was good for anymore. Not that Marik could be considered young, strictly speaking. How did Jane Austen put it? At 27, one was no longer young. And Marik was ten years beyond that landmark.

At 27, Nonny was a wife, a mother to Gerry and Dahl and poor Flo, and pregnant with the next one. That baby would be Dan, father of this dear troubled granddaughter. Dan had taken it hard when his oldest left home like that, without warning and far too young. He hadn't wanted to know that she was a woman, although too young a woman, much too young, to leave home. How he had wanted to find someone to blame! It had been a shock to her, his accusation that it was her fault. She was Marik's grandmother, the family matriarch, she should have seen it coming! As though with age came clairvoyance!

What a painful, sorry time that had been, for the whole family, but most especially for Dan and Rose. They'd pulled themselves together, for the sake of their younger ones, but the hurt and the blame had torn at the already-weak fabric of their marriage, and Nonny had been helpless to mend it. Prayer had been all she could offer them, even though they had no faith in prayer. Prayer, in Nonny's experience, did work; and eventually her prayers had been answered, as Dan and Rose began to rebuild their marriage. It was stronger than it was before, as mended things sometimes are. Marik's disappearance, oddly enough, had the beneficial effect of forcing both Dan and Rose to re-examine themselves, their relationship, and their whole way of being in the world. Eventually, Marik had been located, although she had never been back to Chesney Creek except for the briefest of visits. They had the comfort of knowing that she was still alive in the world, although the fear of losing her forever was never far from them. It grieved them that she wanted little or nothing to do with them. Still, where there was life, there was hope, and Nonny had prayed every day that Marik might return, so that this wound in the family might to be healed. Once again, her prayers had been answered. Thank you God!

"You'll find your way back into the pattern," she said now. "Do you know the story of the Prodigal Son?"

"He ran away and lived with pigs, and then came home again. Right? That's me, the prodigal daughter," Marik tried to laugh, but choked on it. This was the feeling that she stuffed down, this complicated sense of shame and wrong-doing, her profound reluctance to let these innocent people know just how much she had loathed them, and how in her loathing she had come so close to destroying herself. Living with pigs, indeed! Loathsome, drunken, drug-addicted pigs! And she had become one herself. The hot tears of shame welled in her eyes, but at the same time, she was proud of herself, because she had pulled herself back out of the depths. There was more. She was proud of herself as well because she had the courage to return to the place and the people where she had gone wrong. She had the courage to start over again. She scrubbed her eyes with the sides of her thumbs. Somehow or another, she would get right again, right here in Chesney Creek. It wasn't really starting over. Like Terri had said, you can't go home again. You can't ever go back and start over, you can only go forward, making a fresh start. She had more than one fresh start behind her. She knew how to do that.

"The wonderful part of the story of the Prodigal Son is what happens when he returns," Nonny continued. "His father immediately calls for a celebration. There is no talk of forgiveness. You only need to forgive those whom you've held in resentment. No resentment – no need to forgive. No need to ask to be forgiven. Just celebration. That's how your family feels about having you home again, my dearest."

"I wish I could believe you, Gran, but that seems to be too good to be true, at least for me. It's more than I deserve."

Nonny picked up her cup. She let her other hand drift softly over the kitten's fur, and wondered how to comfort this unhappy, remorseful grandchild. She may not be clairvoyant, but she did have a clear vision of how a family, her family, ought to love one another. Sometimes it took all the strength she could muster to lift them up. Her son Dan, much to her surprise, required little lifting up this time. She was proud of him. He accepted his daughter's return with grace, as if he were the Biblical prodigy's father himself. He made it look easy. It was not so easy for the returned one. Here was their family prodigal, asking for help, but there was no mention of the grandmother in the Bible story. She had not idea how to convince the girl that she already had a place in the family pattern, that indeed she had always had a place, even when that place was not here in Chesney Creek. Nonny's cup rattled in the saucer as she replaced it.

"I'm sorry, Gran. I've worn you out," Marik exclaimed. "I shouldn't dump on you like that."

What a descriptive expression that was, the old woman thought, smiling inwardly as her gaze wandered out to the familiar, distant peaks across the valley. One might say that she had spent a lifetime listening to what others had to dump. What good did any of it do? She sagged against the cushions. Useless old woman that she was! What made her think she could help any of them?

Marik looked on with compassion as the veined eyelids drooped over the sunken eyes, and the loose old lips sagged.

Rose warned her that the old woman would do this sometimes, slip suddenly away into sleep in the midst of a conversation. Her mother was deliberately re-orienting her to the family, warning her about the differences she would see, such as Aunt Daisy's imminent diabetes and her ageing grandmother's tendency to slip away into sleep at unexpected moments, so that these changes didn't disconcert her. A bubbling snore spilled from the old woman's slack lips, the lower one grown pendulous, the upper decorated with a few strong dark hairs. Marik leaned forward, gently removing the cup and saucer from the gnarled fingers. They reminded her of the roots of old, tough trees, strengthened by adversity. Dear old Gran! If for no other reason, Marik was glad that she'd come back to Chesney Creek in time to get to know her grandmother as a person, rather than simply a role, the way children see the adults around them. She had missed that opportunity with her Grandfather. She had missed a lot in twenty years.

She heard the screen door brush open behind her. Aunt Dahl, coming out to check on them. "Gran's dozing." The door closed again, quietly, but it was enough to disturb the old woman, who snorted herself awake.

"I wasn't sleeping, I was thinking. If you don't want to stay with Dan and Rose, why don't you move out here? Dahlia would welcome another pair of hands in the house. In the barn, too. You always did like the horses, didn't you? You had that collection of plastic horses that your Aunt Dahlia collected when she was my little girl. She gave them to you. I remember how thrilled you were when she did that!"

Nonny chuckled reminiscently, then sobered. She laid her withered hand on Marik's knee. "You could replay her, give her a hand around here in return."

It was true, she had been horse-mad as a child. It wasn't practical, her parents said, to have a horse when they lived in town. Even if they could keep it out at Gran and Poppa's farm, it wouldn't work. They'd had all sorts of reasons why she shouldn't and couldn't have a horse. Yet when Liz or Robbie wanted something, a flute to play in school band or a basketball hoop beside the driveway, they got what they wanted. It was only Marik, the oldest one, the responsible one, who was expected to do without. She never got what she wanted. Her lips tightened on that old familiar hurtful thought before she remembered to ask herself if it were really true. Her years in recovery taught to question herself and her analysis of the events from her childhood.

She ran from home shortly after Dan got on at the fire hall. Since her father came home every night, she told herself, her mother didn't need a little slave anymore. So she left. She walked out to the highway at the outskirts of town with one little bag of her most precious possessions, and stuck out her thumb, and left. What a fool she had been! She had forgiven them for their part, but how on earth could they forgive her?

Nonny was waiting for her answer. "Let me think about it, Gran."

The screen door slapped behind Fleur as she followed Dahlia, Daisy and Rose out onto the shaded veranda, coffee mugs in hand. The others settled onto the shabby wicker seats while Rose leaned against the railing, her back to the lowering sun. How the girls had teased Dan when he came home with another "flower girl" as his bride.

Nonny wondered, now, why she'd chosen to name all her daughters after flowers. Lincoln wanted family names for the boys. She'd been fine with that, but the family names on her side had seemed too old fashioned, too European. She wanted something different. Like her mother before her, she had always loved flowers. Her own darling Granny, her mother's mother, told her about the patch of pansies that she had tended so lovingly years ago, on the barren rocky land of an island croft. They'd saved her sanity, she said, those few small flowers lighting the bleakness of her isolated life. Flowers were a precious part of her maternal heritage. So Nonny's girls were all named for flowers, and then Dan had brought home another one, his Rose. "Come sit with me," she said now to Rose, pulling her afghan aside to make room on the wicker loveseat. "I've been suggesting to your dear girl that she come and stay with us. You wouldn't mind, would you?"

"It's time for your lie-down, Mom" Dahlia reminded her. "You know what the doctor said."

It was a relief to let herself be pulled upright onto her feet, to shuffle into the house and retreat to the comfortable sofa in the front room where she could stretch out. The seed was planted. They would arrange matters so that Marik could move here to the farm where she was needed. The murmur of their voices outside on the veranda came to her ears, though not the words. A pity; at one time, her hearing had been acute enough to hear what the children were plotting when they sat on the veranda at the end of the day. Fleur and Frank... She was worried about Fleur, without Frank to look after her. She hadn't wanted them to marry. Fleur was gifted with domestic skills, but Nonny and her dear Lincoln had decided that marriage would not be right for this pretty daughter. They understood her limited mental capacities. Robbed of oxygen at birth, Fleur's brain was different. The best thing would be to keep her at home with them. She would have done well as the daughter-at-home, Nonny thought ruefully, better than her Dahlia.

Fleur had been her third baby, although she would have been fourth if Nonny had carried her predecessor to term. She still wondered if the late, painful miscarriage the year before had done something inside, something that made Fleur's birth so long and difficult. She had developed more slowly than the others, and the doctors had not been able to tell them exactly what to expect. In fact, they'd been lucky. Fleur was just a bit slow, slow to walk, slow to talk, slow in school. Slow to develop. Not great wife-material, they'd thought, but Frank, a young widower, had fallen in love with her gentleness and her loving nature. She adored his little Brad, and Frank knew she would look after him with all the motherly love that his biological mother hadn't been able to give. He had recognized Fleur's limitations, but they didn't matter to him. He promised faithfully to look after her, to appreciate her virtues and to be kind to her small faults, and so they'd given their grudging consent to the marriage. It had turned out far better than they had dared to expect. Not only that their daughter in good hands, but Frank himself was a treasure, a gift that Fleur had brought into the family. Dear Frank! Dozing, Nonny's thoughts drifted contentedly along the cloudy edges of memory and dream.

Out on the veranda, the others were discussing Marik's future plans.

"I'd love to have you here," Dahlia told her.

"Trust your grandmother to come up with an inspired idea," Rose added.

"You sure you won't mind, Mom? You won't feel like I'm abandoning you – again?"

"Not at all, but weren't you talking about renting an apartment? Maybe you could pay Dahl rent. That would be fair. But won't you have to find a job soon?"

Marik bit her lip. She wanted to blurt, "I've got all the money I need, Mom!" but she hadn't told anyone about the lottery win. Not one single member of the family knew she was secretly a multimillionaire with an income that would always be more than sufficient for her needs. She told them that she had 'savings'. That was true, she did. What they didn't know was how huge those "savings" were. Rose's logical assumption that she was living on her savings and would use them up soon, was just that, an assumption.

Now she had the opportunity to come clean, to confess that she was an extremely wealthy woman. Her mother had always been money-conscious, or rather, lack-of-money conscious, always fearful that there might not be enough for the next month, or for next year. It would be wonderful to give her a share of the lottery money, enough to free her from that long-held fear! Yet how could she do that without everyone finding out? She wasn't ready for that. Before she admitted to her riches, she wanted to know if she could be accepted as part of the family, part of the community, in the way that she would have been if she hadn't run away. Time enough to be the family's Mrs. Moneybags, later. She squashed the impulse to confess. This was not the right time. Once they knew about money, everything would change.

"Or you could come and stay with me, darling Marik," Fleur said. "I'd like that."

"What about me?" Daisy exclaimed, laughing. "I could use another woman in the house. I should get Marik!"

Saved by the Flo, Marik thought, relieved laughter bubbling up inside. Rose's uncomfortable money-questions could be answered some other time.

"Of course I'd pay you rent-money, Aunt Dahl." It would be generous rent, too, if she had anything to say about it. "Room and board, that's only fair. And maybe.....maybe you could find a horse for me, one I could buy? I'd pay room and board for that, too."

Rose picked up the coffee tray, and loaded it with their cups. "That's settled, then. Good."

Later, after the others went back into town, Dahl pulled on her flannel shirt and went outdoors to bring Skudder into the barn for the night. It was cooler tonight, with a wind picking up. The other horses were fine out on pasture, but her old pensioner needed the shelter of the barn on such an end-of-summer night. She slipped his fly-sheet off in the alleyway between the box stalls, and began the ritual of grooming him, one experienced hand drawing swift circles with the rounded spring-steel curry comb to loosen the dust, the other flicking the dandy-brush to lift it out of his fine chestnut coat. She was pleased that he had put on weight over the summer, his skin rounded over the old bones. She had been worried about him in the spring, he had been slow to recover from the winter. She ducked under his neck to do the other side, and he nuzzled her, the loose old lips pulling at her rolled up sleeve.

She thought of Marik, asking for a horse to buy. History repeats itself; a horse had been what she had needed, in order to re-integrate herself into life back home, when she returned to help nurse her father through his last illness. Her mind ranged over the horses out in the pastures. None of them would do for her niece, she needed a younger one, one that could take her for a gallop, or a good long trail ride. The horses Dahl kept were too senior for that. She purposefully bought these older horses who had outlived their usefulness. Rescuing them supplied her with quiet, amiable animals, a perfect match for the needs of a riding-school, especially with the handicapped youngsters in her Ability Riders group. How they flourished, put up in a saddle! She thought of Roger Pasqualli, crumpled up in a wheelchair for most of his young life, but oh! Lifted up onto a gentle animal, reins clasped in his cramped hands, and steadied on either side by volunteer-helpers, he was in control as he could never be, otherwise. He was a cowboy, a jockey, a knight in shining armour! He was a master of life – that was the gift that her horses were able to give. Dahl buckled the stable sheet under Skudder's belly, and loosed him into the box stall. That was one of her antiques put to bed. Now to get her mother up the stairs and into bed. If only the old woman would agree to move downstairs, how much easier life would be. If only!

Nonny was sitting in the front room with her current crochet project, another afghan for the Boomer Project, moving steadily through her hands. It was a comfortable room, with pale yellow walls above the white wainscoting, and deep couches and chairs covered in worn plush and chintz, evidence of the good taste of the woman who had furnished and loved it for these many years. Nonny had come to the farm as a war bride, inheriting her mother-in-law's stiff Victorian and Edwardian furniture. Those had been good years in the Canadian agricultural industry, and Nonny had quickly put the comfortable stamp of her Scottish country background on this North American dwelling. She made a lovely picture now of peaceful old age, in her wing-back chair with the soft glow of the lamp light turning her white hair into a halo, and the kitten, Domino, purring on the back of the chair. "It was a beautiful sunset. Did you see it, from the barn?"

Dahlia pulled the heavy green velvet drapes, lined with warm peach, across the window, shutting out the night. She had seen the sunset, glowing from behind the rise of the hills, filling the whole sky and the valley below with a vivid rosy light before it faded to blue and turquoise and mauve and then into darkness.

She helped the old woman to her feet, handed her the rubber-tipped walking stick, recaptured the ball of wool from Domino, and followed both of them upstairs. It was a slow progression, the old woman stopping twice to catch her breath. She shook Dahlia's hand off her elbow impatiently, and soldiered on to the top of the staircase, one hand on the rail, the other leaning heavily on the old carved walking stick. Dahlia admired her independence as much as she was exasperated by it. At last, they were both in their bedclothes, the old woman sitting up against her pillows in the high bed, the soft angora bed jacket she'd knit for herself around her shoulders. Dahlia sat on the end of the bed in her old red flannel dressing gown, Domino on her lap.

"Take down my hair, dear." This too was part of their evening ritual, the unpinning of the long white braid that Nonny wore as a coronet around her head in the daytime. She was able to braid it and pin it up herself, in the morning, but by the tired end of the day, she appreciated help.

"Mother, we need to talk about having Marik here. I like the idea, I do, but I'm wondering which room we should give her. Whichever one we choose, I'm going to have to find time to clear it out." Dahl's shoulders sagged at the thought. As though she needed one more project to do! Her helper girls, Alika and Bonnie, had kept the unused bedrooms dusted. Housework and barn chores paid for their riding lessons, but they were both leaving Chesney Creek to go to college. Like most unused rooms in large houses, the extra bedrooms had become convenient depositories for the whole family's unused or unwanted items. Whichever room her mother chose for Marik would be Dahlia's responsibility. It would need de-cluttering and deep cleaning, and probably new paint and wallpaper as well.

"I think she should have this room. It's the biggest." Nonny looked thoughtfully around. "We'll move my bed and dressing table downstairs. There are enough other pieces in the house to furnish this room as a sort of bedroom-sitting room. Marik will need a space to herself so she can get away from us old women."

"You mean – you'll move downstairs?" Dahl stammered. After all these months of resisting the idea, her mother's sudden capitulation caught her off guard.

"Yes, of course," Nonny snapped. "You young people think that old folks can't change, you think we're stuck in our ways, but that's just not true. I can make changes if I need to! I may be old, but I'm not stupid." She sank back on her pillows, exhausted by her display of temper. She was getting too old to be acerbic, it took too much out of her. Unfortunately, by the end of the day she didn't have the energy to hold herself up to the standard of kindness and consideration that she expected herself, as well as others, to display.

"But where downstairs? Which room could you go into? Surely not the back bedroom, you said when Daddy died that you never wanted to be put in there." She held her breath. The choice was obvious. The farm office would be perfect. Back when the house was built by Dahlia's great-grandfather, the large room off the kitchen had been designated for the cook/housekeeper. It had been used as the farm office now for decades. The smaller back bedroom under the stairs by the back door was built to house the farm hand. For some reason, her father had chosen that room as his invalid room, the room he'd died in. She could understand her mother's reluctance to move into it. The farm office was larger than the hired hand's room, but even so, it certainly wasn't large enough to house all of Nonny's heavy, handsome bedroom furnishings.

"The girl's room, of course. I was looking at it this evening, while you were outdoors. You'll have to cut the lilac back, I don't know why you've let it get so overgrown. You'll have to move all your bookshelves and the computer and everything into the dining room. We never use it anymore, you may as well turn it into an office. It has a view of the barn and the yard, you should like that, and you won't be so isolated like you are there, back off the kitchen." It was as if the old woman was trying to convince her that the move made sense!

"Maybe Marik should have the girl's room, since she'll be housemaid and farm hand combined." Dahl regretted the words as soon as she spoke them. What a foolish thing to say! She crossed her fingers behind her back. She found herself arguing with her mother all too often. She didn't understand why she was driven so often by the impulse to disagree with the old woman. This time, thank goodness, her mother ignored her protests. She insisted that Marik must have the big upstairs room.

"If she's going to pay room and board, she should have the best we can offer. That means I have to give her my room."

"Moving the office into the dining room is a good idea," Dahlia said. "I hadn't thought that far ahead." They didn't use the formal dining room. Back when all five of them were growing up on the farm, Nonny gathered them around the big table for meals three times a day, along with any friends, neighbours or workers who happened to be on hand when food hit the table. Now with just the two of them in the big old house, they lived mostly in the front room and kitchen. Visitors, too, congregated around the dented scrubbed pine table in the big farmhouse kitchen. Eating there made it easier to serve and clean up. The dining room would be no loss.

"I'll start moving things tomorrow. And I'll cut back the lilac, you are right, it does block too much of the light." She would give Dan a call. Her brother was usually good for a helping hand when she needed it. Dahlia got to her feet and dropped a kiss on the old white head. She glanced back from the door, seeing the kitten curled up by the old woman's side. It would be strange to see her mother in a different setting after all these years, she thought, but thank goodness she was willing to make the change. The end of one era meant the beginning of another. There would be no more worrying about the old woman falling up or down the stairs. Feeling lighter hearted than she'd been for more months than she cared to count, Dahlia closed the door and went thankfully to her own bedroom across the hall.

CHAPTER SIX
Running Shoes

The maple and alder leaves were golden under Marik's feet, and above her head as well. She loved this particular part of the trail around Chesney Lake, especially at this time of year when the arched deciduous trees began to drop their leaves. The filtered afternoon sunshine glowed through the autumn leaves above and below her, so that she felt as though she were walking through a golden cathedral.

These daily walks had become a habit for her. Now that she wasn't waitressing, she found that she missed the physical activity that work had entailed. Being in motion had been part of her daily life for years. Although she certainly didn't miss waitressing, she did feel the need to use her muscles. The rough terrain of the trail, she noticed with appreciation, was an immense improvement over the concrete floors of the Olde Beanery, and how good it felt to be out in the open air. Later today, she would go out to the farm, as she did almost every day now.

Yesterday, she and Aunt Dahl had painted Gran's new downstairs bedroom. The paint would be dry now, and her father had promised to organize some of his fellow fire-fighters to come out in the next day or two to move the bedroom furniture downstairs. Once Gran was settled in, Marik would be able to redecorate the big bedroom upstairs as her own new home. She would buy new linens and drapes, as well as new furniture. She would get a really comfortable mattress, she thought eagerly, unlike any she'd ever slept on, and Egyptian cotton sheets. A new start! It would use up some of the cash that had been accumulating in her new checking account at Valley & District Credit Union. She would have to find a logical explanation for her mother, however, to explain why she wanted to splurge on all these new things.

She could just imagine what Rose would say. "You don't have to buy everything new all at once!" she'd say. "Take some of the things from here, from your old bedroom! Don't spend all your savings! You'll regret it if you do." Poor Rose, always so anxious about money. Even now, with no children at home and two good incomes coming in, Rose still worried about money. She and Dan were secure, but now she was concerned about the next generation. Marik's brother Rob and his wife had three little children now, and were still in a rental. Liz and Zachary should be putting away money for their boys' college funds! Marik listened to the litany of anxiety, knowing how unnecessary it was, but as Lizzie said, worrying about money was virtually a hobby for their mother.

Marik scuffled her shoes through the leaves, lifting them with her toe so that they showered around her feet. There was a jogger coming up behind her, she could hear the footfalls growing closer, but she resisted the temptation to turn around. It might be Stan; he had never called her, and, much as she hated to admit it to herself, some part of the reason for her daily walks was the hope of running into him again, if only to snub him. He'd had two weeks. It wasn't unreasonable, was it, to expect him to make good on his promise? If he hadn't intended to call, she wondered, why had he taken her number? And on the other hand, what on earth was she doing, hoping for a call from a cop, or hoping to run into him again here in the park?

The jogger coming up behind her wasn't Stan, but rather a young woman with earphones and shiny pink wrist- and ankle-weights. She gave Marik a nod in passing, and ran on. A serious runner, with all the proper gear and muscular legs; no doubt that was the sort of woman a guy like Stan would be looking for. All these serious exercisers! The park was not as peaceful as it used to be. In Marik's memories from childhood, it was only in the summer time that hordes of people filled the park, gathering on the beaches around the lake. Large rural properties like her Aunt Daisy and Uncle Will's surrounded it, and the only people in the park once summer was over were occasional fishermen, or teenagers avoiding parental supervision. Over the years that she had been away, Chesney Creek had grown. House prices had soared in the urban centres to the east and south, and since prices were so much lower here, more and more people were willing to face the commute.

"We've been turned into a bedroom for Quinton," her father grumbled. Her conversations with Dan often seemed to end with his being irritated about something. Despite the way the women of the family had welcomed her with open arms, her relationship with her father remained strained. That troubled her, but she didn't know what she could do about it. It would be better, perhaps, when she wasn't living in his home. She raised her head, taking a deep breath of the fresh morning air, and reminded herself to appreciate what was good about this moment. The bottom line was that Chesney Creek's population had grown, and consequently more people were using the park all year around, including this seemingly endless parade of sleekly-dressed suburban runners.

"They're training for Chesney Creek's first Half Marathon event," her cousin Edward told her when she'd met him on one of her very first morning walks in the park. "We started it at the Chamber of Commerce. We're challenging local businesses to enter teams." Edward Karlsson was a maternal cousin, her Aunt Lindy's son. She had been dismayed when he jogged up beside her, gave her the usual runner's nod of greeting, and then pulled up short. Ed was the last person she wanted to meet when she was out for a peaceful stroll, and by herself.

"Marik! I heard you were back in town!" He grinned, flashing that dimple that so women found irresistible according to her Aunts Joan and Jan, those inveterate gossips. They told her about her cousin while they were picking berries. Divorced, he had a reputation as Chesney Creek's resident Don Juan, according to the aunts. Marik could believe it.

"It's great to see you, you're looking good." He slowed his steps to match hers. He wore an orange tee, just snug enough to show off his muscular torso, loose grey jersey shorts and the gaudiest shoes that she'd seen on any runner, orange and purple and green. It was all she could do to be civil to him.

"I'm training for the half marathon. It's just about killing me, but I've got to do my civic duty." He told her about the fund-raiser. "It's for the local food bank. I'm president of the committee this year." He explained his involvement in the project, making it sound as if the idea had originated in the offices of Bolster and Nod, perhaps even in the mind of that brilliant young barrister Edward Karlsson.

"So I'm in training, three days a week. Why don't you join me? You'd look good in running ... shoes." He flickered a flirtatious blond eyebrow, letting her see that his focus on her good looks was well above shoe level. Other women no doubt found his innuendos amusing, even flattering, but Marik was immune to his charms. There was no denying that he was good-looking, by any woman's standards. He had the rugged good looks of his Scandinavian heritage. The blond hair, worn just a little bit too long, and the blue eyes framed by unusually dark lashes, were his inheritance from his father, Jack-the-Jerk-Karlsson. He'd inherited his father's high opinion of the Karlsson sex appeal, too, an opinion he apparently expected her to share.

Marik bit back the words that sprang to her lips. She didn't tell him to F-off, although those were the first words that sprang to mind. She wasn't a street-person anymore; she could discipline herself enough to exercise some discretion about what words came out of her mouth. Instead, and for the sake of family peace, she only said, coldly, "I don't think so," and "Don't let me stop you from your exercise."

"It's not my favourite exercise, but it will have to do," he'd said, treating her to a wink and a raised eyebrow. He jogged on ahead of her down the trail, turning for just a moment to flash his dimple in a grin that was just barely not a leer.

Revolting man – her stomach was in knots after the encounter. Meeting him brought back the memories that she longed to forget. If only she could! He had been the bane of her childhood, her most-hated enemy. She thought she had put that behind her. She knew when she came back to Chesney Creek that she would inevitably run into him. She expected it to be at a family gathering, surrounded by others. She would brush him off, move past the uncomfortable memories. She had been sure she could do that, sure that the work she'd done in recovery had reduced any lingering disgust to a manageable level. He would be just another family connection.

Instead, she'd run into him one-on-one in the park. It had been worse than she expected. Apparently she hadn't put those feelings as far behind her as she had hoped. Nonetheless, she told herself now, she had handled the uncomfortable, unexpected meeting very well. She'd stood strong in her own power, had acted and spoken with control and dignity. She had refused to be disconcerted by his appalling sexual innuendos. She hadn't been drawn into conflict. She had set the limits of their conversation, because he no longer had any real power over her. She had brushed him off, she told herself, in a highly civilized manner.

He might be the same, full of himself and his macho bravado, but she was no longer the little girl cousin, to be bullied and dominated by him. Nor was she the reactive street-person that his little girl-cousin had become. Instead, she owned her own reactions and deliberately chose how to conduct herself. If she ran into him again today, she'd brush him off again. Sue-Ellen, her sponsor, would have been proud of her. She was proud of herself! Edward Karlsson no longer had any power over her. In short, Phoo him. The expression made her laugh. She had gone into recovery with a mouth like a sewer. Someone, maybe Sue-Ellen or some other long-term member, had suggested that she clean up her language. "Euphemisms can be fun," they'd said, and she had discovered the truth of it, and learned to laugh at herself. Phoo him indeed!

Nonetheless, after that encounter with her cousin Edward, she decided that early morning was not, after all, the ideal time to be in the Park. Instead of being dropped off by Rose on her way to work at the Library, Marik washed up their breakfast dishes and made the beds before driving down to the Park entrance off north Main. A brisk walk before lunch was just as good as one right after breakfast.

She drew in a deep breath of the crisp mid-September air. No need to dwell on uncomfortable memories. It was too lovely a day a day for that. More leaves, russet and deep burgundy as well as golden, carpeted the trail with each passing day. High above, beyond the thinning canopy, dark clouds were massing. There would be rain before the day was done. Two more joggers passed her, chatting as they ran. She turned off the main trail to go down a narrow, less-used path leading down to the lake shore. Years ago, this had been a mere thread of a trail through the brush, used only by exploring fishermen looking for the perfect spot to cast a lure out on the quiet water. Alongside the water, the walkway had been widened, low spots built up on a kind of dyke for dryer footing. It was still pleasantly wild and private, enclosed on one side by the thick forest undergrowth of ferns and shrubs, and bordered on the other side by the tangle of reeds and swampy vegetation rooted deep in the marshy edges of the lake. There was a scent of rain-to-come in the wind blowing off the water, and she wished for a moment that she'd worn a heavier jacket.

Yesterday when she had come this way on her walk, there had been wild ducks, black and white, where the lake opened out into deeper water. She'd looked them up in her father's shabby old bird book. From her description, Dan said, they were mergansers or possibly buffleheads, one or the other. Amateurs often confused the two, although they were completely different types of ducks, he told her. With luck, she would get another look at them today, even though, darn it, she had forgotten to bring Rose's light-weight binoculars. She would buy a pair of her own, a really good pair. She meant to do that yesterday, but she hadn't gone shopping. She still wasn't accustomed to the idea that she could simply go out and buy virtually anything she wanted. In hiding the fact of her wealth from others, she reflected, she had almost hidden it from herself. Last week when she had her monthly call with Ken Rheddenk, he'd chided her for not using up the monthly 'allowance' that automatically deposited in her checking account.

"Use it!" he said, "Go shopping and enjoy it, that's what it's for. There's plenty more where it came from!" Shopping, however, had never been a favoured recreation for her, the way it seemed to be for so many women. Anything extra she'd earned as a waitress, above and beyond her daily living expenses of rent and food and comfortable work shoes, she hoarded to pay for her college courses.

She took one or two courses every year, although not for the sake of a degree. It wasn't that she wanted to get a better job with higher wages. She liked waitressing. She liked the way that she could change how people felt, just by being kind to them. She was content with what she earned, especially with the tips. The reason she took the college courses was that she simply enjoyed learning, exposing herself to new knowledge and new ideas.

Consequently, her courses were all over the map. She had studied everything from art history to sociology, from history to psychology, and even philosophy. She'd especially enjoyed the Modern Philosophy course. That professor had touched on neuro-science and a host of other topics, eastern spirituality, the law of attraction, quantum energy, and other ideas that he referred to as "the Woo-woo fringe of philosophy".

The speculative discussions, lively and sometimes even vituperative, entranced Marik. Once she was settled here in Chesney Creek, she would have to find out what courses might be available through the community college down in Quinton. Spending money on tuition interested her far more than spending her money on the latest fashion trends. Maybe, she thought, she just wasn't the type that should have a whole lot of money. Her only extravagant spending this month was the paint for Gran's room and her own. She'd gone to the new big-box home-store out at the east end of town, and bought the most expensive, full-coverage, environmentally safe, toxin-free paint she could find. Gran and Dahlia offered to pay for the paint, but she'd brushed them off, saying that it was part of her moving-in budget. Neither of them realized just how expensive and up-scale the paint was, but it was worth every penny, she thought. She was so looking forward to living out at the farm. It was a childhood's dream come true.

While they were painting Gran's room yesterday, Dahlia told her that one of the horse-rescue organizations she worked with had a young mare that might do for her. That evening, she borrowed Rose's computer and sent Terri an email about it.

"I'm going to get a horse!" she told her friend. She could imagine what Terri would think. Her old roommate would give her head a shake, and accuse her of going redneck. "Aunt Dahl's found me a rescue horse, which means it will cost virtually nothing. I could buy a registered Quarter Horse or a full-blood Arabian if I wanted," she typed, "but if I did, I'd blow my cover! Everyone would know I've got money up the yin-yang! That's the last thing I want, so here's hoping this rescue critter will work out."

She found the idea of rescuing an unwanted horse far more appealing than buying an expensive, highly-bred one, the sort that would always be assured of devoted care. She was horrified by Dahlia's stories about the NorthWind horses. How could people treat animals that way? She would give her new horse the life it deserved. She let her imagination run forward, into a future when she would ride this lovely trail along the lake on horseback, rather than walking as she was today. She would buy that pair of expensive, up-scale binoculars this afternoon, she decided. She would carry them with her when she rode by the lake or up into the hills beyond. She saw herself cantering across sunny meadows, the fresh wind blowing in her hair and her horse's long mane.

Suddenly her daydreams were exploded by a shout. "Halt right there!" The sun on the trail ahead framed the silhouette of a man, one arm raised in a peremptory gesture as he barked an order at her again. "Don't come any closer!"

She could see now that it was a runner, bare legged and tee shirted. These people training for the marathon seemed to think they owned the whole park! She strode boldly forward.

"Lady, stay where you are!" he ordered.

"Says who?" She yelled back at him. How dare he tell her to stop? "I've as much right to walk here as anyone!"

"Police!" He snapped back at her, and stepped in her direction. "Don't come any closer, ma'am, you don't want to see..." His voice trailed off. "Marik? What are you doing here?"

"Stan?" It was him, she realized, recognizing the big grey dog who sat with patient alertness behind him. "What's going on?"

"You don't want to know. Can you stop anyone else that comes down the trail your way? I've got backup coming, they should be here soon." He glanced behind him, in case anyone was coming from the other direction.

There was no one else on the trail. She took a step closer, until she could look down the steep lakeside bank behind the man and dog. The growth of reeds and brush was dense, but through their shadows she could make out the pale shapes of bare arms and legs. It appeared that a jogger had fallen of the trail, the body twisted down half hidden in the swampy undergrowth of the lakeside. His extended arms trailing down into the water and one bare leg was exposed. On the motionless thigh, blond hairs gleamed in the sunshine.

"Aren't you going to help him, get him up?"

"He's past that."

"Past that? What do you mean?" She drew back. "He's dead?"

"I'm afraid so. I've called backup." The wind came up then, shifting the reeds to reveal the gaudy, multicolour running shoes. Marik hand shot up involuntarily to cover her mouth, as though she were pushing herself back even as she leaned forward, trying to make out more.

"Get back, Marik, you don't want to see this."

"I think I know who it is." She recognized the grey shorts, the gaudy orange tee that was crumpled up under his arm pits as he lay face-down in the muck. The blond hair on the back of his head matted and dark. "Oh God – it is. It's him. Is he...?"

"Yes, most definitely. I checked." They could hear the sirens now, coming into the park, and then cutting off abruptly as they got to the parking lot out at the end of the park.

"I hated him," she gasped, "but not enough to want to see him like that!" Her gut revolted. She spun on her heel, fled to the other side of the pathway away from Stan, and crouched, heaving, until her stomach was empty. Stan touched her on her shoulder, offered her his water bottle. She rinsed her mouth, spat and rinsed it again. He was on his cellphone, directing the police.

"The south parking lot. Take the jogging path to your right – west. There's a trail....Hold on," he turned to Marik, "Can you - ?"

She understood. He needed someone to direct them.

"I'll send someone out to the turning. A bystander."

She handed the water bottle back him, and turned to go back out to the jogging path to meet them.

"Wait! I don't want you out there by yourself, it might not be safe." He tapped his thigh, and the big dog jumped up to join them. "Trigger will go with you. Go on, go with Marik!" he commanded, gesturing. "Go on up the path, he'll come with you. No one will bother you."

Marik broke into a jog up the narrow path through the trees, with the big grey dog pacing beside her. When she reached the bark-mulched running trail, she saw four officers trotting towards her, garbed in heavy black jackets and duty belts, with all their official accoutrements bumping around their hips. She waved to them, catching the leader's attention. They were probably Chesney Creek's entire available lineup of law enforcement on this quiet Thursday afternoon, she thought. She stood aside as they turned to head single-file down the narrow trail. The third one noticed the big dog beside her, and paused just long enough to cast a glance over her. Other than that, no one paid any attention to her, or even looked back as she and Trigger followed back to where Stan waited. The one woman, her straight blond hair pulled into a no-nonsense ponytail on the nape of her neck, dropped back to speak to Marik. "Stay here, but stay well back. I'll have a look at this, then I'll want to talk with you. You were the first one here, right?"

"After Stan, yes."

"Officer Albescu," she said tersely. The message was 'don't call my men by their first names.' Or perhaps, 'my man'? Marik waited patiently while the officers inspected the body and strung the yellow scene-of-crime tape up, blocking off the path from both directions. She stepped back to stay on the outside of the barrier. A few drops of rain were stippling the silvery surface of the lake. There were still no ducks to be seen. Clouds, heavy with rain, covered the sky above the lake as far as she could see. A young woman pushing a stroller came down the trail, but halted before she reached Marik, when she saw the yellow tape and all the activity. She spun the stroller around and retreated. Moments after she disappeared back up the trail, she was followed by a lanky, grey-haired man in khakis, his sports jacket damp on the shoulders.

"Bob Pasqualli," he introduced himself to Marik, "from the Chesney Recorder. I heard it on the scanner. What's going on?"

Before she could answer, the female officer was beside them. "Talk to me, Bob."

"I heard it on the scanner, you've got a body?" He ducked under the tape, and followed the female officer, their voices kept low. Marik saw her gesture to Stan, jerking her thumb over her shoulder to send him away from the reporter. He came back to join Marik and Trigger.

"You okay? It will be awhile, but June will need to talk to you. To both of us." He glanced back at his fellow officers, an unreadable expression on his face. "She doesn't want us talking to Bob, not yet anyway. I told her you knew the guy. I did too, once I saw his face. Ed somebody, isn't he? He was a couple years ahead of us, a big hero on the ball team, as I recall."

"Ed Karlsson." She grimaced, not wanting to talk about him, but knowing she would have to, there was no escaping it. "He's a cousin."

"Okay, I don't need to know anything about it. You can tell June about it when she gets rid of Bob. I won't have any official role in this investigation, unless they decide that since I found him, I'm a suspect. A cousin, you said. You have a lot of family in Chesney Creek, don't you? I seem to recall that. You were with all your aunts, weren't you, picking blackberries?"

"You didn't call." That was a mistake, she hadn't meant to say anything about that. "Not all my aunts, just Daze and my twin aunts, and..." She realized she was babbling, trying to turn his attention away from the blurted accusation.

"Yeah, I'm sorry about that, I meant to call but then, well, stuff happened," he paused, as though wondering how much to tell her. "I would like to see you again. I mean, not like this," he added ruefully. "This isn't quite the ideal first date, is it, stumbling across this...situation."

June was escorting the newsman back past them, away from the action. "No names, Bob, and not interviewing, not yet. You can just say 'found by joggers.' Please. Until I have a chance to hear what they have to tell me. I know it will be the biggest story in Chesney Creek right now, but I don't want their stories messed up by twice-telling."

Bob tucked his notebook back into the inside pocket of his jacket. "Alright, but you owe me one. I'll call you later for their contact info." She nodded in reluctant agreement.

"I'll see you two later," Pasqualli said to Stan and Marik. "Chesney Creek has a right to know much more than Ms. Detective Halston wants to tell me. I'll be in touch, later this afternoon or early tomorrow." With that, he strode away.

"It will be the headlines on Saturday, Goddamn it," June said angrily. The Chesney Creek Recorder published three days a week, Tuesday, Thursday and Saturday. "Unless we're lucky enough to be hit by a giant meteor between then and now. Alright you two, let's have your story. You were together when you found him?"

Some of the tension seemed to go out of her as Stan explained that he was the one who discovered Ed's body and that Marik had only come along after he'd called it in. She was an innocent bystander who had volunteered to go and meet the officers so that Stan could stay with the body.

She made a note of Marik's phone number, warned her not to leave town. "I'll need for you to come in to the station this afternoon to give me an official statement, for the record." She pulled her phone out a pocket, brought up her scheduler, and told Marik she would expect to see her at 1:15.

"I'll ask you to keep this to yourself until then. Try not to be talking about it to everyone you meet, especially not to Pasqualli. He's liable to be waiting for you, so just tell him I told you to keep your mouth closed." The rain was coming down harder now, although it was still relatively dry under the shelter of the trees. "I'll rephrase that: I'd prefer that you not talk to people about this until we can inform his immediate family." Marik hadn't had a chance to tell her that the victim was one of her cousins. "This town has a flourishing grapevine, I'd rather that the gossips are kept busy with the usual who's-meeting-whom behind the barn, for the time being. So keep your mouths shut, both of you. Please. Albescu, I'll see you at the station later on."

"I don't need to identify him or anything?" Marik asked. She'd read enough detective stories to know that it might be her uncomfortable duty to take a closer look at her cousin's body. "I know who he is."

"We already know who he is," June said impatiently. "This small town, everyone knows everybody, one of my officers was in school with him. Go on now, you don't have to stand here in the rain. God forbid that I ask a citizen to do that!"

Marik turned to go, but Stan stopped her with a hand on her arm. "I'll call you," he said. He ignored June's dark look. "I mean that, this time for real."

CHAPTER SEVEN

Father and Daughter

Dan was just getting up after sleeping off his night shift when Marik came in, dripping wet, from her afternoon walk. "Will you be here? I've got something to tell you," she blurted, "but I have to get dry first." She bolted upstairs.

Dan cringed in dismay. Now what? He ran his hands through his thick grey hair, a nervous habit that seemed to help him think. He didn't know how to respond to his daughter, this stranger who'd come to live with them. Rose seemed able to put the past behind her, to forgive and forget and move forward, but Dan found that impossible. He and his daughter spoke to one another as two well-disposed strangers might do, polite but distant. He was unable to bridge the twenty year gap that lay between the two of them, unable to connect this 35-year-old woman with the little girl he had loved so much. She was his daughter, but not his daughter, and that was fine with him. The girl had hurt him too badly, running away like that. The shock and trauma of it had left scars on his life that would be with him to his dying day. He had recovered, they all had, but that event had changed everything, including his marriage. The damage couldn't be undone.

She came back downstairs and sat down at the kitchen table and told him about finding Edward

Karlsson. He could see that she was upset, but all he could think of to say was, "They'll be back at the cop-shop by now. You'd better phone, and get down there."

"I hate talking to cops!"

"That's stupid," he snapped back, and immediately regretted it. He wouldn't speak like that to a stranger. He muttered an apology, not looking at her.

"No, I'm the one who's sorry, Dad. It's just that.....well, I've had some bad experiences. You're right, I'll give them a call right now. Who should I call? Not 9-1-1, right?"

"No," he agreed, and reached for the phone book in the kitchen drawer. He flipped it open, found the non-emergency number and handed her the book. He was right, Detective Halston was back at the station and wanted to see Marik as soon as possible.

After Marik left, Dan retreated to his workshop in the garage. Today, he wanted to finish sanding down the matched pair of rocking horses he was building for Rob's twins, his new granddaughters, but he couldn't concentrate. He found himself staring out the dusty workshop window, remembering Rose's hysterical phone call when she came home from the library and found Marik's note, all those years ago. He had been on shift, at the fire-hall. Looking back, it seemed to Dan that the girl had thrown a bomb into his life that day, causing an explosion that changed everything. God but he had been angry! He'd blamed everyone, Rose, the school, even his mother and sisters. Weren't the senior women of the family supposed to look out for the younger ones? Bottom line was, they hadn't.

Dan picked up a cloth and rubbed some of the dust off the workshop window, fine sawdust from the projects he'd completed in the past few years. Maybe when the rocking horses were done, he'd take a break from making things. He'd take time to give the workshop a thorough going over, maybe even frame in the windows as he'd been meaning to do for years. He rubbed his hands over the smooth wooden saddle as his thoughts drifted back to those awful months after Marik disappeared. She had almost destroyed his marriage. He and Rose had said far too many ugly things to one another. Always outspoken, she had nonetheless been able to tell him things about himself that he'd never heard from her before. He was completely self-absorbed, she'd told him. He didn't care about Marik, or about Liz and Rob either. He always put himself and his needs first.

"You don't give a single damn about what Marik might be feeling, about what she is going through! It's all about you, about what she's done to the almighty most-important person in the whole wide world, YOU."

The accusation stung, although he denied it. He broke his own habit of reticence, and told her a few home-truths about herself as well. The things they said to one another were unforgivable. They never should have been said, not by either of them.

Funny, you think you have a good solid marriage, until something happened to blow it apart. Naturally enough, once the honeymoon was over, it was over. The romance had been sweet, but once they started raising a family, their relationship changed. It had to, in his opinion. Each of them had their own part to do, to make life as a family run smoothly. Rose worked part time, so it only made sense that she had took on more of the day-to-day chores of raising a family than he did. If she blamed him for not being as hands-on with the kids as she was, then she should have asked him to help out. It was ridiculous to blame him for what Marik had done. He was a good father, a good provider, even willing to go live away from home for months at a time when that had seemed like their best option, financially speaking. But after Marik ran away, it seemed that Rose had nothing to say to him except to criticize his every action, his every word. They'd had a good marriage, or so he had thought, until their oldest disappeared and Rose began to treat him as if he were the worst man in the world. She seemed to think it was all his fault. Their marriage was headed for a smash-up, he could see that as clearly as if they were driving towards the edge of a cliff. Then he'd lose the other two, sweet little Lizzie and Robert his son. His hands caressed the smooth wood of the rocking horses that he was making for Rob's little girls. God grant that they not bring him the kind of sorrow that Marik had brought him!

Marik! Maybe the first mistake he'd made was in letting Rose give their first-born such a crazy name, the name of some fictional character in whatever book she'd been reading at the time. But

Dan learned early-on in their marriage that his sexy, delightful, loving wife was a woman of strong opinions, and so he hadn't opposed her choice of names for their first-born. The poor girl had a rough time explaining who she was, once she got to school.

"Tell them it's like Mark with an 'I' thrown in," he suggested. That didn't suit his fiery 7-year-old.

"That's a boy's name!"

She was her mother's daughter, no doubt about that. He picked up a piece of sandpaper and smoothed a patch of rough wood that his searching hands had discovered in the intricate carving of the rocking horse's mane. They were such different people, he and Rose. She was outspoken, he kept most of his thoughts to himself. She worried about money, he didn't. There were a host of differences between them, but their love dissolved all differences. Their love was the solid, unshakeable foundation of their life together. So he thought until Marik ran away and that illusion was blasted apart.

Rose demanded that they go to counselling. He was furious. Like some asshole sitting in an office could change anything! He went – twice - driving all the way down to Quinton, spending an hour listening to the guy's bogus bullshit. "The stages of grief." "The hidden benefits." He had no interest in some outsider's opinions about their 'family dynamic'. It didn't bring the girl back, didn't erase what had happened.

The guy made them pay for a block of six sessions, but after the second one, he dug in his heels. He wasn't going to waste his time on something that could make no difference. The girl was gone. If she hated them that much, that was her decision, and they would just have to live with it. Rose could go to the counsellor by herself, if she thought it would help her.

Rose, not wanting to waste the money they'd invested – a crazy reason, but he knew enough not to say so – continued to make the weekly trips down to Quinton on her own. She didn't tell Dan what they talked about or what the guy said, which was fine with Dan. He made his disinterest clear. Apparently talking it out with a "professional" helped Rose. She settled down and stopped blaming him and treating him like a pariah. Eventually, she even began to mention things that she thought he was doing right. They talked, but only about the present, not about the past; never about the past. He'd been fine with that. He didn't need to blow off his feelings, didn't even want to. What good did it do to talk about something when there wasn't a damn thing you could do about it? He was happy that counselling was helping her to be a more pleasant wife, but it wasn't what he needed. He had his own ways of dealing with things, he didn't need to talk about his feelings. He preferred not to feel them at all.

He reached for the fine-grit sandpaper, and continued his slow patient smoothing of the carving. These rocking horses were the best pieces he'd ever made. Once he painted them, they would look more like cavorting carousel steeds than traditional rockers. Painting wasn't his greatest field of expertise, he could only hope to do them justice. He was good, he knew, at roughing out the shapes with the saws, at refining the lines by hand chisel and then with the sandpaper. The fine grain of the wood stood up well to the sand-papering, first with the heavy-grade, because you had to start with the roughest, and succeeding with finer and finer grade until the wood became smooth as glass.

His brother Gerard, he remember ruefully, had gone at him with the heaviest-grade sanding grit when he stepped in and gave Dan the rough side of his tongue. Rose had nothing to compare to what Gerry had to say. It had been a year, almost to the day, after Marik's disappearance, when his big brother walked into the fire-hall at the end of Dan's shift, and demanded to talk to him.

"Get in the truck," he snapped. It had been years since they were kids, but the habit of obedience to his elder was still there. Gerard told him years later that he had been elected family spokesman. "I didn't think it was my business, but Mom and Dad thought otherwise. We were both in the midst of raising families, they thought that would give the message more impact. So I got to be the one to talk some sense into you."

The final straw for the family had been at Daisy's birthday get-together, the summer following Marik's disappearance. Willard Chalhey, Daze's husband, had offered the men beers, nothing unusual about that, except that Dan had spiked his from a pocket-flask, and was seen doing it. When the burgers were finally served, and they gathered around the picnic table to eat, little Robbie, reaching for the chips, knocked over a punch glass and spilled it all over Lizzie's party dress. Lizzie shrieked in dismay, and Dan reached across the picnic table to give Robbie a cuff. "Be careful what you're doing, you little idiot!"

"Dan, for Heaven's sakes! Little boys spill things!" Daisy cried. "There's no need to smack him!"

Furious at being reprimanded by his little sister, Dan smashed his fist into his half-eaten burger. "Rose, are you and the kids coming with me? Because I'm not sticking around to be told how to raise my son!" He had stormed out, leaving them gaping.

He was watching sports when Rose and the kids got home. She put them to bed, and went to bed herself, without saying a word to him. He guessed that the counsellor had told her not to speak out until she had simmered down. It was a relief to him. He had enough of the rough side of Rose's tongue. The next day, Gerard showed up at the fire-hall. Apparently he was the topic of conversation among the adults, after he left the party.

"Your drinking has got to stop," his big brother told him when they were seated in the truck outside the hall. "You're turning into a damned alcoholic."

It was the pressures of the job, Dan defended himself. He hated it that as a fire-fighter he was also the first responder every time there was an emergency of any kind in Chesney Creek. He was the first one who saw the heart-attacks, the strokes, the accidents, the blood and the bodies. "You don't have a clue what I have to deal with!"

"Bullshit. I may be an old high-mountain rancher from the plateau, but I know bullshit when I hear it! You knew what you'd have to deal with when you signed on, you were a volunteer long enough to know about that shit." Back in those days, twenty years ago, the department was made up of a mixture of professionals and trained amateurs. Volunteering was the fastest, if not the only, route to full time employment. Volunteers were still a major part of the town's protection.

"No, little brother, you know and I know that your drinking started when Marik ran away. Shit happens, man. You can't let it destroy you, or your family. That little boy of yours is scared of you now, scared of his Daddy! Is that how you want him to be?"

Dan reached for the door handle, meaning to jump out of the truck, but Gerard hit the master lock on his door. "You've lost one child. You're going to lose the others if you go on drinking the way you have been." God, how he had resented that! What gave his big brother the right to tell him he was drinking too much? Gerry had no idea what it was like, living with a wife who despised him, even if she didn't say as much out loud anymore.

"Marik ran away, she said you were lousy parents. It looks to me like you are proving her right! You are doing everything you can to destroy the family you've got left, just because your oldest one had a brainstorm and made a bad decision."

"A bad decision," Dan repeated sarcastically. "Yeah, that was one bad decision. The stupid little bitch!"

"Alright, you're angry at her. It's a lot easier to be angry than it is to grieve for her, isn't it? You're right, she did make a horrible decision, an inexcusable decision. I'm not denying that. Teenagers do stupid things. I'm sorry for you, man, but you've got to pull yourself together. Life isn't over. Prove that you're a good father by being one. Make your other two happy. Get focused on them, instead of being furious at your oldest and sorry for yourself. Get focused on what's good in your life. You've got two healthy children at home. You've got a lovely wife who has the patience of a saint with you! It's time to pull up your socks, Bro."

"What makes you so effin' smart?" he snarled, stung to the quick by his brother's words.

Gerard refused to be pulled into a fight, verbal or otherwise.

"What made me so effin' smart?" He pulled a bag of rolling tobacco out of his shirt pocket, and proceeded to roll a cigarette while he considered his answer.

"I was raised by smart people, and I married into a family of smart people." He swiped the edge of the paper with his tongue. "Kinda' like you. Besides that, I spend a lot of time out on the range, alone. Gives me time to think." He pointed to the dash. "See that? I even ripped out the wiring for the radio. Got tired of listening to other people, decided to listen to myself instead. That's how I got smart." He looked at the cigarette he'd rolled, twirled it in his rough fingers, and then flipped it out the window. "Quitting. I roll 'em but I don't smoke them anymore. Stupid habit. I'm too smart for that. Just like you are too smart to go on drinking."

Much as he'd hated to admit it at the time, Gerard had been right. Booze and television had been his escapes from inescapable pain. Once his brother had rubbed his face in it, he couldn't go on doing what he'd been doing. The change didn't happen overnight, but looking back, he knew that he had been lucky that Gerard caught him in time, and turned him away from that particular path of self-destruction.

He mended his fences with Rose over time. Bless her, she'd forgiven him far more quickly and easily than he'd deserved. It had taken longer to win back the trust of the two little ones. He stopped using his shift work as an excuse, started making the effort to be there for them. He took Liz to her gymnastic classes as often as possible, even if Rose was available to take her. He coached Robbie's soccer and baseball teams for years, all the way to the league championships. He had been lucky, and he was still reaping the harvest. His marriage was better than ever, better even than those honeymoon days before children. What was it they said? 'Life begins when the kids grow up and the dog dies.' Now he had grandchildren. Grandchildren! Liz's boys, and Robbie's little girls were the joy of his life, and of Rose's too.

Dan finished the final sanding, and was indoors building himself a cup of coffee and a sandwich when he saw Marik's pickup pull back into the driveway after her interview with the police.

"They seem to think I did it!" she blurted, throwing her purse on the table and collapsing into a chair.

Dan poured a second fragrant cup from the freshly brewed pot and slid it across the table to her before sitting down across the table with his sandwich and steaming mug.

"They think I did it, Dad! That I killed Ed." He looked across the table at her, this grown woman with her wide, distressed eyes, like a child pleading for help. His child, looking at him in the old familiar way.

"The boys broke my bike, Daddy! You can fix it, Daddy, can't you?" The front tire of her bicycle had been bent almost double. Marik and Lizzie were staying with their Aunt Daisy while Rose was in hospital giving birth to their third baby, his son. His son!

Willard and Daisy's boys were mad about bike-stunting that summer. They showed him the track they'd built in the field leading down to the lake. They could rip down the slope, over some jumps and then launch themselves off the plywood ramp into the lake. The little pink bike, the joy of Marik's 8-year-old heart, must have looked like another BMX-bike to them. Boys - he had one of his own now! His heart was too full of joy to scold them.

"I'll see what I can do, Sweetheart." He put the little bike in the back. If only all her problems had been so easy to solve.

"They told me not to leave town."

"That doesn't necessarily mean they suspect you of murder," he said reasonably. "It's just because you were there, a witness. It was probably an accident, anyway. There's no murderers in Chesney Creek, that's big city stuff."

"They wanted me to account for every minute since I got up this morning! I wish I hadn't waited. If I'd gone earlier, with Mom, like I did last week, she would have vouched for me! Only then, I would have been in the Park when he was running." She paused to think about it. "That wouldn't have worked either, would it? They'd be even more convinced that I'd done it."

"We'll talk to the neighbours," Dan suggested. "One of them may have seen you leave. I don't think you need to worry about it, honey. If we need to, we'll hire a lawyer for you. It'll be OK."

"Thanks, Dad." Calmed by his attitude as much as by his words, she sipped her coffee. He was right. Surely no one could honestly think she'd killed Ed Jamieson, not even Detective June Halston.

The murder of Edward Jamieson, for it was murder according to the Recorder, not an accident as Marik had hoped, was the talk of Chesney Creek. The Recorder reported that he'd been found by an off-duty officer, although neither Stan's name nor Marik's were mentioned.

"I supposed we have your Detective Halston to thank for that," Rose said. She was hearing far more than she wanted to, about the murder. The gossips had a field day speculating about it. Rose's shifts on the front desk at the library were peppered by library patrons asking if she'd heard anything new. The library had always been a clearing-house for news.

"They have different ways of phrasing it," Rose told Marik as they were getting dinner on the table, "but then, when they realize that he was my nephew – they drop it like a hot potato, thank goodness."

"The fire hall too," Dan remarked, coming in from his workshop, where paint was drying on the rocking horses. "Except that mentioning he's our nephew doesn't stop them. General consensus is, it was a husband or boyfriend, someone who freaked out when they found out he'd seduced their wife or girlfriend."

"It probably was something like that," Rose agreed. "Ed was his father's son in more ways than one. My poor Lindy, though. Despite everything, he's still her son." She turned to Marik, to fill her in on another missing piece of family history.

"Your Aunt Lindy's been pretty much estranged from Edward since he abandoned his family, just like his stupid father before him." She stabbed her fork into a saucepan, testing the vegetables for doneness. "You knew he was married and had a son? But Edward was still Lindy's little boy, despite everything. She's all broken up. Bloody Karlsson men! How I wish she'd never married that jerk! He brought her nothing but heartache, and now this, all because Ed learned how to be a 'man' from his father." She banged the lid back on the empty saucepan. "It's no wonder he's ended up murdered! It's a wonder Jack wasn't murdered before him." She turned and set the dish of sautéed vegetables on the table. "But my poor sister! Her heart is just broken all to bits. There's nothing worse than losing a child. Nothing!"

"Can we not talk about it?" Marik asked. "It doesn't make good dinnertime conversation."

"You're right." With a deep sigh, Rose let go of the subject. She handed Dan the last serving dish to put on the table. "I've heard enough about it at work to last me a lifetime. How's it going out at farm? Is your room about ready for you? Not that I want you to leave." She reached out to touch her daughter's shoulder. "It's been wonderful having you here, hasn't it, Dan?" She sent a warm, intimate look across the table to her husband. It wasn't the first time that Marik had noticed the difference in her parents' relationship. It had changed dramatically since she was a child.

"But we do understand your wanting to live elsewhere," Rose continued, "Goodness knows we'll see you often enough, the way this Palmer family is!" The Palmers had been a surprise to Rose, when she and Dan were first married. They were the antithesis of the nuclear family. Instead of mom-dad-and-the-kids, their sense of family included everyone who was remotely related. The siblings were much closer than Rose and her sisters were. Even as children, the Delganee girls had spent little time together. Their mother had set the example as a loner, whose motto might have been I'll-do-it-all-myself. The close bonds of the Palmer family came as a surprise to Rose, especially when she found herself being treated as one more Palmer sister. She thrived in the atmosphere of family closeness.

Nonny and Lincoln expected their daughters, and their sons too, to share the work and play of raising families. No one needed to do-it-all-myself. The example set by her sisters-in-law, with all their shared work-parties and other get-togethers, had inspired Rose to develop closer bonds with her own sisters. It had been easy with the twins, Jan and Joan. They had embraced the Palmer connection. Unfortunately, Lindy's difficult marriage had made it hard for her to feel at ease with the others. Their contentment in marriage was too sharp a contrast to her unhappiness.

"I'll be able to move in this weekend," Marik reported. "I'm thinking of going into Quinton tomorrow to choose my bedroom furniture. It's your day off, isn't it? Do you want to come with me?" She was proud of the new relationship that she and Rose were building. A shopping trip together would help to cement the sense of friendship and equality between them. On the other hand, Marik thought with some trepidation, it would also be fraught with the stress of keeping her wealth a secret. Rose had such a sharp eye for financial matters! It would be difficult to buy what she wanted with her mother looking at the price tags.

"I start afternoon-shift tomorrow," Dan reminded Rose. She knew what he was saying. Before their daughter came to stay with them, they had treasured the rare days when Dan's morning off coordinated with her days-off from the library. As empty-nesters who both worked shifts, they appreciated the delights of a long, leisurely morning together

"I think not, Marik. I want to pick up Darrin and Lincoln after school, after Dad goes to work. We are planning a puppet show for Thanksgiving, the boys will be delighted to have time to work on their puppet-heads." Her five grandchildren, 7-year-old Darrin and 9-year-old Lincoln, along with Rob's three younger ones, were the joy of Rose's heart. Rose had started her library career as the children's librarian, back when Marik was in middle school. The opportunity to work with children again, in the form of grandchildren, delighted her. Marik was still not completely adjusted to the idea of her parents-as-grandparents. She had known about the births of her nephews and nieces, but only as distant events among people far away. The family had grown. There were new family members, children and in-laws that she would have to get to know, as well as re-acquainting herself with the ones she left behind.

"Why don't you ask Lizzie to go with you?"

"That's a good idea, Mom," Marik agreed. She hadn't seen much of her little sister since she'd been home, other than the big family dinner when Rose was delighted to announce that their big sister had come home to stay. Lizzie and Rob had been happy to hear it, but more for their parent's sakes than for themselves. They were both too busy with their young families to have a lot of time for their prodigal sister. "I'll give Liz a call after dinner."

It would be good for them to have a day out alone together. Marik had been Lizzie's protector when they were children, although her little sister probably hadn't known that. Perhaps having maternal feeling for younger siblings was natural, even though Marik had known even at that young age that she never wanted nor intended to be anyone's mother. That was way more responsibility than she wanted, thank you! It would be good to build a friendship with her sister. She missed the camaraderie of her friendships with Terri and the others at the restaurant. She would have to create a new network of friends here in Chesney Creek, perhaps reconnect with some she'd known before, if they were still in town. Before she began reaching out for those, however, she wanted to renovate her connections with family. One thing at a time, she reminded herself. That was something she'd learned from Sue-Ellen, in those early years without drugs. One baby-step at a time.

CHAPTER EIGHT

Sister Love

"I love the padded headboard you bought," Liz remarked over a late lunch. "It will be so comfy to lean on when you read. You are still a big reader, aren't you? It's kind of weird, not knowing you, even though you are my sister."

"I suppose it is," Marik agreed. Last time they'd spent any time together, Marik had been an unhappy 15-year-old, while her little sister was only 11. "We don't know each other as adults." She hoped that today's shopping trip would mark the beginning of a new, close relationship, like the older generation of their family shared. It would be wonderful if she and Liz became good friends as well as sisters.

They were sharing an extravagantly expensive bottle of white wine with their meal. The meal would be Marik's treat, she had insisted before they stepped into the elegantly-appointed restaurant. She waited until Liz went to the washroom before she ordered the half-bottle of the German Gunderloch Riesling. It cost more than both their meals put together, but their waiter had recommended it highly as the perfect accompaniment for the entrees they'd chosen. Liz, bless her heart, hadn't said anything about the amount of money Marik was spending on this trip.

It made her a comfortable shopping companion, far more so than Rose would have been.

"Remember those Nancy Drew books that the Aunt Twins used to give us, for birthdays & Christmas? You were always through yours, and wanting mine, before I was done with it! The four-year-advantage. What do you read now? Detective novels still?"

They talked about books, about the family, about the twenty years of Liz's life that her big sister had missed, her teenage and college years, her marriage and children. Liz was happy to chatter about herself and her own concerns, with very little curiosity about the intervening years of her big sister's life. "I don't get a lot of adult-conversation, except other moms, and then we mostly talk about our kids. I'm so, SO glad you've moved back to Chesney Creek!"

The wine, as Marik had foreseen, was helping Liz relax. She tipped the end of the bottle into the younger woman's glass, excusing the uneven division by the fact that she was driving. In truth, Marik was very careful of her alcohol use. She had never been one to drink much – it was street-drugs, not alcohol, that had been her downfall, but she was wary of her addictive personality, and restricted her share of the wine with conscious deliberation. She was content to let Liz have the lion's share of both the wine and the conversation.

After lunch, they browsed through a book store, and then through a local branch of 'The Store (for Your Home)', where Marik bought blankets and linens, and Liz fell in love with a pair of floor lamps in the form of elongated giraffes. "They would be so perfect for the family room! Zach's family is Dutch, Boer you know, and I'm decorating in an Afrikaans theme. The boys love it." When Marik offered to purchase the lamps for her, she gave in after only the slightest hesitation. "Thank you, I just love them!" she exalted. If Big Sister wanted to indulge her, she was all for it. "You single women are lucky, you can buy whatever you want with no one to answer to."

Little did she know just how very lucky Marik was; being single had nothing to do with it!

"What can I get for Mom and Dad? I want to get them something in return for having me, they've made it really easy to come back home to Chesney Creek."

Eventually they settled on a feathery Angora-blend throw that their parents could toss over their legs when they snuggled together on the recliner sofa to watch TV. It had surprised Marik the first time she caught them doing that. Obviously her parents had renewed their marriage in the years since she left home.

"It makes my heart sing to see how the folks are, now," she said as they waited for the cashier to ring up their purchases. The lovely soft throw would be "a symbol of their daughters' approval," Liz said, laughing. "Dad will be comfortable with the colours, dark green and burgundy plaid are very masculine. That's important to him!" She caressed the fine wool. "And Mom will love the softness. Good choice, Sis."

Inevitably, the topic of their cousin's murder came up, although not until they were driving back to Chesney Creek. "Remember when he used to babysit us?" Liz asked. "Why was that? I don't remember."

"Dad was working away, at the mining camp up north, remember? I think that finances were a big problem that year. Really a problem, not just Mom's usual anxiety. That's when she got the job at the library. I was only 11, too young to be in charge of you and Robbie after school, so she hired Ed. He was older, almost through high school."

"He used to bring us movies, I remember that. Not every day, but a couple times a week, right? I loved those after-school movie-afternoons! He'd get me and Robbie settled in front of the TV, and then you two would disappear, to do 'big kid' stuff, remember? What did you..." her voice tailed off as she glanced at Marik, whose hands were white-knuckled as she gripped the steering wheel, her eyes fixed on the two-lane highway ahead, her face frozen in a tight-lipped grimace.

"Marik? What did...?"

"I don't want to talk about it."

"Oh my God. He was abusing you, wasn't he? Wasn't he? That's what he meant by 'big kid stuff'."

Tears spilt down Marik's cheeks, but she didn't appear to be aware of them. She nodded, two small tight jerks of her head, without moving her eyes away from the road.

"Why didn't you tell? Good Lord, Marik! That's so.... gross." Liz sat back, absorbing the shock of the discovery.

"He said he'd hurt you and Robbie if I told anyone. I was afraid. So afraid. It would have torn the family apart." She pulled off the highway, and let the truck roll to a stop. "I really don't want to talk about this with you, but since you ask, alright, I will. Only I certainly can't drive as well as talk about it." She dug into her purse, tucked down beside the driver's seat, and pulled out a tissue to mop up her eyes and blow her nose.

"There, that's better," she said, tucking the tissue in the garbage bag that hung from the truck's gearshift. If there was one thing she had learned in recovery, it was to face her devils bravely.

"Ok, I'll fill you in on a little family history." She rested her hands on the steering wheel, gazing out at the fields and farms beyond the highway. "You know about Jack-the-Jerk, right, how he left Aunt Lindy and went off to live with that tart Suzie for a year or so? That's when Mom hired Ed to look after us, because his Mom and him and Helene needed the income. Ed moved back in with them, after Uncle Jack got arrested about Suzie."

She took a deep breath, and blew it out with a gusty sigh. "Jack-the-Jerk." She had come to a kind of peace with this part of her life-story, through the 12-Step work she'd done in recovery. It was a common enough story among women in that sort of program, even Sue-Ellen, her sponsor, had suffered from sexual abuse as a child. Sue-Ellen had brought a law suit against her abuser, but as she told Marik, winning the lawsuit had been a big disappointment. She thought it would help her to put it all behind her and heal, but it hadn't, not in any real, deep way. She'd had to forgive. She'd helped Marik to walk that same path, at least getting her to the point of wanting to forgive her abusive cousin, even if she couldn't take that final step of actually forgiving him.

"They talk about dysfunctional families. In some ways, that's what it was all about. Ed was the victim of Jack, of Jack's attitudes and ideas about sex and women, and Jack was the victim of his father, and on and on back through the generations. I have yet to forgive him, in my heart of hearts, but I can – sort of – understand how he came to be the sort of guy he was, and to do what he did to me." She took a deep breath, and then another, before continuing.

"I didn't tell anyone, because I was afraid for you and Robbie and because it would have stirred up such a hornet's nest in the family. I couldn't bear to be the one to do that, to destroy our family myth of "everything's OK." He was Mom's nephew, after all. It would have hurt her that way, too. Not to mention Aunt Lindy! Maybe I was wrong – I was only a dumb kid, 12 and 13 years old, after all - but that's how I thought."

Eyes fixed on the scenery in front of her, she searched for words to explain how it had been for her. "I thought that if I told, I'd be the one to blame for destroying the family. I couldn't imagine how we, all of us, you, me, Robbie, Mom....how we could survive that. Or what Dad would do. So, I didn't say anything. I was protecting all us, at least in my own mind. Weird, eh?"

The silence stretched out between them, as Liz fought to absorb this new information, and fit it in with what she knew about her big sister and about how the family had been back then.

"I was too young to know anything. I'm so sorry," she said finally. Compassion was all she had to offer. The motherliness that had awakened in her through the birth of her two sons made her want to reach out and comfort the child that Marik had been, but the two of them did not have that sort of relationship yet. They were still strangers to one another. All she could do was touch Marik's arm in sympathy, and meet her brown eyes with her own tear-dimmed blue ones when Marik turned at last to face her. "You must have hated him."

"I did," Marik said boldly.

"But not enough to...!"

"No, it wasn't me who killed him!" She snapped. "How could you even think that?" It was easier to be angry at Liz than to feel the horrid weight of the pain and shame that she carried every day of her entire life.

"Oh Marik, of course not! That was just stupid, I didn't mean it. I'm just so shocked!"

"Well, it's true," Marik admitted, "I did hate him. But not enough to want him to die like that. No one ought to die like that, with their face held down in the dirt until they couldn't breathe anymore."

"No," Liz agreed. "I don't think any of us liked him, none of the cousins I mean, he really was a nasty person, and in more ways than we knew. But to die like that!"

Marik turned the key in the ignition to restart the truck. They pulled back out onto the quiet highway and drove in silence for a few miles, both busy with their own unpleasant thoughts. When Liz finally broke the silence, it was to ask a question. Was Ed the reason Marik had run away at fifteen?

"In a way, yes. I had to wait until Ed was gone, until he finished high school and joined the military. Even when Daddy came home, and got on with the fire department, Ed still..." Her voice trailed off. "He was still a threat. I was afraid if I weren't there, he'd be picking on you instead. And you were so little, I couldn't bear the idea of him forcing you that way. That's what it was all about, him forcing me to do what he wanted. It wasn't sexual at all, at least not for me. For me, the awfulness was being forced to do what he wanted me to do. I just wanted to – oh, I don't know. Go read a book. Hang out with my friends. Whatever. Not lay down for Ed to...." She paused, wondering just how much more graphic she needed to be, to explain it all to Liz. She probably shouldn't tell her any of it, but it was too late now, it was spilling out of her, finally, to a member of her family. Maybe that's what she had been needing, all these years.

"It wasn't even sex, if you want to be technical about it. There wasn't any actual penetration, he just rubbed it between my legs. But

I didn't have any choice, he forced me to do what he wanted me to do. No choice! I still can't stand being told what to do. People don't understand that, that the sexual abuse of children isn't sexual, really. It's about power, and the loss of power. That's why people like Ed, abusers, do it, not so much for sexual gratification – well, that too, I suppose. But what they really want is the feeling of power over another person. The feeling of dominance, of being the controller. That's probably what Ed wanted with all those other women, too, that feeling of power, of dominating. And it's the loss of power that is so destructive for the abused ones.

"That's what damages the child, being forced to do something against her will, something that she knows to be wrong. And then having to keep it secret, living in that fear." She paused, swallowing hard in an effort to stay in control of herself.

"I even had a psychologist, once, try to convince me that I enjoyed it. Gawd! What an idiot!" It had been her one and only attempt to make use of formal counselling. Sue-Ellen, and the whole 12-step-program, had done her more good than that stupid 'doctor'.

"Anyway!" she continued, "Edward was gone, into the military after high school, so you were safe. And then I had the horrible Mr. Bosick for my home room teacher when I started second year in high school. Did you ever have him for a teacher? He was another one from the same mold as the damned Karlsson men, with his stupid attitudes about women. Maybe I was hyper-sensitive about it, but I didn't think any man had any right to judge any woman, or tell her what she could do or couldn't do. It made trouble for me and Dad, too – not sexual, I mean him telling me what to do, or not do. We were fighting about my makeup, the clothes I wanted to wear, short skirts, stupid stuff like that, typical of fathers and oldest daughters. You probably didn't get that as much?"

"No...." Liz agreed.

"I'll take credit for teaching him to lay off about that," Marik said with a lopsided grin. "But to my 15-yr-old brain, it was just another man trying to tell me what to do. So I left... And that's the story, Liz. Sorry to puke it all up, all over you."

Liz waved her hand dismissively. "Can I ask you another question? You don't have to answer it if you don't want to."

"Sure," Marik grimaced. What would she have to confess next?

"All this stuff about Ed – is that why you never got married? Unless you did and didn't tell us about it!"

Marik laughed. "Nope, never married. Because of what went down with Ed? I don't think so. Maybe that affected me – well, of course that affected me, sexually speaking, but no, I just never met anyone I wanted to marry."

"Aww..."

"Maybe Dale, when we first got together, but that was just 18-year-old fantasy."

"That's the guy you lived with?"

"Yes, for a brief, horrible year. He was abusive. Not physically, emotionally. After I caught him in bed with a friend of ours, I found out from friends that she was by no means the first one. He'd started sleeping around when we had only been together for a couple months. You might say, he never stopped sleeping around! I was just a convenience, chief cook and bottle-washer sort of thing. Anyway, my heart got smashed 'cause I thought I was 'in lerrrrve' with the brute. It put me off men for years, other than for some very brief affairs and one-night-stands when my hormones were raging, you know how our bodies are. I'd get out of control and fall in bed with the closest 'stud' – most of whom were duds. Or maybe I was the dud, I can't say that I enjoyed being with any of them." She paused. "You sure that you want to hear all this?"

"I want to get to know my sister!" Liz declared. "I'm not here to judge you, we lived different lives, that's all."

"Alright, true confessions time: I ended up meeting a man worthy of me, about 7 years ago, but – well, he was married. He and his wife had one of those 'open-marriages', or so he said, and I found him so magnetically attractive that I couldn't resist. I'm ashamed to tell you that even when I saw the ring on his finger, I made the running. I didn't want to marry him – I had pretty much decided that I wasn't interested in that sort of thing. He was a really special man, but difficult, not marriage material. I don't know how his wife managed. A strong woman, that one.

"We had an on-going, sporadic affair, I'd see him, oh maybe once a month or once every couple of months. When I say 'see' I mean – we'd fling ourselves into my bed together. Oh Lordy, it was so good, the man played my body like a harp!" Marik realized that she'd let her memories run away with her. "Sorry, Liz, too much detail, eh? But sex with him – well, he taught me to enjoy being a woman, to enjoy my female sexuality. So I was crazy about him, still am in some ways, and at the same time I'm glad I had the strength to tear myself away from him. I broke up with him a few years ago. If you want the truth, I'm ashamed of myself for ever succumbing to him. Talk about out of control!" She hesitated. "You're not saying anything. I guess this is more than you wanted to know, eh? A little too much for a suburban housewife?"

"I'm a little more than that," Liz defended herself. "I had my moments, too, when I was in University, before I met Zachary." A wicked grin flashed across her face. "As for Zach, he plays my body like Jimi Hendrix played the guitar! So there, Mrs. Sophisticated Big City Harp Woman! Us Palmer-girls, we're hot stuff!" she giggled as they pulled into her driveway.

"Thanks, Lizzie!" Marik had hoped they would become friends, and now it seemed they were. Nothing cemented a relationship better than knowing, and accepting, some intimate truths about one another. "Thanks for today, for – everything."

They went around to the back of the truck to lift the two lamp-boxes from the corner of the bed. "This has been wonderful, Mar."

"Even despite the pukey story, Ed and all that? Listen, Liz, I hope...I mean, please! Don't talk about all that, OK? You don't have to tell Zach, do you?" She had no idea what the dynamics of her sister's marriage might be, whether it included confiding everything she did or talked about or heard to her husband. She hoped not. Truth and honesty were all very well, but there should be some limits to them as well. She had spoken in confidence, or so she thought.

"Of course not!" Liz leaned the tall boxes against the tailgate, and opened her arms to give her sister a strong hug. "He knows what goes on at the mall, stays at the mall. Anyway, he's not interested in my girl-talk. He won't even ask, beyond, 'did I have a good time?' and 'I hope you didn't overspend yourself.'" He'll be delighted that my giraffees were a gift, not one of my big spend-ups."

"I'll tell Mom you're back, she can bring the boys over when they are done with their puppeteer project. That was the plan, right?"

"That would be great. Tell her, no rush. Zach will be home soon," she chortled, "and I'm feeling musical."

"You had a phone call," Rose told Marik when she got back home after delivering the boys. "Stan Albescu, he's the one who found Edward, isn't he?" Marik had given her mother an abbreviated version of her role in the Park that day, after her interview with Detective Halston. The detective had made her sign of copy of her brief and unadorned statement about her role as a pedestrian bystander, and warned her not to leave town, but that was the last Marik had heard from the local police force.

According to the Chesney Recorder, the murder must have been a personal vendetta. "Police sources say that there was no danger to other Park users." Nonetheless, Marik had abandoned her morning walks. Instead, she was up early each morning to go out to the farm. It was a comfort and joy to spend time there. The house, standing across from the big barn with the hard-packed barnyard between them, was the same as it had always been. Even the flower beds, with Gran's big mop-headed dahlias, looked the same.

Gran had moved downstairs into her new bedroom, with her high old bed and the ponderous dresser and dressing table that Dan and his friends from the fire-hall had manhandled down the stairs. They moved the rest of her bedroom furniture into one of the spare bedrooms. Marik's new pieces would be delivered tomorrow, and then, she told Rose, she could have her sewing room back. Meanwhile, Rose wanted to know why Officer Albescu was phoning for her daughter.

"I went to school with Stan," she explained, "and then I met him that day we did the blackberries, remember? I might meet him for coffee one day."

"That's good, I was hoping you'd find some of your old school friends still around town. He said he'd call again." Over the dinner table, she told Marik about the cute things the little boys had said, and about the puppets they were making for Thanksgiving fun. If Marik was a little more quiet than usual that evening, Rose didn't notice. She'd had a wonderful day, first with Dan at home all morning, and then the afternoon with the boys. Even the sight of all Marik's purchases didn't distress her. To her daughter's relief, she didn't ask what any of it had cost. It was enough that her two daughters had spent the day together, being friends. Rose revelled in the knowledge of renewed family ties.

Cinderella

Marik moved out to the farm on the weekend. In the following weeks, the three women began to develop a new pattern of life together. Dahl was free at last to focus most of her energies outdoors, doing the work she loved. Marik and Nonny shared the cooking, and the younger woman took on the housework routines, the making of beds, the dish-washing and laundry, that Dahl had been doing very haphazardly since her student-helpers Alika and Bonnie went off to college and university. Dahl was apologetic about the dust on the furniture and the dust-bunnies under it, but Marik delighted in the work.

"I love this," she told her Aunt over lunch. "It's like nurturing my roots when I take care of these things that my maternal ancestors. Besides, it's rewarding to get things looking good again. Gran understands, don't you, Gran?"

"But Dahlia never will," Nonny laughed. "If it doesn't have hair on it, she's just not interested."

"I've done my best!"

"I know that. I'm just very grateful that Marik is here, and that she likes doing the work," Nonny explained peaceably. "I'm grateful for all you've done, too, especially because I know your heart isn't in it. I appreciate the effort you've made. We aren't all made alike, and thank goodness for that. I could see that the housework was a burden for you, you know. I may be a useless old woman," she added tartly, "but I'm not a stupid or insensitive one."

"I want to help with the horses, too," Marik interjected. "And the chickens. You'll have to teach me what to do." Dahl accepted the offer thankfully.

Marik drove into town before dinner on Sunday to bring her Aunt Fleur out to the farm.

"Darling Marik, you must have a tour of my garden!" She was excited about the fountain she would install in the spring, back by buddleia bush, with concrete butterflies that would spout tiny streams of water as antennae.

"I didn't think I could afford it," she said happily, "but darling James is helping me about that. Oh!" Her hands flew up to her mouth. "I'm not supposed to tell about that!" She looked at Marik, wide-eyed.

"I'm sure it's OK, Auntie Flo," Marik comforted her. She didn't know James, except to know that he was Carol, her cousin's, ex-. They had divorced several years ago, when their two daughters were still in diapers. She had been disappointed to learn that both Carol and Helene, her closest cousins, no longer lived in Chesney Creek. She had hoped to renew those old friendships, but so far she hadn't had the opportunity to do so. "So James still lives here in town?"

"Oh yes, darling James is wonderful, he does lots to help me. Maybe it is OK that I told you," Fleur added, picking nervously at the buddleia shrub's purple plumes. "He asked me yesterday who else might be interested. He might come and talk to you, because Rose said you had savings."

Her aunt's words didn't make a lot of sense to Marik, but that didn't surprise her. The words of their childish ditty came back to her. "Poor Aunt Flo, she's really rather slow." She knew that Fleur's sisters, and Rose too, were concerned about her, living on her own since Uncle Frank passed away a few years earlier. Both Dahlia and Daisy, as well as Rose, dropped by the house frequently, to be sure that she was still taking care of herself. Dahl brought her out to the farm several times a month, ostensibly to help look after Gran, but really, to be sure that her sister had company and stimulation on a regular basis. It seemed that her ex-son-in-law shared their concern, and was doing his part to help her. Life as a widow is challenging for anyone, and more so for Fleur, with her limited capabilities.

"I'm glad you are coming out to stay with Gran. Dahlia says we probably won't get home tomorrow until late. We'd better go now, Gran will have dinner ready."

After dinner, Marik and Dahlia went outdoors for what Dahl called 'evening stables,' leaving Fleur to do the kitchen clean up. They delivered hay out to the rack in the pasture and topped up the water in the old bathtub that served as the horses' water hole.

"That's it for tonight, except for Skudder." The ancient horse was in what Dahl called the Home Paddock, behind the barn. "The others are fine outdoors at this time of year, but this guy is better indoors. Why don't you go do the chickens while I give him a quick grooming? Then I can just put him out in the morning and we can be on our way." She unbuckled the sheet, pulled it off the old horse and tossed it over the half-door of the stall.

There were only a dozen birds in the run. Marik remembered the much larger flock her grandparents kept when she was a child. Gran supplied the family with the good eggs, and sold the excess from a stand at the bottom of the driveway, down by the corner of Mountain and Mountain Retreat roads. Marik glanced into the nest-boxes. There were only two, laid after her grandmother did the morning collection. She slipped the two dirty eggs into a cardboard carton, locked the hens safely in their little house for the night, and met Dahl in the mud room, where they both shed jackets and boots before stepping into the kitchen.

"I'm going to pay for the gas and lunch tomorrow," Marik reminded her, "since we're going to get my new horse."

"Maybe get you a horse," Dahl corrected her. "We won't know until we look at her. We don't have room in the barn for another rescue horse unless she is the right one for you. It's easy to get hung up on the idea of rescuing these critters, all and any of them, but that's a dangerous pitfall. Been there, done that, learned the lesson. My job is to rescue the useful ones. The others have got to be some other person's responsibility. If we tried to rescue every poor horse that needs rescuing, we'd be up to our eyebrows," she paused and started to laugh. "Up to our eyebrows in you-know what."

Since Marik's pickup didn't have a trailer ball, the two-horse trailer was hitched to the back of Dahl's big Buick Roadmaster, ready for an early start as soon as their 'morning stables' were done.

Fleur was up early to make breakfast for them while they did the outdoor chores. Now, Marik and Dahlia had their travel mugs of tea ready to go, tucked into makeshift cup-holders on the old Buick's front seat. Dahlia led Herald, the big pinto gelding, up the ramp into the trailer. They were taking him along as a companion horse for the young mare, in case she was trailer-shy.

"Herald is my best helper," Dahlia declared, slapping the big splotchy rump affectionately as she reached for the plastic-encased chain that secured the dividing wall between the two sides of the trailer. "The newbies always adjust more quickly once he takes them under his wing...or mane?" She stepped back off the trailer-ramp, and bent down to lift it up into place as the tailgate. Marik moved quickly to the other side to help her. "Use your knees, not your back! Heave-ho, we can do it!"

"I can see I'll be building some muscle, hanging out with you," Marik laughed as they swung the heavy ramp up. "For a not-very-big woman, you certainly are strong, Aunt Dahlia."

"Wiry, they call it. Well, it's amazing what a person can do when you don't think you can't. You've heard stories about mothers lifting whole cars to get them off their baby, haven't you? There's really no limit to what we can do when we have to. I tell myself I can do it, and so I can. It's easier that way." They dogged down the clamps on either side of the tailgate. "That's my hope for senior senility, touch wood I don't go that way," she interjected, tapping the side of her head with her knuckles, "but if I do, I hope that what I forget is all the stuff I've been telling myself I can't do. Maybe I'll write a novel or become a great painter when I have Alzheimer's."

They checked the lights on the trailer, Marik standing behind it while Dahlia flicked the turn-signals and tapped the brake, before buckling themselves into the comfortable plush seats.

"I think you should drop the 'Aunt Dahlia', and just call me Dahlia. Or Dahl, that's what my friends call me." She shifted the Roadmaster into gear. Fleur waved at them from the veranda as they pulled out of the barnyard and down the curving driveway onto Mountain Retreat Road. "I worry about her, since Frank died. We all do. She shouldn't be on her own, but oh my goodness, I can't imagine having her out here to live with us full time. That, I don't need! At any rate, she won't leave her garden, so I guess the question doesn't arise. At least not yet."

Dahlia swung the car and trailer off North Road onto the highway. They headed eastward with the rising sun on their faces, through Rainbow, where Marik's maternal 'Aunt Twins' lived, and on into country Marik hadn't seen before.

"Auntie Flo said something odd to me, when I picked her up yesterday, when she was showing me around the garden." She repeated what Fleur had said about James helping her to buy a fountain for her backyard. "Then she said she wasn't supposed to tell anyone. Any idea what that's about?"

"No idea. James is a bit of a financial whiz-kid, though. You know about him and Frank?" Here was more family history that Marik had missed, in her twenty years away. As the miles slipped away behind them, Dahl explained how Frank had hired James after Brad, his son from his previous marriage, made it clear that music, not insurance, was his life's passion. Frank had built up a good solid business, a growing business, specializing in home and farm insurance.

"He developed it into a brokerage, trained his salesmen to do the leg-work. Frank said that hiring James was one the smartest he ever made. James is one of those natural-born salesmen, a real boon to Frank's business. They expanded the business, Frank and James together. Then when Carol married him, Frank made the two of them minority partners, one-sixth each or something like that." It had worked well, Dahl said. James had some good ideas for building their business, and Frank was more than willing to go along with them. Carol wasn't really involved in the day to day running of the business. She had enough to do, she was teaching full time even after the little girls came along.

"Then Frank started having heart-problems. When that happened, James naturally stepped up to take over more of the day-to-day operations in the

office. Frank got bent about it. I'm guessing that he
was feeling out of control. Reminded me of when Bill
– do you remember him? Your Uncle Bill?" she
asked. "Maybe not. You would have only been
maybe two or three when he passed away. When he
was first diagnosed with the leukaemia, he got
obsessive about control – wanted to dictate how the
spoons were stacked in the cutlery drawer, silly stuff
like that. Compensating for not being in control of
the disease. I think it was something like that for
Frank.

'He was in hospital for quite a while after that first
heart attack. There were complications, then he had
a long convalescence when he couldn't do a whole
lot. A couple of the women who had been with him
since he started the business retired, and James
hired their replacements, younger people who were
more computer-savvy. Frank saw red about that! It
was the control-thing again. He didn't like
technology, said insurance was a people-business,
not a machine-business. Carol sided with her dad.
You can imagine what that did to the marriage.
Although," she added thoughtfully, "from what I
could see, the marriage wasn't exactly a happy one
to start with. Your Gran thinks that was James' fault,
but I don't know. It takes two, you know.

    "After Frank passed on, James naturally
expected to take over the business completely. But
that didn't happen. You can imagine the shock when
he discovered that Carol had told Frank – not
James, but Frank - that she wanted a divorce. Frank
was virtually on his deathbed, but he called Bolster

& Nod and changed his will anyway. All that poor James ended up with was his little one-sixth partnership. Bolster & Nod, the executors, sold the business just as Frank had directed. Fleur inherited virtually the whole thing. Of course, the money is well-protected, she lives on some sort of trust fund. Frank understood my little sister" she said with a snort of laughter, "very well. Bless him." They drove in silence for a few minutes before Dahl continued.

"I think Flo feels sorry for James. Carol took the girls and moved off to Quinton, but James stuck around. He's really been very good to Flo. The rest of us appreciate that. Neither Carol nor Brad have stepped up to the plate, and you know your Aunty Flo – she needs some looking-after."

"Thanks for telling me all that. I'd wondered about James, after what Aunty Flo said, but it was just because I didn't understand their relationship, because I didn't know their back-story. I've missed so much of family history. My own fault, of course, but I'm glad to be filled in about." She was grateful that the road trip had loosened Dahlia's usually taciturn tongue.

They stopped for an early lunch at an old-fashioned rural inn, just off the highway. Dahlia wanted to give Herald a break, even though they had only been on the road for a couple of hours. The inn was a 'horse hotel', with plenty of room to turn the trailer, and small exercise paddocks for animals staying overnight.

"We won't be stopping on the way back, unless you or I need a potty break. I won't want to unload the horses like this. It might unsettle the new one if she hasn't been handled much. I want to get her home as soon as possible." They dropped the tail-gate, and Dahlia moved up to untie the big pinto.

"Here's hoping this little mare we're going to see turns out to be right for you, I'd hate for this to be a wasted trip." Dahl backed Herald down the ramp, and walked him for a few minutes. "Lucky it's a nice day, he can stay out while we have our meal. These older horses, they don't do well in the trailer for too long without a break. Even a short rest now like this will make it an easier day for him. It will be five or six hours coming back, a long ride for this old boy." She tied the big pinto to the side of the trailer, with a flat-sided rubber bucket of water hung from a hook on paddock fence beside him. He was hidden from traffic on the highway, but visible from the window beside their table. The waitress, grey-haired and smiling, poured coffee into the big flowery mugs. The specials, she reminded them, were on the sign by the door.

Their salads, when they came, were generously heaped on large plates. "You can see why I like this place," Dahl said, digging her fork through the toppings into the mixed greenery. "Healthy food, and lots of it!"

When they'd finished, and Dahl went off to the washroom, Marik pulled a $100 bill out of her wallet and folded it to fit under her empty mug. One of the delights of being so wealthy was being able to leave ridiculously good tips. After all her years on the lunch shift at Bob's Olde Beanery, she knew just how notoriously bad the 'ladies who lunch' were, when it came to tipping. Pat had lost it one day when she overheard one of her customers warning her companions that "we mustn't tip too much."

"What are you worried about?" she purred to them with a very professional smile, "Afraid that I might be able to buy my kids new shoes, instead of pawing through your rejects at the Thrift Shop? Wouldn't that be just awful?"

Marik finished serving the table, and handed the tip, 15% to the penny, over to a very apologetic Pat. "We all have PMS attacks occasionally. Don't worry about it."

They all agreed that if – when - they won the lottery, they'd make it a habit to tip BIG, every single time, regardless of the level of service. Even servers could have a bad day and provide less than top-notch service, as they all knew well, but even the worst kind of day in the service industry could be turned into a good day if a poorly-served customer left a ridiculously big tip. None of them had experienced that, but they could imagine what fun it would be.

What fun it was now to know that this hard-working, pleasant, grey-haired woman would be absolutely flabbergasted when she cleared the table and discovered the folding money that her lunching ladies had left for her. It was so much fun to be anonymously generous! Even before she'd won the lottery, Marik had tipped as well as she could.

"Another hour or two," Dahl said as they pulled back onto the highway, "and you'll get to meet this new pony. I hope she's the right one for you. She sounded good. Young, they said, and recovering well after being pretty much starved for a couple years. God, sometimes I hate human beings!"

"And then there are human beings like you," Marik reminded her. "I'm delighted to be part of this rescue, Aunt...I mean, Dahl." It was a hard habit to break. If she'd stayed in Chesney Creek, she thought ruefully, she would have grown out of the habit of addressing the older generation in so respectful a manner. They would have morphed naturally from Aunt-This-or-That into "Lindy" and "Joan" and "Dahlia" and so on. As it was, she was leaping from child-of-the-family to fellow-adult without the usual transitional phase to ease her through the change. "I'm enjoying the trip," she added, rather lamely. "It's good to have this time with you." The conversation, as they drove, had ranged from horses to family history and back again, from Dahl's work with the handicapped children to some of Marik's history in the years she'd been away.

"How are you feeling now, about finding Edward and all that?" Dahl inquired. "It must have been such a shock."

"I just wish they'd find out who did it, and we could put the whole thing to rest. It's worse for Aunt Lindy, of course. She doesn't want to have any sort of memorial service, or 'celebration of life' until they know who did it, Mom says. It's like a black cloud hanging over all our heads. I just wish it would go away! Blighted Ed, he always was trouble!"

Dahl cast a quizzical look at her, raising an eyebrow as if to ask where that was coming from. "Ed's the victim here, remember?"

"I know. I just never liked him, we had some history together. I can't help but think that he drew the situation upon himself, you know what I mean?"

"Psychology of the Individual," Dahl said, "that's what Poirot always said. You know Poirot – Agatha Christie's famous Belgian detective?"

Marik laughed. "Oh yes! I'm a reader too, Aunt, I mean, Dahl. Psychology of the Individual is probably right, aren't they saying that it was probably a disgruntled husband or boyfriend or something? That would be because of his 'psychology'."

"Maybe," Dahl said. "Maybe it was his philandering ways that caused him to end up murdered. But that's only one piece of his psychology. Nobody's one-dimensional. Maybe it was about something else in his life. I wonder what lawsuits or legal brouhaha-s he was involved in."

"You mean a disgruntled client, or someone who lost a case because of how Ed defended the other guy?"

"Sure. Or someone else he offended, in some way. Your cousin Edward was a brash kind of guy, a bit of a braggart, a 'big man about town' in his own estimation. He tended to throw his weight around. Remind me to tell you about the time he got mixed up in a problem I had with one of my riding school clients. I'm here to tell you, Edward Karlsson was not always the Mr. Nice Guy that he wanted people to think he was."

"I know that if anyone does," Marik muttered.

"The problem is that the shadow of suspicion falls on everyone who ever had anything to do with him. After what I went through with him, I could even be a suspect! That's how it will be until we know exactly who did it. Everyone's a suspect until we find out who the 'bad guy' actually is."

"So which comes first – knowing why he was murdered, or knowing who did it, and figuring out the reason from there?"

"Motive and Opportunity, that's what we're supposed to look for. We don't know who murdered him. That's the big secret, after all. We'd better start with the reason he was murdered."

"What, do you think we are going to play detective? You and me, Aun, I mean, Dahl?"

"It doesn't seem like the police are getting anywhere with it, if the Recorder is to be believed. It's been, what, a week or more?"

"Not that long. Five days. Believe me, I know." Marik pinched her lips together. She was not at all sure she wanted to be talking about this.

"Then there obviously isn't a quick answer! The police don't know who did it, and they may or may not figure it out. I think it is the duty of every citizen to apply their brains to this sort of puzzle, especially if they have insider knowledge, which we certainly do!

"Not because you found him!" she added, seeing Marik's grimace. "I meant because we are family, we know a lot more about him and what made him tick than the police, the official investigators, can possibly know. We know his father, and his mother for that matter, and what he was like as a child, and what he was up to as a teenager and all that stuff. We know his psychology!"

Marik knew his psychology, all too well. She toyed with the idea of telling Dahl about her own history with Ed, but this wasn't the time or the place for that confidence.

"So, what does his psychology tell you about who might have murdered him?" She would play along, she decided, with what appeared to be a kind of game for her aunt.

"Nothing, so far." Dahl's fingertips did a little dance on the steering wheel, and she shifted in her seat. "So, what do we know about him? He was a skirt-chaser; he was a lawyer, and a pretty good one from all accounts, I'll give him that even if I was on the wrong end of it; he could be an arrogant jerk. Without even trying." She ticked them off, raising a finger for each characteristic as she identified them. "He was also, on the plus side, known to be very honest and straight-forward about money. They'll be eulogizing him about that, just you wait.

"Remember when I was talking about sister Flo earlier, about Frank and James? I can tell you this about Frank and Edward. Frank trusted him implicitly when it came to money. He even told me that, when I was having that problem with the riding school. Edward Karlsson would never, ever, trick or mislead anyone about anything having to do with money, I could trust him for that. Financially, he was a one-hundred-percent honest lawyer."

"Nice to know he had one virtue," Marik said drily. They were off the highway now, coming down into the rolling eastern foothills among broad hay fields, with dairy farms, and even a few scattered vineyards where the harvest was starting, the vines being stripped of their fruit by the big mechanical harvesters.

"It's rich country," Dahlia remarked. "You'll love this place we're going, it's beautiful, a real up-scale training stable with no expenses spared." Her prediction proved true. Marik was impressed as they pulled in down a long, tree-lined lane. Beyond the trees, white board fences enclosed pastures dotted with grazing horses, thoroughbreds Marik thought, with their long clean limbs and graceful necks. At the end of the lane, in the center of the raked gravel parking area, a life-sized sculpture of a rearing horse rose above a carpet of gold and burgundy chrysanthemums. "They do horse-rescue on the side, I suspect for the tax write-off. If this mare is right for you, they'll want a receipt from me, for the donation. They love it that Northwind Ability Riding is a registered charity, makes it a win-win situation all around. Hello Susan!" she called to the tall, slender woman who had emerged from the long low barn. "She's head groomer. Nice woman." She introduced Marik.

"Welcome to Sutton Place Stables," Susan said, grasping Marik's hand with a surprisingly strong grip. "Come on in, you two, I want to introduce you to your new pony."

"I'll just get Herald out of the trailer, let him stretch his legs."

"You can turn him into the ring, no one's riding today. Hello Herald, old boy," she added, giving him a pat on the shoulder as he backed down the ramp. "Why don't you take his sheet off," she added. "He can have a nice roll." Clearly this was a woman who loved horses, even an old fellow of no particular ancestry like Herald.

"I've brought the mare in for you," Susan explained as she led them into the barn. On either side of the long central alleyway, sliding stall doors of gleaming varnished wood with black steel hardware stood open, their occupants out on pasture. Monday, Susan told them, was their down-day, a day of rest for the horses.

"For me too," she added, "but I wanted to be here to show you this girl." The little bay mare stood on cross-ties halfway down the alleyway, her delicate black-tipped ears tilted towards them. "We call her Cinders, short for Cinderella. Isn't that a good name for her? I've been cleaning her up for the ball." She picked up the clippers that lay on a tack box beside the animal and wrapped the cord neatly before returning it to the box. "She's not too crazy about the process! I've done her chin whiskers and front fetlocks, but not the rear. And not the bridle path either, I think that will have to be done with scissors. She's a little head-shy."

Dahlia led Herald up, let the two animals greet each other nose to nose, blowing their breaths at one another. Satisfied, she took Herald down to the other end of the barn, where the central alley opened out into a covered riding ring, floored with sand.

"I covet this riding ring," she called over her shoulder. She releasing the lead from Herald's halter. "Our ring isn't covered," she explained to Susan as she came back to join them. "Means that in bad weather, the kids can't ride. We teach them horsemanship, but it's not the same thing. Now, let's have a look at this Cinderella of yours."

"You can see she's not very big, probably not even fourteen-three." Marik knew what that meant, that horses are measured in four inch "hands". Most of the old Northwind Stables horses were around 15 hands high.

"You're just used to your thoroughbred giants," Dahlia laughed. "She's plenty big for Marik here."

Marik stood back a bit, watching these expert horsewomen at work. Would she ever become as confident around the animals as they both were? Dahl ran her hands down the mare's front legs, first one then the other, then moved to the mare's hindquarters. She was reaching down to check the off hind leg when the mare's hoof lashed back, missing Dahl's knee by inches.

Marik, at Cinder's head, jumped backward, but all Dahl did was make a kind of shushing, hissing noise. "Calm down now, pet," she said quietly. She rested her shoulder against the mare's side, one hand on the Cinderella's angular hock. Again she ran her hand down the black leg and pastern. Cinderella trembled, but stood still. Dahl repeated the process, standing in close, on the other side.

"Nice and clean, and good black hooves as well. Have you lunged her at all?"

"No. You know the deal. We rescue them, but don't rehabilitate them. That's your part, to turn them into useful equine citizens. Our part is to feed them up, get them back on their feet. Which reminds me, we did have the farrier check her out when he was here last week to do some re-shoeing. You can see her hooves have been filed. They were way overgrown. She was in a swamp, from what I gather, out back of a dairy farm. It had been sold up a couple years ago, after some kind of tragedy with the family that owned it. I guess the dairy corporation that bought it couldn't find a buyer for an untrained yearling. I doubt if they even bothered to look for one before they turned her out in the swamp. Basically they just forgot about her. Another victim of the demise of the family farm, just like my folks.

"Luckily for Cinders here, a neighbour who was going in through a back lane to get firewood early last spring after the snow-melt, saw her and called the rescue line. She was obviously starving, but she had spirit! They had a hell of a time getting her out of there. Basically she was wild, untouched.

She's come a long way since then, haven't you, Cinder-baby? I must say, I like working with these rescue horses we get in. Quite a change from our pampered darlings."

"You've done a good job," Dahl responded, moving up to the mare's head. "Even clipping her little chin whiskers. We don't do that much with my bunch," she added for Marik's benefit, "but any sort of handling is good for them when they are like this. They have to get used to the human touch. Let's take her out, see how she moves. Have you trailered her at all since she's been here?"

Susan explained that they'd been feeding her in what the other groomers called their Rehab Palace, an old two-horse that wasn't used on the road any more. "It's what we usually do, with any of our own who are trailer-sour. It happens, even with these big-money horses, if they've had a bad experience, been hauled too long or been in an accident. Horses can be temperamental, especially these hunter-jumper thoroughbreds. They usually settle down once they get the idea that 'the trailer equals lunch'. Cindy should be fine going into your trailer, especially with your old Herald to show her how."

"I only hope she'll be fine once we start moving!"

"I'm sure she will. She's really an amiable little girl once she figures out what's expected of her."

Susan's prediction proved true. Cinderella hesitated for a moment, front hooves on the ramp.

They let her stand there while Marik led Herald clattering up beside her and into the trailer. Reassured, the young horse followed and was soon secured, happily attacking the hay-net that hung in front of her.

"I'll just sign off on the Rescue Forms, and we'll be on our way." They followed Susan into the barn office, where Marik admired the equine photography and the multitude of big, rosette prize ribbons while the other two murmured over the paperwork.

CHAPTER TEN
Woman Talk

They headed home, facing the sun as it sank down past its zenith towards the westward mountains. Both horses were quiet in the trailer behind them, to Dahl's relief. "I had a bad time, once or twice, with horses that started to panic when the trailer started moving. That hasn't happened since I've been taking Herald along as a travelling companion. His calm seems to be contagious. We'll keep them together at home, until she settles in. Then we'll have the long job of teaching Cinderella how to be a riding horse."

"And me to be a rider," Marik added. "I hope I can handle it!"

Dahlia reassured her. It would take time, but as long as Marik made time to work with Cinderella consistently, every day, they'd both do well. "But what about that? Are you going to have the time? I know your Mom said you have savings that you are living on, but you're going to have to get a job eventually, aren't you?"

It was tempting to say, "No, never!" Dahlia could probably be trusted to keep a closed mouth, but Marik simply wasn't ready to reveal her secret yet. On the other hand, she feared that the longer she kept quiet about her wealth, the harder it would be to explain herself, if and when she did decide it was time to come out of the closet about the money. If and when! Maybe her family need never know that there was a multi-millionaire in their midst. Wouldn't that be an experience, to keep it a life-long secret! She realized that her aunt was still waiting for an answer.

"There's no rush," she said. "I'll have plenty of time to work with Cindy, and help you with everything else on the farm as well. I have a.... sort of an online job. With an accountant I worked with, before." This was the story she'd told her mother a few days ago. Other than the library systems she worked with every day, Rose had little interest or knowledge about computers and the online world. She could only hope that Dahlia was the same.

"He pays me pretty well, I have all the income I'll need." That was as close to the truth as she wanted to venture. Oh what a tangled web she was weaving for herself, she thought ruefully, wishing she could take back the lies that spilled so easily from her mouth. More lies! She didn't want to deceive anyone, not her mother, nor this dear aunt, nor anyone else. But how else could she maintain her privacy when people kept asking questions? It would only be for these first months, she told herself again. Once she felt established here in Chesney Creek, she would come out and confess. In the meanwhile, people kept asking questions and she felt obliged to respond. She had no choice but to spin a web of lies. There was, however, one web of lies that she could sweep down.

"We were talking about Ed, earlier. I can tell you something more about him, about his 'psychology.' If you want to know it."

Dahlia glanced at her, puzzled perhaps by the tight tone of her voice.

"He was sexually abusive to me, when we were kids," she blurted. There! The truth was out, to one more person.

"Oh Marik! I'm so sorry to hear that." Dahl took her hand off the steering wheel long enough to touch Marik's knee. "I mean, sorry that you had to experience that, not sorry to hear it. Not sorry you told me. You haven't talked about this to many people, have you?"

"No." Sue Ellen, her sponsor, had been the first, and then her sister Liz. Now Dahl knew the ugly truth, and she supposed it would be common knowledge before long.

"Women often don't talk about it," Dahl said. "Yet it's common as dirt. The male of the species have been abusing their female relatives since the days of Thog-the-Caveman. Sometimes I think that is why virginity came to be considered so important, because it was so rare. And thank God humans advanced enough to consider virginity a virtue. For the men, it meant that using their young female relatives sexually would reduce their marketability. The boy-oes of the family had to restrain themselves if they wanted to benefit from their young female relatives' commodity-value. What a blessing that must have been to primitive woman!"

She glanced over at Marik, who was staring straight ahead, her face frozen. "Sorry – I tend to go 'intellectual' when I'm uncomfortable. I start talking history and philosophy or something. Silly, really, and what's even sillier that it makes me feel superior. You know what they say, 'Small minds talk about people and events, but superior minds talk about Ideas.' I talk about ideas. That makes me superior, right? Except that talking about ideas, for me, is really only a nervous habit. I blather. Forgive me, I don't mean to diminish your experience."

"That's okay." Marik looked out her side-window. She wished they hadn't started talking about Edward Karlsson.

"No it's not," Dahlia said. "You do know, don't you, that I was in social work when I lived out east? Before I moved back here?"

Marik hadn't known that. How very little she did know, not only about her aunt, but about any of her family, and not because they were keeping secrets! That was her way, not theirs. The thought shamed her.

"I worked with families, and I hate to say it, but sexual abuse was a pretty common theme." She took her eyes off the road long enough to glance at Marik again, hoping she was taking this as meant. "It is way, way more common than people like to think. Perhaps not as common for your generation as for mine. I'd like to think it is a diminishing phenomenon, despite our de-valuing of virginity. But being common-as-dirt doesn't mean it isn't important. It is!"

"Yeah," Marik muttered sullenly. "I just wish it wasn't."

"It's nothing for you to be ashamed of! The shame is his, not yours. Women take on the shame, along with the abuse. Sometimes I think that's the worst of it. Being shamed by something that happened, something that you would never have chosen, that's horrible. I can only imagine, or rather, I can't imagine."

She could see trickling tears glistening damply on the younger woman's flushed cheeks. Dahlia's heart wept in sympathy, even though she knew very well that her words were causing the tears. She was the one with the scalpel, cutting into this tumour of shame. It was necessary, but not fun for either the surgeon or the patient. It reminded her of why she'd abandoned her social-work career. One hand on the steering wheel, she reached back to grab the box of tissues that she kept tucked behind the passenger seat.

"You are ashamed, aren't you? There's no need for you to feel that way. It wasn't your fault."

"I know that, but I still feel it! I've been living a lie because of it." Marik groped blindly for words to explain it. "I was always pretending that everything was OK, when it wasn't! It wasn't!"

"Of course not!"

"I'm ashamed of being abused, but I'm even more ashamed of lying about it, if that makes sense. I hated it! Lying to my parents, to everybody, keeping a secret. That was the worst of it, living a lie that way. I've been living it all my life, pretending I wasn't damaged."

"Damaged!" Dahlia cried, "You weren't damaged, for goodness sakes!"

"I was. I lost.... truth."

Dahlia took a moment or two to absorb this. "Lost your integrity, would you say?" she asked. Marik made a small sound of agreement. "Yes, I can see that living a lie, the loss of integrity, is damage. You are absolutely right. Sorry. I didn't get that at first." She paused, wanting to organize her thoughts in order to speak in a way that might help.

"It's good that you are getting this out in the open now, Marik, even though it is surely painful to do so, painful to admit to all of it. Maybe not so much to admit you've been abused – you couldn't help that – but to admit that you've been out of integrity for all these years. That you've been living a lie, pretending that the wound, and the scarring, didn't exist. Have I got that right?"

Sue Ellen had said something similar, that she needed to forgive both Ed and herself and accept that the abuse was simply part of her life's experience. Only then would she be able to let go of the complex of guilt and shame that destroyed her self-respect. She hadn't understood, at the time.

"Were you....?"

"No," Dahlia replied, "By God's Grace, I never was, but I do know lots of women who were, friends and friends of friends who were in support groups about it, as well as my clients. I probably know even more, women who've gone through it but never admitted it. You aren't the only one who's chosen to hide your scars, I'm sorry to say. Like I said, common as dirt. No less reprehensible, but certainly not unique. You aren't alone in this, you know."

"In a way," Marik mused, "it makes me feel better to know I'm not the only one. To know that lots of other women have lived through the same thing, and still made a success of their life. Not all of us ran away from home and became druggies," she added ruefully. "But how weird to say "us" - the sisterhood of ...what? Relative abuse?"

"Something like that. Thank you for trusting me with this, Mar. I can appreciate that it isn't easy to break the habit of keeping it hidden, as if it were something to be ashamed of, even though it's not."

"I still feel the shame, even though I know intellectually that I shouldn't. Maybe feeling ashamed is just a habit, the way I'm accustomed to feel when I think about all that. Do you think these feelings of being ashamed will fade, the more I come out of the closet about it?"

She told her aunt about her conversation with Liz. "It seems to get easier to talk about," she admitted, "though I don't know if it is easier just because it is you, or because you are the second person back home here that I've talked with, about it."

"Hard to say. We'll hope so. And good for you for daring the experiment. You're a brave woman."

A brave woman. That was a new perception of herself. "Thank you, Aunt Dahl. That means a lot to me, coming from you."

"I don't know, though, if that sheds any light on Edward's murder," Dahl added, "if you don't mind getting back to that?" She glanced over at the younger woman.

"No. It's weird, but I feel less...." Her voice tailed off as she sought the right word. "Less angry at him. It's as though I'm starting to see him as a whole person, the miserable asshole. One thing I know for certain, he didn't get killed because of what he did to me. Ergo, it must be because of something her did to someone else. Or didn't do?"

"That was the original question, wasn't it? What was it about him that motivated someone to smack him in the back of the head with a rock and then finish the job by forcing his face in the mud until he smothered? That was pretty brutal! Whomever that was, they were pretty determined to turn his lights out."

Marik was grateful that Dahl had changed the direction of their conversation. "Maybe instead of the victim, we should be looking at the psychology of the person who did it," she suggested. "Work out his 'psychological profile' – or hers, since I guess it could have been a woman - and then see if we know anyone who fits that description? Seems to me that's the only way that we can help, if it's someone we know, or at least know about. Who do we know that thinks violence is good way to solve problems?"

"I wish we could learn more about the parts of his life that we don't know about," Dahlia grumbled. "If it's something to do with his law practice, or some woman he mistreated, we might not even know who the players were. We might know someone who fits the psychological profile, without knowing that they had any connection to Edward. On the other hand, they say we're only six connections away from anyone else on the planet."

"Maybe the police already know who did it," Marik said. "That would be a relief." She felt herself growing tired of talking about anything connected to Edward Karlsson, including the murder. It had been a long day, and there were still miles ahead of them. Deliberately, she changed the subject.

"You know that riding ring back at Susan's place? How much would it cost for us to have one of those, at Northwind?"

"To put a roof over ours? Oh, I don't know. Ideally, I'd have a whole new ring built. We just started using that area, fenced off one side of the home paddock, but it isn't in the ideal situation."

"What would the ideal situation be?"

"Like at Sutton Place – a ring that's an extension of the barn so that you could go right into it from the stalls without having to go out and around like we do now."

"So how much would that cost? Thousands? Tens of thousands? Hundreds of thousands?"

"Oh – tens, I suppose. Maybe 50 thou, something like that. It doesn't have to be as elaborate as Sutton Place, we don't need seating and washrooms and a fancy office, just a roof wide enough to offer some shelter for parents and so on, if they're standing around watching. Not to say fancier wouldn't be better! But it's all a pipe-dream, anyway. Not going to happen."

"Aren't there grants or something?"

"I've looked into that a bit, but no."

"Would you mind if I talked to Ken Rheddenk about it? My accountant? My boss I should say." She corrected herself, then wished she hadn't. She didn't want to build a bigger lie, but it seemed to just happen, out of her control.

"Why? I'm curious, not sceptical," Dahl explained, "but why talk to an accountant about it?"

"Maybe he'll know something that we don't. He, well, he works with some charities." She knew she was getting herself even more entangled, spinning more strands into her web of deceit. "I'll talk to him," she said dismissively. "You never know."

The autumn sky was stained the brilliant colours of sunset by the time they turned onto Mountain Road, with just a mile to go before unloading the horses. By the time they came into the house, after putting Herald and Cinderella in neighbouring stalls with fresh hay-nets and buckets of water, Fleur had dinner ready and waiting for them. She would spend the night again, since it was late. Tired from their long day, Marik and Dahlia had little to say. Fleur was happy to fill in the gaps in conversation with happy chatter about the baking that she and Nonny had accomplished.

"Your freezer is full of apple pies, four of them, and cinnamon buns. And I made some of those branny-bun muffins that Mummy likes, you can have them for breakfast."

Dahl appreciated all that her sister had done. There could never be any question about the goodness of Fleur's heart, but it had been a very full day. She was glad when she could escape upstairs to her bedroom, and open her laptop. She clicked on the "Guided" icon, and let her fingers rest lightly on the keyboard.

Dear One, thank you for our time together. We want to assure you that what you want is in the process of formation. Be patient. Your activities today have been formative in ways which, in ways that we can't explain to you because there is no language – other than mathematics, to some degree – to define how your thoughts and longings affect what we might call the unformed-energy. You did good work today. We will talk more on this another time, but for right now your body needs sleep, your psyche or nervous system needs to rest and recuperate. When you are in this state, this less-than-optimal, in fact less-than-usual (!) state, it is difficult for us to communicate, or rather, for you to receive our communications. Bless you and goodnight. Your questions will be answered, be patient. Goodnight.

CHAPTER ELEVEN

Distrustfulness

The following afternoon, Marik drove down from the farm to meet Stan, who had made good on his second promise to call. They would meet at Coffee Creek, in the shopping plaza that served the Sanson Vale and the rest of the upscale development that was creeping north from the old Chesney Creek. They'd grab a coffee, he suggested, and then perhaps go for a hike? Not by the lake, but up in the hills beyond the new suburbs.

"I'd like that," Marik said. "I'm used to being more active than I've been lately."

The shopping plaza was built in an area that had been bush and swamp when Marik was growing up. She changed out of her stable-clothes, into clean well-fitted jeans, a new peach turtleneck, and a light khaki jacket. She added a touch of mascara to her usual lip-gloss-and-go routine.

He got to Coffee Creek ahead of her and was waiting for her on the mezzanine overlooking the barista station. She heard her name being called as she headed for the lineup. "Marik, look u-up," he sang. "I'm up here." It was a playful, low-pitched voice, utterly different from the voice of command that he had aimed at her last time they met. She caught sight of him leaning over the balcony railing straight up above her, and he laughed at her startled expression.

The grey-haired woman in front of her glanced up at him as well. "You're supposed to be the one up there, Juliet" she remarked with a chuckle before turning to get her coffee from the sleek young barista. Marik ordered a skim-milk latte.

"Make it a large," she added extravagantly. She had forgotten for a moment that she could have the most expensive concoction on the big blackboard if she wanted. Even after two months, three if she counted the month-of-silence they had imposed on themselves after hitting the jackpot, she still wasn't accustomed to the idea that she could buy virtually anything she wanted.

The austerity habit was too ingrained to be easily changed, she thought wryly. Her wants and desires hadn't yet caught up with her unlimited budget. Her old friend Terri was doing a better job of it. According to her most-recent email, she'd bought the condo of her dreams, and was filling the closets with a complete new and extravagant wardrobe. Marik was embarrassed to reply that she hadn't spent even half of the 'allowance' that was automatically deposited in her checking account each month. Ken Rheddenk has insisted on that.

"Your latte, ma'am." She paid the barista and carried her latte carefully upstairs.

"You look great! That colour really suits you." He was wearing a soft dark blue flannel shirt, the sleeves rolled up to expose muscular forearms. He pulled the chair out for her, and handed her a napkin to mop up her saucer where the latte had splashed over the brim of the cup on her way up the stairs. "What have you been up to? Settled back into Life in Chesney Creek? It must be quite a change from the city."

"It is, and I like it." She still had reservations about seeing a cop, but to her surprise their conversation flowed easily. He was interested enough in her to ask questions, and open enough to tell her about himself. He had come home to Chesney Creek after 'paying his dues' as he put it, in the city.

"My parents were still here, but getting older. And I never really was a city boy. I like the pace of life here." He'd been married, he admitted, but very briefly. "It was over before it started, to tell you the truth. A mistake for both of us, but we parted amiably. We both realized that small-town life was not a fit for her. What about you? Most of us have been through one marriage, at least, by our age."

Without going into details, she told him that marriage had never been part of her life plans. "I had a short, and ugly, live-in with a man who turned out to be a complete and utter rotter. Once bitten, twice shy, you might say." She told him about Cindy, her new rescue-horse. He knew about Northwind Stables. "It's an institution around here," he said. "Bob Pasqualli, from the paper, remember? He has a disabled nephew who rides with the Ability Riders program. Bob does a feature about the stable just about every year, helps with the fund-raising projects. It is a fine thing your aunt is doing, with those kids. I didn't realize she did horse-rescue, as well. Not that I know much about horses, I'm more of a dog-person."

Stan eventually brought up the Ed Karlsson murder case. She told him that she hadn't heard anything more from the Police Department after her initial interview. "That's fine by me, I don't want to even think about it."

"You must have convinced June – Detective Halston - that you were just an innocent bystander," he said. "She even thought about suspecting me, you know. The one who discovers the body is always a suspect. She didn't pursue it, she realized how ridiculous it was. June is tenacious, but reasonable. There's no connection between me and Karlsson. I've never had any need for a lawyer, and as far as I know, my ex- is not a notch on his bedpost, although there seems to be a lot of those! The man sure couldn't keep it in his pants, could he?"

Marik ducked her head as she felt the hot blood flushing up in her face. "I don't want to talk about him," she muttered. "I don't want to talk about him, think about him, or have any more conversations about him with anyone, alright? He's dead, and he can blighted well stay dead!"

"Sorry! I guess I shouldn't have brought it up." He reached across the table to cover her hand with his large warm one. It was a strong, broad hand, with just a few dark hairs across the back, the nails cut short and blunt.

Marik pulled her hand away, refusing to look up at him. She didn't see the concern in his eyes.

"I was forgetting he's part of your family."

"Yes he was, worse luck! But like I said, I'm not interested in talking about him. Or about the murder."

"I'm sorry I brought it up."

"Bullshit!"

She pushed her chair back and stood up. "Detective Halston set this up, didn't she? And I thought she was done with me!" She was furious at being tricked. This 'coffee date' was nothing more than part of their investigation.

"No!" The table wobbled as he started to stand.

She snatched her jacket and bag off the chair. "Now I understand why you never phoned, not until after finding Ed's body! I was fool enough to think this was just going to be a chance for us to get to know one another better."

Stan tried to interrupt her, but she wasn't listening. "You figured that if you invited me here, made me think it was a 'date', you'd be able to find out more about me, right?" She shoved the chair out of her way. "I don't have anything else to tell you except what I said that day in the park. I hated Ed Karlsson. I wish I'd never heard of him, I wish to God I hadn't been in the park that day! I'm sick of everyone wanting to talk about him. He's not that important, and he never was!" She spun on her heel and hurtled down the stairs, abandoning her unfinished latte.

"Marik, wait!"

He caught up with her just before she reached the parking lot. "You've got it all wrong! I'm sorry, you misunderstood me. I'm not 'investigating' you! Not at all. I have nothing to do with the investigation. Nothing!" She glared at him. "I said the wrong thing, obviously, but I didn't mean to upset you."

"Well, you did!" He sounded sincere, but she couldn't trust him, he was a cop. She knew about cops.

"Please, forgive me. I really am sorry." He reached out as if to take her hand. She swung her arms behind her back. "Marik, please. Come on back in, come and finish your coffee." His voice was kind, conciliatory.

Marik chewed her lip, not sure what to do. She hadn't had a flashback like this since she'd come home to Chesney Creek. She thought she'd left that old street-girl persona behind, but apparently she hadn't.

"We don't have to talk about the case. I'm sorry I brought it up. I want us to get to know each other better, that's all. Really. Let's go finish our coffee."

"Alright," she conceded. She would give him another chance. "I probably overreacted."

"You did," he agreed, "but I shouldn't have said that about your cousin. Not very sensitive of me."

She didn't want to go back into the shop. They had provided enough entertainment, her grey-haired friend from the lineup was probably waiting for the next act. Romeo and Juliet indeed! Stan seemed to have come to the same conclusion. "Look, why don't we go back to our original plan, go for a walk? I've got Trig in the truck, I was going to take him for a run after." He glanced down at her feet. "You've got sensible shoes on. Why don't I go back in, I'll get a couple to go, and we can go up the Sanson Trail for a bit, like I suggested when I called. Can we do that? I promise not to mention another word about the case."

Marik followed him back into Coffee Creek, keeping her head down as she crossed the room. In the tiny washroom, she splashed cool water on her cheeks, and ran a comb through her unruly dark hair. She was growing it out, she didn't need to keep it short since she wasn't in food services anymore. So many changes in the past months, she thought, no wonder she was a bit out of balance. Lots of changes, but some things remained the same, like the hellish influence Ed still had on her life. Still! Even after all these years, even with him being dead. She'd thought she could escape from that, when she ran away from Chesney Creek all those years ago, but she knew now that it was impossible. The long arm of past experience still had the power to reach out and strangle her emotions. Curse Ed! Tomorrow was his memorial service. Her Aunt Lindy had given in and agreed that they needed to do that. Another whole day devoted to Edward Karlsson! Perhaps when she got through that she could finally leave him, and all that he'd meant in her life, behind.

Meanwhile, there was Stan. He was a nice man, a good man, and he was waiting for her. He happened to make his living in law enforcement. She needed to get past that particular prejudice, her dislike and suspicion about cops. That was one of her city-ghosts that she thought she could leave behind, by moving back here. How ironic, she thought as she untangled her comb, that she'd run away from the city just like she had run away from Chesney Creek all those years before. She had come back, ready to confront her Chesney Creek ghosts. Apparently she had her city-ghosts to confront as well.

She jammed the comb impatiently back in her purse, and with her head held high went out to join Stan. She added a little more low-fat milk to her cup before following him out the door. His truck was parked not far from hers, with the big grey dog leaning out the driver-side window. His broad pink tongue lolled out the side of his wide doggy grin. Stan pushed him back and got into the truck. "I'll follow you, meet you at the trail-head."

"You'd better lead. I'm not sure I remember how to get up to Sanson Trail, if I ever knew." Things had changed. She needed to do the same.

The drive took only a few minutes, but it gave her time to gather her resolve. If it was true, as she and Dahlia had agreed, that she had nothing to be ashamed of, then she should be able to talk about her history with her cousin without getting caught up by the sort of emotional whirlwind that had overwhelmed her a few minutes ago. Stan had apologized for upsetting her, but in truth it was she who owed him apology. She had overreacted, badly. She hoped she could muster the courage to admit that to him. How else could she expect to build an honest friendship with him?

She zipped up her jacket while he clipped the leash onto Trigger's collar. Sanson Trail was marked "challenging" on the trail map. It headed steeply up from the parking lot, winding through the trees alongside a rippling waterway, and then levelled off where it met the power lines stretching north and east from Chesney Creek. Stan seemed surprised that she was able to match him, stride for stride.

"Years of waitressing. I'm used to being on my feet." She wasn't accustomed to walking uphill, but the exercise felt good and she liked the feeling of working her muscles. Still, it was a relief to reach the power lines, where the trail levelled out, but it was still deeply rutted from trail bikes and ATVs running up and down it, and treacherous with loose rock.

"I want to tell you why I said that about Ed, why I hated him."

"We don't have to talk about it…"

"I want to. I need to explain."

Stan unsnapped Trigger's leash. The dog bounded into the brush alongside the trail, nose down and tail lashing with enthusiasm. Eyes down to watch her footing on the rugged trail, she told him briefly about her ugly history with her cousin. It was, she said, one of the reasons she'd left Chesney Creek. Now, she wanted to put that part of her life behind her, to forgive, forget and move on.

"I've discovered I can't do that unless I admit to what happened, years ago. So now you know why I hated him." Marik finished her capsule history of her relationship with Ed Karlsson just as they reached the turn-off up to the highest viewpoint.

"Want to go on up?" he asked, gesturing at the steep incline.

"Let me catch my breath first." She wasn't as prepared as she thought she was for the fast pace that he and the dog set.

"Marik, I don't know what to say. Except that I'm sorry that happened."

"Whether I like it or not, that experience is part of who I am. I'm tired of being in denial about it. That's what it has amounted to – denial. I'm done with that."

"I can't blame you for not wanting to talk about it, especially to someone like me."

"Because you're a cop?"

"Because I'm a cop, because I'm a man, because.....well, you don't really know me. You didn't exactly remember who I was, did you, that day I met you in the park. The day you were picking blackberries, I mean."

"It took me a moment," she admitted.

"Thought so. You ready for the next lap?"

Marik was game for it, so they hiked up side by side without speaking, saving their breath for the hard pull up the last steep, rocky stretch. The view from the lofty mountain top was magnificent. They gazed out over miles of valley, over a landscape that had been carved out eons ago between the two encircling mountain ranges. How peaceful it looked, with little Chesney Lake placidly blue under the sunny pale sky.

When Marik had caught her breathe again, she completed her story. "I thought I had gotten over hating Ed, when I decided to move back here," she said. "But the truth will out, as they say, when the pressure is on. The pressure was on, once he became the center of attention by getting murdered. The hatred came out. That's why I reacted like I did, running out of Coffee Creek like that."

She had never talked about it to a man, other than that useless psychologist she'd mentioned to Liz. There had been a few men in her life, between that first, disastrous relationship with Dale and this return to her hometown, but none of them had heard a word about her distant, despoiled past. Now, after telling Liz about it, and then talking with Dahlia, the memory of what had happened to her as a child simply didn't feel so intense anymore. It was losing its emotional impact. This return home to Chesney Creek was paying unexpected dividends, challenging her old perceptions, forcing her to grow in self-respect and self-acceptance. More than just resolving old issues, she felt as though she were developing into a new sort of person. She was proud of herself for opening up to Stan. Perhaps the new person she was becoming would be a woman who could have a decent, lasting relationship with a decent man. Wouldn't that be a change!

Having drunk their fill of the view, they started back down the steep trail. Trigger reappeared out of the brush, an over-sized stick clutched in his broad, drooling jaws.

"Give it up," Stan told him. Trigger released his grip on the stick, tail wagging in gleeful expectation as Stan lifted it high over his shoulder, and flung it down across the power-line trail into the trees. They followed the dog downhill at a more moderate pace.

"Marik, I hate to be the one to tell you this, but you're going to have to add this stuff about Ed to your official statement."

"What do you mean!" she exclaimed. "No way. I'm not doing that!" She felt like kicking herself, trusting fool that she was. Obviously he was a cop first, and only a fellow human-being and potential friend as a very distant second! How could she have been so stupid, telling him her story? What was it about this man? She was making the same mistake over and over again with him, trusting him.

"I'm not going to talk to them again," she said flatly. "Why should I?" Once was enough. She had reported what she'd seen in the park. She had signed her statement. It was done. She hated dealing with the police. Now he wanted her to go back and reveal – what? That she herself had a motive for murdering the ass-hole?

"Because he might have gone on abusing children, after you were fone. Maybe that's why he got killed. You're going to have to talk to June – Detective Halston. She already knows about your saying that you hated him."

"   Oh." What he said made sense. She hadn't thought of it, she was too caught up in her own perspective, her own little drama. "Ok I will." She felt spent. Her reserves of emotional as well as physical strength had been used up on this hike. "But can we drop the subject now? I really can't bear to talk about it anymore."

"Sure. Consider it dropped." He whistled for Trigger, took the stick from his jaws and threw it ahead of them again down the trail. Marik decided to take control of the conversation. She would put the pressure on him, tit-for-tat and a change was as good as a rest.

"I've got a question for you," she said. "Why is it that you always say 'June' and then change it to 'Detective Halston'? If you don't mind my asking?" She realized with a mixture of guilt and glee that he didn't like the question. The straight black brows drew together to form a dark dividing crease up his forehead. Ha! He'd been perfectly willing to talk about things she'd rather not discuss. "Your turn to be on the hot spot," she added coolly.

"Alright," he said reluctantly. "The thing is, I made the mistake of getting involved with June, and I still tend to call her by her first name. Professionally, she is Detective Halston. That's how I ought to refer to her, and I do, most of the time. She deserves the respect, she's worked hard to get where she is." He whistled for Trigger, and then whistled again.

"Darn it, dog, come on!" Clearly June Halston was a topic of conversation he didn't enjoy.

"Anyway, that's in the past. But you still need to go talk to her, tell her the rest of it about your cousin."

"Yes," she said shortly, and started back down the trail, man and dog a step or two behind her. A rock rolled under her foot suddenly and she might have fallen if he hadn't jumped forward to grasp her arm and keep her upright. She shook off his helping hand impatiently.

"Look, Marik.... I seem to be doing what you just did, slipping up. I don't want to lose my footing with you, but I've said the wrong thing a couple times now."

"So you have."

They had reached the more level part of the trail now, down from the high lookout. "I'm not very good with relationships, with women, but I'd like us to be friends. Can we put the misunderstandings behind us and try again?"

Marik twitched her lips back and forth a few times as she considered his request. "Alright," she said, "Here's the deal. I told you about Ed, and me. That was hard, that made me feel pretty vulnerable. So how about telling me something about you? I don't mean about you and June-Detective-Halston, that's none of my business. But you need to tell me something...I don't know. Embarrassing. True. Intimate, even."

"Whoa!" He threw up his hands and recoiled in mock surrender. "That's a lot to ask from a man. Embarrassing, True and Intimate? We men don't talk about stuff like that!"

She giggled. "Yeah, right, you want to look at my cards but hide your own. Well, that won't work. I told you, Mr. Policeman – under my sophisticated veneer, I'm a street-girl. I don't put up with any manly bullshit." It was true, there was a part of her that was a tough street-chick, who knew how to take care of herself, and who couldn't be bullied. She felt like she was integrating a little more of her past into the present. It was fun to amuse herself a bit at his expense. She waited to see how he would respond to this challenge she'd given him.

"Give me a minute." It took more than the minute for him to gather up his nerve. They walked silently together, matching strides. They were almost back to the parking lot before he answered. "OK, here's something about me and my past. When I was in high school, 16 or so, I had a crush on this girl who didn't know I existed. I really liked her, you know how kids do?" He slid his eyes sideways at her.

"So this girl – she was really pretty, gorgeous in fact, and smart – but she left, moved away. I never got to tell her that I had this big crush-y thing about her. But I've never forgotten her. Is that pitiful, or what? I've been carrying the torch for twenty years for the girl that got away! I think that's part of the reason my marriage went sour, I was hoping Gillian could replace the one who went away, but of course she didn't. No one has ever been able to take the place of my high school crush."

"So?" This seemed like a pretty lame story to Marik. It didn't compare in any way to what he knew about her now. "Is there more to the story?"

Stan clenched his jaw, tensing the strong muscles around his mouth as if to keep the words from escaping. Finally he blew his breath out in a gusty sigh. "Yeah. There's more. This is embarrassing." He opened his truck door so Trigger could leap in. Slapping it shut, he leaned back against the truck, one booted foot up against the door. He patted his dog absently, and fondled the cropped ears.

"Here's the embarrassing part: That girl? I saw her again, a few years later, when I was in Vancouver." An impish grin began to form, spreading from his eyes to his curving lips. Marik wondered where this story could be headed, to cause such a play of emotion, from grim on moment to amused the next.

"I stopped her for a minor traffic violation, didn't know it was her until I got out of the car and asked for her driver's licence. You know the story: I didn't give her a ticket. I've regretted it ever since." Marik's eyes widened. "Yup. That girl was you. Pretty pitiful story, eh?"

Marik was at a loss for words. It was difficult to believe that any boy had been interested in her, back then. She thought that only girls developed crushes like that, like she'd done in Grade 9. She still remembered the boy, although she hadn't thought of him in years. It came back to her now, how thrilled she'd been to see him in the hallway, or watch him on the basketball court. Apparently Stan had felt the same about her, and had never forgotten. How weird was that?

"So here's what I've been wanting to do," he said, lowering his foot to the ground. He lifted her chin with a finger, stepped in close and captured her lips with his. His arms slipped around her as he gathered her against his broad chest, and took the kiss deeper. The man knew how to kiss, Marik thought as her lips responded to the tender, demanding warmth of his.

"That's my confession," he said, releasing her gently. "I've been wanting to do that for a VERY long time." He smiled into her eyes, and touched her lips lightly with an extended forefinger. "No need to say anything."

He opened the truck door, giving Trigger a push. "Get over in your own seat, buddy. I'll be in touch," he added through the open window. Then he was gone, pulling out of the parking area, leaving her stunned speechless by the unexpectedness of it. At last she stirred herself, and got into her own truck. That was certainly an interesting development, she told herself. Kissed by a cop! Not only that, but she'd kissed him back, and enjoyed it. The man certainly knew how to kiss.

CHAPTER TWELVE

Sympathy for the Devil

It was raining when Marik came into town to join Rose and Dan to attend Ed's memorial service. Rose had a casserole dish in a quilted carrier. "The Church Auxiliary Ladies are providing refreshments for the reception afterwards," she explained, "but I wanted to bring something. Poor Lindy, this day will be hard for her."

Dan, looking uncomfortable in his dark suit, came around to open the car door for his ladies. The church parking lot was filling fast. Women in somber rain coats, accompanied by their dark-suited men, hurried into the church. Marik took an order-of-service folder from a tall blonde woman at the door as Rose led the way quickly to the second row of chairs at the front of the sanctuary. Liz and Zach were there ahead of them. They shifted over to make room for the late-comers. Aunt Lindy, looking haggard in a dull black skirt and jacket, twisted around to greet them from her front row seat. Marik didn't recognize the younger couple, with a lanky teenager, seated on Lindy's left.

"That's Ed's ex," Liz whispered. "She had left town, and remarried, but she stays in touch with Aunt Lindy, because of Connor. Ed's son, her grandson. Good of her to show up."

When the blonde woman who'd handed her the order of service slipped into the seat on Lindy's right, Marik realized with a start that this must be her cousin Helene. She touched her on the shoulder. "Sorry – I didn't recognize you at the door." Helene returned the greeting quietly, rustling the paper she held on her lap as she turned around to face front.

Marik glanced around at the congregation. The Delganee family, the aunts and uncles and cousins she shared with Edward, filled the first few rows, twin Aunts Joan and Jan with their flighty grey hair done up in knots, their husbands, like Dan, looking uncomfortable in dark suits. She was surprised to see that her Aunt Fleur was there as well. She was on the other side of the central aisle, several rows back, with a darkly handsome, broad-shouldered man sitting beside her.

She turned to Liz, sitting next to her. "Is that James, the ex-son-in-law, with Auntie Flo?" Her sister glanced back, and nodded. "Why would they be here?" Fleur was a Palmer, not a Delganee.

Her sister shrugged. "Ed was her lawyer, I think," she explained sotto-voce. Marik felt mildly reprimanded.

The quiet organ music faded to silence as the minister, a stocky woman with cropped grey hair, came in, pausing briefly to greet Lindy before stepping up onto the raised dais. It had been many years since last time Marik was in a church. Aunt Lindy's was a larger, more modern building than the old white-clapboarded church with its high, cross-topped steeple where the Palmer family worshipped, and where Marik and her Palmer cousins attended Sunday-School. There were no stained-glass windows in this building, and rows of folding chairs took the place of wooden pews. The starkly naked cross on the high front wall was the only decoration other than the minister's white robe and the colourful woven stole that draped around her neck. A framed photo of Ed, professionally posed and smiling, stood on a small table in front of the pale wooden lectern. The minister lit the candle in front of the photo, and led them in a recitation of the Lord's Prayer. The words were comfortably familiar to Marik's ear, despite the modernization of a few phrases. The service proceeded through hymns and readings, and a lengthy eulogy by old Mr. Bolster, titular head of the law firm where Edward had served the community for the past decade and a half. Apparently what Ed had told her that day in the park was true, he had been about to become the newest partner in the firm. "We would have been proud to see his name added to the firm's title, Bolster, Nod & Karlsson. But it wasn't meant to be."

The minister held the old man's arm as he stepped carefully down and returned to his seat. Then it was her cousin Helene's turn. Marik found it difficult to see, in this tall, elegant woman who stepped up to the lectern, the skinny little girl she remembered, lank straw-coloured hair hanging in a curtain around her ears, freckles scattered across the nose that had always seemed a little large for her face. She'd grown into it.

"The best thing I can say today," Helene began, "is that my big brother has finally escaped from the heartaches and regrets that marred his life."

A murmur rippled across the room. "I know – few people if any knew the real Edward Karlsson. Most of you knew my brother as a confident, successful man – a respected lawyer, a valued volunteer in the community, and a charmer in every sense of the word.

"All of which is true. If you had any dealings with him in a professional capacity, you know that he was worthy of your deepest trust and respect. As Mr. Bolster told you, he was a conscientious, dedicated lawyer. He had a great respect for honesty, especially in regard to money. Ed would NOT have submitted billable hours unless he'd actually worked those hours, and more as well." Her small, sad smile gave them permission to chuckle. Lawyers were always good for a laugh. She straightened her papers, and continued.

"As you've heard from the previous speakers, my brother Edward was a man who gave back to the community in service. He believed in Chesney Creek, believed it was a good place to live, a good place to raise families. One of his deepest sorrows was that he'd made a mess of his marriage. Just like his father before him." Her eyes, and all of their eyes, swung over to the far side of the church, where Jack sat, one hand shadowing his eyes. For the first time in Marik's life, she felt sorry for him. Jack-the-jerk had lived up to his nickname, but now he was nothing but an old man with nothing left, even his son taken from him.

"And it is also true that Ed liked women; he really did. He adored our mother, and he was always so kind, so loving, to both of us. Anytime I needed help, any kind of help, I knew I could count on Eddie. I couldn't have asked for a better big brother." She choked on a sob, then collected herself and went on.

"What you didn't know about Ed was the agony of his inner life. You didn't know that he wasn't living the life he'd hoped for; you didn't know his pain, his suffering." She hesitated, pinching her lips together.

"Well, that's how he wanted it. He didn't want you to know that he was a disappointed man. He didn't want me to know either, but – you can't care about someone as I did for my big brother, and not know the truth of his heart, much as he tried to keep it hidden. Maybe he knew that pain like his is toxic. Did he know that, did he try to hide his pain in order to protect us from being infected as he was? I don't know, but for whatever reason, he kept it hidden. He didn't want you to know that his life was imploding inwardly.

"Consequently, you probably don't know that he longed for a different life, a different career. You don't know about the dreams he gave up to please others, and you don't know how deeply he regretted that, through his own mistakes, he destroyed his marriage.

"Instead, you knew him as the man he wished he could be: Worthy of your respect. Loveable. Honourable. Happy. Ironically, what he thought of as a false-front, a pretence, was actually exactly who he was. Edward Karlsson was worthy of your respect. He was honourable. He was loveable. You know that. But he didn't! That is the tragedy of his life. He wasn't given time to discover that he was exactly the man he longed to be. That was taken from him. And this good, honourable, giving, loving man was taken from us. I hope to God that they find who did this to him, and to us!"

She turned her page over. "Whoever did this, I want you to know: you stole something from us, from all of us here. Given time, and life, Ed would have rebuilt his inner life, he would have found a way to be as strong and good and happy on the inside as he appeared to be on the outside. If nothing else, he for sure would have gone on being a treasure to those who knew and appreciated him, as we are all treasures to one another. Someone stole our treasure, and took him from us." With tears trickling down her face, she folded up her notes and stepped out from behind the lectern. She stood there at the front of the church, and looked up. "Ed – if you are there – I hope you know how much we miss you. Big brother, we love you."

Marik pulled a tissue out of her bag, and wiped her eyes. All over the sanctuary, people were doing the same. The minister stepped up to lectern again, gathered her congregation with a short prayer, and then offered the Benediction that traditionally ends such a service.

"Coffee and tea and refreshments will be available downstairs in the Fellowship Hall. We ask that you let the family have a few moments, then they will join you to receive your commiserations and remembrances of Edward Karlsson: beloved son, brother and fellow struggling human-being, who is missed so very much."

As she stood up, Marik was surprised to see June Halston step out into the aisle from the back row of seats and head for the exit to the parking lot. Marik had called the department to make an appointment, as Stan had suggested. She would go in for a talk with the detective the following afternoon. She hadn't expected to see her at Ed's memorial service. Perhaps, however, it was standard procedure for a murder-case? If so, she doubted that the detective had learned anything that would help uncover the murderer. Surely he – or she? - was not to be found among those who were mourning her cousin's death! She followed her parents downstairs

.

The Fellowship Hall was crowded, the volume of noise growing as people filled plates, clinked cups against saucers, and found others to chat with. Marik found herself beside Helene, offering her condolences. "That was beautiful, your eulogy," she told her cousin. "I think you gave all of us a different picture of Ed."

"Thank you. It wasn't easy." She changed the subject. "Have you met my nephew, Connor?" The teen ran true to the Karlsson type, a tall Nordic blonde who seemed to owe nothing to the slight, dark-haired woman who was standing next to him. She introduced herself.

"I'm Connor's mother, Tiffany. Your cousin's ex," she added, and introduced her husband, who set his plate down long enough to shake Marik's hand. "Connor's step-dad." The lanky teenager turned away.

"Are you in town for long?" Marik asked, making conversation.

"We have to talk with your police again tomorrow." Tiffany grimaced. "Apparently they aren't satisfied with Connor's story, they've got more questions to ask him. I did my best to smooth his relationship with his dad, but you know what teens are like; Connor and Edward didn't get along all that well after the divorce." She excused herself, and the family turned away, making their rounds. Marik was glad that Detective Halston had left directly after the service. Surely she couldn't suspect this gangly, spotted teenager of patricide? It seemed absurd to think that someone, anyone, had hated Ed enough to commit murder. Yet it had happened, and perhaps the detective was right in looking for a suspect amongst the very people who should have cared most for him.

She spotted her Aunt Flo standing alone and looking a little lost beside the glass doors that led out to the patio. Poor Flo! She made her way across the crowded room to join her.

"James said he'll be right back. He went out to talk to someone." A few people stood on the patio, huddled in jackets with their backs to the wind, in order to smoke their cigarettes. "That's James, in that nice charcoal-brown suit." James apparently noticed them watching him. He and the other man quickly exchanged business cards before he opened the door and came in.

"Too cold out there for me!" His ruddy cheeks wore a hectic flush, and he rubbed his palms together as if to warm them up.

"This is my niece, darling Marik."

"Good to meet you, I've heard lots about you." His brows were lowered above his deep-set blue eyes, but his full, rather sensuous lips curved into a friendly smile as he asked, "What's Mama Fleur been telling you about me?" He grasped her hand for just a little bit longer than necessary in his large, surprisingly muscular hand. "Nothing bad, I hope."

As if Aunty Flo could ever say anything bad about anyone! He relaxed his grip as Marik replied, "Only that you were outdoors. It's quite a crush. I didn't realize that Ed was involved in so many community programs."

"I'm going to grab a coffee, want one?" He came back to them quickly, as if worried that she might get away before he had a chance to get acquainted. "Mama Fleur tells me you've just recently moved back to Chesney Creek. How do you like it? Quite a change from the city?"

"It's great," she said agreeably. "I decided I prefer small town living."

"I understand you saved up, so you could move back, not need to work for a while. What sort of work did you do?"

"I was a waitress."

He stepped back. "Really? I would have pegged you as a corporate ladder-climber. Waitressing, eh? It must have taken a long, long time to save up enough, working as a waitress."

Marik had decided long ago that it wasn't worth the energy to defend her career choice. If people thought less of her because of what she did for a living, so be it. "I did alright," she said flatly.

He realized he'd offended her, and apologized. "I guess it must have been one of those high-end places? Good tips?'

She nodded, feeling slightly ashamed for being so touchy. Some people were perfectly comfortable discussing their own and other people's financial situations, but she was Rose's daughter, she couldn't get away from feeling that one's finances are one's own personal business.

"I get down to the coast occasionally, to meet clients, so I'm always on the lookout for great places to eat. What was its name, that place you worked?"

"Bob's Olde Beanery," she replied, and instantly regretted it. What if he was one of those people who followed the lottery news, and recognized the name? She had been so careful to maintain her secret identity as a multi-millionaire. The last thing she wanted was for her anonymity to be ripped open. She would choose her own time and place to do that, and it certainly wouldn't be in the middle of a crowded room, talking to a stranger!

"Sounds familiar," he said casually, but then a different expression passed over his face as he murmured the name thoughtfully to himself. "The Old Beanery. Very familiar."

She had to change the subject, fast. "What do you do?" she asked. In her experience, men preferred to talk about themselves rather than about her. She'd taken advantage of that fact more than once, to turn a conversation when it threatened to become uncomfortable.

He was an investment consultant, he told her. Before she could ask what that meant, he changed the subject himself, putting the focus back on her. "Fleur tells me you've recently acquired a new horse. You must tell me about that."

She explained that Cinderella was a rescue animal. He was suitably shocked to hear how she'd been abandoned. "That's appalling! How can people treat animals that way? How good of you to want to take her on." Fleur listened happily, glad that her niece and her dear friend were enjoying one another. Occasionally she contributed a comment, usually simply an echo of what one or the other of them said.

"Mama Fleur has rescued me, you know." James said. He wrapped his arm snugly around Fleur's shoulder. Her aunt was suitably and attractively groomed for the occasion, as she always was, in soft navy-blue suit that subtly flattered her well-kept figure. "I would have been abandoned, out in the cold after Carol and I split up if it weren't for dear Mama Fleur. It takes an exceptional mama-in-law to be so good to an ex-son-in-law."

"Oh, but you are good to me, darling James!" She turned soft eyes up to him. "He is such a help to me. Every way," she added.

"No more than you deserve, but let's not talk about that now." He gave her shoulder a little admonitory shake. "You don't want to embarrass me. I think we should go now. Fleur thought she should come, since Edward was her lawyer," he explained to Marik.

"Nice of you to come with her."

He reached into his jacket pocket, pulling out a silver card-case. "Here's my card, let's stay in touch now that we've met. I'd love to see this rescue horse of yours, maybe there's something I can do to help. Fleur has your number?"

He held Fleur's pretty floral raincoat for her, and tucked her hand firmly into the crook of his elbow as they said goodbye and made their way through the crowd away from Marik. Liz appeared beside her. "Looks like you made a conquest there, sister-dear," she laughed. "It's OK, I'm sure Carol wouldn't mind. She doesn't want him!"

"They had a bad divorce?"

"Not a good one," Liz replied, "from what I heard. I don't know the details, Carol and I were never as close as you and she were, and then of course, she got the teaching job down to Quinton when they split up. The family doesn't see much of her."

"I was disappointed when Mom said that Carol didn't live in town anymore."

"You should go down and see her! Auntie Flo goes down to visit occasionally, to see the little girls, but you know her. Time away from the garden is time wasted! They might come out to the farm over the Thanksgiving weekend next month, see their great-granny and all. It's sad, the way family ties get broken. It's like by divorcing James, Carol ended up divorcing her own family. If Zach and I ever broke up, it would be him leaving town, not me!"

"I don't think I learned anything today that will help us figure out who killed Ed," Marik told Dahlia later that afternoon as they were stripping the bitting rig off Cindy. The young horse had accepted the restriction of the reins with only a little head-tossing before settling into her good, even trot around the circle on the end of the long lunge-line. Dahl was pleased with both of her protégées. "Helene's eulogy for him was.....well, it changed my attitude about him. I'd like to see justice done for Ed. I want his murderer found out."

"I'm glad to hear that. Means you are coming to terms with your past." They turned Cindy out into the front field with Herald and some of the others. As soon as Marik slipped her halter off, she spun around and took off down field at a run, her long black mane and tail tossing in the wind of her passage. "Plenty of energy!" Dahl remarked, "But we're going to have to break her of that spin-away habit, that's dangerous!"

They walked together into the kitchen where Nonny, engulfed in an oversized apron, was cutting dough into circles for her famous baking-powder biscuits. Moving downstairs had been good for her, in more ways than one. She seemed energized, and had surprised them all by deciding that lunch was now her responsibility, and on days when both the younger women were busy, she helped out by starting dinner. She promised to teach Marik to make some of the family favourites, such as the special pot-roast that was simmering on the stove.

"That smells marvellous, Mum! We haven't had your pot-roast in ages." Dahl and Marik went upstairs to change out of their horsey clothes.

Over dinner, Marik told them about the service and the gathering in the Fellowship Hall.

"I met Carol's ex, James. He was there with Auntie Flo. Apparently she wanted to attend because Ed Karlsson was their lawyer, hers and Frank's."

"Nice of him to go with her," Dahl remarked, but Nonny had a puzzled look on her wrinkled face.

"That's odd. I'm pretty sure Fleur said the other day that it was his idea to go to the service."

Dahlia snorted, sounding almost like one of the horses. "He wouldn't have any reason to go. You know Flo, Mum, if she can get things muddled up, she will."

"Not that sort of thing, Dahlia!" Nonny replied sharply. Her dear middle daughter might be easily confused by some things, but if she said James had invited her to come with him, then that is exactly what had happened. She didn't have the imagination to make up details like that. Her siblings had never understood their sister as she and Lincoln had done. They had made a study of Fleur, just as they had of each of their others, in order to help each one develop to their truest potential. "You don't give your sister enough credit, Dahlia, for what she does do right."

How she missed her dear Lincoln, so perceptive and yet so compassionate of others.

Dahl laid her strong, calloused hand on Nonny's bony old wrist. "I'm sorry Mum." She hated to see the old woman distressed, especially when her own careless words were the cause of it. She turned to Marik. "What did you think of James?" she asked.

"He seemed...pleasant. A good conversationalist. He was interested in what I am doing with Cinderella, in the whole horse-rescue thing."

"Sure it wasn't you he was interested in?" Dahl teased. She might be right, Marik reflected, although it seemed odd that she was having that effect on men, now she was back in Chesney Creek. First Stan-the-cop, now James-the- ....what? He had been a partner in Frank's business, she knew, but that was before. She had no idea what an investment consultant did to earn a living. Neither did Dahl or Nonny. Fleur was the only one in the family that had kept up the connection with him.

"Maybe he misses Carol, sees me as a way to get back in her good graces?"

They speculated about what else might be motivating him. Like most women, they were driven to try to understand their fellow creatures. It must be difficult, Dahlia suggested, for a person who had been absorbed into a family the way the Palmers absorbed the in-laws to suddenly be cut off from those connections.

"Imagine how he must feel, suddenly back on the outside looking in, banished from his place in the family circle."

"And not by his choice," Marik added sympathetically. "I gather it was Carol's decision to break up the marriage?

"It was," Dahlia confirmed. "Poor James, pushed back out into the cold after having been part of the Palmer clan. You should get in touch with him, invite him out here. Especially if he has an interest in our horse-rescue. Maybe he'll volunteer to help with the Ability Riders."

Nonny reserved her opinion. There had always been something about James that she didn't quite like, even when he and her dear granddaughter Carol were first married. Frank and Fleur had both been so pleased to welcome him as their son-in-law. Frank had been badly disappointed by Brad's decision to pursue a musical career instead of taking over the family business. That made James, with his commitment to the business, even more warmly welcomed as part of their family.

Dahl pushed back her chair, and pulled on the old flannel shirt she wore for evening chores outdoors now that the weather was colder. "I'll do evening stables tonight," she said, "and the chickens too. You've done lots already today." The door slapped shut behind her.

Marik began clearing the table. "Pull my chair back for me, Marik dear," Nonny requested. By this end of the day, she appreciated having the strong young arm to help her heave herself upright out of the low dining room chair. She shuffled into the front room, and picked up her crochet bag before sinking into her favourite high-seated wing-chair by the fire. Her kitten, Domino, followed her, replete from her own dinner of kibble and left-overs. She leaped lightly up to settle on the back of Nonny's chair. It was her favoured perch for a nap, in the glowing warmth of the lamp.

It hadn't taken long for both Frank and Carol as well, Nonny remembered, to become disenchanted with James. Neither of them had confided the reasons why things were going sour with him. The family seemed to think they were protecting her, when they didn't tell her of their troubles. Didn't they know that she sensed their pain, that it sent burning arrows through her when they weren't happy? Far from protecting her, it made her feel worse. She was being left out in the cold, a negligible old woman who had no role in their affairs. She was left to bear the pain of their pain on her own. So she had done the same thing for her beloved son-in-law Frank and her dear granddaughter Carol that she did any time when there were upsets in her extended family. She prayed.

There might be different words for it, but the prayer was the same: Dear Lord, Let there be a fast and ease-full resolution to their problems; let them come through the chaos to a new and higher place in life, let them grow in wisdom; let them be enriched by the experience, uncomfortable as it might be as You lift them up to a higher place in life.

That is how it had been for her, all the years of her life. It was only by soldiering through the pain and chaos of the bad times that one was lifted up to the enrichment better times, better circumstances. Her prayers had always been answered, although rarely in the ways she had imagined.

Here was her dear Dahlia, no longer a sad young widow but a vigorous young senior, still doing such useful work amongst the people who cared for horses. It was a pity she hadn't remarried, it would be good to have some male energy in the house, but it wasn't to be. Not yet, at any rate.

Here too was her lost granddaughter, busily tidying up the kitchen after dinner, returned into the fold of the family. Soon she would find her true place, her role and her work. Please God, let it be soon. Let her be happy, useful, at peace. Her prayers continued, crocheted into the looping yarn of the afghan that was growing under her gnarled, skillful fingers. Thank you God that I can still be useful. That I can pray still for my children, and my children's children.... and my children's children's children, she added with a small bubbling laugh at herself. How odd to be a great-grandmother when, within, she was still as young as a new bride. The transparent, veined eyelids drooped, her hands fell still as she allowed herself to dream of those days when she had come here, to this farm, to this land, with straight, stalwart, kind Lincoln at her side, so loving.

Marik, finished in the kitchen, came in to ask if Gran wanted anything before she went upstairs. She saw the seamed lips curved in a soft, slack smile, and left the old woman to enjoy her after-dinner/before bedtime snooze. Dahl would be in shortly from checking on the horses and closing up the chickens. She tiptoed quietly away upstairs to check her email, hoping for an update from Ken Rheddenk about freeing up fifty grand to renovate their riding ring. There was nothing from him, but to her surprise Stan had sent an email. He must have dug up her e-address from the murder files. He attached a copy of his schedule, wanted to know if she would accompany him for a jaunt across the valley next week, for dinner and a concert. Curious about what sort of music he preferred, she emailed her acceptance. If she were honest with herself, she was interested in more than his taste in music. She was building a new life here. Perhaps he was part of it.

CHAPTER THIRTEEN

Civic Duties

The police station in Chesney Creek is part of the new Civic Center complex. When Marik left home twenty years ago, the two blocks of little war-time houses between Third and Fourth streets had just been torn down, leaving a wasteland behind the handsome old Carnegie Library on Big River Road, the old highway through town. The Civic Centre and Municipal Gardens revitalized Chesney Creek's downtown core, just as the town council had hoped it would. It includes the fire-hall as well as the cop shop, the district and municipal offices and the much-enlarged library where Rose worked.

The first time Marik visited the Civic Center, on the afternoon after Edward's body was found, the gardens around the complex had been rich with late summer blossoms. Today, there was a woman in coveralls raking September's fallen leaves from the walkways. She paused when she saw Marik locking the pickup.

"Marik Palmer! I heard you were back in town." Marik searched her memory, but came up empty. This wasn't the first time it had happened. She found it amazing that so many of the people she had gone to school with were still living in Chesney Creek, apparently perfectly happy to grow old in the same place where they'd been born. "Nice to see you! How are you?"

"Nice to see you too!" Marik replied. What was her name? "Sorry, I can't stop to chat right now, I have an appointment." She could feel the gardener's eyes following her curiously she pushed open the heavy glass door marked "POLICE Services."

She gave her name to the stout uniformed brunette behind the thick reception window. This one didn't recognize her. There were some new-comers in Chesney Creek, thank goodness, as well as the stick-in-the-mud people from the old days. "I've an appointment to see Detective Halston." The brunette directed her to take a seat and wait. The hard plastic chair was a perfect match for the discomfort that she already felt. She hated this! She wouldn't have come if Dahlia hadn't given her that extra push that morning while they were cleaning stalls. They each had five to do. Heavy rains meant that most of the horses spent the night in the barn.

"It's your civic duty," Dahl said as she moved into Herald's stall, slipping her manure fork neatly under a pile, and tossing it into the barrow by the door. "They need to find that pile of you-know-what who killed Ed. Anything we can do to help, we have to do."

"I hate the idea of talking to the police again when I don't have to!"

"Keep your ears open, Detective Halston might let something slip while you are talking to her, something that will help us figure out who did it, since her bunch don't seem to be accomplishing much." Dahl moved the barrow aside, and picked up the rake. "We'll work Cindy later this afternoon. Susan said she had a nice temperament, but I didn't expect her to be this easy. Let's put the reins on the bitting-rig when we lunge her today, since she was so good yesterday."

"I'm meeting my cousin Helene for lunch today after the interview," Marik reminded her.

"No problem. The Ability Rider kids will be here until 3:30 or so. Take your time, you'll have lots to talk about."

"Ms. Palmer." June Halston stood in the open door, waiting for her. She wasn't in uniform today. She looked like a prosperous business woman in her well-cut jade jacket and the dark slacks that flattered her slim curves. Her heavy blond hair hung gracefully in a long bell, framing her subtly made-up face. Marik felt dowdy in comparison, in her jeans and casual sweater. The detective was probably past 40, Marik thought, but from the way she moved, she was in good shape, probably considerably more fit and strong than most women her age. She followed the detective down the bare hallway. There were no doorknobs on the doors, just keypads. The other woman stopped, slipped a card into the slot and tapped the numbers, shielding the door from Marik's view as she did so. The stark room they entered was windowless, its only furniture a table and several utility chairs.

"You wanted to see me, something to do with the Karlsson case?" She sat down on the far side of the plastic-coated table. "I'm recording this, for the record. Sit down. Please."

There was no small talk, no 'Hello how are you' or 'Thanks for coming in'.

"So, what have you got? This a confession? You gonna tell me you did it? Or are you just here to check out the competition?"

"No! I wanted to..." Competition? What did she mean by that? Marik shook off her confusion and took a deep breath. "I thought you ought to know...that is, you might not know that Ed was..." This was harder than she'd expected. "He was an abuser. Sexually abusive." The detective's hostile attitude wasn't helping. She clenched her hands in her lap, hands that were developing new calluses from the new work she was doing. It was good, satisfying work, as well as good exercise.

"We know that," Detective Halston sneered. "He was a stud, or he thought he was. If that's all you've got, you're wasting my time." She started to stand up.

"I don't mean that. This isn't about that. When we were kids – well, he was a teenager – he abused me. Sexually."

Detective Halston gave her a sceptical look, as if she were taking this with more than a single grain of salt. "So, what are you saying? You came back to town to murder him, because of what went on between you as kids?" She rested her weight on one fist, looming over the table. "You know that giving a false confession is considered obstruction? We already checked out your story. The neighbour across the road said your truck was in the driveway at your parents' place all morning, he saw you leave the house at 10:15, he happened to notice the time. The medical examiner says the guy was dead by then, didn't you read that in the paper? We're not stupid, you know!"

"No! I didn't – no, of course not!" Marik could feel her temper flaring up. The detective was baiting her, playing bad cop, and it was working all too well. "I talked about it to Stan, and he said I ought to tell you, maybe it would give you another thread, another perspective to pursue, since you're getting nowhere with the case!" No way would she be bullied. Her old street-kid persona was kicking in, sharpening her voice to match the detective's. "I'm trying to be helpful! If this is how you treat people who try to help, it's no wonder you can't solve anything."

"Sit down!"

Marik sank slowly back onto the hard chair. She planted her feet firmly, well apart, and sat up straight. She was back in control of herself.

"Alright. All I wanted to do was come in here, tell you what I knew about Ed Karlsson. I thought that it might help, give you another direction to investigate. According to the Recorder, you haven't gotten anywhere with the case so far. It said you don't have any suspects."

"Damn Bob Pasqualli anyway! He'll say anything to sell another paper."

"Are you telling me he's got it wrong, that you're closing in on the guy?"

"What guy? You watch too much television," June curled her lip. "Everybody thinks that police work is simple, that we should be able to solve every f-ing crime in an hour, with time out for commercial breaks. Well, it doesn't work that way. We may never know who killed Karlsson. Never! It could have been completely random, he might have stumbled on something he wasn't meant to see, in the wrong place at the wrong time. Meanwhile, you come in here wasting my time with some common-as-dirt accusation about something that went down years ago. Who cares! The sorry s.o.b.'s dead, d-e-a-d, dead," she said furiously. "Isn't that enough revenge for you?"

Marik recoiled at the other woman's angry vehemence. Where was that coming from? Had the detective been another of Ed's bed partners herself? And if so, what did that imply?

"At this point, everybody and nobody's a suspect, including you. So don't push me, I don't have time for it. Karlsson's isn't the only crime I've got to deal with." June made a disgusted sound in the back of her throat. "It's not like I've got a team of assistants in this two-bit town. I sure don't need you coming in here with some lame story about what happened when you were a kid. Get over it! You're wasting my time." She keyed the door open, and stood back to let Marik proceed her out into the hallway.

"And while you are getting over that," the detective added, "I'll tell you another thing you might want to get over." She glanced down the hallway. It was empty. "You might as well get over Stan Albescu. Maybe you don't know that Stan and I are together. We're in a 'relationship'." June sketched the quotation marks in the air.

It was a silly term, she thought, but what else could you call it? It was certainly more than a friendship; different from a friendship, too. Even though they were going through a rough period just now, she felt sure that they could work it out. Stan was a good man, a solid dependable man as well as being a good cop. "He's not available, so you can get over being 'interested' in him." She keyed open the door into the lobby.

"Don't bother coming back unless you have something worthwhile to tell me!" She turned on her heel, letting the heavy door slam shut between them. Back at her work-station in the common room, she re-opened the Karlsson file and completed a brief interview report. Like every other interview she and her half-time partner Tomas had conducted, this one had led nowhere. God it was frustrating! She scanned back through the pages. The man was ordinary: competent civil lawyer, divorced dad, skirt-chaser, community volunteer. A dime a dozen. There's was no reason for him to get himself killed that way.

He took up running for the Chamber's big whoop-up fund raiser, that's what had put him in the park. But who had he met there? There had been other people in the park that morning, some of them had come forward in response to Pasqualli's editorial. A dog-walker had 'heard raised voices,' but couldn't be sure of the time; someone else claimed they might have seen 'someone hiding off the trail, in the trees' but couldn't say if it was a man, woman or child. More likely it was a hallucination. Not one of them had anything useful to offer. She'd hoped the interview today would give her a break, but it was nothing. Stupid whining civilian. Curse it! She smacked her fist down on the desk, hard enough to joggle the keyboard-shelf.

"Hey, settle down over there!" a voice called from another workstation at the other end of the room. She couldn't tell who it was. The work-stations, with half-walls topped by pebbled glass uppers, made it impossible to see, yet equally impossible to miss hearing, what was going in the room. Stupid etched glass! She wondered what genius in city hall had come up with that rocket-scientist-idea. It must have cost a mint. What a waste of good money, money that would have been better spent on sturdier desks, or even – God forbid - more comfortable chairs, ones that would fit an average-sized woman's butt instead of being built for a fat-ass 200 pound man. She sat back, arching her lower back to relieve the nagging pain. She unbuttoned the waist band of her slacks, and pushed the zipper down an inch. It helped, but not much. The man-sized chair didn't help at all.

Maybe that's why they'd gone for the etched glass, to add an artsy-fartsy gender-neutral touch to the place. Each glass plate depicted a different scene, waterfalls and trees, lakes and flying birds. The ones around her work-station were mountains, like the mountains that formed this valley. As if she needed more mountains to look at! There were times when she longed with her whole being for a wide open view, a prairie view, where a person could see for miles rather than being hemmed in and walled in by goddam mountains! She'd been thinking of applying somewhere else, some bigger center than this piss-ant Chesney Creek, but she'd be damned if she'd apply while this Karlsson case was still wide-open. Sure, every force on the planet had unsolvable crimes, cases that were still open fifteen or fifty years later because no one had been able to figure them out. But dammit if she was going to apply with something like that on her resume. She could just imagine it: "Couldn't figure out a simple small town murder? Somewhere where everyone knows everyone else's business? Sorry, we've decided to hire someone else."

Dammit, they'd have to get a break sometime, the sooner the better. Someone knew something that they weren't telling her, but who? She drummed her fingernails on the desktop, lightly so no one else in the big room could hear, and scanned the list of names again. She was waiting for one to pop out at her, the next person she should talk to, but none of them did. Certainly not this stupid Palmer woman. God, the things some women would do for attention! Pitiful. She dug into her big black purse, tucked under the desk at her feet, and finally pulled it onto her lap to search a little deeper. Wouldn't it be nice if these desks had drawers, instead of the cheap-o open shelves? A girl could keep a few personal items on hand instead of having to cart around with a giant purse.

She pulled out the pink, zippered packet of tampons that she'd been seeking. Sometimes, she muttered to herself, it was just too much fun being female. That was probably why she'd been so cranky with that damned Marik Palmer.

She shouldn't have said that about Stan, not very professional. It needed saying, nonetheless. She and Stan had some issues, but they'd sort it out. She outranked him, but she couldn't help that. She was more ambitious than he was, that was the problem. He could advance if he wanted to, he was certainly smart enough, but he seemed perfectly happy to stay where he was, stuck in the mud. That was another reason for getting out of Chesney Creek. He needed the stimulation of a bigger challenge, same as she did. It was hard enough to make love work, as her mother often said, when the man in the case was a cop. Harder still, then, when both of them, man and woman alike, worked law enforcement. Maybe that was the reason her mother had protested so much when June announced her intention to go to the Police Academy, to follow in her Dad's footsteps. The profession was not conducive of domestic bliss, maybe, but then, unlike her Mom, domesticity was not her bent. She was a professional. She closed the Karlsson file, pushed back the heavy chair and headed to the washroom

.

Meanwhile, Marik was walking slowly back to her truck. Had there been anything in the interview that was worth passing on to Dahlia, for their own consideration of who had murdered Ed? Probably not. She certainly wouldn't be telling her aunt about what the detective had said about Stan.

She parked across the street from Rocky's Diner on Second, where she and her cousin had agreed to meet for lunch. Helene, seated in a window booth, waved a menu to get her attention. The restaurant was decorated to look like a step back into the 1950s, with shiny red aluminium-edged tables set in padded tuck-and-roll vinyl booths.

"If it were a car," Helene laughed, "It would be a bright red convertible, say a 1959 Pontiac Impala – or do I mean Chevrolet? I'll have to ask my husband, he's the car-guy in the family. I'm having a glass of wine with lunch. You too?"

Marik slid across the plump red vinyl, its fat edges trimmed with white piping. The place mats were white paper, scalloped around the sides. There was a little quarter-a-tune juke box on the table-top, flanked by pressed glass salt-&-peppers and a shiny spring-loaded napkin dispenser.

Their waitress, a pony-tailed blonde in a flared skirt and a name-tag that read "Sarra", brought Marik a chilled glass of Chablis, and took their orders. They each ordered the butternut soup, and decided to split a Reuben sandwich. "Can you tell we're related?" Helene laughed. "Stu thinks sauerkraut is Disgusting with a capital D."

Marik felt the tension drain out of her shoulders as their old friendly camaraderie washed away the stress of her interview with Detective Halston. They sipped their wine, and bridged the years between with quick summaries of their lives. Helene was married to Stu, they had a girl and boy. "I wish we had stayed closer, when we got to be teens," she said. "I never really understood why you ran away – do you mind my asking?"

"There are so many reasons – I don't really know myself, anymore. I was a dumb teenager, I guess that about sums it up." She and Helene, with only a year between them, had drifted apart starting when Helene went into high school. "Seems like that should have been you running away, doesn't it, with your parents divorcing when you were, what, 13 or 14?"

"I was so much into golfing by then, it didn't really matter." Helene had gone on to compete nationally as a junior, travelling with her mother around a country-club circuit that took her far away from Chesney Creek. They both agreed, looking back, that they had occupied different worlds by the time they were teens. "I'm sorry I wasn't around for you, back then. Maybe all you needed was a friend."

Sarra arrived at their table then, delivering their soup. It was served in old-fashioned pressed-glass bowls, an island of yoghurt floating in the creamy gold broth, and a sprinkling of nutmeg dusted across the top. It smelled heavenly and tasted even better.

"Your folks were rich, that was the difference. I remember my mother being envious of yours, wishing she'd married a rich professional man instead of Dad – except for the fact that Dad was..." she groped for the right word.

"More dependable," Helene supplied, with a rueful look. "My father figured as long as he was a good provider, then that was all that was necessary. Poor Dad. I think he came to regret his ways. Actually, I know it." She grabbed a paper napkin out of the 50-s chrome dispenser, and dabbed at her eyes. "Like poor Ed. The Karlsson men are geniuses when it comes to making messes of their personal lives."

Their Reuben arrived, divided onto two plates with a single-serving bag of potato chips on each plate. "Clever!" Marik remarked. "A little generosity like that goes a long way to ensure repeat customers." Helene gave her a puzzled look. "Sorry – once a waitress, always a waitress. I meant that some places would have made us share a single bag of chips, since we only ordered one sandwich. This way, they spend maybe 25 or 50 cents extra, and buy a whole lot of goodwill." They tore open the packets and ate in companionable silence for a few moments.

"I find it interesting," Helene remarked, "that you look at the business aspect of restaurant service. Most people come into a restaurant, all they are thinking about is the food, the service. You didn't own a business, did you?"

"Me? No!"

"I don't know if anyone's told you that I own a business?"

Marik shook her head, her mouth full of sandwich.

"I'm in network marketing, if you know what that is. Some people don't." She rattled off some examples: Tupperware; Mary Kay; Epicure Selections. "Home-Based businesses, that's what some people call them. Mine's USANA. It's a good way to earn extra money, if you are interested?"

"Not at the moment." She was tempted to explain why she didn't need any extra income. She had enough trouble figuring out what to do with what she already had, never mind having any interest in earning more. "How did you end up getting into that business?"

The Karlssons, as Rose used to say, always did have an eye for money. Jack-the-Jerk had done very well as a mutual-funds salesman and financial advisor. He had been Chesney Creek's one and only notary public as well, back when they were growing up. It seemed that Helene as well as Ed inherited the Karlsson flair and acumen around money, along with their Nordic cheekbones.

Helene told her about trying USANA's good nutritional supplements, liking them, and checking out the business. "Basically, that's the business plan: try the supplements, like them, share the enthusiasm with others. They try them, they like them, they share the enthusiasm, those people try them, like them, et cetera, until you have dozens or even hundreds of people using the products, and you get paid a little commission on everything that everybody buys. That can add up to a really good income. That's how it was explained to me. I'd been looking at a couple other network marketing companies, and USANA seemed like the best one to me, so I got Ed to look at it, give me his legal opinion. He had no interest in this sort of business, but I trusted his legal smarts. I'm going to miss him, so much! " Her eyes puddled with tears once again. " So much."

Marik's heart ached for her. She hadn't realized the impact Ed's death would have on so many people. She and Dahl were treating it as a puzzle, a whodunit, but his murder was more than that. As her cousin had said in the eulogy, there would be no peace for those who had loved her brother until the mystery about his death was solved.

"I don't think the police are getting any closer to figuring it out, either," Helene added. "Not that they'll tell us much! They just drag us in for interviews and more interviews, like they did poor young Connor. Just because he's a teenager, wham! He's a criminal suspect." With their meals finished, they both ordered tea when Sarra came to take away their plates, but refused the dessert menus she offered.

"We must be related!" Marik laughed.

Sarra thumped the heavy brown teapot down between them. Helene picked it up and poured the fragrant brew into the thick white mugs. "I'm just afraid that they'll never figure it out, never get to the point where we can close the book on it and say, 'That's it. It's done. Rest In Peace dear Ed'. Meanwhile there's no rest-in-peace for anyone. My poor Mom is a wreck. Thank goodness your Mom is being there for her. Auntie Rose is a rock."

"A rock? My Mom?"

"She always has been! Mom always says that without her big sister, she wouldn't have survived her divorce, or her marriage either, for that matter. Dad has a lot to answer for. Auntie Rose has been coming over to Mom's just about every day. Didn't you know?"

"No. In some ways, I don't know my mother very well. I keep discovering that there are big gaps in what I know about everybody in the family. I missed so much! Everything that has happened in the past twenty years is just part of it. I don't know the senior generation – your folks, mine, all the aunts and uncles – as adults. I love my mother, but now that I'm getting to know her, I'm learning to respect her as well."

If Edward hadn't been murdered, she reflected, this conversation might never have taken place, and she might not have learned what a staunch tower of strength Rose was in the family. She was proud to be the daughter of 'Rose the Rock".

Sarra returned with their bill and they tussled briefly over it. "It's a tax-deduction for me," Helene declared. "As long as I mention my business, it's a business luncheon as far as the tax man's concerned. I make too much money, I need all the deductions I can get."

"If you put it that way," Marik surrendered. She didn't know much about up-scale brands, but it was obvious that her cousin's matching shoes and handbag were of fine Italian leather. Apparently her business paid extremely well. Helene had no need of her charity.

"Then I get to leave the tip." Marik strolled back to their booth to tuck a $10 bill under the cold teapot. She was careful here in her hometown. Her anonymity could be blown if she splashed her abundant money about too openly. That was the last thing she wanted. For all its growth in the past twenty years, Chesney Creek was still a small town, with small town gossips. The grapevine had been fast in the old days; social network systems like Facebook had brought it up to warp-speed. She needed to be careful.

Her family and friends were accepting her easily back into the fold, but that could change in a moment if they discovered her immense secret wealth. Once the word got out, it would be no time at all before the entire Delganee and Palmer families, along with their extensive network of local acquaintances, would know that she was wealthy beyond anyone's imagining. The time would come, she knew, when her financial status would become public knowledge. But not now, now yet! In the meantime, she could do good in small, quiet ways. Sarra would be more than happy with her $10 tip. If she was going to be a greater financial benefactor here in her hometown, she would do it secretly. She hadn't heard back from Ken Rheddenk yet about the anonymous donation she wanted to make for Dahl's riding ring. She would email him again this evening.

"It's been great seeing you again, Helene."

"I'll be back in town fairly often. Mom has Rose-the-Rock to depend on, but she still needs me. Thank goodness, with this business my time is my own. Time-freedom! What a blessing." She paused on the sidewalk before getting in her car. "I'll let you know when I'm coming up, we'll get together again. It's been wonderful, Mar."

Marik walked across the street to her truck. It had been wonderful to see Helene again. One by one, she was reconnecting with the family, finding her place in the pattern of home-town life. How weird it was, she reflected, that Ed's murder was helping her to do that. His death brought him to the center of everyone's attention. The topic couldn't be avoided. That was the reason she had opened up to her sister and her aunt about the childhood abuse. Their loving, wise responses had helped her to come more to terms with that part of her past. It had reduce the emotional charge. Those conversations had deepened her relationship with each of them, and they only happened because Ed, brutally killed, was on everyone's mind. Despite all the pain he'd caused her, she knew she would never have wished such an appalling fate for him. Her long-held hatred was being diluted by pity. Dahlia was determined to help discover his murderer, and she would do whatever she could to help. Perhaps when that was done, she would be able to finally forgive him, and close that chapter of her life forever.

She turned onto Main, passing the gates of the Park on her way back to the farm. Murder was wrong, but she was grateful for the sharp twist it gave to the lens through which she viewed her life and the people in it. Helene had given her a new perception of her mother, as a woman of strength in the family. Then there was Stan. She couldn't help but wonder if he would have called, as he had promised that first day, if they hadn't met again when he found Ed's body? Her mind shied away from that memory, skipping forward to Stan's 'confession'. Imagine him having a secret crush on her! Was there still an uncertain teenager just below the surface of the confident man? Is that why he hadn't called? Because her cousin's death was an issue between them, they were coming to know one another much better than they might otherwise have done. Ed's death had catapulted their relationship forward. It was another benefit that she was reaping. However, she reminded herself, it remained to be seen whether or not getting to know Stan would be a good thing! She parked beside the barn. Cinderella stood in the ring, head over the railing as if waiting for her lesson. Marik was more than ready to get into her work-clothes and join her. Horses were simple and easy. No wonder Dahlia preferred their company!

CHAPTER FOURTEEN
A Real-Life Whodunit

Dahlia taught two groups of adult riders on Saturday mornings. The early group of advanced riders trailered their own mounts up to the farm for their lessons. Marik joined the second group, the beginners, riding Herald or whichever one of the Northwind horses weren't being used by the others. Dahl liked to switch them around. "You'll learn something different from each horse," she told them. On this Saturday, two of the beginners had cancelled their lessons.

"Are you up for a trail ride?" Dahl asked Marik after lunch. "Neither Stoneyman nor Irish Empress got worked today."

Marik gave her an uncertain look. She was still learning the horses' names and how to identify them.

"Stoney's the black with the crooked blaze. The kids say it looks like he wiggled his head when the white streak was being painted. Empress is the coppery chestnut with the star. You can ride her. You'll find her a bit livelier than old Herald. You need to get used to a zippier ride. That's what you'll be getting, once we get your Cinders under saddle. She's going to be a real treat, but you need to be ready for her."

The sun broke through the cloud-cover as they headed up the old road behind the barn, both horses with heads held high and ears pitched forward, eager to be out on the trails. Marik couldn't help but admire how easily her aunt rode, her body moving as if she and the chunky black gelding were one being. Would she ever be that relaxed on horseback?

Stoneyman, Dahl told Marik as they rode, had been her Uncle Gerard's best roping horse. The two of them had competed on the rodeo circuit. "I wasn't sure how he'd take to the slow pace around here – sometimes working horses aren't happy about being retired, same like people, even if they are too old and decrepit to do the work anymore. Gerard could have turned him out on the range, or turned him into dog-food." She gave a snort of sarcastic laughter. "Turning him out on the range would have amounted to the same thing. Gerard says they've got wolves moving in up there on the plateau. Bloody wolves or grizzlies, either one would have made short work of an old crock. Luckily, Stoney turned out to be a good teaching horse. He's started more than one rider on the path to equestrian skills." She patted the dark neck affectionately. "Ready to pick up the pace?"

Marik squeezed her knees against the mare's ribs, as Dahl had taught her. To her surprise, Empress responded by accelerating instantly into a swift smooth trot.

"Whoa ~! This is different from Herald!" It required considerable leg pressure before the big old pinto would break from the walk. More often than not, the pressure had to be followed by a solid thump on the ribs before he would break into a trot. "She doesn't make me feel like a sack of spuds, either!" Even after several lessons, Marik still found it difficult to sit Herald's jarring trot.

Dahl laughed. "Not the bone-rattler you're used to, eh? The Empress is a saddlebred, she used to be a show horse. She has wonderful gaits, those long sloping shoulders and pasterns have plenty of play to absorb the shock. I knew you'd enjoy her."

They wound their way up the hills, through the steep pine-forests and out into the high meadows where they could see for miles. They pulled up to give the horses a breather after the last hard climb.

"I've been thinking more about Ed's murder." Dahl remarked as they admired the panorama of hills and valleys that stretched for miles before them, dappled now with cloud shadows. "It seems like the investigation is stuck, so far as the police are concerned. From what Detective Halston told you, it sounds like they don't even have a suspect!"

"She seems to just want to sweep it under the rug and forget about it!" Marik fumed. "Another unsolved mystery, oh well."

"That's just wrong! After all, Ed isn't the only one affected."

Although she didn't mention it to Marik, Dahl was quoting from her guided writing. After her meditation-time last night, her guides had written about Ed's death: "Murder is wrong not so much because of what it does to the victim," they wrote. "Only those who believe themselves to be mortal are THAT upset by dying; after the fact, they are fine. What is wrong with murder is the deleterious effect it has on the ones who are still alive in your world, both the person who committed murder, who must go on in physical life with that self-knowledge; and all those who have a connection with either one of them, either the victim or the perpetrator, all the people whose lives are affected by the event, their families and communities. Murder is a potent event, its energy ripples out like the circles when a stone flung in the water. Murder touches more than just the murderer and murderee."

"Ed's the one who is dead," Dahl continued, "but his murder touches everyone who knew him." She felt slightly dishonest, pretending that this insight was her own when in fact it was borrowed from her guides. She had never, ever, told anyone about her lifetime habit of channelling. She was tempted to show the writing to Marik, and teach her how to do it, in the same way that she was teaching her to ride and work with horses. The timing didn't feel right, however. Her Guides would tell her when it was. Too bad they couldn't, or wouldn't, just tell her who had murdered Edward. Then she could be done with it.

They said it was not their role to do that. 'We know who did it, of course; but from our perspective, revealing that is not particularly important – we do not see "justice" as you humans do! What is important are all the hurts, misunderstandings and misperceptions which are being brought forward into your collective awareness by the energy of the event. These errors-of-thought both precede and proceed the moments of murder. If all those affected by this murder could use it as a spur to forgive themselves and others for such errors, it would be transformed in their experience from a negative experience to a positive one. Out of Chaos accepted comes growth.

'It is important for your growth, Dear One, that you embrace your role in this drama. How will you act, in response to this event that has touched your life? Will you use your considerable intelligence and powers of observation to discover the murderer, that the innocent may be absolved of suspicion?

"If the police can't figure out who did it," Dahl said, picking up the reins, "then it's up to us."

"How are we going to do that? Look at Means, Motive and Opportunity, like detectives always do in books?"

"Fiction? No, I think the place to start is with the people, the ones whose lives were most affected by Ed's murder."

"But that's everyone! My life was touched by Ed's murder – if he hadn't gotten killed, I wouldn't have gone to his memorial service. I wouldn't have bought the jacket I got to wear for it. I wouldn't have met Helene and gone out for lunch and left a tip. You could even say that Sarra, our waitress at Rocky's, was affected by Ed being murdered because as a result, she got a tip."

"That's a pretty tangential connection!"

Marik considered that objection for a few moments. "Then would you say that the people who were most powerfully impacted – the ones closest to Ed – would be the more likely suspects?" She searched her mind for a metaphor to clarify her thoughts. "It's like the murder is a pebble dropped in a pond. The strongest ripples are the ones closest to the center."

"Exactly. Your waitress – Sarra? - is a pretty distant ripple. But I'd have to see it on paper. How about if we sit down after dinner, draw up the concentric circles of people affected. We can see whose names are closest in to the center, and start with them."

She glanced up at the sky. "We'd better get headed home, I don't like the look of those clouds." She turned Stoney down the sloping hillside, following a narrow path. "I'd like to bring my trail-riders up here, give them a look at that view," she said over her shoulder. "I need to check out this route back down. Too bad we can't go by way of the hill meadows, but they are in hay all summer." The hill meadows, she explained, were on Palmer land but leased to the Kings who owned the neighbouring ranch.

"I'm pretty sure this route we're taking is easier than going back the way we came. Coming up, that steep hill-climb up to the high meadow isn't bad. That's the way I usually go back, but it's too steep for amateurs. I don't dare take folks who aren't regular riders back that way. They would have hissy fits if I tried to get them to ride down it."

"I'm trying not to have a hissy fit about this!" Marik exclaimed. "It might not be as bad as the way we came up, but it is still a pretty sharp drop."

"I want to do more trail-ride outings next summer. The horses I have now are up to it and trail rides pay more per hour than teaching. Maybe by next year, you and Cinderella will be able to lead a few rides."

"I don't know about that." Marik didn't like the look of the hill they were about to descend, even if it wasn't as steep as the one they rode on the way up to the high meadow.

Dahl brought Stoney to a stop and leaned down to check his saddle-girth. "You better do the same. No, don't dismount, just slide your fingers under it to make sure it's still snug. I don't want you slithering off over Empress's head. She wouldn't like it any more than you would."

Marik followed the instructions, bending her knee up and back, using her foot to lift the heavy saddle fender away from the soft, wide cotton-rope girth that secured the saddle. Empress, well-accustomed to fidgety riders, stood calmly. "I think it's good."

She tried to hold her nervousness in check as Empress picked her way down the narrow trail. Dahl and the horses seemed completely relaxed about it, but Marik didn't like the feeling of riding downhill. She had to trust Empress to pick their route, since she couldn't see what the trail looked like with the mare's head in the way. If this was less steep than the way they'd come up, she was glad that Dahl had chosen a different route. She would have bailed off and walked, if the route were any more perpendicular.

"Cattle and deer makes these trails," Dahl explained. She twisted around in the saddle to chat, resting one hand on Stoney's broad rump as the horse negotiated the narrow way.

"It doesn't seem wide enough for anything bigger than a jackrabbit!"

"I used to know these little high-country trails like the back of my hand," Dahlia told her. "I rode all over the hills when I was a youngster, my first horse was a real good little trail horse. I think this route will take us down into the canyon north of the Kings' place. We can cut around from there onto Mountain Retreat road and then it's just a mile or so back to the barn. A good circle for longer trail rides next summer, I want to do more of those. Maybe even add an over-night camp-out, take tents ..." Her voice trailed off. "Well, pipe-dreams! We'll see what happens. I need to do something to create a bit more revenue."

By the time they reached Mountain Retreat Road, the last lap of the ride, a light rain showered down on them. "A good ride, despite getting wet at the end of it," Dahl said.

"Except for the scary part coming down off the high meadows," Marik complained.

"We'll have to take some tools up next time, widen that cattle path if we're going to use it for trail rides. Won't be until next spring." They rubbed down the horses and turned them out into the front paddock, where they both collapsed onto the turf for a roll before shaking themselves off and dropping their heads to graze, indifferent to the misty late afternoon rain. They went indoors, Dahl to have a rest, and Marik make dinner. Nonny came out of her bedroom where she'd been napping to greet them.

"What have you been doing this afternoon, Gran? Did you have visitors?" A pair of tea cups and saucers were drying on the embroidered tea towel beside the sink.

"Old Mrs. King called in, although I shouldn't call her that, she's younger than I am. The senior Mrs. King, I mean. We've been neighbours all our lives." Marik hadn't met the Kings, but she knew the two properties shared a boundary fence. They'd ridden along it today on their way back down from the higher hills.

Nonny turned to Dahl. "It's bad news. They found out today that it's metastasized. I'm talking about the younger Mrs. King," she explained for her granddaughter's benefit. "Annalise beat the cancer ten years ago, but it looks like this time the cancer is winning."

"I'm so sorry to hear that, Mom," Dahl said, her voice low with pity. "No wonder they call breast cancer the plague of the middle-aged middle-class. Poor Annalise."

Marik stepped into the pantry for a pair of acorn squash, and cut them in half while the other two talked. She would scoop out the insides and stuff them with a savoury mixture of sausage meat, apple and fresh herbs.

"Lavinia King came down after they'd talked to the oncologist, she wanted to give the two of them some time to absorb the news. Poor woman, she's wearing herself out trying to look after both of them, and both houses." Nonny compressed her wrinkled lips. "It will only get worse, now. Gordon is taking it hard, of course. He's too young to be a widower, poor soul." Her gaze flickered over Dahl's face, as if looking for some expected response.

"Don't give me that look, Mother." Old Mr. King, Gordon's father, had been Dahl's mentor in horsemanship when she was a teenager. She spent most of her free time up at the King's, working with her young horses. Gordon, a year or two her senior, had a young horse of his own. They helped one another with the training. Both of them knew that their families entertained hopes for their future together. Despite that, even despite her feelings for Gordon, Dahl had other plans. She wanted to live her own life, experience life outside of the Valley. She would sell the two well-trained riding horses, and go to University out east. That's what she did, and that was where, after university, she met Bill. Wonderful Bill! He was the man for her, the man she adored, the man she married. She loved him with all her heart and all her soul and all her body, too. The fact that he had died so young made no difference to her love. Her mother might think that Gordon King, widower, was part of her future, but Dahl knew otherwise. "I'm going up for a lie-down," she said now.

"The stuffed squash will be done in about an hour," Marik reminded her.

"That's fine." Upstairs, Dahl stretched out on the smooth counterpane, too tired even to meditate. This excessive weariness at the end of the day was something she battled far too often. Even with Marik to help with the house, and the worst of her worries about her mother allayed by her move downstairs, there were times when Dahl felt overwhelmed by her responsibilities. If only she could earn more money! She could hire more help, make some of the needed improvements to Northwind, build the covered riding ring...but it was all a hopeless dream. The only way to earn more was to work even harder than she already did.

I'm getting too darned old, she told herself, to carry on working as hard as I do. But what choice is there? She and Marik had talked about hosting overnight trail rides. That could be profitable. It would tap into a new market, people would come from further away for a horseback holiday than they would for simple day-rides. But oh! The sheer hard labour it would entail, not just the rides themselves but the marketing, the planning! If Marik became her partner, sharing the workload, they could probably do it. The problem was that Marik was young, there was no guarantee that she would want to stay and work with horses on a permanent basis. She considered asking her niece outright if she planned to remain on the farm permanently, but it was too soon. Marik was enamoured of her new lifestyle, but that was no guarantee that she would stay once the novelty wore off.

Perhaps, Dahl thought, her guides could give her some advice. She reached for her laptop, on the bedside table, but caught a glimpse of her clock. The hour had sped by. Somewhere along the way, she must have dozed off. She swung her feet off the bed, sat up and stretched her back. Tomorrow would be another day, she told herself. She went downstairs where the savoury scent of dinner filled the kitchen. By the time dinner was done, and she was back in the house after stabling Skudder, she was more than ready for her bed.

"I'm just too fried to start drawing circles and considering suspects," she told Marik. "We'll do it tomorrow."

"No problem, I don't think my brain's at 100% tonight either. Too much fresh air, maybe."

Upstairs again, with the night dark outside the upper windows, Dahl stripped down and stepped into the shower to wash away the accumulated dust and sweat of a long, active day.

She reached out for the towel to wrap around her wet hair. The mirror above the sink was steamed up, again. She had forgotten, again, to turn on the exhaust fan. A 'Freudian slip' perhaps, she told herself with sardonic amusement. The steam had misted the long mirror on the back of the bathroom door as well, and that suited her just fine. Soft focus was just what she needed. She didn't like the sight of her naked body, the way her abdomen jutted out between her hip bones, the small sagging breasts, the ropey muscles of her arms and legs. She was fit, her muscles were strong and useful, but the picture as a whole was undeniably unattractive. She had turned into a baggy mismatched conglomeration of parts. Thank goodness for steamed-up mirrors. Nostalgically, she remember the sleek, softly-rounded body of her youth, that body that Bill had caressed with such delight. She remembered the joy and pleasure of moving naked in his encircling arms. Such pride she'd felt, such pride in being young and beautiful, and belonging with Bill. He had teased her, called her "3B", Bill's Beautiful Beloved. So long ago, so very long.

Perhaps it was just as well he hadn't lived to see the wreckage the years had wrought. No one would call this bone-rack of a body beautiful. Which being the case, she told herself with a twisted grin, what was she doing contemplating the remains in the steamy mirror? All that accomplished was to grieve and annoy her. She wrapped herself in her faded flannel dressing gown, and made her way to bed.

CHAPTER FIFTEEN

Opportunity Knocking

James phoned the farm a few days later, and asked to speak with Marik. "How about if I come out later this afternoon? I want to see this rescue horse of yours, and you too, of course."

He arrived while Marik was working Cinderella in the riding ring. It was on the high side of the barn, a long oval, fenced all around with white palings. The mare was settling down nicely, despite not having been worked for three days, due to the rain. No wonder Dahl wanted a roof over the ring! Wet weather meant no riding lessons, and no horse-time for the Ability Riders, either. Marik sent an email to Ken Rheddenk, the accountant, to ask if the fifty thousand dollars she wanted could be a worked as a donation to the Ability Riders. With a covered riding ring, the program could run right through the winter. He promised to do some research.

"I'm sure we can manage it, it just might take a little time to get all our T-s crossed and our I-s dotted, make it legal and tax-deductible. I'll let you know."

"It has to be anonymous!" she reminded him. "I don't want anyone to know it came from me!"

Today the rain clouds had finally blown away. The ring was dry enough to use, although still wet in places. The weatherman promised another week or more of the slanting autumn sunshine. Marik had Cinderella on the long lunge-line, making her walk, then trot and canter in a circle around her. It steadied the mare in her gaits as well as giving her some good exercise. Marik gave the line a quick tug, signalling Cinderella to stop. She gathered up the rope, hanging the long loops from one hand as the bay mare came quickly and easily to her at the center of the ring. It was quite a change from their early days together, when she had fought the varied commands of halter and line with all her might. Dahlia taught Marik to encourage the animal's sporadic good behaviour, however, and it hadn't taken Cinderella long to grasp what was expected of her. Now she knew that after her exercise there was a treat in store. She nuzzled at Marik's jacket. Both of them were wet and muddy to the knees.

"Patience now, my girl," Marik laughed, pushing the eager muzzle aside as she dug into her pocket for the alfalfa 'cookie'. The mare lipped it from her flattened palm, and then followed her placidly over to the gate, where Marik exchanged the long line for a soft cotton lead rope. She snorted and pulled back as James strolled over from his car.

He wore a long-sleeved plaid shirt, drawn tight across muscular shoulders and arms. It was tucked firmly into his jeans, held in place on his hips by a tooled leather belt with a silver buckle. Marik was suddenly conscious of the shabby old barn-jacket she wore, and of her hair, pulled back on her nape in a frizzy ponytail. Knowing he was coming out, she had taken time to do a quick job with mascara and eyeshadow before lunch, but there was no getting around the fact that her boots were caked with mud and that her jeans bore the stains of the morning's stall-cleaning chores.

"Told you I'd get here!" he greeted her. "Sorry I'm a little late, I guess you are finished already?"

Marik explained that they did lunge-line work first, before beginning the training session. "It takes the edge off her energy. It reminds her that she's a nice tame domesticated creature who obeys directions, right Cindy?" She scratched around the mare's ears and smoothed her forelock. "It makes her more amenable to the rest of the weird things we expect her to do."

Dahl came around the corner of the barn, a high-backed western saddle hung over her arm. "Oh good, you made it! Marik said you were coming out to watch. You're dressed for the part," she added with a slanted grin. She swung the heavy saddle over the railing, and handed Marik a thick woollen saddle-blanket.

"Let her smell it again," she instructed, "before you try putting it on her back." She turned back to James. "Marik's ridden her a few times now. She's not real happy with the idea, but she's getting there. It's a challenge with a green 4-year-old like this. Much easier to train them if you start when they're foals." Dahl slipped naturally into teacher-mode, as she did with any new person around the barn. Marik chuckled. James was cast into the role of horsemanship student, whether he liked it or not.

"We can look at conformation," Dahl explained while Marik began the slow saddling procedure. "We can check for physical flaws, poor bone structure or weak hooves, but temperament? That's chancy. You have to be around a horse for quite a while, expose them to a lot of different situations, before you really know the sort of personality they are. Kind of like human beings, you might say."

She went on to tell James about the steps they'd taken so far in training Cinder to be a riding horse. James obviously wasn't a horseman, but his paternal grandparents, he told them, had farmed, so he had been on horseback once or twice as a child.

While James and Dahl talked, Marik let Cinderella sniff the saddle. She smoothed the blanket into the hollow of the mare's back, and then slowly lowered the saddle over it. The mare flinched as the weight came to rest on her back and swung her head around to see what was going on. Marik gave her another of the alfalfa cookies. At last, the saddle was on, the soft cinch snugged lightly around the mare's belly and the stirrups dropped down on her sides.

"Walk her around, we'll see how she does with some distractions."

Marik led the saddled horse around the ring while Dahl smacked the rails and clapped her hands.

"Give me some help here," she said to James. He thumped the rails tentatively at first, then followed Dahl's lead and added his whistles and shouts to hers. Cinderella looked over at them with curiosity, but followed steadily as Marik led her towards them. James hooked a booted foot up on the lower rail, and clapped his hands.

"That's good, we can stop now."

"That was fun." He hadn't expected to enjoy this part of his visit.

"Bring her out of the ring. We'll get James to drive his car past her. Would you mind...?"

"Sure, just tell me what to do."

"We've led her around the parked vehicles," she explained. "She's alright with them, but she might decide to throw a fit about a moving one. We need help with that. I can't drive the car and train the pair of them at the same time. Marik isn't experienced enough to deal with an upset pony all on her own. I'd appreciate it if you'd help."

James folded himself into the car, pausing to thump his boots together to knock off the dirt before bringing his feet in.

"Turn around up behind the house, by the chicken run, and drive back down here past us. Take it slow the first couple passes. We'll see how she reacts."

Marik took a strong grip on the lead-rope as James' car rolled by a few feet away. The mare tipped her ears forward and snorted.

"Good, she's not alarmed. Just interested and curious," Dahl observed. James had stopped a few feet past them. "Pick up the speed a bit coming back," Dahl called to him.

He turned the car around in the Y where the driveway split, the short side ending in front of the wide front veranda while the other branch continued up past the barn. After the fourth pass, James stopped the car. He had rolled up the sleeves of his plaid shirt, resting his stocky forearm out the window. "Now what?"

"Come closer," Dahl gestured, but when he started to open the car door, she said, "No, I mean drive slowly straight towards us, see what happens."

Satisfied at last, Dahl allowed James to park the car in front of the house and told Marik to mount up. She stood at the mare's head, ready to intervene, as Marik gripped the reins against the saddle horn and got her left foot into to stirrup. The mare sidled nervously.

"James, come and help. Go around on her off-side. It's ok, she won't bite," she laughed, "you can get right up close to her."

"We usually just put her against the rail when I'm mounting," Marik explained over the mare's back. Poor James, he obviously wasn't used to horses, nor to bossy horse-women.

"She needs to get used to standing in the open while you get up. Try again now." This time, the mare stood quiet as Marik swung her leg up and over her back.

"I feel like an Ability Rider," Marik said as she cautiously lowered her weight onto the saddle. The Ability Riders were always 'spotted' by assistants, one on either side to make sure the rider stayed centered on the saddle, while the third held the horse's head.

"To Cinders, you feel more like a cougar. Be ready to steady her," Dahl warned as Cinderella flicked her ears back."

Marik froze. "A cougar! I hadn't thought of that!" James laid his hand on her thigh.

"Relax!" Dahl said. "If you get tense, she'll get tense. You know that. Ok, I'll get the gate, you can take her on into the ring.

"Phew!" James stepped back. Marik wondered if he was relieved because she was safe or because getting away from the horse meant that he was.

"How did you get into doing rescue?" he asked Dahl as they watched horse and rider trotting their long figures-of-eight up and down the ring. "Isn't it awfully expensive?"

Dahl told him about Skudder, her first rescue, and about how the animals paid their own way now, as well as hers, as mounts for her students and the Ability Riders program.

"Mother's doing her baking today. Want to come in for a cup of tea with us?" Dahlia asked when she was finally satisfied that Marik and Cinderella had done enough for the day. "I'm not sure what she's making today." Baking was one of her mother's favourite amusements. She liked to try new recipes as well as the tried-and-true ones that had delighted her family for decades.

"Lead on! My Mama Fleur uses some of her recipes. They are terrific!" He followed Dahlia up the back steps and into the mudroom. She admired the beautiful tooled leather boots that James pulled off.

Hands washed, they stepped into the kitchen where Nonny, engulfed in her purple apron, was taking a tray of oat scones out of the oven.

"Grannie!" He saluted her cheek with a kiss as she straightened up.

"James." She set the tray on a cooling rack, and took off her apron.

"Did you have your lie-down, Mom?" Dahl's anxiety about her mother was less intense since they'd moved the elderly woman downstairs, but she still worried. If only she could be in two places at once! Her mother had more energy since she didn't have to climb up and down the stairs. Unfortunately that meant she sometimes skipped the afternoon rest that her doctor recommended. When she missed her nap, Nonny grew as petulant as a tired child as the day wore on. Her response to James, with its slight edge of crankiness, suggested to Dahl that today might be one of those days.

"Yes I did, I had a lovely nap. And when I woke up I saw the blue car out there by the barn, so I knew we had company. I thought you would enjoy something special with your tea." She filled a basket with the hot oat-scones and brought it to the table along with the blue butter-plate and two of her favourite cut-glass dishes brimming with blackberry jam and apricot preserve.

Marik came in, and ran upstairs to change before joining them in the kitchen. The kettle was on the boil by the time she returned, so she filled the big teapot, and plunked it on clay trivet in the middle of the scrubbed table. James took a seat on Nonny's left, across from Dahlia.

"Mug or cup?" Marik asked. "Dahlia and I are muggers, but Gran likes a 'proper' cup and saucer."

"This is a treat! You ladies could start a restaurant, a country tea-room, you could make a lot of money serving up feasts like these!"

"More money would be a fine thing," Dahl agreed. "But I don't think a tea-room is quite the solution for us."

"People might object to finding horsehair floating in their teacups," Marik laughed.

James had a thoughtful look on his face as he stirred a teaspoon of sugar into his mug. "More money would always be a fine thing," he echoed. "If you really do need more income...can I make a suggestion? I might be able to help." He glanced around the table. He had their full attention.

"Like I told you the other day, Marik, I'm an investment consultant. That means I help people find investments so they can earn decent income based on money they already have. For example..." he hesitated again, as though not sure whether or not he should confide in them. "This has to be confidential. I have a friend who has invented something....if you're interested?"

"Always curious," Dahl remarked.

Marik was reminded of the remark Fleur let slip, that evening when she picked her aunt up to stay with Gran while she and Dahlia went to collect Cinderella. Hadn't Fleur said something about

James helping her get money to buy her new fountain, and it was supposed to be confidential?

"I don't know if any of you know much about computers, about computer games?"

"Marik's our computer expert," Nonny volunteered. "She even has a job....what do you call it?"

"An online job."

Nonny was proud of her granddaughter, who not only understood computers, but used one to earn her living without having to leave the house. Such a thing was simply unheard of, in Nonny's day.

"It's not a big deal, Gran. Lots of people work from home these days."

"You didn't say anything about that! What do you do?"

"It's just – office work." Marik flushed, conscious of James' interest in her, and ashamed that she was building an even larger web of deceit. "Data-entry so to speak." Surely data-entry was boring enough to disinterest anyone.

"Know anything about the online gaming world?"

"Not really. Do you, Aunt Dahl?"

"I use the computer for record-keeping, notes, that sort of thing. I don't know anything about.....what did you call it?"

"Online gaming. I'm not sure how much to tell you about this." James pushed his plate aside. "We don't want it to get out, someone might try to steal the idea before we get it off the ground. But I guess I can trust you ladies to be discreet." He accepted another cup of tea, and continued.

"My buddy Doug has invented this computer program where people will be able to design their own playing-fields, so to speak, for the games they play. That's a huge industry, online games. Huge! So there is an immense market for what he's developed. I'll tell you, the man's a frickin' genius when it comes to computer programming!

"Unfortunately, it costs money to get something like this into the marketplace. My buddy knows computers, but he isn't really savvy about how to develop this from a brilliant idea into something marketable. That's where I come in, because I understand marketing. My background is in sales, as you know. I know we can make a killing with this! But like I said, it takes money to take it to the next stage.

"That's where our investors come in. That's my part. I'm looking to find the people who are ready to get in on the ground floor with this. With a little investment, you'll be in line to make some really good money. Really good!"

"Unfortunately, we don't have any money to invest," Dahl said. She reached across the table for their plates, brushing all the crumbs onto one and stacking it on top of the others. "Wish we did!"

"But that's what I do!" James explained, handing her his knife. "I help people resource their unrealized monetary capabilities, their borrowable assets. Marik here has savings, you probably have a retirement plan – if you don't, then you certainly should! Dear Gran owns the farm, right? Those are all accessible, and it is just plain expedient to make use of them. Lots of people make the mistake of leaving their money tied up, when you could be putting it to work for you. Smart people, wealthy people, know that. You have to invest money to make money. That's all that the banks do – they invest your money, and they make money with it. With your money! Isn't that pretty crazy?"

Even Nonny had to agree with him. Having grown up in a depression, the "dirty thirties", she could understand mistrusting bankers.

"That's why you need to look at investing for yourselves, or get an expert to help you. Something like this Playing Fields System is ideal! You need to put your money into something that is going to make you some real money – and let me tell you, this is going to make a bundle of money for our friends who take advantage of the opportunity. This is special! I'd love to see you ladies benefit from it!"

"I don't know much about that sort of thing," Dahl said dismissively.

"Aunt Dahlia, all you need to know is that this is an opportunity like you've never seen before! I'll bet there are things you'd like to do around here, with the stable business, right? We could make that happen, you and I together. I'm telling you – I've never been so excited by a financial opportunity as I am by this one. And I've seen lots! Our investors are going to make a killing!" His face flushed with enthusiasm. "It's a once in a lifetime opportunity. I'm putting everything I've got into it!"

"There are a lot of things I'd like to improve around here. That much is true," Dahl agreed. She set the dirty plates by the sink, and leaned back against the counter.

"Is there another cup in that pot?" Nonny asked, before turning to James. "You're really that confident about this – what did you call it – Playing Field?"

James covered Nonny's hand with his. "Gran dear, yes I am! I know how much this is going to benefit people who have the b--, that is, who are smart enough to get in on the ground floor with us. My buddy and I are both determined to make this available to ordinary people, our kind of people. People like you and Dahl and Marik, here. I mean, why should the rich people make all the money? This time it's OUR turn!"

He turned to Dahlia. "Ask yourself this: If you don't grab this opportunity to make good money, what will you do instead? Marik told me about how you've been rescuing them, and I think that's great. Those horses of yours deserve the best! For that matter, so do you. With an investment in Playing Field, think of how much more good you could do! I can see you rescuing a lot more of them, wouldn't that be great?

"The thing is, though, we have to make up our minds pretty quick. Make hay while the sun shines, right Gran? Once we go public, it will open up for other people to invest. I want to see Family get the first kick at the cat, if you'll pardon the expression!" He pushed back from the table and stood up. "Gran, those were the best scones I've ever tasted! If you decide to open that tea-room, let me know, I'll be your first and best customer!" He chuckled. "Seriously, though, I suggest that you gals talk about it this evening, make up your minds, and I can pop back out tomorrow and we'll figure out how to free up the money so that you can make some money!"

"Whoa down," Dahlia said. "I don't think I know enough make that decision. Marik's the only one of us who knows much about computer games. What do you think, Mar?"

Put on the spot, Marik didn't know what to say. James had a suggestion. "Why don't you and I get together, then, tomorrow? Could we meet for lunch, or maybe coffee? I can explain more about this, help you make an educated decision. We can't delay too long, though. Like I said, we'll be going public soon. Oh! That reminds me: We are not public yet, so this has to be kept under our hats. I trust you won't talk with anyone about it, I had some trouble that way with one of my other investors." He scowled, and it was as if the sun had gone behind a dark cloud. "I don't ever want to go through that again," he added fiercely. "This has GOT to be kept confidential! Do I have your promise, no one else will hear about it from you?"

They agreed to that condition. He shook hands, solemnly, with each of them in turn, to seal the agreement. "Marik and I will discuss it tomorrow, and then we'll move on it. You'll be glad you did." He pulled on his handsome boots, and Marik strolled out to the car with him.

"Thanks so much for helping with Cinders. That was great!"

"I enjoyed myself," he assured her. "Like I said, I'm impressed with what you are doing, rescuing those poor animals. That's part of the reason I decided to tell the three of you about Playing Field. I hope the other two understand just how big this is going to be." He took her hand, then leaned in to give her a quick kiss on the cheek. "See you tomorrow!"

"Sure." Another kiss, another coffee date, with another man. Marik shook her head in wonder, and went back indoors to wash up their tea things and the utensils Gran had used to make scones.

Concentric Circles

After dinner that evening, Dahl asked Marik to help her draw up a chart of possible suspects. "I want to see all the names, how they're connected." While Nonny dozed by the fire in the front room, with her crocheting and her book and her kitten, the other two withdrew to the dining room next door, which Dahl now used as her office.

"We'll use a sheet of newsprint," Dahl said, tearing a long piece off the big roll. "My riding kids use it for horsey art-work on rainy days, when we can't use the ring. Oh, for a roof over the riding ring!"

They spread the page out on the big old table, taping it down at the corners to give themselves a flat surface for their brainstorming. Dahlia picked up a black felt pen and wrote "Edward" in the very center of the paper. She drew a circle around his name. "That's our stone thrown in the middle. How many ripples spread out from it?"

They decided that seven would be sufficient. In the first circle, closest to the golf ball, they put in the names of Ed's closest connections, his parents Lindy and Jack, his son Connor and ex-wife Tiffany. "What about her husband – what was his name?" It took Marik a moment to recall his name; Helene had introduced them at the Memorial Service. "But he doesn't go in the first ring, more like the 4th or even 7th. There can't be much emotional-connection there."

"Is that what we're looking for, emotional connection?" Dahlia queried.

"Emotional, or maybe financial?"

Dahlia picked up her red marker and wrote the two words at the top of the big sheet of paper.

Marik considered them. "Should we identify the emotions? You know, jealousy, revenge, rage, envy....or are jealousy and envy the same thing?"

Dahlia chuckled. "It's a subtle difference: Envy is 'I want what you have'. Jealousy is 'I don't want you to have what you have'. "

Marik considered that for a moment, and nodded. "When I said 'emotional connection' I guess I was thinking of the Motive. You know: Motive, Means and Opportunity. The murderer has to be someone who has all three."

"Right!" Dahlia listed the three words down the right edge of the paper, outside of the concentric circles.

"Means – that implies a man, doesn't it? Someone strong enough to knock him down, knock him unconscious?"

"Twenty years of hard physical work," Dahl said, flexing her bicep. "I wouldn't have any trouble knocking down a city-boy like your cousin Edward."

"With a bit of luck, I suppose any fairly strong person could have done it," Marik conceded. "Male or female. Say his head hit a rock, he might have been knocked unconscious. Then it would be easy to hold his face down in the mud until he smothered. That's what the Chesney Recorder said, he was smothered."

"There wasn't anything about his head hitting a rock, though, was there? Darn it, we just don't have enough details!"

"Let's put 'strength' under Means. We know he was on the ground when he died. There must have been a fight, and knocking him down would take more strength than the average person has."

Dahl wrote the word with the blue pen. "When it comes to Opportunity," she mused, "the question is whether the person who fought with him intended to kill him. Or did he – or she - take advantage of the fact the he was unconscious? Was it a sudden impulse to kill when opportunity knocked?"

"You mean, it might have been someone else, someone who came along afterwards, found him unconscious and decided, 'Yippee, here's a golden opportunity to kill the sorry s.o.b.'? That seems pretty unlikely!"

Dahlia gave a snort of laughter. "You're right. I think we can assume that the same person who knocked him unconscious finished up the job by smothering him. I meant: Was it deliberate? Did he somehow lure Ed to come down off the jogging trail, intending to kill him? Or did they just meet to discuss something and it accelerated out of control?"

"We can't know that, can we? Not until we know who it was, and maybe not then. Does it really matter, do you think?"

"I think it does. I learned a long time ago that there are different kinds of people. If we are looking for a deliberate murderer, that's one sort of person. An opportunist, that's a whole different type. When you do the kind of work I did when I was young, social work, you learn to assess people pretty quick. I'll tell you, people run true to type! Plotters are always plotters. Opportunists are always opportunists. Like they say, 'How you do anything is how you do everything.' We're talking about Opportunity. We have to ask ourselves, did someone make an opportunity, or just take advantage of an opportunity that showed up?"

Marik nibbled thoughtfully at her lower lip. "Since we don't know – maybe write "Plotter" and "Opportunist" under the Opportunity heading – with question marks."

Dahl nodded, and made the notes as Marik suggested.

"Let's get more names in our concentric circles. Then we can start dividing them up, as Plotters or Opportunists."

"Psychology of the Individual, Hercule?" Marik giggled. "I guess that makes me....what was his name? Dr. Watson?"

"Capt. Hastings. Dr. Watson was Sherlock Holmes. Capt. Hastings was Hercule Poirot's sidekick."

"As Capt. Hastings, then, I suggest we add a blank line inside Ed's golf ball."

"A blank line?"

"For the murderer," Marik was serious again. "They're in it together, right? When we know who the murderer is, there will be other people in the circles. He - or she - will have a mother, father, family and friends as well. How awful for them."

Dahlia drew the blank line as Marik suggested. She looked at what she'd done for a moment, then shook her head. "We don't know who those people are. Let's focus in on Edward, on his connections."

"But what if this whole thing is something to do with his law practice?" Marik objected. "The murderer could be someone he put in jail, or something like that."

"Not likely. Bolster & Nod does civil law, real estate and wills and tax-law, not criminal law."

"Oh. I guess that's not the sort of thing that people murder about. But still, there could be something. Maybe someone was cheated out of an inheritance by something Ed did, something like that? I think we have to put 'Bolster & Nod' in the second or third circle, they'd be affected by Ed's death, and their clients too, whoever they are. How are we going to find that out?"

Dahlia added "B&N etc." to the third circle. "We have no way of knowing about Ed's professional life," she said rather impatiently. "Presumably the police will have checked that out. They're the ones to look at anything to do with his law-practice. They're good at that sort of thing." She bounced the pen on the table top. "He was a community volunteer too. Food bank and that sort of thing. He showed up a couple times at Chamber of Commerce meetings, too."

"I didn't know you belonged to the Chamber of Commerce!"

"Sure! That is, Northwind Stables does. They've done a lot for me, especially for the Ability Riders program. But let's not get side-tracked." She added "C of C" and "Food Bank" in the third circle with Bolster & Nod.

"Shouldn't we have individual names in that circle as well?"

"This is just a reminder. We're going to have a lot of investigating to do. We'll fill in specific names later. There was a lot of talk about the murder at our last Chamber meeting, but it was just gossip. No one said anything helpful."

"No one looking relieved because he'd dead?"

"Not that I noticed. Hopefully the police will check that out, too. Like his law practice, that's their department."

Marik folded her arms, stepping back from the table. "So what can we do, that the police can't? We can't look into his law practice. We can't check into his community groups." She pointed to the top of the page. "If it is financial – maybe he discovered somebody trying to abscond with the food bank funds, something like that – we have no way of finding out about it."

"That's not our department," Dahlia said firmly. "We can't do what we can't do. What we know about, far more than the cops, is his personal life. Let's get the rest of Ed's family on the chart, your cousin Helene and your aunts and cousins and so on."

"I hate to think that one of my own relatives killed him."

"You can't be sure. It could be anybody. You said your cousin Helene gave a really touching eulogy, but how do you know she wasn't just pulling the wool over everyone's eyes?"

"Aunt Dahlia!" Marik cried, appalled at the suggestion.

"Well, you don't know. He was abusive to you, who's to say he wasn't the same with her?"

"His own sister?"

"Another convenient younger female, why wouldn't he? I'm sorry Mar, but like I told you before, it's common!"

"I don't think Helene could have murdered him, not after what she said at his service!" She pinched her lips together, struggling to control her anger and revulsion at Dahlia's comments.

"That's the problem! Until we find out – or the police do – everyone is a suspect. I'm sorry Mar, I didn't mean to upset you."

Marik took a deep breath and blew it out with gusty sigh. "I keep thinking I'm over it, and then, Wham! Someone mentions abuse, and I'm off the deep end again. I just hate to think that Helene might have suffered the same thing I did. Worse for her, since he was her brother." She remembered the eulogy her cousin had given, and the way she spoke of her brother when they met for lunch at Rocky's. Surely her affection was genuine.

"No," she said, "I don't think there was any abuse there, Dahl. I ....." Her voice tailed away as she remembered how her Aunt Lindy had taken Helene away on their golfing trips. Had that been a way to separate the siblings? "I hate this! I hate to think my family is full of dark secrets."

"That's why we have to solve this! We can't know anything for sure until we figure out who did it. That's why we need to put everyone's names down here on our chart. Everyone's. Then maybe we can start eliminating some of them. Maybe your cousin Helene was somewhere else when he was killed. Let's get the names written down, and then we can start working on them."

"You're right. Okay, well, the Aunt Twins – their husbands... " Dahl wrote down the names as Marik rattled them off.

Nonny heard the familiar names, and pushed herself up out of her wing chair. Domino, the black and white kitten, pounced on the ball of wool that dropped from her lap. Marik heard Nonny's exclamation and glanced over her shoulder. She ran to rescue the yarn from the kitten's claws, and handed Nonny her heavy black cane. She picked up the little cat and followed her grandmother back into the dining room. Dahlia explained what they were doing.

"We're looking at the people who are connected to Edward in some way. Who were connected, I should say. Somehow, some one of them must be the one who murdered him. Unless it was completely random, which we don't think it is."

"I should think you should include everyone who came to his Memorial Service," the old woman pointed out, peering at their chart. "Those folks acknowledged their connection to him. Don't they say that the murderer always returns to the scene of the crime?" She too had read her fair share of detective fiction.

"We've already got most of them."

"Not Aunt Flo." Marik lowered Domino to the floor. "You stay away from Gran's wool, naughty kitten! Auntie Flo was there, and she was one of Ed's clients, right? So that's one person who is connected to him via the law office. Don't worry, Gran! I don't suspect her of being the murderer!"

Dahlia laughed. "She fails the Means test – it would take a strong woman, and that's not my little sister! But I'll put her name in anyway, since she was at the memorial service. Third ring?"

"No." Nonny was adamant. "You can't suspect your own sister! You said she didn't have the strength, even if family loyalty doesn't stop you from suspecting her!"

"You're the one who said we should include everyone who was at the service."

"Not your own sister!" She banged the heavy cane against a chair leg for emphasis.

"Alright Mom, we'll leave her out. Don't get yourself worked up."

"We can talk with her, though," Marik pointed out. "Even if she couldn't have done it, maybe she knows something that could help."

"Good luck getting it out of her," Dahl muttered. "What about James? You said he was with her."

"Yes," Marik agreed, "but that was because of his connection with Auntie Flo, not with Ed. Maybe put him out in the fifth or sixth level. It's a pretty remote connection."

"Ask him if he knows anything about Ed when you meet him tomorrow," Dahl suggested. "Maybe he can suggest some other connections that we don't know about. Maybe even about his affairs with women. We haven't gone into that at all. Who was the woman he left Lindy for?"

"I don't remember. I can ask Aunt Lindy, I guess, if it will help our investigation."

"I don't like the idea of you two 'investigating' as you call it," Nonny grumbled. "I don't want Marik going out like one of those stupid women in those silly fluffy books you read." She sketched quotation marks in the air. "'I think Bob's the axe-murderer, so I'm meeting him tonight at midnight, at the abandoned slaughterhouse outside of town....'"

Dahlia made an exasperated sound. "I know this isn't fiction, 'every year, another body.' I don't imagine there will ever be another murder in Chesney Creek. Don't worry about it."

"Somebody has to," Nonny snapped. "It's one thing to discuss Ed's murder, or even draw up lists like this, but when you start asking questions, it could get dangerous. This is real life! It's a murderer you're talking about. Someone who isn't afraid to kill."

"Someone has to do this," Dahlia said fiercely. "Like I told Marik, it is our duty! It's our civic responsibility. Imagine if everyone in Chesney Creek put their minds to it! We'd figure out pretty fast who the murderer is! But everyone wants to bury their heads in the sand."

"Just don't forget what kind of human being – or un-human being – that you are dealing with. Murderers aren't like the rest of us. They are sub-human. That makes them dangerous, like a rabid animal!" She thumped her walking stick on the floor again for emphasis. "Dangerous!"

"Alright Mom, don't upset yourself." Dahl pushed the pens aside and began to roll up the big sheet of paper. "We've done enough for one evening. We'll talk about it again in a day or two. Meanwhile we can put our thinking caps on. And if the opportunity to talk to someone who's involved comes up, I'm taking it. I have to."

"Do you want help into your bedroom, Gran?"

"No," she said stoutly. "I'm fine on my own tonight."

The black and white kitten followed the old woman into her bedroom, and sprang up onto the foot of the bed. Nonny undressed slowly, hanging her dress away in the wardrobe and slipping the voluminous nightgown over her head. She padded into her bathroom, the linoleum cold against her bare, blue-veined feet. Her toenails needed cutting, again. This time, she would ask Marik to do it. Dahlia, poor thing, would rather deal with horses' dirty hooves than her mother's bare toes! She ran a sink full of warm water, and had what her mother had always called 'a birdbath', washing her face first, and then hitching up her nightgown to finish the job. She pulled the pins out of her hair, let the long white braid loose down her back, and climbed carefully into her high old bed. The curtains were pulled back, so that she could see the night sky where the waxing half-moon glowed dimly behind a high autumn-night haze.

Lying there with Domino warming her feet, she thought of Dahlia and Marik playing foolishly at investigating murder. Dahlia certainly was old enough to know better, however naive the younger woman might be. The person who could stoop to murder was an aberration, a monster! Confronting such a beast was a job for a professional, someone who was paid to face the danger. Only a fool would think it was a game, a puzzle to amuse an idle hour. "Lord keep them safe," she prayed. She opened her old worn Bible that she kept at her bedside, and read through Psalm 91, the Psalm that promises safety to those who believe.

"If it is Your will, distract them. Give them something else to think about." Surely it was His will to keep them safe. If only they didn't use their own foolish wills to take them into danger! Why on earth, she wondered, did people always think that the exercise of their free will meant choosing the wrong way, the dangerous path? They could just as easily use their free will to align themselves with God, with goodness, with peace. Her responsibility, however, was her own soul, not the souls of others, even if the others were her dear ones, so she prayed for herself, "Lord, help me to practice peace. Even if for some bizarre reason it is necessary for Dahlia and Marik to investigate murder, let me be at peace. I don't know enough to decide what is right for them. Help me to choose Thy will even when it makes no sense to mine." She breathed slowly and evenly, experiencing the peace she prayed for, trusting from long practice that she and her loved ones were in God's hands. She set the Bible back on the table, and switched off the lamp. Her head on the pillow, she and the kitten slept, old age and youth sharing the peace of their common trust in God.

CHAPTER SEVENTEEN
The Man About the Money

"Do you need anything from town?" Marik asked as they finished breakfast the next morning. She took the household grocery wallet, to which they all contributed equally, out of the drawer. It was her delight to do the weekly grocery shopping. She could buy the best cuts of hormone- and antibiotic-free meat, fresh seafood and as their own growing season wound down, imported organics fruits and vegetables. Neither of her elders had tumbled to the fact that she was supplementing their shared grocery fund. Dahlia didn't pay much attention to what she ate, and Gran had accepted her explanations that "it was on sale" and that "there's still plenty in the grocery-kitty."

Marik pushed the grocery list into the back pocket of her expensive new jeans.

"You look very nice, dear," Gran told her. "Pretty." She caressed the soft wool of Marik's light sweater. She paired the jeans with a lacy shirt and the loose cardigan with a fluted hemline.

The clothes were all new, part of what she brought home from another shopping trip with Liz. Lizzie prided herself on her dress-sense and wasn't afraid to tell her big sister what to buy, especially when

Marik daringly admitted, "I won some money on a lottery ticket. I can be a bit extravagant." She handed Liz a hundred dollar bill. "Now you can be extravagant too!"

Liz didn't ask how much the lottery win had been. She was too thrilled about having extra spending money to question where it came from. "Let's go into the spa! Maybe we can book pedicures right now," she suggested, and Marik breathed a sigh of relief.

Marik dropped the grocery kitty into her leather handbag. "Give me a kiss goodbye," Nonny requested. She was happy to comply. They were both nurturing this new loving friendship that was springing up between them, a precious growth.

"I'll do the shopping after I meet with James. I should be home in time for lunch."

He was just getting out of his car when she pulled into the parking lot, wearing a dark suit with a blue striped shirt, but no tie.

"Glad you showed up!" he greeted her. Marik glanced at her watch. She was on time, early if anything. "Sorry. That didn't come out right. I meant, I'm glad you're here."

"I remembered why I thought that place you used to work sounded familiar," he told her as they walked across the parking lot. "You mentioned it the first time we met. Bob's Olde Beanery, right? I knew I'd heard something about that place."

Her heart sank. She'd been afraid of this, afraid that someone would discover her immense wealth.

"You heard about that bunch of waitresses there, winning a great big lottery? I bet you wish you hadn't quit, eh?" He nudged her with his elbow. Already off balance, she lost her footing and stumbled.   "Careful!"

Marik was speechless.

"Just think - you wouldn't be driving that beat-up old Datsun pickup if you'd stuck with your job!"

"Toyota."

He ignored the interruption. "Talk about bad luck!" he laughed. "You quit to move back to little old Chesney Creek, and wham! Your ex-co-workers hit the jackpot. Talk about bad timing!" He held the door for her. "You must be just pissed!"

"Uhhh..." she murmured, at a loss. "Excuse me, I have to hit the washroom." Thank goodness, she thought, James had a reality of his own, one in which rich people drove fancy cars and wouldn't ever live in small towns. Her careful dissembling, her pretence of being ordinary, held. Nonetheless, it had been a narrow escape. She washed her hands and touched up her lip gloss before rejoining him.

"What do you want? I'll buy," he offered, "since you missed The Big Win."

"I sort of ... don't like to talk about it."

"Yeah, I can understand that." He shook his head. "It's kind of a sore spot, eh?"

"Something like that."

They ordered their hot drinks, plain coffee for James, her usual choice of a skim-milk latte for

Marik. "I can't drink that fancy stuff," James said, "too much caffeine for me!"

Marik considered telling him that caffeine wasn't an issue since her latte was made with espresso. The darkest of dark roasts, most of the caffeine was destroyed by the time the beans came out of the oven. His ordinary coffee may have been weaker in flavour, but not in its caffeine punch. The moment passed. James, she suspected, was a man who preferred that people agree with him. He hadn't liked it when Dahlia teased him. She'd met men like that before, men who were defensive about their ideas and opinions, the silly things. She chuckled to herself as she led the way upstairs. She felt no need to argue with James. She stood aside to let him chose their table, curious to see which one he would pick. Although they were the only customers upstairs on this quiet weekday morning, he led the way to the table tucked into the window nook. He was a man who valued privacy, she concluded. That was probably a good thing in an investment counsellor.

"What did you ladies decide about Playing Fields?" he asked as he hung his suit jacket over the back of his chair. "We have to jump on this right away."

"We didn't really talk much more about it," Marik apologized. "We were focused on other things last night. But I would like to meet your friend, what was his name? The guy who came up with the idea."

James frowned. "I'm afraid that's impossible. He's one of those reclusive computer geeks, doesn't like talking with people." He tore open a pair of sugar-packets, and poured them into his mug. "Now don't be giving me the look," he chuckled. "I know I shouldn't drink sugar. This doggie's too old to change now, I've been drinking my coffee regular all my life." He stirred in the sugar and took a sip. "Ahhh, perfect. But to get back to my computer geek buddy, you wouldn't be able to meet him anyway. He's down in....let me think, this week...." His dark eyes shifted back and forth as he searched his memory, "Mexico City this week. He's got some computer-buddies down there who are going to help, we're taking this international, you know!"

Marik was disappointed. "I really wanted to meet him."

"I'm sorry, but like I told you, he's not in town, so you can give up on that idea, there's no time to meet him. In fact, I'm flying down to Belize next week to join him, we've got important meetings arranged." He picked up his cup. "What that means" he explained, "is that this is your only chance, you've got to jump on this now, this week. I need to show up with the cash to do our part." He sipped his coffee, waiting for her reply. "See what I mean?"

A flush had spread up his throat, engulfing his face. He tugged at his collar. "Too much caffeine, it hits me like this sometimes." He reached behind his chair to pull a cotton handkerchief from his suit jacket pocket, and used it to wipe away the sweat that beaded his brow and temples. "Now, where were we? Oh yes – so what did you women decide?

You've got to jump on this. I'm telling you, Marik, it's the opportunity of a lifetime!"

"That's why they wanted me to meet with you today, to learn more about it. Aunt Dahl's definitely interested. Do you need a glass of water?" Once a waitress, always a waitress, she told herself as she hastened down the stairs. He accepted the icy glass with thanks.

"One thing I really regret about breaking up with your cousin Carol," he said, setting the empty glass down, "is that I've gotten out of touch with the family. I always liked being part of the Palmer clan, but I didn't feel right about visiting anyone except my Mama Fleur after Carol left me. That's why I'm showing you this Playing Fields investment. I want to get the Palmers involved. This is my way of reconnecting, you understand?"

Marik nodded. He was obviously sincere in his desire for a stronger connection with the family. "Sure. I know how that feels."

"I really want to help the Palmers. The family deserves it, all of you. You deserve to get in on this, make some real money for once. Maybe it will make up for your missing that big lotto-win!" he teased.

Maybe if they all make a bunch of money with this, Marik thought, it won't be such a big deal when I tell them about my riches. She brought her mind back to James and their conversation.

"I appreciate that you want to help us. Gran and Aunt Dahlia wanted me to talk with you because I know more about computers, but to tell you the truth, I've never gotten into game-playing, though I know a lot of people do that. It used to be 'the big pollution' on Facebook."

"What we're talking about is a little more sophisticated than 'Farm Space' and 'Jewel Hunter'" he laughed scornfully. "The kind of gaming I'm talking about, it's the big money. Big! This kind of gaming is a billion-dollar, a multi-billion-dollar industry. People spend big money just to get in on the games. The thing is, it's a fad, and with any fad, if they don't keep adding new features, people get bored and go looking for other amusements. So there is huge value in any new idea, especially in a new feature like Playing Fields." His eyes radiated enthusiasm.

"With the Playing Fields application, people will get interested and stay interested, because they can actually see themselves being creative, it gets them excited and into the games at a deeper level, more involved, more engaged. I'm telling you – this is going to be HUGE!"

He sat back and picked up his coffee, his gaze still intent. "I'm telling you, Marik, the internet is a gold mine. You know that! But you have to know how to work it. That's why Don's such a genius, he understands the internet and what a person can do with a new idea. You mentioned Facebook. Can you imagine if you'd gotten in on the ground floor of that? Or E-bay or Amazon or LiquorList, any of those giants? You see what I'm saying?"

She nodded thoughtfully.

"Good! You tell Auntie Dahl and Grannie, and we'll get this business underway."

His excitement was contagious. "I'll talk to them," she agreed. "Like I said, we've been focused on other things, especially Aunt Dahl. But it sounds like she needs to do this. I know she'd like to have a better income than what she earns with the horses and teaching and all."

"I get it that money is a major concern for her," he nodded. "Running a riding stable can't be a real high-profit occupation. This is going to solve that problem. That's why I'm inviting her in on the ground floor. Gotta help family first, and she's the one who needs it most! No wonder she's a bit pre-occupied. I would be too if I had a barn full of hay-burners to feed!" he laughed.

"It's not that, really. Of course, the horses are always on Dahl's mind, Northwind Stables is her business, but that's not what she's been preoccupied about." She twisted her cup around in a circle on its outsized saucer. "It's this thing with my cousin Ed Karlsson, the murder. Well, you know. You were at the service. Aunt Dahl is – well, she's almost obsessed with figuring out who did it, so that's what we were talking about last night, instead of about your Playing Fields thing."

"What do you mean, she's obsessed? Doesn't she get it that this is her entire financial future we're talking about? That's what she should be obsessed about, if anything!"

"She says we have a civic duty to figure it out who did it. You know: look at means, motive and opportunity, follow up on all the clues, that kind of thing. I think she read too many Nancy Drew books as a kid." Marik laughed. "Her generation was enamoured of Nancy Drew, girl sleuth. Mom tried to get me to read those books when I was a kid. Sheesh! That Nancy Drew was the ultimate twinkie, if ever there was one." She drained the last of her latte.

"Anyway, Aunt Dahl wants to solve this mystery of Who Killed Ed Karlsson. She says it's our civic duty." She held up one finger. "Means: that's easy, just about anyone could do it. But," she said, lifting a second finger, "we're stuck on Motive. I can't imagine how anybody could bring themselves to kill another person! Can you?"

"Sure I can! If someone were threatening your safety, trying to do you down, wouldn't you do whatever it took to protect yourself?" His face flushed again, but with anger this time, not caffeine. "Fight or flight, right? I certainly wouldn't run away if someone were threatening me! We have a right to protect ourselves!"

Marik was taken aback by his vehemence. "It seems to me there are better ways to deal with a problem than getting into fisticuffs about it, much less murdering someone."

"Sometimes you have to do what you have to do," he said fiercely. "If someone came in here, threatening you, don't you think you'd want to fight? I sure would!" His jaw thrust out, and she could see his shoulders tensing under his shirt, the muscles of his arms bunching against the confining fabric.

"I don't get a testosterone-rush from violence, especially not imaginary violence," Marik replied with a vehemence that matched his. "It's pretty ridiculous to imagine anyone strolling into Coffee Creek and threatening us!"

"How can you be sure of that? You never know when your life may be threatened. You have to be prepared to do what it takes. In everything."

"I'd hate to think that way."

"You're the one that brought up Karlsson. Face it, we live in a violent society."

Marik realized she had no desire to continue the argument. "I guess it must be a male thing, that protective instinct." She had learned long ago how to lather on the soft soap of flattery to calm down an angry man.

"That's right!" he agreed. "Men know we have a right to protect ourselves, and others too." His tight shoulders relaxed, his jaw lost the pugnacious thrust. "You talk about our civic duty. Protecting ourselves is just as much a 'civic duty' as anything else."

Marik didn't agree with him but she refused to get drawn into a pointless argument. Despite her regrets about the path her life had taken, life on the street had taught her the useful skill of controlling conversations. More than once her safety had depended on her ability to change a man's mood almost instantly. It was surprisingly easy. All it took was a sentence or two, a little flattery, a little distraction. She had become an expert at the subtle art. As a waitress, her ability to change the mood around a table netted her good tips. She did it almost without thinking, quickly and easily. She did it now.

"I'd probably run shrieking and screaming out of here!" she said, flapping her hands like a comedienne.

James laughed, as she'd meant him to. He had no idea that he'd been manipulated.

"That's about what I'd expect from a woman. Men don't let themselves get pushed around like that."

"I suppose that's true, at least about a lot of men." He had no idea that he'd just been pushed around. Pugnacious men, who thought all problems could be solved by a fist, were not her favourite sort. James might be a whiz-kid when it came to money and investments, but he seemed to be sorely lacking in emotional intelligence. Was that the reason his marriage with Carol had failed? Had his willingness to get physically violent had been the problem? She had no idea. There was still so much she didn't know about her family. They may have welcomed her home like the prodigal child, but there was no making up for all the years she'd lost. The roots she'd yanked up so precipitously all those years ago would take more than a few months to regrow. Perhaps they never would. Regrets, however, were useless. She shook off the mood, and changed the subject.

"This is one of my favourite new places in Chesney Creek," she said. "I like the artwork." The pieces displayed this week were hand-tinted photos, black-and-whites to which the artist had added hints of translucent colours. They chatted about the displays for a minute or two before James tenaciously brought them back to the Playing Fields investment.

"The thing is," he warned her, "we have to keep this under our hats. I don't want word leaking out before we are ready to launch! There's always that possibility that someone might be able to scoop us, beat us to the market. It might be a remote possibility, but it's still there. That's why our investors have to sign a Confidentiality Statement. In fact," he added, pursing his lips, "I should have made the three of you sign before I told you first thing about this! I'm too trustful sometimes. You haven't talked to any outsiders about it, have you?"

She hastened to re-assure him that they hadn't talked to anyone. The truth was that they hadn't given it another thought after he left the farm the day before, but he wouldn't want to hear that. There was no point in creating discord.

"You don't have to worry about it, not with us."

"I've thought that about others, and been wrong," he muttered. He glanced at his watch. "How about if I come out to the farm with you now, get all three of you to sign the agreement? Then you can get to the bank tomorrow, get the money, and we'll be good to go."

"I've got the grocery-shopping to do, and other errands," Marik explained. There was a boutique clothing shop in Chesney Creek now. Its window display had attracted her. She wanted to get something special to wear for tonight. She was surprised by how excited she felt about spending the evening with Stan.

"I've got a confidentiality statement in my briefcase, in the car. I want all of you to sign one. Come out with me." He pushed his cold coffee cup aside. "You can sign yours now, then I'll drive out to the farm and get Dahlia and Grannie to sign theirs. I never should have talked to any of you about this before getting your signature on the Confidentiality."

By the time she got back to the farm, James had been and gone. She put the groceries away, and went downstairs to take the sheets out of the washing machine. "One of these days," she told Nonny as she came back up to the kitchen, "I'm going to attack the laundry area with a giant scrubbing brush!" The laundry appliances and wood-burning furnace had occupied a corner of the unfinished basement for years. "There are cobwebs down there that I'm sure were built about the same time as the Egyptian pyramids!"

Nonny laughed. "It's not quite that bad. Lincoln always promised that he'd finish the laundry room one day, wall it in and make it more pleasant, but somehow that just never got done. It was never a priority."

"Would you mind if I did that? Or hired someone to do it?"

"What are you hiring someone to do?" Dahl asked, slipping off her boots in the mud room and coming in to the kitchen for lunch. Marik had bought cold cuts, and constructed sandwiches using Nonny's handmade multi-grain buns. She piled them with lettuce, and stabbed them with toothpicks so they wouldn't fall off the plates. "Hero Sandwiches" they'd been called at Bob's Old Beanery. Every time there was a new hero in the news, the chef had created a new version with a different selection of cold cuts and cheeses, reflecting the news-maker's interests or ethnicity. Marik brought her towering constructions to the table, and explained her plan for the laundry room.

"It's about time! If this thing with James pans out, we'd be able to afford it easily." Dahlia was excited at the prospect of making good money.

"There's something about that young man that doesn't sit right with me." Nonny shook out her napkin and laid it across her lap. She bent her head for a moment, calling a silent blessing upon the food and thanking the Provider. "I signed the paper, but I'm not at all sure I want to put any money into his thing. Lincoln was so proud that we never had to take out a mortgage on the farm! Even when..." Her voice trailed off. There were some memories not worth visiting. "I'm not sure it's a good idea."

"Oh Mom!" Dahlia said impatiently. "You know as well as I do that 'you have to spend money to make money'. We can't keep pinching pennies forever! It was fine to be careful back then, but times have changed. We've got an opportunity here, we don't want to miss out on it."

"I just don't have a good feeling about that James. There's something about him that rubs me the wrong way."

Dahlia glanced at Marik and rolled her eyes expressively. The childish expression struck Nonny's funny bone. "I saw that, young lady! Don't you go rolling your eyes at me!"

It made them all laugh, and broke the tension. "Fleur brought that expression home from grade school," Nonny explained to Marik. "She must have seen one of the other children doing it. She thought she'd try it out on her Dad, when he told her to help with the dishes or something - something she didn't want to do. Oh my goodness how we laughed afterwards! Those big blue eyes of hers were perfect for making that particular face! Our little girl grew out of it – but it looks like her big sister didn't."

"OK, Mom. I get the message." Dahlia took another bite of her sandwich. "I'm still going to go for James' offer. I agree, his personality leaves something to be desired, but what difference does that make? He's got the money-smarts, that's what counts. A chance like this doesn't come along very often. We'd be crazy not to jump on it! I've got money in my retirement savings, but not enough to retire on. If I can invest it like this, make some real money, I might actually be able to retire someday. I hope."

She picked up her teacup and drank deeply. "Luckily, I'm not in any hurry to quit working," she continued. "On the other hand, I would love to be able to hire some good help. That would make my life easier. I know I could make Northwind into something more than this jury-rigged operation I've got going. All I need is the money. Now, finally I've got a chance to get it. Of course I'm taking James up on his offer! Just imagine, I can finally get that roof built over the riding-ring like I've been talking about for the past ten years!" She turned to Marik. "I'll even renovate the laundry room for us, how's that?"

"I was thinking of paying for that myself. I've got the money, if you'll let me do it?"

"Go ahead," Nonny shrugged. "It makes no difference to me. My laundry-duty days were over, thank God!" Thank You God, she added, turning her mind upward with a sense of gratitude. Thank goodness for Marik! Lincoln would be so glad that the Palmer family home being cared for, not just maintained but improved, by this new generation. She had fretted about what would happen to the house when she was no longer there to look after it. Certainly Dahlia was not the one for the job. She would be happy to have the farm, yes, but she was no kind of housewife. Love for her home simply wasn't part of her character. She had looked after the house these past years before Marik came, but only as a caretaker, not as a homemaker. Now that her granddaughter had come home to stay, Nonny knew that her dearly-loved home had found a chatelaine who could and would love it. Her daughter would never have thought of improving the laundry room, or any other room for that matter, but her granddaughter did. Marik saw the potential for making it better, and did. Who had bought the paint for their bedrooms, chosen new draperies and helped her decide how to arrange her furniture in her downstairs bedroom? Marik.

How extraordinary that this child, the one who had run away from home, was in fact the very woman she'd been waiting for, the woman to whom she would entrust the family home. In Marik's care, the farmhouse would continue to be the center of the Palmer family life. The family needed this, a place in the world where they belonged, together. That was what made them a family. Even though times had changed, and the farm itself was no longer an inheritance to be passed from generation to generation, the family still had a home, embodied in this house.

This making of a home for the entire, extended family had always been in the hands of the women. The sons had inherited the farm, and their wives had cared for the home. It had passed from Lincoln's grandmother to his mother, from Lincoln's mother to Nonny herself. But times had changed, and it was not Gerard, the oldest son, who would live here next. He'd been perfectly happy to hand the diminished farm over to Dahlia's care when their father passed away. Dearest Lincoln!

Now she, Nonny, would pass this home into Marik's hands. She had prayed for someone, another woman, who would love the home as she had. She had served this home and this family to the best of her abilities, and God had answered her prayers. She was blessed to be able to pass the mantle on to another who would love it. Even if

Marik never married, never had children, the inheritance of home-making would be passed on. God would provide another woman to love this home and keep it in good heart for the sake of the family, just as he had provided Marik. He had been good to her, and was still being good.

"Mother!" Dahlia's voice jerked her from her reverie. "You looked like you were about to fall asleep in your plate. You'd better go for your lie-down."

Caretaker, that's what her daughter was, all she could ever be. She didn't have the softness to be anything else. "Yes, alright. I need your hand, Marik. Pull me up out of this chair."

Dahl watched the two of them move slowly towards the bedroom door, the older woman leaning heavily on the arm of the younger one. Thank goodness for Marik! Her niece was exactly what they needed. The mood of gratitude stayed with her as she went upstairs for her own after lunch rest-time.

Dahl slipped out of her work jeans, wrapped herself in the old red dressing gown, and relaxed on the smooth counterpane. Marik, bless her, had made the beds and swished the bathrooms before going out to do the errands and meet with James. She pulled the afghan over her bare legs. She began her breathing exercise, drawing the clean fresh air deep into her body, holding her breath for a moment before releasing it with a sigh. She repeated the cycle until the exhalations slowed and became as relaxed as her inhalations. Her after-school riders would begin arriving in just over an hour, but for now her time was her own. She settled into slow-breathing peacefulness, and opened her laptop.

Dear One, thank you for this time together. Please know that we are always with you, guiding you, as near as your next breathe, as near as the air. Yes, you are doing the right things. Yes, the steps you are taking today will lead you to that which you desire, although perhaps not in just the way you are expecting. The arrangements we are making are invisible to your human eye and so you are tempted to believe that 'nothing is happening' in response to your desires. That is not quite correctly stated: Rather than 'invisible' we would say, 'misinterpreted', for you do see things happening, events and interactions occurring. You simply don't recognize that these occurrences are the currency of your desire. It is as if we were paying you in Malaysian money, and you think, "I can't use this! This isn't money!" because you don't realize you are in Malaysia. Do you understand? The events of the past few days and weeks are all serving the manifestation of your dearest desires.

She took her hands from the keyboard and rested them on the bedspread. Enigmatic as usual, she reflected impatiently. Sometimes her Guides' writings were incomprehensible. Malaysian money indeed! It was more like Martian money, and she knew very well she wasn't on Mars! If only they'd give her straight answers to her questions. Was investing in James' computer-project going to provide her with the money to shift Northwind Stables into a higher strata? Would she be able finally to build a covered riding ring, buy new tack and more rain-sheets for the horses, hire help, and make all the other improvements that she'd love to make for the business? What about the murder? Why couldn't they give her a straightforward response about that? Either, "Yes, you will discover who killed him" or "No, give it up, you are wasting your time and energy obsessing about it." Oh for a few simple straightforward answers!

Dear One, the future is never completely predictable, even by us, because you – YOU! - are constantly in the process of creating it. What you do, what you think and feel, or rather, the vibrational frequency and amplitude of your behaviours, your physical, mental and emotional behaviours, are creating the circumstances of your life. Further: it is not up to us to dictate to you what to feel, think and do. That is your part. Our part is to help you live consciously, with awareness of yourself. From that awareness, you can choose. What is the choice?

For all humans, it is the same: "Shall I do what I know in my soul to be right...or shall I do otherwise? Shall I follow the dictates of my higher wisdom, or of my willfulness and desires? Shall I trust in the goodness of life?" As long as you act in harmony with your soul's desire for peace, your soul's desire for happiness, you will create a future in which you will experience peace and happiness. If you prefer drama and excitement – as so many of you do - then you will choose actions and thoughts and emotions which are harmonious with that desire. Ask yourself: Do I desire to feel peaceful & happy? Do I desire to feel optimistic and trustful of life's goodness? Or do I think it is fun to be challenged, to prove my strengths against adversities? It doesn't make a whit of difference to us which way you choose.

Dahlia let her hands come to rest yet again. Which did she prefer? Peace and happiness, for sure, but in the meantime, she had all these issues and concerns to cope with on a day-to-day basis. Peace and happiness simply weren't consistent with her circumstances.

You are looking at the difference between living as a unique and individual soul (peace, trust, happiness) and your imprinted patterns; from the perspective of love, or the perspective of fear. Understand this: So long as you feel that your choices of behaviour, thought and feeling are right and true, you are making right choices for you.

You ask, do we know who killed Ed Jamieson? Yes, we do. However, no one would be served by our 'telling' you, whereas many will be served by the fact-quest you are doing, and which you know to be right. It will benefit you to go through the slow, human process of discovery. Others, too, will benefit from being engaged in that process, including the poor soul whose path collided with Ed's so violently. Many lives have been thrown into chaos by that event, and here's the most important thing: CHAOS is not 'bad'; Chaos is simply the name that you give to the time between the old order-of-things and the new-order-of-

things. Do not think that the Chaotic Circumstances in which you find yourself are 'bad' or 'dangerous' – if you think they are, that is what you will experience! On the other hand, if you simply recognize, 'Oh, this is Chaos....I wonder what the new pattern will be?' then you will waltz through it (to the degree that you can practice this state of disinterested curiosity, the more dance-like the experience will be) KNOW THIS: the new pattern will be better – BETTER!!! Than what-was.

Dear One, we sense that you are tired and confused. Please put that aside, and trust that as you do what is right and true and harmonious, the decisions you make and the actions you take will lead you to a new & better life tomorrow. To the degree you can practice (practice practice practice!) trust in the goodness of life, to that degree you will experience it. And take note, that your trust-practice so far has brought Mar back into your life. See how her presence here has blessed you? Yes indeed! And you ain't seen nothin' yet. We are so glad that you are becoming more and more trustful in the goodness of life. Now trust also that you are making 'right' decisions, although there are no right decisions, really, but only, Decisions. When you make a decision, when you choose course A or course B, it is you who are stepping onto the course. The course isn't very important; the circumstances aren't very important. YOU are the important factor in whether, in hindsight, you'll say, "That was a good decision" or "That was a bad decision". Its goodness or badness doesn't arise until after you become engaged with it. There is no goodness or badness to Course A or Course B in-and-of themselves. It is only how you live, post-decision, that matters. Flip a coin! (Notice which side you are hoping will be up, while the coin is still spinning in the air....and if you experience no preference, then go with the side that shows up.) That is all from us for now, and more than enough it is. We love and will always be as near to you as the air. Our blessing upon you.

Dahlia imagined flipping a quarter into the air. Heads, she'd invest with James, tails not. The simulated, imagined coin-toss was more than enough. Her decision had already been made. She was going to do it, come what may. Goodness would come, that's what they said. She would trust in that.

CHAPTER EIGHTEEN

The Icing on the Cake

After her coffee with James, Marik went into Dorothea's, the new boutique across from the library. She found a draping, elegant bias-cut wool skirt to wear over her knee-high leather boots. The boutique owner, Dottie, suggested that she top it off with one of her artisan-made pieces, a fitted toreador jacket.

"It's one of a kind," she said, "and it looks like it might have been made for you! A very nice fit." It was expensive, probably one of the most expensive items Dottie stocked, but it was the perfect foil for the skirt and Marik agreed that it flattered her curves irresistibly. Showered and dressed for her evening out with Stan, she came downstairs to show her Gran the new outfit.

"He's here already," Nonny called from the office. "That is," she added, "if that's him, that good-looking young fellow who's out there talking to Dahlia. Does he drive a little foreign sports car?"

Marik joined her in the farm office that used to be the dining room. Nonny leaned on her stick to peer out the window overlooking the barn and stable yard.

"Yes, that's Stan," Marik confirmed. "Last time I saw him, he was driving a beat-up pickup." He had his arm stretched over the front paddock fence to let Cinderella snuffle his hand. Marik hoped that her aunt wasn't cross-examining him about the Karlsson case. She knew by now how tenacious Dahl could be. That was a gift, a strength, but like most such gifts, it could be over-used. "I'd better go out and rescue him. Goodnight, Gran."

"This is your rescue horse?" Stan asked as he greeted her with a quick stolen kiss. Dahl raised her eyebrows, but refrained from commenting. "She seems like a nice little mare. It sounds like you're doing a good job of training her, too." Marik was relieved. Apparently he and Dahlia had been talking about horses, not murder. It sounded as though he was fairly familiar with horses, too. That was another mark in his favour.

He held the car door for her. "What happened to your truck?" She folded her bottom down into the curve of the worn leather seat, and swung her booted legs into the low well in front of it. Stan tucked her skirt in after her before closing the door and coming around to join her. He slipped in behind the wheel.

"I didn't think you'd care to get covered in dog-hair," he explained. "I use the truck when I've got Trig with me." He turned the key and the engine purred into life. "I call this my date-car," he explained with a flirtatious lift of an eyebrow. "Much more appropriate than the truck, don't you think?"

"What kind of car is this?" She buckled her seat belt. "I've never seen anything like it." The curved wooden dash was mounted with domed-glass dials and little chromed toggle-switches. "I can see that it is vintage, but I'm not very good with cars, they aren't my field of expertise by any stretch of the imagination."

He shifted into second gear as they rolled down the curving drive onto Mountain Retreat road. "She's 1956-vintage, classic Porsche, what they used to call the 'bathtub model' – quite rare. I found this one a couple years ago, my Dad helped me restore it. I let him drive it sometimes," he told her as they descended the hills towards Chesney Lake, "but not when I've got a hot date."

He glanced over at her as if to check on how she would respond to being called a hot date. She met his gaze with an enigmatic smile. It was an expression she'd used a thousand times before, dealing with flirtatious male customers at the Beanery. It was a smile that said, 'behave yourself if you want to remain friends.' He could flirt if he wanted to, but she was by no means sure whether her interest in him was anything more than friendly curiosity, the same that she might have about any new acquaintance, old or young, male or female.

"I'm glad to see you dressed warmly. We aren't very air-tight." He reached through to the shelf behind their two seats, and handed her a folded blanket. "Here's a plaid, you can use it to wrap around yourself if you get cold. It's a little late in the season to be driving her, but sometimes I can't resist." He was wearing a dark turtleneck under his leather jacket, and warm black wool slacks.

Marik relaxed into the soft curves of the leather seat. He was a good driver, playing through the gears as they rounded the turns down into town and on through the quiet streets to pick up the two-land highway that stretched across the Valley. They picked up speed going past the farmlands and the orchards where the trees were beginning to shed their red and golden leaves.

"Your aunt – she is your aunt, am I right? She was asking me about the Karlsson case."

"I was afraid of that. She's got a real bee in her bonnet about it," Marik replied, disgruntled. Apparently she was wrong with her assumption that all they'd discussed was Cinderella. "She's been talking to all sorts of people, trying to get a lead on who might have done it. I hope you didn't mind her questions?"

"I'm afraid I was a disappointment to her. I don't know any more than anyone else. I'm strictly a dogs-body constable, the guy on patrol, not a detective. Well – I'm also the department armourer, but it's such a small department, we all have to do some kind of double-duty. Being armourer gets me out of doing traffic patrol some of the time, but serious crime? Nope, not my detail. I didn't have anything new to tell her."

"She's been trying to figure out what might have motivated the murderer to kill him. You know, motive, means, opportunity, that sort of thing."

"Murder's a job for professionals! She'd be better off leaving it alone."

"She says that all citizens have a duty to help the professionals," Marik said mildly. "I think she's right. It concerns all of us, the whole community. One of us might know something, might figure something out, which will give you professionals the break you need to solve it. Isn't that why you wanted me go to Detective Halston, about my history with Edward?"

"Fair enough," Stan conceded. "I can see your point. So what has your aunt decided? What does she think motivated someone to kill him?"

"We haven't a clue!" she admitted. "Somebody suggested that safety could be the issue, that he was killed because somehow or other he was a danger to his murderer. But that doesn't make sense because safety only become an issue after a crime has been committed, right? If the murderer is afraid someone will point the finger at them, like if they've killed someone before, then they have to kill that finger-pointer as well. That means safety-motivated killings are second ones, not firsts. Who was murdered before Ed? No one! He was a first-murder, not a second one, so safety doesn't come into it as a motive."

"Sounds like someone reads too many detective novels." He glanced over at her with a grin that took the sting out of his words.

"Maybe we do," Marik defended herself, "but the fact remains that Ed wasn't a threat to anyone."

"He wasn't a threat to anyone that you know about," Stan corrected her. "Maybe there was a 'first crime' as you say, but only the criminal and Ed knew about it. How about that for a scenario? Ed confronted the guy, whoever he was. Then instead of admitting to a previous crime when Ed accused him, the guy killed him."

"If that were the case – what was the first crime? We haven't heard about any murderer, or any other big crime that happened before Ed got killed, have you? There hasn't been anything in the paper."

"That only means that the cover-up worked! Ed was the only one on the planet who knew about it, so his death meant that the secret remained a secret. That would work in a book," he chuckled, "maybe. Frankly I don't much believe in the 'secret crime' idea. There are very few secrets in the world. They have a way of leaking out."

Marik winced. She didn't like being reminded of her own secret. It worried her that the truth about her extreme wealth might somehow leak out before she was ready. She could imagine what would happen if the whole family, the whole town, suddenly discovered how extraordinarily rich she was. It would poison every relationship that she had worked so hard to strengthen in these weeks at home, this new relationship with Stan as well as with her family.

People don't like it when they find out that they'd been fooled. Being secretive was dangerous, but she simply wasn't ready to reveal hers riches. First, she wanted to be accepted for herself, the basic Marik Palmer, not Marik-The-Wealthy-Woman. She felt that she was finding a place in the pattern of life here. So far, she was being accepted, but would that continue when they discovered that she had lied to them? Unfortunately, what Stan said was true. Secrets did have a way of leaking out. Soon, she promised herself, soon she would begin to tell a few people, her parents first of all, then Dahlia and Gran and the others. For now, she could only hope it would remain her secret, and hers alone.

Splurging for this new and expensive outfit for this evening with Stan had probably been a mistake, especially since she'd bought it right there in Chesney Creek. She'd been surprised by the quality and range of the stock in the boutique. The owner, Dottie, had been pleasant and helpful without pressing for the sale, and Marik had felt good about buying from a home-town merchant. Nice as she'd been, though, it wouldn't be any surprise if Dottie went home gloating about the woman who'd come in and paid cash, big cash, for everything she needed from the skin out. It was probably her biggest single sale of the week – of the month, even! Her husband and all her friends were sure to hear about it. Darn!

"Hello?" Stan was waiting for her response.

"Oh, sorry, just thinking about what you said, about secrets leaking out." She shook off her thoughts about her own situation. "I agree with you, although maybe for different reasons. If my cousin's murder was safety-motivated, the next question is, 'what secret did he discover?' And why did Ed happen to confront the guy in the park that particular day? It just seems too completely odd and coincidental to me. That's why I don't think this whole secret/safety thing is very probable."

"I expect we'll eventually find out who did it," Stan said dismissively. "Most crimes do get solved, if you work patiently enough for long enough. June's good at what she does, and she's persistent, too. I expect that she will go on putting one foot in front of the other until she finds the guy. That's what I told your aunt. We can trust June to do it. It's really not anyone else's business to figure it out what happened to him."

Marik couldn't have agreed more. She had gotten sucked into Dahlia's obsession, but she would be just as happy to forget about it. She had given more than enough attention to her cousin Ed recently. "I'd like to see his murder solved once and for all, and then I could put everything about him behind me. I'm pretty tired of Ed Karlsson!"

"Let's start by putting him behind us now," Stan suggested. "I hope you are ready for some surprises this evening. You haven't been to Giller since you moved back home, have you?"

"No. My mother's aunts lived there, but they are long gone."

"I grew up Giller. Well, until I was 12," he said. "That was before Giller re-invented itself, big time. Wait until you see what they've done."

Marik knew that many communities in the Valley had suffered from the failing economy during her growing-up years. Times had been hard. In Chesney Creek, businesses that had been part of the community for generations were shut down. She remembered the downtown shops being boarded up, with locked doors. Her own parents had suffered from the economic down-turn of those years, when her father had worked away from home, and her mother called herself lucky to get the part-time job as Chesney Creek's children's librarian.

In Giller, Stan told her, the slow-down in the lumber industry, and the subsequent closure of the saw-mill had thrown virtually the entire population of out of work.

"I was lucky, my Dad was able to transfer into the Chesney Creek school district, so we didn't move to the city like so many folks did. But I sure missed my buddies."

The sun was setting by the time they got to the old mining and logging center. When his family left, Stan said, Giller was rapidly turning into a ghost-town. Then the town fathers, in a daring last ditch effort to save it, managed to get a loan to hire a PR firm from Toronto. They challenged their public-relations-experts to develop a plan that would re-vitalize the town. They succeeded beyond anyone's wildest dreams.

With an inspired idea from the marketing gurus, and the co-operation of its last few loyal citizens, Giller had re-invented itself as a living-history museum. It became a destination-stop for tourists from around the world, and was home to a thriving artistic community. Marik was as surprised and delighted as Stan had predicted when they drove up the main street of town. She had vague memories of Giller, of the faded clapboard buildings with their high false fronts, from visits to her great aunts. Now, instead of being a uniform weather-beaten grey, they were cheerfully painted in various shades of blue and green highlighted by contrasting colours on the name signs and trim around the doors and windows. Many of them bore murals illustrating the town's history. The low trees lining the main street were hung with fairy lights that were blinking on as they drove through to the municipal parking lot.

"I made a reservation for us at The Bedouin Horseman." He locked the car doors. "I hope you'll like it." It was a new middle-eastern eatery, he explained. It occupied the top floor of the old sawmill, where logs from the mountain ranges above the town had been transformed into lumber for building. Now, the lower level of the mill-building was home to a high-end antique mall that they entered from the parking lot.

He reached for her hand as they strolled along the wooden walkway that wound between the sales stalls. It had been a long time since she had walked hand-in-hand with a man, perhaps not since the very early days of her relationship with Dale, the man she had lived with for two horrible years. Dale had held onto her as if she were his possession, something he had to control. This man's clasp made her feel cherished. She liked the feeling of connection she got with her hand wrapped warmly in his. Strange how much one could sense about another person simply by walking hand in hand with them.

Display cases featuring photos and memorabilia from the town's heyday as a logging and mining center were scattered between the shops. They paused to examine the model of the mill in its working days. "These days, they export the logs whole. No more sawmills 'round here," he said. "They make them into boards overseas. Then if we need lumber here in North America, we have to pay to have it shipped back. Crazy, huh? But that's modern economics. Giller isn't the logging town it used to be. Different folk living here now."

They made their way up the stairs, built of rough-cut planks, to the foyer above where the rough-cut lumber gave way to the lush tapestries and tasselled hangings of the Bedouin Horseman.

"Use your imagination," Stan whispered, his warm breath caressing her ear. "The Sheik has invited us into his palatial tents for a fabulous feast with exotic dishes of unknown origin. Are you with me?"

She giggled, entering into the spirit of the fantasy, and leaned against his broad shoulder to whisper in his ear, "I hope you have your scimitar sharpened, just in case he wants to grab me for his harem. You never know, with these wild desert sheiks. I wonder what he will serve us. Not sheep's eyeballs, I trust."

Stan admitted that he had never tried middle-eastern cuisine. "I had a feeling that you were the adventurous sort. I hope I'm right – you don't mind trying something a little out of the ordinary, do you?"

"Not at all! I never thought of myself as adventurous, but sure, I'm up for trying new things. If it turns out we don't like it – well, then we'll know, and we won't have to eat it ever again."

Their host, garbed in a long loose djellabah, escorted them to one of the curtained alcoves that lined the long narrow room. He bent down and pulled out the low table so that they could fold themselves down onto the brightly-covered, plump floor cushions, to sit side-by-side against the padded and cushioned back wall. He pushed the table close in over their extended legs, and lit the candle lamps before handing them the over-sized menus, their leather covers embossed with the beautiful Arabic script. "You will have a drink to begin with." It was more statement than question.

"Wine?" Marik suggested. Stan agreed, and ordered a bottle of a bold dry white that turned out to be the perfect foil for the richly seasoned food.

"That was a fabulous meal." Stan stretched and leaned back against the wall. They had ordered coffee to complete their meals, and he sipped cautiously from the tiny cup. It was so densely brewed that it was almost syrupy in consistency. "Who knew vegetables and lentils could be so good!"

"Are you sure it wasn't just the belly-dancer that you liked?" she teased him. The languorous music had been playing while they ate, weaving an entrancing spell around them. When the dancer swayed sensuously into the room, shaking her chimes in time with the music, they had been discussing dessert. Stan dropped the menu to watch. Enticing glimpses of gleaming skin flashed amongst the diaphanous veils that swathed her arms and upper body, leaving her supple midriff bare from below her breasts all the way down to the loose band of her skirt. Open-sided, it hung so low that Marik half expected to see the sheer fabric slither to the floor as she gyrated. Caught up in the music, she didn't realize that her own torso was shifting in time with the beat until Stan wrapped his arm around her shoulders and pulled her in close to him. When the dancer moved on to shake her belly for another table of diners, Marik relaxed luxuriously against him. The setting, and perhaps the wine, were having their intended affect. He really was a very attractive man, she was drawn to him by an appeal that transcended the purely physical. Where this attraction might lead she did not know, nor, at this moment, did she care. She decided to give herself in trust to the embrace of the moment and the man. It felt, she thought, very, very good. They decided against dessert, as it was getting close to concert time. Stan left most of his coffee still in the tiny cup, but Marik finished hers. She liked the depths of richness it held.

"Are you ready for some innovative and unusual music?" he asked as they strolled up the hill to the renovated Strand Theatre. Marik was fascinated to read the history of the building, written up on the back of their programs. Built as a venue for travelling players back in the booming late 1800-s, it was richly decorated with a host of gilded plaster cherubs surrounded by intricately molded garlands. Private boxes faced the stage from both sides.

"Why would anyone want to sit in the boxes?" Marik wondered. "They'd have the worst view, set off to the side like that!"

"I think the point was not to see, but to be seen!"

In the early days of the film industry, the theatre had been modified with a big silver screen, and a piano in the small orchestra pit, so that the miners and loggers could come into town and spend 25 cents to ogle Greta Garbo and laugh at the antics of Charlie Chaplin. It had been long closed and abandoned when Stan and his family lived there, but modern renovators had removed the screen, sanded the boards, and renewed the heavy plush stage curtains, turning it back into a live-performance center. "There is a movie screen mounted in the flies," the program notes bragged, "which is used year 'round for Films on Tuesdays." It finished with a list of classic and 'art' films to be shown over the winter months. During the tourist season that was winding down now, the offerings ranged from Shakespearean classics to corporeal mime shows, from comedy to rock and roll.

"Tonight's concert," Marik read aloud, leaning comfortably against Stan's shoulder, "is a unique presentation of innovative music as we bring together performers from around the world, playing some of the most unusual instruments in the world. Expect cutting-edge modern Swiss Hangs as well as Australian didgeridoos and Peruvian nose-flutes, and much much more. Prepare to be surprised."

Marik sat back. "Confident, aren't they? What's a Swiss Hang?" Stan didn't know either, but they both fell in love with the sound when the two musicians took the stage with their drum-like instruments.

The grand finale of the concert brought all of the musicians back on stage together, in an improvisational session that left Stan and Marik breathless with admiration. They clapped their hands sore in appreciation as the performers took a second and third encore.

"I envy the way musicians can communicate with each other," Stan whispered as they rose to their feet for the last time. "All they have in common is the music. They obviously don't all speak the same language, and they come from totally different cultures, but - it works!"

"A universal language," Marik observed. She took the hand he offered, and followed him out into the night. The waxing moon was high in the sky by the time they were back on the road. Marik was glad to wrap herself up in the plaid blanket. "What a wonderful concert."

Stan agreed. "A wonderful evening, all around." He reached over to tuck the blanket more securely behind her shoulder. The Porsche ate up the miles while Marik, comfortable with Stan's competence at the wheel, melted into a contented doze.

"Wake up, sleepyhead." She woke with a start to find that they were at the farm, the little car pulled up in front of the veranda. He came around to open her door, and to offer a steadying hand as she swung her feet out and stood up. It seemed the most natural thing in the world to end up in his arms. He cupped the back of her head in his hand and captured her mouth, his lips soft and warm on hers. An intoxicating warmth spread through her body. She let her eyes close as she savoured the feeling. Her lips opened to his exploring, caressing tongue as he tightened his arms around her, pulling her even closer against him. He raised his head at last, his breathing ragged, and held her close, her cheek resting against the solid wall of his chest. She was aware of the beating of his heart, and knew her own was beating in time with his.

"You are so lovely," he breathed, and captured her lips once again for a kiss that made her body hum with desire. "I'd better say goodnight. While I still can."

"Do you want to come in and...?" She wasn't sure what she wanted to offer him: A cup of tea, a cup of coffee, herself?

"Best not. It's late."

She stood on the veranda until the Porsche's little oval taillights disappeared down the drive. She trailed in indoors through the front room and into the kitchen. She wanted something, it had been hours since dinner. What a delicious dinner it had been, so enchanting to sit shoulder to shoulder with him, and what fun to watch the belly dancer, and to tease him a little bit about her. She opened the refrigerator, gazed aimlessly at the full shelves, and closed it again. Stan had awakened hungers in her that had been dormant for a very long time. She wanted chocolate. There was chocolate ice cream in the big farmhouse freezer, but it was downstairs, and too much effort. She opened a drawer, took out a spoon, and dipped a spoonful of peanut butter. It was far from satisfying the hunger in her, but it would have to do. She headed up to her bedroom at the top of the stairs.

She was not, she told herself as she brushed her teeth, ready to leap onto the pink cloud of being in love, but the more time she spent with him, the more she liked him. Despite what June Halston said, she didn't believe that Stan was in any way committed to the other woman. He said that it was over with June. She believed and trusted him. That in itself was odd. She had never been a trusting woman, most certainly not trusting of men.

That deep-seated distrust had protected her well during her years on the street. Without that, who knows where she might have ended up, or what she might have ended up doing? She had seen other girls, her own age or even younger, dragged down to destruction by men whom they never should have trusted. That was how hookers and heroin addicts were made. She spat in the sink.

Thank God, she hadn't she followed that path. She'd had been one of the lucky ones, one who knew something that most young girls didn't know, poor things. Like that stupid old Cyndi Lauper song said, "Girls just want to have fun." There should have been another song to warn them: "Boys just want to have sex." Lucky for her, she had known that, back when she was a young girl on the street, and had been able to avoid the pitfalls.

How, she asked herself as she flossed, had she known that? Why had she, unlike so many other little street girls, been so violently distrustful of men? Because of Ed. He was the one she had to thank for making her wary of predatory men. She swished the astringent mouthwash around her teeth. Why did every train of thought have to circle back to Ed? All she wanted to think about was Stan, who wasn't like that at all, but here she was, back to the cursed Edward! He may have helped to street-proof her, but she wasn't a street-girl anymore, she was done with that era of her life. It was long, long gone and done with!

She turned the water back on to swirl the mouthwash down the drain. She was a Chesney Creek girl now. It was time to put the lost years behind her, along with all the perceptions and misperceptions of that era. Stan was trustworthy, June Halston notwithstanding. Even if it turned out that he wasn't, which was certainly always possible, who cared? She was not a girl, she was a woman. If Stan turned out to be a disappointment, well, she could handle a little disappointment. He was only one part of her life, after all, and not by any means the main part. Her story was not about finding romance. It never had been. Nonetheless, this developing relationship with Stan was a very pleasant, an extremely pleasant, part of her new life here in Chesney Creek. She smiled reminiscently as she kicked off her slippers and climbed into bed. It was delightful that they were getting to know one another better. It would be good to spend more time with him. He was becoming a good friend and it had been a wonderful evening. That was enough for now. The future would take care of itself. The fact that his kisses were positively addictive was simply the icing on a delightful cake. Life back home in Chesney Creek was good and getting better. She drifted smiling into sleep.

CHAPTER NINETEEN

Engaged in the Process

Rose let herself out the staff door of the library, and walked down Third Street to the fire-hall to say goodnight to Dan. He was on evening shift this week. After her long day behind the checkout desk, it felt good to get out in the air. She could have gone through the Complex, since all the various areas were connected by hallways, but it was too pleasant an evening for that. Winter would come soon enough, with snow and rain to keep them indoors.

This habit of meeting after her work-day had become a ritual with them, started when the children were in school. Because of his shift work, it was often the only time in the day that they saw one another. Back when they were raising their family, Rose had felt a little guilty about their differing schedules. Her nine-to-five hours meant that she almost always got a full quota of sleep, while poor shift-working Dan had to snatch naps where and when he could.

He said it made up for his having worked in camp so much when the children were small, when she had been alone with them, sometimes for months at a time. She had missed a lot of sleep in those early years. The fireman's shift-work came as a welcome improvement. His children saw more of him, in the morning when he was on night shift, or in the evening when he was on days. The routine worked during the school year, but during the summer, he was Dad-on-call all day while Rose was at the library. She knew that the schedule wasn't good for his health, but she was thankful he'd become such a hands-on father with Liz and Robbie. Marik had missed out on that, more's the pity. Regrets, she reminded herself as she opened the side-door into the fire-hall, served no purpose. They were happy now, and their children had turned out well, even their eldest. He was a good man, her Dan.

"I thought you'd be along pretty soon." He greeted her with an affectionate kiss. "Long day?"

"Not bad, but you know how it is this time of year, the kids come in after school, pretending to do 'book research' – on the off chance there is something they can't learn on Google," she added sarcastically. As a librarian, Rose had been forced to learn some computer skills, but she still believed that books and other printed material was a more trustworthy source of information than anything online.

"Are you going over to Lindy's again tonight?" he asked. Since her nephew's death, Rose had spent much of her free time simply being with her sister, supporting her as she slowly recovered from the devastating loss of her son.

"Not tonight. She's adjusting, and Helene is in town. I called Fleur, I've been neglecting her lately. I thought she might like to meet me at Rocky's Diner for a quick bite of dinner, but she's got James staying with her."

"James? Her ex-son-in-law-James? What's that useless jerkwater doing there?" Dan had never liked the man, although he'd been reasonably tolerant while James was married to Carol and thus part of the family.

"I'm not sure. She was busy making a Yorkshire pie for his dinner, that's all I know. I hinted about being available to help eat it, if she'd invite me, but she didn't take the bait."

"So he's free-loading off of Flo, is he?" Dan scowled. He didn't like the idea of anyone taking advantage of his innocent sister. "If you ask me, the biggest mistake my smart brother-in-law ever made was taking the loser into the business, and then into the family. Frank didn't make many mistakes, but when he did, he went the whole hog."

Dan's low opinion of James was old news, and not something Rose cared to rehash. "I'm going out to the farm for dinner instead," she told him.

They chatted for a few minutes longer, before she kissed him goodnight. He tightened his arms around her, deepening the kiss.

"That comes with a rain-check," he said with a wicked grin when he finally released her. "I'll see you in the morning."

"You got yourself a date, Big Guy." Even after all their years together, Rose reflected as she drove home, it still gave her a thrill when Dan flirted with her. Perhaps it was especially fun because of all the years, rather than despite them! She knew herself to be a fortunate woman. There had been times when she had been sorely tempted to give up on her marriage, but both she and Dan shared one particular value: they kept their word. Thank goodness for that.

As she had told their daughter Liz, on the morning of her wedding day, "Make your promises to yourself, rather than to Zach, or even to God. Vow to yourself that you'll make this marriage work, and I know you will." No wonder mothers of brides wept at weddings. Marriage is a lot to expect, of anyone. She and Dan had talked about that before they were wed. They had agreed that they were committed to monogamy for life, even if temptation raised its diabolical head. They agreed that they were in for the long term, that they would honour their vows as an unalterable agreement. They would, they promised one another, stick with their marriage for the rest of their lives. They knew when they promised "for better or worse" it might actually be "worse" at times, although neither of them had any idea of how cruelly married life would challenge them. The year after Marik disappeared had been the worst.

In retrospect, Rose thought as she waited for a traffic light to change, the year when Marik ran away had been only marginally worse than the year or two leading up to it. Pressure had been building in their family life well before the explosion of Marik's disappearance. That explosion had hit Dan the hardest. Rose, feeling the responsibility for her remaining two, could not and did not let herself fall apart. For reasons she could not understand, Dan was not compelled to do the same. He turned to booze to dull the pain, and it had all but destroyed him as well as shattering what was left of their family life.

Already grieving for her lost daughter, she thought she had lost Dan as well. How terrified she had been that he would never recover, that she would be tied by her vows to a drunken, angry man for the rest of her life. The man she was living with bore little resemblance to the man with whom she'd fallen in love. She was promised to him, and to their marriage, for life, but she had never expected that the "...or worse" would be so hard. There had been moments, and more than moments, when she hated him as passionately as she had ever loved him. She was committed to staying married to him for life, but there had been times, God forgive her, when she hoped that their life together might be cut short by his death. She imagined him killed on the job, perhaps, so that there would be some economic compensation for her and their two remaining children, to tide them over into a new life. She had hated herself for thinking such thoughts, but she couldn't seem to stop herself.

She didn't know what changed for him, but over the course of a few short months, he finally came to terms with what had happened. He'd stopped the drinking, other than an occasional sociable beer. When he finally bounced back, after having sunk so low, it seemed to Rose that he had risen to a higher level of being. He became a better man, a better father, a better husband, a better friend than he had ever been before. Certainly they were happier together now than they'd ever been, happier even than they'd been in their honeymoon year.

It was pretty bizarre, Rose reflected, that she should feel grateful for all the pain they had suffered, but there was no denying the benefits they'd reaped. It seemed that sometimes things had to fall apart completely before they could reorganize in a better way. It was rather like when they renovated the kitchen in the new house. What a mess that had been, ugh! She had been reaping the benefits of the kitchen renovation ever since. The renovation of her life had been even messier, and far more painful, but the improvements were nothing short of amazing. She was more in love and, though she hated to admit it, probably much more loving, than she had ever been before. Marik's departure, with all the agony that entailed, had changed her as well as Dan. Perhaps, she admitted to herself, she had needed renovating just as much as Dan.

She unlocked her front door, letting herself into the quiet house. How fortunate I am, she mused, to be enjoying the rare and unusual benefits of a long-term, currently-happy marriage. Unlike her sister Lindy, she added sadly, and unlike her poor sister-in-love too, poor dear slow Flo. She counted over her blessings as she ran a quick bath. Dressed in a sweater and a comfortably loose pair of jeans, she headed eagerly out the door again to drive up to the farm. She hadn't seen Marik since the funeral two weeks ago. She was glad that her daughter was living at the farm. It was the perfect launching pad for her as she made her way back into the pattern of the extended family. She was in the kitchen, an apron tied around her waist, when Rose got to the farm. "Don't you look right at home!" They shared a quick hug.

"Gran is teaching me to make her famous Yorkie Pie."

"That's what Fleur's making tonight too!" Rose laughed as she bent down to give Nonny a kiss. Marik had moved the old woman's favourite chair, straight-backed and thinly upholstered, into the kitchen for her. "What happened to the rocking chair?" It had occupied the corner of the big farmhouse kitchen for as long as Rose could remember.

"I can't sit in a rocking chair. Or rather, I can't get up out of one," Nonny said. "There aren't any babies in the family these days, so the rocker is banished to one of the unused bedrooms upstairs."

Rose picked up a peeler and started on the carrots that were sitting beside the sink. "I didn't see Dahlia outside. Isn't she here this evening?"

"Still upstairs." Marik stirred the meat that was browning in the cast iron frying pan. "She said today was even more crazy-busy than her usual Thursdays, she needed some down-time. I'll wake her up in time for dinner if she's not up."

Dahl's Thursdays always started early, with the drive down to Green Gables Stable near Quinton where she had a class of five students. They were middle-aged women who boarded their horses at Green Gables but didn't need the specialized show-ring training that was offered by the stable's trainer. Today Dahlia's students had been particularly frustrating.

"Horses need consistent discipline!" she found herself shouting at them from the middle of the ring, her voice echoing against the metal roof above. "Consistent!"

They seemed to think it was too much trouble to practice what they learned. Between lessons, they rode for pleasure, apparently without any kind of discipline for themselves or their mounts. Then they wondered why the horses either ignored or fought the commands of reins and knees when Thursday morning lesson-time rolled around. Dahl knew that shouting at them didn't help, it only frustrated or offended them. She couldn't afford to do that. Scolding didn't give the results she wanted for her students or their horses and it didn't give what she wanted for herself either. She needed the steady income they provided.

"Alright," she called now, "Come to center and line up. Very nice!" These women paid her well for her time, and being able to use Green Gables' covered ring meant she could earn a year-round income as a riding teacher, but she had to keep them sweet. Positive reinforcement and praise was her best strategy.

"Let's take an extra five minutes." It was more time than she had planned, but it was necessary. She sent them back out to the rail, one after another, and applied the soft soap of praise as they trotted and cantered around her.

"Nice change of lead!" she called out, followed by, "Well done, Tessa!" and "You are looking much more comfortable on horseback now, Jane!"

"Just remember," she told Pru, who rode a raking bay gelding, "you have to reinforce what we've done today each time you ride him. You'll be glad you made the effort, especially when we start jumping. He's a great horse, but with a hot-blood like him, consistency is imperative!" Pru liked hearing that Pedro was a 'hot-blood'. Dahl had something complimentary to say to each one of them, either about their riding or about their horse. At last all the ruffled feathers were smoothed and they were once again looking forward eagerly to next weeks' lesson. "We'll be starting over jumps," Dahl warned them, "So come prepared for a workout!"

"You always give us a workout!" Tessa exclaimed.

Dahl left them laughing, but the delay put her behind schedule when she was already cutting it close. She had to get back to Chesney Creek for her appointment with the Investment & Loans Manager at Valley District Credit Union. Yesterday morning when she phoned to make the appointment, they told her it would take 24 hours before the cash would be deposited in her checking account. She should have left Green Gables sooner. She had promised James that she'd have the money for him by midday tomorrow, Friday. She was cashing-out almost the entire amount in her Retirement Savings fund.

Seated in a cubicle, she explained her plan to the Investments & Loans Manager, a rotund little man with thin strands of red hair combed across his freckled scalp. He was reluctant to assist her. He wanted more information.

"I can't tell you exactly what I'm investing in," she'd insisted. "It's confidential."

"But Mrs. Blabon, it's such a radical change in your plans! I can't in good conscience encourage you to do this, without knowing more about it." He pursed his thin little mouth.

"I've signed a non-disclosure form. It hasn't gone public yet, but when it does, I'll make back all of this, and then some! You'll get your money back."

"But Ms. Blabon! You've been investing in mutual funds for years, and they've done very well for you, your future is very secure. You can be proud of that. There's nothing wrong with tweaking your plan little bit, I'd be happy to help you with that. But to make such a radical change, taking out half your investment? That is simply not a good idea."

He pleaded with her at length. "These days, it pays to be conservative in our investing. I cannot in good conscience recommend the kind of a huge change that you are considering. I beg you to reconsider! You know you'll have to pay income tax on all this, don't you? Trickle it out, and stay under the tax man's radar! It's never a good idea to cash it all out at once. "

Dahlia refused to listen. The tax was a small price to pay for the money she was going to make by investing in Playing Fields. Her guides had confirmed her decision. "What you want, all the improvements you want to make in order to serve your community at a higher level, are coming to you. When you align yourself in loving service, the universe has no choice but to agree and give you what you want. Expect the unexpected." They'd had more to say, but those few sentences were all that she had needed to make the final decision. She knew beyond the shadow of a doubt that investing with James would bring her everything she wanted, and more. So there would be some taxes to pay! So what?

The Manager had eventually caved in, and printed out the paper work that would free up the money, despite her steadfast refusal to explain the 'investment opportunity' that had come her way.

"We will have to agree to disagree," she said stubbornly. If she wasted any more time with him, she would be late getting the horses tacked up for her after-school youngsters. "Let's get this done."

Unfortunately by the time she finished signing the multiple copies of forms, it was well past the one o'clock. "That's the cut-off time for receiving your cash tomorrow," the banker told her.

Dahl was furious. "I'm supposed to have the money tomorrow, by noon. That's why I made the appointment for midday today! That's 24 hours."

"I understand that you are annoyed," he said defensively as he escorted her from the cubicle, "but there has to be 24 hours between getting your signature and the cash being made available to you. Has to be, it's the law. It will be in your checking account on Monday morning. We open at 9:30, so you can come in, or write a check, after that. I'm afraid that's the best we can do, with the weekend coming up. Maybe you'll use the time to reconsider this decision."

"Not likely," Dahlia snapped. She knew what she was doing, and no officious twit in a suit was going to tell her different. She jumped into the Roadmaster and sped out of town, only to be slowed down by the yellow school bus trundling along North Rd. On days like this, she felt like she was battling her way up the waterfall rather than going with the flow. She thumped her fists impatiently against the steering wheel. Her youngest riders would be at the barn before she could get the horses in for them. If only the bank business hadn't taken so blasted long! Luckily, the school bus carried on along North, so once she made the turn up Mountain Road she was able to hit the gas.

Happily, there were no parental SUVs or vans in the barnyard when she pulled in. Even better, Marik had all five horses saddled and waiting along the riding ring rail, their bridles hung over the saddle horns. They were the gentlest of her old rescue horses, the ones she used for her youngest riders.

"Thank goodness! I was afraid I couldn't get them brought in and ready before the little ones get here. You have no idea how much I appreciate it!" She was reminded once again of how much easier her life was now that her niece had come to stay. That was one area of her life where things were going smoothly. It would be alright about the money as well. Anyone as money-savvy as James would understand that you can't fight the bank. Their rules and regulations were carved in stone, deeper than any law in the land! James would understand. She would let him know tomorrow that they would have the money on Monday. And then... She would have a covered ring by this time next year! With a smile in her heart, she greeted the first of her students. Life was going wonderfully well for her, minor frustrations and slow school-buses notwithstanding.

Later, after the second bunch of elementary-age students were gone, Marik came back out to help turn the horses out again to pasture.

"Mom's coming out for dinner," she reported as they rinsed the bits and hung up the bridles. "So it will be a little later this evening."

"Good! I'll have time for a shower, maybe even a quick lie-down." Dahl felt the need for a little time-out, after such a day.

Feeling refreshed now after her rest, she pulled on a soft plaid shirt over her turtleneck and came downstairs to the sound of voices and laughter in the kitchen. "What's so funny?" she asked.

"Yorkshire pie is the dinner-of-choice for the extended Palmer family," Rose explained. "Fleur told me that's what she's making tonight too, for James. He's staying with her, apparently."

"He is?" Dahlia exclaimed. "He never said anything about that to us. Did he mention anything to you when you met him for coffee yesterday morning?" she asked her niece.

Marik slid the pie-plate into the oven, beside the covered casserole in which a garden-ripened spaghetti squash was baking. She had picked greens that morning, and a few tiny end-of-season beans and tender broccoli shoots for the salad that was waiting in the refrigerator. "It will be about 20 minutes, right Gran?" She opened a bottle of red wine and poured a glass for Dahlia before answering her. "No, but he did say that he's flying down south on business on Monday, maybe that's why he's staying with Auntie Flo for the weekend? Who else wants a glass of wine while we wait for dinner to be ready?"

"If you ask me," Rose commented, "it's pretty bizarre that Fleur would befriend him, especially considering how much poor Frank disliked James at the end. He wouldn't be happy knowing that Fleur invited him to stay."

"Isn't that Flo all over again! She just doesn't get the idea of "disliking someone."

"Now that's enough, Dahlia!" Nonny intervened. "Fleur is a very kind and gentle-hearted soul, she always has been. The rest of us would do well to emulate her in that."

"It's true, though," Rose defended Dahl's statement. "Disliking people isn't part of Flo's emotional repertoire. I can't remember her ever having anything bad to say about anyone. Even after Carol divorced him, Flo still called him her darling son."

"Maybe this time my little sister has it right," Dahl commented drily. "After all, Carol moved away, down to Quinton. James stayed here. He's been good to Flo." She noticed her mother's scowl. "What? It's true, he is good to her! And look what he's doing for us!"

Rose agreed. "Flo told me he's been helping her with some gardening project. A fountain? And he put the tripod together for her latest reflecting ball."

"Another one?" Dahlia shook her head in disbelief. "Flo's taste in garden ornamentation leaves a lot to be desired."

"There's no garden like it!" Rose said, chuckling.

They shared an affectionate laugh at Fleur's idiosyncrasies. "My favourite," Marik chimed in, "is the gnome that looks like Uncle Frank. Maybe we should find one for her that looks like James."

Nonny frowned, but made no remark. She moved slowly into the front room, leaning on Rose's arm. They settled around the pleasant warmth of the wood-stove, and Rose entertained them with tales of her grandsons, Darrin and young Lincoln, until the oven timer dinged.

"That was wonderful," Rose sighed as she placed her knife and fork side-by-side on the empty plate. "You've inherited your grandmother's culinary creativity along with her recipes."

Her mother's praise warmed Marik's heart. Rose had never been one to gush with appreciation. Her compliments were only given when they were truly earned. "Gran made us an apple flan for dessert. I thought we'd have it after we do the barn-chores." Marik said. Dahlia was already pulling on her old jacket and gumboots. The younger woman followed her out into the dusk.

"I'm glad to have a chance to talk with you alone," Nonny said as Rose helped her up from the table. "I want you to do something for me."

"Of course, Mother Palmer. What can I do for you, bring you something or...?"

"It's about Fleur. I'm not happy that James has moved in with her, not happy at all. Do you know how long he has been living there with her?"

"I don't know. He was with her at Edward's service, which we all thought was a bit odd, and he was there for lunch when I dropped by after church on Sunday, but I didn't realize he was staying there until I called her this afternoon. I'm sorry, I'm afraid I've been neglecting Fleur a little these past weeks."

"You have been a good sister to her," Nonny said firmly. "Better than some of her blood-sisters. That's why I wanted to talk to you, just you and I by ourselves." She lowered herself into her favourite, comfortable wing-chair with a small grunt. "I just don't like James. I know it's wrong to say so, but I never could warm up to him even when Carol was married to him, and I don't like it that he might be taking advantage of Fleur."

"I'm off tomorrow, so I'll go check on them," Rose promised. She leaned over the wing of the chair to give the older woman a peck on the cheek. "I've got to get home now, but if I don't like the looks of things, I'll bring Fleur out here for a visit, and you can talk to her. OK?"

She stuck her head in the barn door to call a goodbye to the other two. Marik came out, her face looking slightly sweaty in the dim yellow glow of the yard-light.

"I'd give you a hug, Mom, but I'm kind of horsey." Rose gave her a hug anyway.

"What about dessert, Gran's flan?"

"I've got a piece to take home to your Dad. I don't need it, not after a dinner like that. It was excellent, sweetheart. I'm so glad you've settled in here with Dahl and Gran. Makes my heart glow."

Marik stood and watched until the taillights of her mother's Camry disappeared in the distance. Her mother had mellowed, she thought, and her heart was filled with gratitude for how good her life was now. Or perhaps, she thought ironically as she turned back into the barn, it was just her full tummy and the wine that made her feel so complacently contented! That might explain her mother's unusual effusiveness as well. Whatever the cause, she enjoyed the feeling of having slipped into this new life, like a hand into a well-fitted glove.

"Let's take another look at our Concentric Circles," Dahlia suggested as she hung up her jacket while Marik toed off her boots. "We haven't done anything with them these past few days."

"Do we know any more than we did before?" They unrolled the newsprint chart onto the dining room table. The room was a perfect office, with its big table and the sideboard that now held books and files instead of Nonny's fine china.

"I haven't used it enough, haven't had the pleasure of eating off of it enough," Nonny said when they asked her what to do with it. "Put it in the kitchen cupboards. It's time we started using it on a daily basis."

Dahl and Marik stood back from their chart, one on either side, and studied the information they'd gathered so far.

"I talked about Edward with my Sunday lunch-bunch," Dahlia said. The lunch-bunch were friends of long standing, some of whom had been in school with her. Despite the very different shapes of their lives, they had been getting together once a month for Sunday lunch for years. "They knew about him. Some of them even knew him personally or professionally. This is such a small town. The only thing I got, though, is that he had a reputation for chasing women. We already knew that. One thing they agreed on was that he didn't go for married women, or those who were in a serious relationship. I guess that fits with the whole macho attitude," she sneered. "No poaching in another man's territory. I think jealousy, revenge, that whole sexual-predator thing, is probably a dead end. It's not the murder-motive we're looking for."

"James said something interesting about that," Marik said. "He suggested that a person might commit a murder to ensure his own safety. It's similar to what Stan said, too." She explained the theory that Stan had advanced, that some secret crime had been committed by someone, and that Edward had known about it and threatened to expose him. That's why he'd been killed, to shut him up.

Dahlia tapped on her teeth with the top of her pen as she thought about that. "That's an interesting thought. It would mean that he was killed because of his virtues, not his sins."

"What do you mean?"

"I've been assuming that Edward was killed because someone was angry at him because of something to do with either a law suit, or something to do with his womanizing. Something he'd done wrong, or that someone perceived as a wrong. Was he killed as a Lawyer, or as a Lover?" she added with a snort of ironic laughter. "That's the question I've been asking myself.

"Problem is, no one I've talked to knows about any acrimonious lawsuits he would have been involved in. That seems like a dead end, and then too, everybody says he was careful who he bedded. He didn't go for women who were already taken, so to speak." She tossed down the pen. "Both Love and the Law are washouts, when it comes to motive! There's no logical reason for his being killed, that's the problem. We've got all these names written down, all these people who were in his circles of influence, but no reason that connects any of them to him in a murderous way. Damn!"

"In that case," Marik said reasonably, "let's talk about the 'Safety' thing. You said, it would be because of his virtues. What do you mean by that?"

"Things he did right."

"Sucks!" Marik exclaimed. "What virtues did he have? None that I know of."

"That's not true. The one good thing that everyone says about your cousin Edward is that he was rock-solid honest about money."

"Money," Marik repeated thoughtfully. "In that case, maybe he was a threat to someone who was cheating about money. Hand me that red pen, let's circle any names here that have to do with money."

"That pretty much eliminates family." Dahl picked up the black pen and began crossing them out. "No one in the family has much money to speak of."

"Except Auntie Flo," Marik reminded her. "Mom told me that Frank left her very well off."

"That's true, and thank goodness for it!"

"We didn't even put her name on the chart, remember? After what Gran said."

Dahl laughed. "She's not watching this time! Where should it go, close or distant?"

"Fairly distant. This fourth circle out, that's where we've put his professional connections. He handled her trust." Marik used the red pen to add Fleur's name to the chart.

"Mom was right, you know. We're grasping at straws if we think Flo had anything to do with his murder! Can you imagine her doing it? I don't think so!"

"Not the murderer, but somehow connected," Marik insisted. "He was her lawyer. That's why she came to the memorial service." She extended a red line from Ed's name, in the center of their chart, out to Flo's.

"Draw a fish beside Flo's name," Dahlia laughed, "because that's what she is, a big fat red herring. Or I should say, a pretty, plump, well-corseted red herring."

"So who else is 'about money' with Ed?"

They wrote "banker?" and "accountant, bookkeeper?" in the third circle out from the center. Dahlia was pleased. "We're getting closer, I can feel it. This is good! We don't have to go out chasing clues, we just need to think it out. This is the sort of brain-storming that more people ought to do, to come up with a solution."

"How about someone from the Chamber of Commerce? Isn't the Chamber sponsoring the Marathon that Ed was practising for? Maybe someone was planning to abscond with the money they raised, and Ed found out about it?"

"Good idea! We put C of C further out, last time. I'm crossing it out." Dahl drew a black line through it, then picked up the red pen and wrote "Chamber" on the line between the second and third circles. "I can talk to some people, find out who is handling the money for the fund-raiser. I had a call last week, they wanted me to donate a trail-ride voucher for the silent auction. I wasn't going to do it, but I can rethink that now. I'll get on to them next week."

Satisfied with their progress, Dahlia rolled up the chart while Marik tucked their pens away in the sideboard. They went upstairs together. "It's been a productive day," Dahlia said. "I think we're making progress towards figuring out who killed your cousin. And I've got the money lined up for James, so that's taken care of, too. Even if it won't be until Monday." She paused outside her bedroom door. "Thanks again for getting the horses ready for the kids. That made my job easier. It turned out to be a good day after all, with more good days to come."

Deeply satisfied with how things were going for her, Dahl fell asleep with a smile on her face, little dreaming of what the next day would bring.

CHAPTER TWENTY

What Fleur Knew

"Good morning Gran." Marik came into the cozy bedroom off the kitchen with Nonny's breakfast. "Bran Flakes, boiled egg with toast-soldiers" she reported. "Is there anything else I can bring you?"

"You spoil me."

"You deserve it." She flipped down the legs of the bed-tray, "and I like doing it."

She realized soon after moving to the farm that her morning routines would flow more easily if she served her grandmother breakfast in bed. It was quicker to prepare a tray than to help the old women get herself up and dressed for the day. Once she had some food in her belly, her grandmother had the strength for almost everything she wanted to do in the day, including taking her much-loved hens their morning mash.

Mixing up the mash was another task that Dahl somehow wedged into her busy days before Marik joined the household, a chore she considered completely unnecessary. "They don't need a mash-up during the summer," she argued, "They'll do fine with just their scratch." Her mother would have none of that. She'd always made a mash for them, just like her mother and grandmother and countless other women had done. The best care resulted in the best eggs, and that, she said, was that. Dahl had given in as she so often had to do before Marik came on the scene. Since the younger woman moved in with them, her mother seemed more relaxed, as well as more energetic. It made her much easier to live with, and for that, Dahl was grateful.

The old woman was up and dressed and at the kitchen table when Dahl came in from the barn. "I have a suggestion," Dahl said as she cut eagerly into her omelet. "How about we do a trail ride when I get back? I'll only be an hour or two. It's a beautiful morning, and we probably won't get many more of them. Mom, would you mind?"

"Not at all. I'm happy on my own, you know that."

"You really think Cinders is ready for the trails?" Marik wasn't sure how the mare would behave outside of the ring. Cinderella had come a long way in the few short weeks since they brought her home. She was a pleasure to ride, responsive to her rider's knees and hands, while Marik, who spent an hour or more in the saddle every day, was a much more confident rider.

"You both are," Dahl said in response to her niece's question. "We have to keep pushing the limits. We won't go far or fast. I want to take Skudder with us, on the lead. He likes to get out on the trails." They agreed to head out as soon as Dahl got back from the fairgrounds over towards Giller, where she taught an early-morning riding class for the Valley Equestrian Society,

"Pack us a lunch," she suggested. "We'll go over to the Hill Meadows. Gordon King told me last week that he had the hay off it now. We can let all three horses enjoy the grazing while we eat our sandwiches."

While Marik was busy making sandwiches in the farmhouse kitchen, her mother Rose was using her free morning to catch up on her housekeeping. As she ran the vacuum over the rugs and mopped the kitchen floor, she considered how to keep her promise about checking up on her poor sister-in-law. She wouldn't phone Fleur, she decided. She would drop in unexpectedly. That would give her the best chance of finding out what was going on with her and James.

Fleur was happy to see her. Rose waited to broach the subject of James until they were settled with cups of tea in Flo's dainty kitchen nook. She was surprised to see breakfast dishes piled on the counter beside the kitchen sink. Flo was usually an obsessively tidy home-maker who washed her dishes or put them into the dishwasher the moment a meal was finished.

"I hear that James is staying with you now."

Flo played nervously with her teaspoon before answering that yes, he was.

This was unlike her sister-in-law's usual calm serenity. "Are you alright with that? You invited him, didn't you?"

Fleur's wide blue eyes trailed over the table, avoiding Rose's gaze. "Not... exactly."

Rose's heart sank. Mother Palmer's maternal instincts must be right. Something was amiss here. She would have to choose her words very carefully in order to get the truth from dear simple Fleur. "Tell me more," she coaxed. "Why is James staying with you?"

"He needed a place to stay. His lease ran out. That's what he told me."

"That's nice of you to have him here. How long has he been with you?"

"I think, a week," Flo replied uncertainly. "Or maybe two weeks?

"Is he paying you rent, then?"

"Oh no!" The big blue eyes brimmed with tears. "He's already mad at me, I couldn't ask him to pay me money for staying here, too. That would be too much!" She dabbed at her eyes, then tucked the lace-edged hanky back into her apron pocket. "I can't ask him for more money."

This made no sense to Rose. Flo was asking James for money? "I had dinner out at the farm last night," she said. "Your mother is worried about you."

"Mummy? But why?"

Rose realized that in Flo's mind dinner at the farm, and her mother's worries, were a whole new topic. She would have to spell out the connection between Nonny's worry and Flo's unwelcome guest. Poor Flo couldn't put two and two together and get four.

"She's worried about why James is staying here."

Fleur pressed back against the upholstered seat, biting at her bottom lip. "I don't want to talk about that. I don't!"

Rose regretted her bluntness. It took a special kind of delicate tact, a skill she didn't have, to get

Fleur to open up when she didn't want to. Her sister-in-law could be stubborn as a mule when she was frightened.

"Let's go out to see your mother this afternoon. I know she would love to have you come for a visit. She always does."

Reassured, Flo's pretty face lit up with delight for a moment, and then fell. "I can't. James told me to stay here. I think he'll be back pretty soon."

Rose started to suggest that they do the breakfast dishes before leaving, but now she hesitated. She wasn't sure why she swept up by a sudden wave of urgency, but she wanted to get Flo out of the house quickly, before James returned. She mustn't infect Flo with her anxiety. That would only slow them down.

"We'll leave him a note," she said cheerfully. "Look, we can use this pretty paper."

She pulled a pad of notepaper out of her purse. It was one that the girls at the library had given her, the lined pages decorated with delicate pink blossoms.

"What should I say?"

"Just that you're going out for lunch with me. I'm sure he'll be fine with that. Here, you can use my special pen."

Fleur rose to the bait. "I am out with darling Rose" she wrote slowly and laboriously. "I will be home..." She paused, gripping the purple pen. "Should I say, 'soon' or 'for dinner'?"

"Just say 'soon.' That's good," Rose assured her. "Let's go now, we'll be just in time for lunch."

At last they were out the door and buckled up in the Camry. Rose pulled away from the curb, relieved that the street was empty. She half-expected to see James' car come hurtling around the corner, but there was no sign of him. She could feel her adrenaline-rush receding as they headed out of town.

She parked by the kitchen door, across from the barn. Dahlia was bringing Stoneyman out of the big barn doors, followed by Marik with Cinderella. Rose had never been really comfortable around horses. She watched from beside the car as Marik led the mare aside, and swung up into the saddle. The animal sidled and tossed her head.

"Is she really tame enough to be out like this?" Rose asked nervously. "What if she starts to buck?" She had a vision of the mare rearing up, of her daughter flying off to land head first on the hard-packed earth of the barnyard.

"She's fine, Mom!"

"Come and hold Stoney for me, Rose." Dahl called. It peeved her that anyone could be afraid of horses, most especially when it was members of her own family. "It's okay, he's a harmless old boy." In her opinion, getting up close and personal with Stoney was the best thing Rose could do, especially now that her daughter was proving such a fine and enthusiastic horsewoman. Rose needed to spend more time around the animals. She needed to get over her foolish fears.

"Let me!" Fleur came eagerly across the barnyard. She patted Stoney's glossy black shoulder.

"I can hold him for you." Even though she wasn't a horsewoman like her older sister, Fleur had grown up on the farm. She loved all the animals, from hens to horses. Stoneyman snuffled at her sleeve as she took the reins from Dahl.

"Want to hop up?" Dahl asked. She steadied the stirrup, and gave Flo a boost so she could swing her other leg up and over. The stirrup leathers were too long. Her feet in her shiny, bling-y sandals dangled loose down the either side of the saddle.

"I'll only be a minute. I've got to bring old Skudder out, he's coming with us." She handed a coiled rope up to Fleur. "Loop that around the saddle horn." She would attach the end to Skudder's halter, so he could follow well behind Stoney when they got out on the trail.

Fleur sat up proudly in the saddle. Rose was glad to see her face light up with a happy smile as she looked around from her vantage point on horseback. It seemed that she'd forgotten about James. Lucky Fleur, who was so quickly distracted from any trouble.

Marik rode over closer to the car. "See, Mom? She's a good girl!" She patted the mare's neck, smoothing the long black mane, and pulling the ends from under the pommel of her saddle.

Dahlia emerged from the barn, one hand resting on Skudder's halter as she led him out. The aged horse paused in the wide doorway. After the dimness of the barn, the bright autumn sunshine made his sunken eyes blink in discomfort.

"You'll need to lengthen those stirrups," she called to Marik. "I used that saddle for one of the kids in my morning group." Marik pulled her foot out of the right-hand stirrup, ready to dismount until her aunt added firmly, "Stay up! She should stand quiet while you adjust the leathers, after all the work we've done."

She nodded her approval as Marik looped the reins over the saddle horn and bent over cautiously to pull the off-side stirrup up onto the saddle. She pushed the heavy leather fender aside to get at the stirrup straps with their big, double-tongued buckle. The mare flicked her ears back, a sign that she was concerned about the way her rider was shifting about on her back, but she stood quietly enough.

Suddenly all three horses raised their heads, ears flicking forward as they looked down towards the driveway. Then the humans heard the car too, coming at speed up the drive. Cinderella shifted restlessly, and Marik clutched at the reins with one hand, holding onto the unbuckled stirrup leather with the other. She steadied Cinders with her knees, speaking reassuringly to her as the turquoise car flew up between the house and barn. The driver slammed on the brakes, bringing the vehicle to a skidding stop beside Rose's Camry.

"It's James!" Fleur squeaked. He jumped out of the car and slammed the door. Marik tightened up on the reins. She turned Cinder's head towards the source of the noise, so the nervous young mare could see there was no danger. James ignored all of the others as he strode purposefully across the yard to confront Dahlia by the barn door.

"Do you have my money?"

"No, I'll have it Monday, the bank said..." She wasn't allowed to finish the sentence.

"I'm leaving Monday morning, I need it today!"

"I don't have it, I'm trying to tell you. The bank won't release it until Monday."

"That's not good enough!"

"James, be reasonable! You know what banks are like."

"Damn the bank! I need the money, we can't wait around on this."

"I fully intend to get the money. This is as important to me as it to you. I told you, I want to invest!"

"You owe me the money today, now! NOW!"

Fleur, watching from the safety of Stoney's back, spoke up suddenly. "That's right, Sister. You have to give him the money so he can pay me, today. He promised."

James, his whole focus on Dahlia and getting his money, hadn't paid any attention to the others until Fleur spoke up. "What the Hell are you doing here? I told you to stay at home until I got back."

"James!" Dahlia snapped. "Leave Flo alone."

"He has to pay me," Fleur interjected. "The same day, every month. That's today. He promised."

"Shut up, you stupid old woman!" He spun back to Dahlia. "I've got to have my money now, today! Get in the car, we'll go to the bank and get this straightened out!"

He reached for her as if he meant to drag her to his car by force. Skudder, startled by the movement, raised his head and James' hand collided with the hard old skull instead Dahl's arm. Skudder yanked back on the halter. James rubbed his fist, his face flushing angrily.

"How dare you!" Dahlia clutched the horse's head against her chest, soothing him with her touch. "I told you, I'll get the money. Now back off!"

Disturbed by the angry voices, Cinderella shied nervously, dropping her head and hunching her back. It was all the warning Marik needed. Her mother's vision of her being thrown in the dirt was about to be true. She pulled on the reins, losing her grip on the unbuckled stirrup leather as she fought to pull the mare's head up to stop her from bucking. The heavy wooden stirrup thudded to the hard earth. Head up, Cinderella started to rear, her front hooves coming up from the ground. Marik threw her weight forward to drive her back down. Even steady old Stoney sidled restlessly. Fleur clutched at the saddle horn.

James glanced at the horses, then turned angrily back to Dahlia. "Get my money NOW!"

"He has to pay me. Every month, exactly on the 15th of every month." Fleur looked over at Rose beside the Camry. "Edward said!"

"Edward? What on earth has Edward got to do with it?" Rose asked, but James' voice rose above hers.

"Just shut up about Goddam Edward! Just shut up!" His voice rose in fury. "I told you. Don't tell anyone, not anyone! But you had to tell Edward, didn't you?"

Marik was still struggling with her mount. The little mare crowded back into Stoney, pushing the older horse against the barn.

"Whoa Stoney, Whoa!" Fleur whimpered. She started to slide off the saddle, but managed to pull herself upright, both hands hauling on the saddle horn.

Marik fought to control Cinderella, clutching with her knees and digging her heel into the mare's right flank to turn her hind quarters away from Stoney. All they needed now was a kicking match between the two horses!

"Who the hell else did you tell?" James raged at Fleur. "Who else knows? I'll get rid of all of them!"

Marik nudged Cinders back towards the riding ring. James was in Dahlia's face again, screaming for his money.

"That's enough, James!" Dahl barked. "Get a grip!"

"Don't tell me what to do!" Out of control, he swung a furious fist at her, and this time there was no old horse in the way to take the blow. Dahlia caught it on the jaw, and stumbled back into the barn door-frame.

"Make him stop!" Fleur screamed. "He'll kill her too!" James spun around and hurtled himself at Stoney.

"I'll do you too, you stupid bitch!" He grabbed Fleur's arm, jerking her out of the saddle. One of her sandals flew off and thumped against the barn before falling to the dirt. Stoneyman danced aside as the loose stirrups swung against him..

"Help!" Fleur howled as James yanked her away from the horse. "Help!"

From her elevated position on Cinderella's back, Marik was the only one who saw his hand wrap around Flo's throat. She clapped her booted heels hard into Cinderella's sides and the mare plunged at James, catching him a glancing blow with her shoulder. Marik hurtled out of the saddle and crashed into his back. Her weight bore all three of them to the ground and broke his deadly grip on her aunt's throat. Flo scrambled to her feet.

"Mummy! Mummy!" she shrieked. "Mummy!" Her remaining sandal flew across the yard as she raced barefoot for the safety of the house. The screen door slapped open. Nonny, leaning heavily on her cane, stepped out to see what all the shouting was about.

CHAPTER TWENTY-ONE

Battle in the Barnyard

Marik pummelled James' back and head with her fists, her knee digging into his back. "Help me!" she cried as he writhed under her.

He brought his head up, spitting dirt and blood and curses, and tried to push himself off the ground. Marik threw herself forward and pushed an elbow into back of his neck. He swung his other elbow back and smashed it across her cheekbone.

"Stop it! Stop it!" Rose raced up to kick at his head. She dodged backward as he snaked his arm at her ankle. She aimed another ineffectual kick at him. Marik grabbed his hair, twisting it into her left fist as she pounded the side of his face with her right.

Dahlia snatched the long lead-rope from Stoney's saddle and threw a half hitch around one of James' flailing feet. His other leg crashed into her shin. She yelped with pain but threw a second loop of rope around that ankle as well. Now both of his feet were trapped in the coils. "Call 911!" she screamed at Rose.

James writhed out from under Marik and twisted onto his back. He caught her with a solid roundhouse punch in the ribs and flung her aside. Feet together, he aimed a punishing kick at Dahlia. She jumped back and he missed. He yanked his knees up, bloody hands groping for the constricting rope. His struggles snugged the other end of the rope around the saddle horn. Stoney, the old roping horse, remembered his training. It was just like all the times when he had a struggling steer to subdue. He backed briskly. The rope snapped taut. James hit the dirt again, his head cracking against the hard earth.

"Stupid bitches, let me go, I'll kill you too!" A stream of invective poured from James' lips. He twisted, turning to reach for the rope that held his legs. Every move he made was a signal to Stoney. The horse stepped back and back again as he dragged James face-down across the barnyard.

"Get his hands!" Nonny shouted from the safety of the veranda. Fleur cowered behind her. "Kick him, Rose! In the crotch!"

"I'm trying, Mom!" Rose yelled back at her.

Dahlia flung herself onto the back of James' flailing arm. He pulled it free and grabbed at Dahl's dangling but Stoney snapped the rope tight again and he missed.

Marik scrambled to her feet, one hand clutching her ribs. "Where's Cinders?"

Dahl had both hands on James' outstretched wrist now, holding it down with all her strength. "Doesn't matter! Get his other arm," she gasped. Marik dropped to her knees on his free arm, pinning it with her weight. Rose had given up trying to kick the struggling man. She ran to her car and scrambled in her purse for her cell phone.

"I'll get you for this! Let me go, goddamn it!" James tried to kick at them but Stoney wasn't having any of that. James gave a grunt of pain as he was racked between the two women who held his arms and the rope on his ankles.

"Don't let him up!" Nonny called. "I called 911! They're on their way."

They didn't need to be told. Already they could hear the sirens coming closer. The firetruck was first to arrive, roaring into the barnyard with blasting horn. The Emergency Dispatcher, unable to make out what the quavering old voice was saying, sent them out as well as the police. The firetruck had barely stopped before it was followed by a police car, and then another. The barnyard was full of vehicles. Rose flung herself into Dan's arms. The other firemen and the police officers surrounded the combatants.

"Got bull-dogged, did you?" one of the cops laughed. Marik recognized Detective Ramirez, June Halston's older partner. "Alright, ladies, let him go. We've got him." The two women rose cautiously to their feet. Dahl went to Stoney's head. "You two alright? Looks like he put up a fight before you 'dogged him."

James sat up, cursing and spitting dirt. "Get that rope off him." A fireman reached down to loosen the tangle around James' ankles.

"But he's the one who did it!" Marik exclaimed. The fireman stepped back.

"They're nuts! They attacked me!" James started to get to his feet, but Stoney wasn't having any of that. He lunged back, tightening up on the slack. James hit the ground hard. "Son of a bitch! I'll get you for this!"

"You'll have to let him go, ladies," Ramirez passed his hand over his thick grey moustache, unsuccessfully trying to hide a grin.

"Come up, Stoney," Dahl chirruped at the horse. He stepped obediently forward. The rope slackened and the young officer knelt down to free James' legs from the rope. Another officer offered him a hand to get up, but James slapped it aside. "Arrest these bitches!" The rope dropped off his legs as he got to his feet.

"But he's the one who murdered Ed!" Marik gasped. "Ask Fleur!"

James launched himself at her. "Shut up! Shut up, or you'll be next!"

She stumbled backwards. Two of the officers had his arms trapped before he could reach her.

"Let go of me!" He fought against them, but they had his hands behind him. The handcuffs snapped onto his wrists.

"Put him in the car," Ramirez said. "Read him his rights. Alright ladies, tell me about this."

Before they could begin, Dan and Rose joined them. Rose picked up the shoe that had flown off when she tried to kick James. "You girls are a mess," she said, looking Dahlia and Marik up and down. They were both covered with dirt, and the swelling bruise on Dahlia's jaw was already purple.

Dan insisted on checking for damage. James's fist had connected with force. "Relax your jaw," he told Dahl. Her brother's hands were surprisingly tender as he explored the line of bone. "Can you waggle it back and forth?" She could. "Does it hurt when I press here?" Dahl winced. "Sorry. I don't think there's any damage, nothing permanent anyway. Marik? How about you?"

Marik's hands and knees were scraped and dirty. "He got me in the ribs, but I think it's just bruised. I'm okay. Thanks Dad."

Nonny stumped carefully down from the veranda and across the yard to them. Fleur, still frightened, clutched the sleeve of the old woman's blue cardigan.

"Alright ladies," Ramirez said, "How about you tell me what went on here."

"He admitted it," Marik insisted. "He's the one who killed Ed Karlsson."

"He came up here to tell you? That's why you attacked him?" He raised a skeptical eyebrow.

"No! He attacked us. At least, he attacked Auntie Flo."

"That's me!"

Ramirez glanced at Fleur, but turned his attention back to Marik and Dahl. "One at a time, please. Mrs. Blabon, why don't you start?"

Before Dahl could answer, the firetruck roared into life. The horses in the front paddock, who had watched the action with amiable curiosity, snorted and trotted away from the noise, heads held high. They saw Dan's arm reach out the window to wave goodbye as the big truck rumbled away down the drive. The police cruiser followed. They could see James thrashing in the back seat. Stoney stood where Dahl had left him, reins dangled on the ground, while Skudder cropped the long grass growing against the stone foundations of the barn.

Marik's voice rose above the noise of the departing vehicles. "Where's Cinders?"

"She galloped off down the drive after you fell off," Nonny said. "You'd better go get her, she'll be out on the road."

"Oh no!" Marik started away, but Ramirez stopped her with a hand on her dusty arm. "I have to go find my horse! She's on the road, she could get hit..."

"Hold on a minute. I want your story first."

"But..."

Ramirez held up his big hand, palm out in the universal signal to stop. Another car, black with dark windows, was pulling up in front of the house. "That'll be June. Figured she'd be along, even though she's off-duty. This is most excitement we've had all week."

June unfolded out of the low car. "What the h..." Catching sight of the old woman, she modified her language. "What the heck is going on here?" She focused on Ramirez. "I talked to the guys going out. The guy was attacked, so you arrested him? Don't you think you got the wrong one?"

They all started to talk. "Enough!" She gestured with her head to Ramirez, and the two detectives stepped away from the Palmer women. "I heard it on the scanner. What the hell's going on?"

The young constable stepped between the two groups as if to shield them from one another.

"Can I go find my horse?" Marik asked.

"NO!" all three officers barked.

"Want me to call Dan?" Rose had her phone in her hand, ready to dial.

"He can't come back, Mom! They'll be back at the hall by now."

"Maybe they'll let him go look for her. A loose horse is a road hazard." She tapped in the number, ignoring her daughter's protests.

Marik turned to Dahlia, worrying her lower lip with her teeth. "What should I do? We can't leave her out, she'll get spooked! She could end up miles away!"

"They won't let us go anywhere," Dahl muttered for Marik's ears only, "until we've answered a whole lot more questions." She draped Stoney's reins over her arm. "I'd like to take the tack off this one and turn him loose." She caught the constable's eye, but he shook his head.

The horses in the front paddock trotted back up along the fence beside the drive. Herald, the big pinto, nickered and was answered. Stan appeared, walking up the drive. The bay mare followed him, her reins looped over his arm. Her saddle was gone.

"Lose something?" Stan called. "I found her up Mountain Retreat road." He glanced around, then led the mare over to where the Palmer women were gathered. "I would have been here sooner, but it took some time to catch her. Between the trucks and sirens and the flapping saddle leathers, she was well and truly spooked." He took in Marik's dishevelled appearance as he handed Cinderella's reins to her. "Her saddle's in my truck. I took it off once I managed to catch her. It was under her belly by that time, she was not happy! I left it in the truck. Trigger's back there to guard it."

He turned away to speak with the other law enforcement officers. "Anything I can do here?"

"Nah, we've got it under control," Ramirez told him. "I've just got to get their statements."

"Wait a minute," June interrupted. "What are you doing here?"

"I heard it on the scanner, coming back from running Trig. Then I saw Mar's horse running loose." He glanced at Ramirez, raising an enquiring brow. "A domestic?"

"You could call it that," June responded. "Tomas was just filling me in, apparently they attacked the guy, roped him."

"They bulldogged him," Ramirez chuckled.

June scowled. "It's not funny, Tomas."

"I think he attacked them first. Don't worry about it. It's just a domestic and I've got it covered. I'll see you back at the station."

"Alright, you were here first," she said, "it's all yours." She looked up at Stan. "What about you? Your shift starts in an hour or so, doesn't it? Need a ride back to your truck?"

She handed the keys to him as they walked to her car, parked in front of the farmhouse. Marik, holding her horse while Dahl ran her hands over the mare's legs to check for injuries, watched the low sleek car glide away down the driveway.

Dahl straightened up with a grunt of pain, one hand pressed into the small of her back. "She's good. We can leave them in the riding ring for now, until Detective Ramirez is done with us." She tossed the stirrup up over Stoney's saddle, unbuckled the girth and slid the saddle off. She slung it over the railing, and winced. She would be stiff and sore in the morning. Oh well. It wouldn't be the first time.

"That's your brother's old roping horse, isn't it?" Ramirez asked.

Dahl was surprised. "You know him?"

"I've been around here for a few years. That crooked blaze down his face is hard to miss. I saw your brother do some pretty fast doggin' off that old boy. He was quick off the mark, that one! They competed nationally, didn't they?" He waited for Dahlia and Marik to strip the tack off the three horses and turn them loose in the riding ring before shepherding all the women together to get their statements.

"Come into the house," Nonny said, "I've got coffee on. And these girls need to get cleaned up."

CHAPTER TWENTY TWO

When the Dust Settled

"I think my tooth is loose." Dahl touched her jaw tentatively. "You can charge him for that, if nothing else."

Ramirez accepted a cup of coffee from Rose. "I'll take you one at time, get your version of what happened here today." He stirred a spoonful of sugar into his coffee. "Where can we talk privately?"

Nonny asked to be first. He followed her into the office and sat down at the big oak table.

"I want to explain about my daughter, Fleur."

"Don't worry," Ramirez reassured her. "My folks knew Frank's folks, they were neighbours. I've heard about Frank's wife. Widow, I should say. I understand that she's not," he hesitated, searching for a word that wouldn't be offensive. "I get it that she's not strong."

Nonny sank into the chair. "But you want to talk with her." It was a statement, not a question. "It's going to upset her all over again."

Her poor, fragile daughter had calmed down after James was taken away. She was distracted by the excitement of firetrucks and police cars, but it wouldn't take much to hurtle her back into emotional chaos. "I don't know that you'll get any sense out of her. It's going to upset her, being questioned by the police.

He looked at the old woman with compassion. He'd been fortunate with his children. He couldn't imagine what it would be like to have a daughter like Fleur, who still needed her mother's protection and advocacy even though her mother was as old as this Mrs. Palmer. Nonetheless, he would have to talk with Fleur. "I'll talk to the others first. Don't worry, we'll be easy on her."

"Will she have to testify, in court?"

"Possibly. But domestic violence – we deal with that on a regular basis. It's not going to make any headlines. Not that I've ever seen anyone roped and hog-tied before!" He chuckled. "Now, what was your part in all this? What did you see?"

The only thing Nonny could tell him was what she'd seen from the office window. She'd heard the car roar up the drive. She came into the dining room because it looked out on the barnyard. "I recognized the car. I was going to invite him in for tea. He's a family connection, you know. But then I saw him take a whack at the old horse! He was aiming for Dahlia, I think. That's when I picked up the phone here, and called 9-1-1. Then I heard Fleur shrieking for me. When I went out on the veranda, the girls had him down, they were fighting with him."

Ramirez made a couple of notes, and then asked to speak with Dahlia. She sank into the chair across the table from him. He could see the purple stain of bruising on her arms as well as her jaw. "Tell me about this barnyard battle. You invited him to come out here...?"

"No! We weren't expecting him. He just showed up and demanded that I drop everything, come with him to the bank. He wanted me to get the money for him immediately." As she spoke the words, Dahl suddenly realized something more. "The bank! I have to call my bank!" She twisted around to grab the phone from the desk behind her. "I really have to call my bank, right now!"

"Hold on!"

"I need to stop the transfer! I'll lose everything if I don't!"

"Mrs. Blabon, you're going to have to explain! What's this about money?"

"James said I could make a bundle, enough for all the improvements I need around here. He's smart about money, he had this invention, his and his partner's, this computer-game thing, and now if he...." She stopped, realizing she was being incoherent. She took a deep breath. "Sorry, I'm babbling. The problem is that the bank is going to cash out my retirement plan today. I've got to stop them."

The detective frowned. "I'll need to know more, but go ahead, phone your bank. I've got a retirement fund myself. Not something anyone wants to mess with." He glanced at the heavy wristwatch on his arm. "Make it quick."

This was beginning to sound like it might be more than a simple 'domestic'. Once you added a money angle, everything got more complicated. Here he'd been hoping that the next couple months would be a nice quiet slide down to his retirement date. Visions of complicated legal proceedings danced in his head. He should have let June take over when she showed up. She would have liked this, a good complicated mess to sink her teeth into.

Dahlia shuffled through the papers on her desk, found the phone number and made her call. She turned her chair away from the table, away from the detective.

"Dahl Blabon here. I need to talk to your Investment & Loans Manager." She crossed her fingers superstitiously as she waited for him to come on the line. "Yes, hello, it's Dahl Blabon. Listen, I need to cancel that transfer! Yes, my retirement plan. I know I did, but... " She glanced across at Ramirez with worried eyes. "No! Can't you just tear it up?" She tapped impatient fingertips on the table top. "Am I in time, or not? Yes, I'll hold.

"Sorry," she said to the detective. "Banks, you know what they're like...

"Oh, thank goodness! That's wonderful, thank you! It's on hold now, for sure?" She hadn't known how tight her shoulders were until she let them drop. "Okay, yes, I'll be in as soon as possible to.... Thank you so much. I'll see you then." She replaced the receiver in its cradle, and turned back to Ramirez. "Thank you. They can put it on hold for me. What a relief!"

"Tell me about this money," Ramirez commanded. "He was here to collect from you? You owed him money?"

"No. I was going to loan him money, or rather, invest it with him. That's what he does, investments. This one is something he and his partner Doug," She paused, a puzzled look on her face, "...or Don? I'm not sure. Anyway, something they came up with. We promised not to talk about it."

"Forget the promises! We need to get to the bottom of this. The money is what sparked the fight?"

"Yes, he demanded I come with him, get the money from the bank for him. But I couldn't do that! I mean, I wouldn't have been able to, the bank wouldn't release the money until Monday. He got verbally abusive, and it..." she hesitated, searching for the right words. "It accelerated from there."

James started by attacking her, she explained. Then he turned on Fleur, her sister, when he realized she was there. "She said something, I'm not sure what, and he started yelling and cussing at her. Then he yanked her right out of the saddle, right off Stoneyman."

"That's when Marik spurred Cinders at him. The next thing I knew, they were on the ground, he was screaming abuse, trying to beat up on Mar. I figured, the best thing to do was try to get him under control. That's why I grabbed the rope. I didn't know it would get caught around the saddle horn like that. It was the long line that I use to lead my old horse, Skudder. We were getting ready to head out on a ride. I thought if I could wrap the rope around James' legs, it would slow him down." She laughed, feeling embarrassed. "I really didn't mean to rope him like a steer!"

Ramirez combed a hand over his grizzled moustache, unsuccessfully trying to hide a grin. He liked this woman's spirit. "So you lassoed his legs. Then what?" It was half an hour or more before he was satisfied with her version of both the fight in the barnyard, and the so-called investment. The man's crazed attack on the women was a pretty good indicator that he was up to something. It didn't take a rocket scientist to know that the whole Playing Fields enchilada was some sort of complicated scam.

"You were seriously considering handing over money for this?" Ramirez shook his head in disgusted disbelief. By the time he dismissed her, Dahl understood that she had been saved from financial disaster.

"I'll see Mrs. Palmer next." He looked at his notes. "Your sister, I mean, not your mother. Rose Palmer. Sister-in-law?" It would take some time to sort them out. Dahl he would remember, there was something attractive about her, even with the purple bruise spreading across the side of her face. Something about her eyes, perhaps. "Was she planning to invest in this 'Playing Fields' scheme as well?"

"I don't know. I don't think so. Can I go get cleaned up now?" She felt heartsick. Her wonderful dream of turning Northwind Stables into a show-place was belly up, and there wasn't a darn thing she could do about it. It had been nothing but a fantasy, an old woman's foolish fantasy.

"Tell my constable to give me a few minutes before he sends her in." He'd have to call the station and tell them to keep the man under wraps until they could learn more about his financial shenanigans.

The interview with Rose didn't take long. Her story of the fight with James tallied with what Dahl told him. Rose hadn't taken any very active part in the battle. When he asked if she had invested any money with James, her adamant denial made it clear that she knew nothing about his financial scheming. It wasn't until he wrapped up the interview by asking "Is there anything else you have to tell me?" that he hit what might be pay-dirt with Rose.

"You knew he was living there, at Fleur's place? That's why I brought her out to the farm today, Mother Palmer wanted to get to the bottom of why he moved in with her. When I went to pick her up, she seemed to be afraid of him. There was something weird going on, I could tell!"

The detective flicked his fingers in a 'give me more' gesture. "I don't know what the problem was," Rose continued. "They were fine together before, as far as I know. But it's a good thing I didn't leave her there with him, judging by the way he acted when he got out here!"

That was all Rose could tell him. She had raised more questions than she'd been able to answer.

Whether or not he'd be able to get any better answers out of Fleur was a moot question. He passed a hand wearily over his head, rumpling his thatch of thick grey hair. He needed to get as many of the facts as possible nailed down before tackling the simple sister. "I'll talk to your daughter next," he said, dismissing Rose.

He took Marik over the familiar ground of the battle in the barnyard. "But the important thing," Marik insisted, "is that he admitted to killing my cousin, Ed Karlsson."

He held up a hand to stop her. "We'll leave that. It was your aunt who accused him, right? You don't actually know anything one way or the other?"

"He admitted it! At least, he said he would kill her too. I mean..." She couldn't remember the exact words. "I think he said he'd kill her like he did Ed. She knew he'd done it. You have to take her seriously. I know Auntie Flo is kind of slow, but the way James reacted, I'm pretty sure she was right. Flo doesn't make things up."

It tied in with what the others had already told him about the man's ravings, but he'd leave it to June to pursue this angle. The murder was her case, not his.

"Tell me about this Playing Fields thing. It sounds like your Aunt Fleur was involved too. Do you know anyone else he might have been scamming?"

"It really was a scam, then?"

"It certainly sounds like it. I'm not sure this so-called partner of his even exists. Your aunt wasn't sure if his name was Don or Doug. Sounds imaginary to me."

"Oh!" Marik was surprised, until she remembered how cagey James had been when she asked about meeting the other man. "Oh dear, Dahl's going to be so ...." Words failed her. "Poor Dahl."

Ramirez drummed his fingers lightly on the table, considering what he'd been told so far. It seemed that there were three different situations here, the domestic dispute, some sort of financial shenanigans, and then the Karlsson case. It sounded like June would finally be able to wrap up the murder, if what the women were telling him was true. It probably was. This is how most murders got solved, more by accident and serendipity than by design. That would be fine for her, but he'd have the rest of the mess on his plate.

They would need to get a forensic accountant in from Quinton before they'd unscramble the Playing Fields scam. The dim sister would certainly need to be interviewed, but not by him, or by June either. They'd have to get another expert up from Quinton, some kind of shrink who could handle her so her story would stand up in court. Damn! So much for peaceful pre-retirement months. He got wearily to his feet and followed Marik back to the kitchen. Dahlia, her hair still wet from her shower, was back downstairs with the others.

"Alright, ladies, I think I've got enough to hold him for now. More than enough."

"Aren't you going to interview me?" Fleur looked disappointed, like a child who had been denied a treat.

"I'll have a special interview with you," he reassured her kindly. "You are a very important witness." He glanced around at the others, not sure which of them to ask. The old lady looked all in, Dahlia Blabon as well. He couldn't ask her to take it on. He turned to Rose. "I'm going to need to arrange for a specialist. Can I ask you to be the contact person for that?"

Rose sat up and straightened her shoulders. She looked over at Nonny, who nodded her approval. "Certainly," Rose said. "I'll be happy to do that. It will be soon?"

"As soon as we can arrange it. Tomorrow at the latest."

"You have my cell number?"

"I've got all the phone numbers. Detective Halston will want to talk to all of you as well. We're far from done."

After Ramirez and his constable left, Marik headed upstairs to get cleaned up while Dahlia went outside to finish with the horses and turn them out into the pasture. There would be no trail ride today. Rose looked at Nonny, slumping in her chair. "You go lie down, Mother Parker. Fleur and I will tidy up the kitchen."

"Why didn't I get interviewed?" Fleur asked Rose plaintively. "I'm the one James attacked!"

"How about if I take you home?" Rose asked. "We can decide what you should wear for your interview. Then we can come back here." She didn't want to leave Fleur on her own.

It was a good thing that her sister-in-law was so easily distracted. Even with James in jail and likely to stay there for the time being, Fleur couldn't be left on her own. Her house would be full of reminders of James. She needed people around her, and time to forget. It wouldn't take long.

"We can bring your things back here, if you want to stay with your Mum for a few days. Or you can come and stay with Dan and me.

"I want to stay with Mummy."

"I'm sure she would like that." Rose would come back to take her for the interview as soon as Ramirez got in touch. "I'll just give Dan a quick call before we go." She pulled out her cell phone and tapped in the numbers. She gave him a quick update. "I'll probably be home for dinner," she told him, "If not, I'll be in touch."

Marik heard that as she came back downstairs. She put on her loosest, most comfortable sweats after a quick shower, clothes that would be soft against her scrapes and scratches. She followed her mother and Aunt out to Rose's car, and waited until Fleur was buckled in before drawing Rose aside.

"Mom, you told Dad you'd be home for dinner, but aren't you going to go see Aunt Lindy?"

Rose was puzzled. "I hadn't planned to." She explained her plan to take Fleur home, get her clothes and bring her back again to the farm. "I'm hoping they'll call to arrange the interview right away. I gave Detective Ramirez my cell number. It might even be this afternoon, if we're lucky. Otherwise I might just stay here as well."

"I'll make up the bed for you, just in case. But what about Aunt Lindy?"

"What about her?"

"Shouldn't one of us go tell her? I don't think the police will do that, and it would be horrible for her to find out by reading about it in the Recorder!"

"Marik, I haven't got a clue what you are talking about!" Rose was growing impatient. She wanted to get Fleur taken care of, and be done. With any luck, she could have dinner with Dan, and end this chaotic day cuddled up on the recliner couch with him. "Why should I tell Lindy about all this craziness?"

"To tell her about James. That he's the one who killed Ed!"

"Oh!" Rose was taken aback. "Are you sure of that?"

"Of course I'm sure! He admitted it, Mom! Didn't you hear him?"

"Oh Lord!" She had heard him, she simply hadn't put the pieces together. "You're right, I'd better be the one to talk to poor Lindy. What a mess!"

They decided that Marik would follow her mother into town, and bring Fleur back to the farm while Rose went on to see her sister. Rose's phone rang while they were helping Flo decide what to put in her pretty floral overnight bag. The appointment was scheduled for the next morning, when the forensic psychiatrist borrowed from the larger force in Quinton could be on hand to help. Fleur scurried upstairs to get a different pair of earrings to wear for the interview.

"I'm sorry to be dumping your Aunt Fleur on you," Rose apologized.

"Don't worry about it, Mom! This is what families are for." She reached out to give her mother the hug they both needed. "I'm glad I'm here to help. Give Aunt Lindy my love."

Later that evening, when they were all settled into their own bedroom, Dahl looked at her laptop but couldn't be bothered to even open it. All of her hopes for a better financial future, those wonderful dreams that had been raised by her Guides as well as by James, lay shattered around her. It was nothing but wishful thinking, completely unsubstantiated. That hurt, worse than her scraped knees and bruised jaw. Her so-called Guides were nothing more than her subconscious mind knowing what she wanted, and promising it to her. She trusted them. She had no doubts whatsoever that she was to have all the money she needed to transform Northwind Stables. And look what had happened! She clicked off her bedside lamp, and pulled the covers firmly up over her shoulder. If I were a crying woman, she thought, I'd be weeping; but she wasn't, so instead she began the slow deep breathing that led into sleep.

The bitterness was still with her the next morning. Her trust in her guides, she thought bitterly as she pulled on her boots in the mudroom, had been misplaced, as misplaced as her trust in

James. She felt utterly betrayed, and there was no one to blame but herself. She'd set herself up for disappointment, all by herself. She stomped her feet down into the boots, and pulled on her jacket. There was nothing she could do about it. There was nowhere to go but forward. The horses still needed to be fed, the chickens needed their trap-door opened so they could get out into their yard - and there was no one but her to do it.

Out in the barn, she tossed a couple bales of hay in the back of the pickup, and drove down the bumpy pasture to the hay rack. That chore completed, she brought old Skudder out of his stall, pulled his blanket off and turned him out with the others. This was how it was going to be. The same old routines, the same heavy work-load. There would never be a covered riding ring, never be hired help to do the chores. There would be no building up of a business that would support her into retirement. Life had stabbed her in the back again, just as it had when Bill got sick and died, and before that when Gordon King threw her over in favour of Annalise.

Somehow, she thought as she began forking manure and soiled bedding out of Skudder's stall, she had survived those cataclysmic events. If only she could remember what she'd done, how she had integrated those particular disasters and moved on! Warmed by the work, she shed her jacket and tossed it over the open stall door. She let her mind run down memory lane as she worked, taking her back to the confident girl she had been. At seventeen, she knew exactly what her life's path would be. She would get her degree in social work. She would come back to Chesney Creek and marry Gordon. Having her degree meant she would have a good income, it would make her a valuable partner as they built his family ranch into something bigger and finer than it had ever been before. That plan had collapsed like a pricked balloon when Gordon met Annalise. She remembered her mother's letter as if it were yesterday.

"Lavinia King tells me that Gordon and Annalise LaChiene are getting married next summer," Nonny wrote bluntly in her biweekly letter. "We'd heard she was spending a lot of time up at Kings, but I didn't realize she and Gordon were getting serious. I hope they know what they are about." There was no padding, no attempt to soften the blow. The best that Dahlia could think was that her mother didn't know how much the news would hurt her. What agony of soul she had suffered, alone and far from home. How on earth, she asked herself now, had her 19-year-old-self managed to pull herself back together when her dreams were blown apart? She simply couldn't remember.

Then there had been Bill. Even now, her mind shied away from the memory of those terrible months of his illness and death. She didn't want to remember the year after of his death, as she tried to come to terms with her widowhood. Compared to that, the loss of Gordon had been a mere pin-prick. Yet even with Bill, although she'd suffered devastating agonies, she somehow managed to pull her life back together. She would do it again this time, she told herself, the same as she'd done before. If only she weren't so old! Too old to put a different life together, too old for the endless, ceaseless ongoing toil of life as it was.

She rested her forehead against the back of her gloved hand as it gripped the handle of the manure-fork. She let the waves of disappointment and fear of the future wash over her as she surrendered to despair. However, a glove used for barn chores is not a pleasant place to rest one's head. Dahl wiped her eyes on the worn fabric of her shirtsleeve, and her nose with the inner elbow, and took the barrow outdoors to dump its contents on the compost pile. Her Saturday students would begin arriving directly after breakfast. Life would go on.

"I'll feel better in a few days," she promised herself, speaking the words aloud as if to some listening spirit. Her breath condensed in the chill morning air, and blew away with the breeze.

Marik was breaking eggs into the blue-striped bowl when Dahl came in, her morning-stables chores complete. "Mom and Fleur are on their way down. I'm making a frittata, it will be about 10 minutes. Coffee's ready. How are you feeling today?"

Dahl touched her jaw. "The tooth is alright, I think. Good thing, I couldn't afford a dentist right now. How about you?"

"I'll survive. A few sore muscles, don't think I'll be doing any more bull-dogging today." Marik laughed, but her heart ached for Dahl's disappointment. Something would have to be done. "Do you think we could maybe do our trail-ride tomorrow? You still want to get Skuddie out for his last stroll before winter, don't you?"

Dahl blew out a gusty sigh. Talk about getting back in the saddle before the dust settled, as Gerard used to say. "Can we make it Monday? I need a day of rest."

Rose came in and refilled her coffee cup. "I called Carol. She and the girls are coming up today, for the weekend," she reported. "A couple days with those busy little girls buzzing around the house will wash the thought of James right out of Fleur's mind."

"That's brilliant, Mom!" Marik exclaimed. "No wonder Helene says you are the rock of the family." She gave her mother a spontaneous hug. Fleur came in, wrapped in a dressing gown to protect the peach-coloured suit she'd chosen for her interview. Today, Nonny too was up and dressed. She came into the kitchen for breakfast.

"Oh! The frittata!" Marik exclaimed. She pulled the big cast-iron skillet off the burner, sprinkled Parmesan cheese across the top and slid it into the oven under the broiler. "3 minutes! Ladies, take your places please!"

After breakfast, Rose took Fleur away to her appointment. "I'll get Carol to call you when she gets in," she promised Marik. "It will be good for you two cousins to get together. Besides, leaving Fleur alone with the two little girls for a few hours is probably the best thing you could do for her, she loves playing

Grammy. You and Carol take all the time you want to get reacquainted."

Marik reported that plan to Gran while they tidied up the kitchen after the others were gone.

"Plan that for tomorrow afternoon. I want all of us to go to church tomorrow morning."

"Maybe they can meet us there," Marik suggested.

"Good! Then you can go off with them, and Dahlia will have to come with us to bring me home, whether she wants to or not." Nonny fought an ongoing battle to maintain the family habit of attending church. Dahl had very quickly passed that weekly Sunday task on to Marik.

"It's not that I'm not a Christian," she explained, "but I don't find that church does much for me. Maybe I'm just not sociable enough, or something. I'd rather give myself a day of rest at home."

"We will all go to church together," Nonny said firmly. "Carol and the girls can come to church too, with Fleur. You two can go off for lunch afterwards."

"Sounds like a plan, Gran," Marik agreed. She and Carol had been close as children. It would be wonderful to bridge the missing years with her, just as she'd done with Helene. Contented, she went upstairs to make the beds and swish the bathrooms before heading out to help Dahlia with the Saturday riding classes.

CHAPTER TWENTY-THREE

Evidence versus Truth

Marik hadn't been to church on a regular basis since she was a child. She was surprised to find that attending with her grandmother each week was somehow satisfying. It was fun to dress up a little bit, in honour of Sunday, in honour of God. She liked the familiarity of the old church, with its old-fashioned boxed pews. The minister was young, closer to her age than to most of his congregation.

It made her laugh, the first time she heard her aged grandmother address him as "Father Mike." How did he get away with that? Most of his congregation were decades older than he was. For that matter, how did he have the audacity to tell these people who obviously had far more experience of life how they ought to behave? Gran approved of him, however. That was the important thing. For herself, she was surprised to discover that she enjoyed taking part in the ceremonies of worship, bowing her head in prayer and raising her voice with the others in the songs of praise.

On this Sunday, the Palmer family pew was well-filled. Carol's two girls, 6 and 9, snuggled in between their Grammy, as they called Fleur, and their Great-Gram. They reminded Marik, sitting behind them, of herself and Lizzie at their age. She remembered sitting between her Daddy and

Granny, watching the play of light and colour in the high, narrow stained-glass windows. Even at that age, she remembered, she'd been an outsider who preferred the sanctuary service to the noisy confusion of Sunday school. No wonder her life had taken the course it did. She prayed that Carol's tender little girls would grow up more happily than she had.

On the far side of Nonny, Dahl was boxed in against the high end of the old pew, which suited her completely. She would rather have stayed at home nursing her bruises today, but duty called. Her jaw was still sore. Happily, her position in the corner hid the spreading purple bruise from the rest of the congregation. Thank goodness they arrived early enough for her to slide into the pew first, and take her usual seat before the rest of the congregation came in to stare and wonder. She could hide in her corner for now, but there was still the social gamut to run after the service. She wondered how many of them had heard about yesterday's 'Big Fight at the Palmers Place'. That's how they'd be thinking of it. Gordon King and his mother were seated in a pew a few rows in front. They'd know about it. Poor Gordon. Compared to him, her burdens were light. She straightened herself up in the pew, smoothing her narrow grey skirt over her knees.

Father Mike had chosen two Old Testament texts for his sermon on this Sunday in early October. The first was from the prophet Jeremiah, 29:11. 'For I know what plans I have for you,' declares the Lord, 'plans to prosper you...to give you hope and a future.'

"Well, Lord," Dahl thought, "Your plans went kinda' sideways this time. That's what happens when you rely on human beings to carry out your plans." Her heart was heavy with disappointment. She knew she was doing good work at Northwind. God must surely approved of it, and she had no doubt that He wanted to prosper her. Nonetheless, hope for the future eluded her. "I suppose I'll get my hope back," she told herself, "I always do. But it won't be anytime soon."

She dragged her attention back to Father Mike, who was introducing his second text. It was from the Psalms of King David, 37:7, who extolled them to "Rest in the Lord, and wait patiently for him, do not fret...."

"If only it were that easy," Dahlia thought in some exasperation. If only she could bring herself to trust and not to fret! That was a lot easier said than done! Easier at any time, but most especially now. It was hard to trust when her plans for a prosperous future had been yanked out from under her like the proverbial rug. She shifted on the hard pew, conscious of the other bruises she'd sustained in yesterday's battle. The Lord's plans for her, she thought grumpily, had gone sadly amiss. Far from resting, she would have to go on working as hard as ever. Harder, probably; and for less return, no doubt.

"I'll bring the car around," she told her mother as they filed out of the pew at the end of the service. She gave Father Mike's hand a perfunctory shake and hurried out, pulling her coat collar up.

Back at the farm, she made lunch since Marik was out for the afternoon with Carol.

Her mother was impressed with how well her young great-granddaughters had behaved in church. "Weren't they good?" She buttered a cracker. "Better than certain other little girls I could name, some of whom are not too far from here," she chuckled.

Dahl didn't bother to point out that Carol supplied both her girls with hand-held games to play with during the sermon. No fault to them. She hadn't listened to the service with any more attention than they gave. She was more interested in the application of the texts, rather than the historical context that Father Mike talked about. She couldn't help wondering why he chose to preach on historical context, rather than current application of his texts. Maybe because there was no current application. "Rest in the Lord" was poor advice in a world where hard work was the only option. Rest would be a nice change, but it wasn't a very likely future, at least not for her.

Nonny finished her soup. "Give me your hand," she requested. "I need a hoist to get up." She leveraged herself up on her daughter's strong arm, grunting with the effort, and reached for her stick. "After sitting in the pew for an hour, I seem to get stuck in 'sit'. You look like you need a good nap today, too."

"Thanks, Mom!" Dahl grimaced.

"You're not as young as you once were, either," her mother pointed out. "After yesterday, well.... It will take you some time to recover. It gets harder as we get older."

"Oh well," Dahl said with a resigned sigh, "I'll feel better eventually." She piled their sandwich plates beside the sink before dragging herself upstairs. It was easy to say she would feel better, and no doubt she would, physically. But 'resting in the Lord and waiting patiently' meant more than simply taking a nap. She wondered what her Guides might have to say for themselves today. She pulled the afghan up over her knees, and opened her laptop.

Dear One, You are making the common human error of basing your judgements on physical evidence, rather than Truth. It grieves us when you do that, when you make your heart heavy for no true reason. You judge by appearances. Appearances mean nothing. Nothing! Your great human failing is to look at an appearance, a piece of physical 'evidence' and say, "This Is. Therefore...."

Understand that when you do this, you block the flow of energy, of love. The energy – this intelligent, loving, kind, expansive energy which underlies everything – which as your physicists and others are now coming to understand, IS everything – wants to expand through YOU. Your focus on physical evidence and your judgements, your 'Therefores', hamper that expansion.

Dear Heart, let go of your Therefores. All things are working together for your good, if you will but let them."

Dahl rested her hands on the soft afghan. Maybe somehow Not Getting the Money, not getting the covered riding ring, not getting to improve Northwind Stables, was the best thing for her. It seemed impossible, but what did she know? She answered herself: Not enough. She couldn't know enough, couldn't possibly know everything. The only thing she could do was go forward, simply continue to put one weary foot in front of the other, and see what happened.

Dear One, do not do not do not make the mistake of thinking you are in any way being punished. We know that thought crossed your mind, even if you didn't quite notice it. There is no desire-to-punish in the energy of the source; it is loving, kind, expansive; and you have done nothing to be punished for, nothing!

All that you have done is that you made errors of judgement, errors of 'Therefores' we might say. Errors are just errors, as if you shot at a target and missed, erred in your aim or your execution of your aim. You aren't punished for that other than as you are punished by circumstances. This affair with your banking, your un-investment, was simply an error, a miscalculation on your part.

Are you being punished for it? No, there is no one and nothing to punish you....except yourself, of course. You are pretty good at punishing yourself, making yourself feel bad – forgetting what is True, which is that you are loved and adored by the Energy which wants to live more expansively through you, if you will allow it to. What you desire,

*which is for the good of all concerned, also desires
to be expressed through you, for it is true, that what
you call "God" does desire 'hope and a future' for
you, if only you would allow that to be. When you
want things to be the way you want them to be, you
forget that there is a higher intelligence than yours.
So you have in every moment a choice: Continue to
insist that your will should have been done, or trust
that there is goodness in store for you. We desire
your happiness, but it is your choice.*

There was a pause in the flow of words. Dahl
waited, flexing her fingers lightly. They felt a bit stiff,
a little bit dry and swollen. Over-worked yesterday,
she thought wryly.

*Hold yourself now in the State of Being that
knows whatever happens to you or around you is
for your good – your GOOD! - and here's the kicker:*

*You can only reap the good if you hold
yourself in the above-mentioned state. If you begin
to doubt, to worry, to believe that 'what's
happening is or might be bad, uh-oh!' you block the
good. It's up to you. We call that Free Will.*

Make a choice.

*Some folks prefer the excitement, the drama, the
fun of battles and challenges. That's okay, we don't
care. Truly we do not. We love you just as much
(100%) when you are worried, upset, anxious,
terrified, as we do when you are calm peaceful and
optimistic. It's entirely your choice.*

*Please remind yourself, as we remind you, that you
are loved, more than you know, and that you can*

trust in that love. 100%. That is all from us for now,
Dear One.

She set the laptop aside, and slid down to rest
her head on her pillow. Sometimes it seemed that
they wanted her to understand in ways that were
simply beyond her ability. Was there really any
choice? If there were, she would choose to trust that
somehow, in ways that she simply could not
imagine, there was good in store for her. She hoped
Marik would be home in time to make dinner and
help with evening stables. If not...but no, there was
no point in dwelling on what she didn't want, she
reminded herself sleepily. She pulled her long braid
out from under her shoulder, and drifted into sleep.

Marik did get home in time to make dinner,
and was bubbly with enthusiasm as she told them
about her afternoon with her cousin.

"She wasn't even surprised about James. She
calls him a vampire – he wants to suck all the energy,
or in this case, money, out of people. She's glad that
he'll probably be put away for a good long time. She
sent her apologies, though, for not warning us – the
family – about what a violent temper he had, under
all that conniving charm. She knew, his
uncontrolled temper is part of why she left him."

"No one's blaming her." Nonny helped
herself to more green beans before continuing. "She
was smart to get away from him, I always said that.
I never liked him. He's not the kind that belongs in
this family."

"No one's disagreeing with you any more,
Mom," Dahl muttered. She was embarrassed that

she'd been so completely taken in by James. All she wanted now was to put him, and everything he stood for, behind them.

"What about our trail ride?" she asked Marik. "You want to go out tomorrow? I still want to get Skuddie out on the trails one last time this fall, poor old boy. This is liable to be our last chance for decent weather. Once the rains start, I can't chance taking him out. The trails get too messy, slippery. It's treacherous for ancient legs." Once the rains started, everything got messy, including the riding ring. She pulled her mind away from that thought. Regret for the Covered Riding Ring That Would Never Be served no good purpose. They'd have indoor horsemanship lessons again this winter, as they had always done. That was all there was to it.

"Sure!" Marik agreed eagerly. "Morning or afternoon?"

They decided to go out early in the day. "I'm going to have to pace myself for the next few days," Dahl said. "Sundays and Mondays are supposed to be my days of rest, and let me tell you, I know I need them this week!" She touched her jaw. The swelling was down a bit. "Not just physically. I need a mind-break, too."

Nonny gave her a sympathetic glance. "I wish...." She stopped herself. "I'm glad we have Marik here now, to help."

Pray God, she thought, that the girl would stay with them. She seemed happy enough, more than happy, to be living on the farm with them, but how long would that last? There was that young man, Stan, for one thing. Women married. She might need to find a job, as well. Who could know what the future might bring? After dinner, settled in her chair by the fire with the kitten Domino on her lap, Nonny bent her head in serious prayer. "Dear Lord, You know what is best for us, and surely that means that my dear daughter does not need to go on working so hard! Let her find a way– she needs to either let go of her need to play with horses, or ...." She wasn't sure what to pray for, her imagination quailed at the unlikelihood of Dahlia ever giving up the horses, but how long could she physically continue to do that kind of heavy physical work?

"Help us all, dear Lord, to accept whatever happens with grace. By Your Grace." Gordon King would be free soon, and she was almost tempted to pray for Gordon and Dahl to come together again, but surely it was wrong to pray for poor Annalise's death. On the other hand, death was not the worst thing that could happen to a person. Her dear Lincoln had welcomed his death when it finally came to him. That last week, how he had hated to wake up in the morning, still alive and knowing he had to spend yet another painful day here on earth. "Dearest Linc, are you happy now?" She didn't expect an answer. She had often felt his presence near her during the first years after his passing, especially at times like this when she struggled to understand what was best for her family. She didn't feel him near any more. She was fine with that. He had other things to do, she supposed.

She lifted her crochet-bag from beside her chair, disturbing the sleeping cat, who jumped down from her knees in hopes that a ball of wool might roll off behind her, to be attacked and subdued. Nonny trailed the end of the wool beside her chair, amused by the little cat's attempt to catch it.

"That's all now, pet." She pulled the wool away from the snagging claws, but let the work lie idle on her lap. Annalise too, she supposed, would welcome death when her time came to move on beyond them. It would be a relief to Lavinia King. Her daughter-in-law had never been her favourite person on the planet. She'd dealt graciously with Annalise, but the relationship had not been blessed with true affection. Lavinia didn't need Nonny's prayers, but Gordon would. She knew that Gordon had loved his wife in his way and to the best of his ability, but it had not been an ideal partnership. He would need her prayers. Dahlia too.

What would happen to her Dahlia as the years mounted up? Nonny knew with the hindsight of experience that the physical body must and would change with age. There was no denying that! Her daughter would not always be able to do all she wanted to do. How would she deal with the frustrations of physical limitation? "Please Lord, give Dahl the grace to accept what cannot be changed; and to do the accepting as rapidly as possible."

Changes in life had to be accepted, and better sooner than later. Would Marik stay? She brought her mind back to the task at hand. "Forgive me

Father, my thoughts go in circles. Hold them all, each one of them, in Your Loving hands. Even James." Praying for her enemies was perhaps the hardest discipline of all. "Forgive us all for our parts in creating our own messes." That about summed it up. Like crocheting, sometimes one slipped a stitch, made a mistake. Unfortunately in life there was no 'frogging back', as knitters called. You can't unravel life and re-work it. You can only go forward. At best, you go forward without resentment towards anyone. You forgive them, and leave them behind you.

"Mother?" Dahlia's voice and a touch on her shoulder interrupted her thoughts. "You looked like you were about to slide out of your chair. Do you want help to get to bed now?"

"Yes, alright, but where's Marik?" Most evenings, her granddaughter helped her to undress and take down her hair. She treasured that intimate time they spent together. The bond between them was strong.

"Just checking the hens." Dahlia heaved her mother to her feet, and handed her the walking stick. She tucked the ball of wool back in the bag. "Sorry Domino," she told the kitten, "you're out of luck." The little cat followed their slow progression through the kitchen to Nonny's bedroom.

"I'll be right there," Marik called from the mudroom. Gratefully, Dahlia wished them both goodnight. Tomorrow, they would have a good ride. They would pick up where James had so rudely interrupted them. Life would get back to normal again, and she was more than thankful for that.

Dahlia walked out into the damp, chilly morning before breakfast, to turn the horses out of the barn. She would keep Cinderella in today, since she would be ridden, as well as Skudder. She hesitated in front of Stoneyman's stall, stroking the crooked white blaze. "You've earned another day off, haven't you?" She clipped the lead onto his halter, and took him out to the front field to graze with the others. She would ride Herald today, he was certainly steady enough to be a lead-horse. They could head out as soon as the stalls were done.

Marik was in the kitchen when Dahl came back in. "I'm making sandwiches, we do want to take a picnic today, don't we?"

"For sure. A big one, I think."

Marik laughed. "Sounds like you're ready for breakfast."

Once again Marik waited in the yard for Dahl to bring Skudder out of the barn. It was Friday all over again, but this time there was no Rose and Fleur watching, no turquoise car roaring up the driveway. Cinderella and Herald had halters over their bridles, with long lead-ropes tied to the saddles. Dahl swung up onto Herald's broad back and nudged him into motion.

"We'll be taking the easy trails today, up the back of Mt. Sanson. There are a couple nice wild meadows up there, good feed for these ponies while we picnic," she said, giving Herald's shoulder an affectionate thump. She led off down the drive,

Cinderella walking comfortably beside Herald, with Skudder on his far side. "I'll let you go ahead when we get onto Mountain Retreat. Best to be careful if there's any traffic. If she starts to get antsy I can bring these two up beside her as a buffer. But I think she'll be fine."

"I guess we have to thank James for that – he helped us car-proof her."

"I hate to think we have to thank that asshole for anything," Dahl growled, "Pardon my language, but words fail me when I think of what he did, or tried to do. Curse him!" She touched her cheek. "It's fading, isn't it?"

Marik assured her that the bruising was beginning to fade. No longer deep purple, it was a pale mauve stain now, running away down her jaw and down onto her neck, fading to sickly green and yellow as it healed. "Yes. Mine too. We could put it all behind us now."

There was no traffic on the short stretch of Mt. Retreat, and Marik's confidence in her mount improved as they turned off the pavement at the trail-head. Ears and head alert, Cinderella seemed to enjoy being out and away from the familiar surroundings of Northwind Stables.

"She's going to make an excellent trail horse," Dahl remarked as they made their way up through the woods, taking it slowly for old Skudder's sake. "I bring the trail-riders up this way," she explained. "This part where it flattens out is a nice stretch if they want to take it up to a trot or a canter. I'll stick to walking today, with Skudder, but if you want to let Cinders out a bit, go ahead."

Marik decided not to be that venturesome. She was beginning to feel the residual aches and pains of Friday's battle. Her ribcage sported a bruise not unlike the one that decorated Dahl's jaw. She was thankful that there was not worse damage, she could put up with a few bruises and sore muscles. It could have been so much worse. Nonetheless, she was glad when they reached the meadows high on the eastward slopes of Mt. Sanson. She dismounted, a little stiffly, while Dahl unsnapped the lead line from Skudder's halter. The old horse dropped his head and began eagerly to crop the late season grasses.

"Pick a spot," Dahl said with a gesture that encompassed the whole grassy spread. "It flattens out a bit over against those boulders. They make a good backrest."

They loosened the saddle-girths and stripped the bridles out from under the halters so that Herald and Cinderella could join Skudder. While Dahl staked out the horses, Marik carried the saddlebags over to the boulders. She spread out a small red gingham tablecloth on the grass, and unpacked their picnic.

"What a spread!" Dahl settled down on the dry grass beside the makeshift table, and helped herself to a sandwich. In addition to the sandwiches, Marik had packed containers of pickles and olives, as well as a few devilled eggs and one of the newly-ripened King apples from their small orchard. A thermos of hot tea completed the feast. "I love the view from up here."

"That's down towards Rainbow, where my Aunt Twins live, isn't it?" Marik asked, pointing towards the folded hills below them.

"Mmm," Dahlia agreed, mouth full. She swallowed. "But if it weren't for the power lines, you might think this was as wild as it was a hundred years ago." She leaned back on one arm, lifting her face to the thin autumn sunshine. "Maybe next summer we can do Gourmet Picnic Trail Rides, how would that be?"

"Aunt Dahl, I have a confession to make." Marik set her enamel tea-mug aside and wrapped her arms around her knees.

"A confession?" Dahl grimaced. She really didn't want to the burden of another emotion-fraught story, but the girl obviously needed to talk.

"Actually, some news and a confession."

Dahl's heart sank. She braced herself. Marik was planning to leave them. That was all she needed, yet another disappointment! She didn't know how many more she could take. "Go ahead, then." She sat up straight, dusting sandwich crumbs from her hands and forcing herself to be brave. "Tell me the worst."

"It's not the worst! Ok, Confession first: I haven't told anybody else, and I don't really want everyone else to know, so I hope you'll kind of keep this under your hat. Just for now, I mean. Eventually everyone...." She stopped and took a deep breath.

"I'm sorry, I'm babbling. This is harder than I expected."

Dahl's mind went racing ahead. What on earth was the girl trying to confess? Maybe she pregnant? Or...?"

"Okay. The bottom line is, I'm rich. I mean, really, really rich. The waitresses where I worked, at the Old Beanery, we won a great big lottery." She paused. Dahl looked puzzled. "I was part of the group, we won a huge lottery. We're all multi-millionaires." She heaved a gusty sigh. "Phew, there it's out. Now you know."

Dahl was stunned. A multi-millionaire? Her niece? Surely not! She didn't look like a multi-millionaire, in her stained jeans and sweatshirt. She didn't act like a multi-millionaire. "But your truck....and moving back here to Chesney Creek, living at the farm when you could have bought a mansion? Are you sure?"

Marik laughed. "Oh yeah, I'm sure. Kind of shocking, isn't it?

"A multi-millionaire." She stared at her niece, mouth open. "Wow. Golly." It was literally jaw-dropping news.

"There's something else I have to tell you. Remember I said that I would ask my boss about getting some money so we could put a roof over the riding ring?"

"I'd forgotten about that. He was going to see if he could get us a charitable donation or grant, something like that, wasn't he? Because of the Ability Riders, right?"

"That was just my story. I didn't want you to know it was me supplying the money, so I made up a stupid story about it. I've made up a bunch of stupid stories, because I didn't want everyone to know about the money. Ken Rheddenk isn't really my boss, I don't actually work for him, he works for me. He's my accountant, my money manager or whatever you want to call it." She took a deep breath. "Anyway, he emailed me last night, he's depositing the money in my account tomorrow. We can get started on the roof right away."

"You mean...," Dahl stuttered, "You mean you want to give me the money for the roof?" It was almost more than she could take in.

"Yes. As a donation, to the Ability Riders. Ken told me a long time ago that I'd have to find ways to reduce the taxes, so it works for me too. We can make Ability Riding a year-round program if the ring gets rebuilt, can't we?"

Dahl leaned back on her elbows in the short dry grass and began to chuckle. "They were right." The chuckle turned into laughter. "It's like there is a plan for me, there really is!" She could almost hear her guides, their laughter joining hers in the clear mountain air. The three horses raised their heads from the grass for a startled moment.

"Are you alright?" Marik had never seen her aunt laugh like this. She seemed almost hysterical.

Dahl wiped the tears of laughter from her cheeks with her shirt tail, still chortling. "Alright? No, far more than alright." She stretched back onto her elbows. "Far more than alright," she repeated. "I've had a lesson, that's all. I should have known that something good was going to happen, along with all the other good things that have happened in recent months. I'd forgotten, that's all." She stretched her arms upward, clenching her hands into fists above her head. "This is such wonderful news!" The weight of her doubt, her fears and worries, were rolling off of her and away down the mountain side. "My niece, the multi-millionaire. Well!" She sat back up and grinned at Marik. "I don't know what to say."

"That's okay, don't say anything. I mean, really don't say anything, ok?" she added sheepishly. "I don't want everyone to know."

"You'll have to tell your Mom, both your folks."

"I know. They are next on the list. I'll tell the whole family eventually, but just for now, I'd like to keep it as quiet as possible."

"No problem!" Dahl reassured her. "How could I be talking about it to others when I can barely believe it myself?

Marik was relieved. Her aunt was taking the news of her big lottery win very well. God grant that the rest of the family would do the same. She would find out over the months to come.

"Do you think I should tell them at Thanksgiving," she asked as they were picking up their picnic things. "Would that be a good time?"

"Sure. That will be fun. I can hardly wait to see their faces when they find out."

"I don't know if they'll all be as happy for me as you are," Marik said doubtfully. "People can be weird about money."

"Expect the best," Dahl advised with a laugh. "It makes the best more probable."

~ The End ~

After Words

I trust you enjoyed your visit with the Palmers of Chesney Creek. Their stories will continue in Volume 2, which I expect to release early in 2017. If you enjoyed the book, be sure to tell your friends and join me at www.BookLovingLadies.com to find out more about the books I write....and the ones I read.

Happy Reading, *Elaine*

PS: Here's a short chapter from the next Chesney Creek novel:

HOW TO MEET A PRETTY WOMAN

Tomas Ramirez opened the back door and let it slap closed behind him.

"Papa?"

"Hola. Yes, it's me. What's cooking? Smells good, whatever it is." He sniffed the air appreciatively as he ambled into the kitchen.

His daughter Francisca gave him an affectionate peck on his rough cheek, and turned back to the stove. "Roast and Yorkshires. Not traditional Sunday dinner for you and me, but it is Todd's favourite, and it is his birthday after all. What's new? Met any gorgeous women lately?" It was her standard question. She wanted her father, widowed these ten years, to find someone to fill the empty part of his life, especially now that he was in the process of retiring from Chesney Creek's small police force.

"As a matter of fact...." He pulled out a chair and perched on it, facing backwards.

"Really?" His daughter's pretty face, with the generous red lips and sparkling dark eyes of her Latino heritage, lit up with delight. "Who is it? How did you meet her? Tell me all!"

"Where are Todd and the boys?" His two grandsons were young teenagers. He missed the old days when Grand-Papa's arrival was a major event in their lives.

"Watching the game. You're safe. Tell me about all her."

"You know that Karlsson case, the guy that was killed last month?" Tomas was a detective with the Chesney Creek Police Department, although he only worked half-time now.

"Sure. You solved that one, didn't you?"

"Not me personally. Matter of fact, no one actually solved it, the guy confessed accidentally when he was spouting off about something else. That's how I met....this woman. She was the one he was threatening. You remember..." He still didn't know what it was about her that attracted him so much. She certainly wouldn't qualify as one of Francisca's 'gorgeous women', particularly not when he met her, with her torn shirt and her bruised cheek, and smelling of horses and sweat. He chuckled. It had been an absurd scene, the bad guy roped and hog-tied by a couple of women and their horses. Police work had its funny moments.

Francisca slid the tin of savory Yorkshire puddings into the hot oven. The roast was resting, tented with aluminum foil. She toed the kitchen door open, and shouted, "Fifteen minutes, you lot!" She turned back to her father. "So, that was a month ago. Are you seeing this woman? Have you asked her out?"

"No!" He rubbed his forearm across his chin. "It's been 40 years since I dated. I don't know what I'm supposed to do. Invite her for a movie? I'd feel like an idiot. Besides, I met her professionally, interviewed her for the case. We don't know each other socially."

Francisca pursed her lips and shook her head. "Oh Papa, you do make things difficult for yourself." She pulled a stack of colourful plates out of the cupboard and handed them to him, along with a handful of cutlery. "Make yourself useful." She turned back to the stove, checking under pot-lids. "What else do you know about her? There must be some way you can get acquainted. Maybe you can arrange to run into her in the grocery store."

"You want me to stalk her? I don't think so."

"Don't be silly. But if you want to get to know her, you're going to have to get creative. So, what else do you know about her?

"She's got that riding stable, out Mountain Road. You know, they do riding for handicapped kids, there was an article about it in the Recorder."

"Oh that one! Dottie' nephew rides with them. He's got CP." Francisca worked part-time at Dorothea's, Dorothy Pasqualli's art and fashion boutique in Chesney Creek's small downtown. "I'll ask her if she knows – what's this woman's name?"

"Blabon," he said shortly. "Dahlia Blabon." He shouldn't have said anything. Francisca was relentless. Next thing you knew, she'd be setting him up on a blind date with the woman. Madre Dios! "Don't go telling everybody your old man is interested in her," he grumbled.

"Don't worry, Papa. You know me better than that. I can be subtle." He made a rude noise. "What? I can! But you've got to find a way to meet her socially, if you want anything to come of it."

"Then what?"

"Then ask her out. Just something simple, ask her if she'd like to meet with you for a coffee, something like that. If it goes well, crank it up a notch. Ask her out for dinner, for a movie or a concert or something. After that, it's her turn. If she's interested, she'll invite you to do something with her. That's the way the dance is done, these days."

"Huh! And what if she doesn't know that dance? We're both old fogies," he grumbled.

"Maybe you could volunteer, help out with her handicap riding program. They are always in need of more helpers, according to that article in the Recorder."

"Want me to slice that roast? What is it, elk?"

"Ok, Papa, I get the hint, I won't say any more about it. For now," she added under her breath as she picked up the heavy cast iron Dutch oven to decant the gravy into the serving boat. "Call the boys for dinner, por favor." Her mother had been gone for ten years. Her boys hardly remembered their abuela. It was past time for her father to find someone to make him happy. He was too good a man to be left unclaimed. She would have to check out this Dahlia Blabon woman.

Later, after her father was gone and while the boys were fighting companionably over the dinner dishes, she mentioned the matter to Todd.

"The riding school," he repeated thoughtfully. "That's the Palmer place, corner of Mountain Road and Mountain Retreat." Todd started driving truck for Andersson's Building Supplies, his family's business, when he was seventeen. He knew every road and backroad within a twenty-five mile radius of Chesney Creek. "Palmers," he repeated, reaching for the TV remote. "Didn't we go through school with a Marik Palmer, elementary and middle school at least? I don't think she was still around in high school."

Francisca nodded. "That's right, I'd forgotten about that. I wonder if it's the same family? She ran away or something when she was a teenager, but she's back in town now. I heard that she won some kind of humungous lottery. Dot says she's been in the shop a few times, but I haven't seen her."

An angry exclamation from the kitchen interrupted their conversation. "Stay here, birthday boy," she said, giving Todd a quick kiss. "I'll settle them down. Boys~!" No wonder she longed for the day when her father would bring another woman into the family. She would help to dilute the testosterone tide that was rising up around Francisca as her sons grew up.

Made in the USA
Charleston, SC
06 July 2016